"She said 'rosebud'?"

"The nurse heard her," Betty said. "On account of Maesie was screaming."

"But she didn't even approve of *Citizen Kane*!" I objected. "I mean, when she finally saw it, she admitted it was a great movie, but she never approved of what it did to Marion Davies."

"The last I heard it was going to be *Camille*," Betty said.

Maesie had spent years planning her death. She would scour classic movies to find just the right exit line. Now she had died, and she hadn't been anyone she wanted to be at all.

"*Camille!* I ask you! Maesie was hardly the suffering martyr type, now, was she? But 'rosebud'?" Betty added.

"So why did she say it?" I asked.

Betty hunched closer. "Wouldn't you just love to find out?"

Books published by The Ballantine Publishing Group
are available at quantity discounts on bulk purchases
for premium, educational, fund-raising, and special
sales use. For details, please call 1-800-733-3000.

FADE TO BLACK

Della Borton

FAWCETT GOLD MEDAL • NEW YORK

A Fawcett Gold Medal Book
Published by The Ballantine Publishing Group
Copyright © 1999 by Lynette Carpenter

www.randomhouse.com/BB/

Library of Congress Catalog Card Number: 98-96686

ISBN 0-449-00407-4

Manufactured in the United States of America

First Edition: April 1999

10   9   8   7   6   5   4   3   2   1

To George Johnson
and
Jerry and Kathy Amato

two generations of owners
of the Strand Theatre,
Delaware, Ohio,
who kept the dream alive,
and
in memory of
Cindy Johnson—
θυμούμαστε

Acknowledgments

Thanks to George and Cindy Johnson, Kathy and Jerry Amato, and Kevin Johnson for sharing their theaters, and to Detective Sgt. Russell L. Martin of the Delaware, Ohio, Police Department, whose beat used to cover the Strand, for sharing his expertise. Thanks also to Frances Bartram and Stuart Krichevsky for reading and commenting on drafts of this book. And last but not least, I'd like to thank my computer consultant, Web master, and cat-sitter, Jeremy Bargar, who saw me through various technological crises with patient good humor.

The Liberty Family Tree

Adam and
(Adolph and

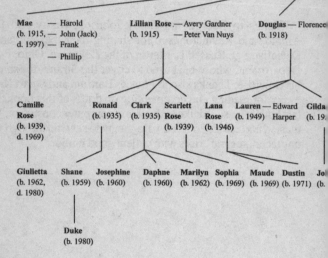

Mae — Harold
(b. 1915, — John (Jack)
d. 1997) — Frank
— Phillip

Lillian Rose — Avery Gardner
(b. 1915) — Peter Van Nuys

Douglas — Florence
(b. 1918)

Camille Rose
(b. 1939, d. 1969)

Ronald
(b. 1935)

Clark
(b. 1935)

Scarlett Rose
(b. 1939)

Lana Rose
(b. 1946)

Lauren — Edward Harper
(b. 1949)

Gilda
(b. 19...

Giulietta
(b. 1962, d. 1980)

Shane
(b. 1959)

Josephine
(b. 1960)

Daphne
(b. 1960)

Marilyn
(b. 1962)

Sophia
(b. 1969)

Maude
(b. 1969)

Dustin
(b. 1971)

Jo
(b.

Duke
(b. 1980)

Liberty
(Liebowitz)

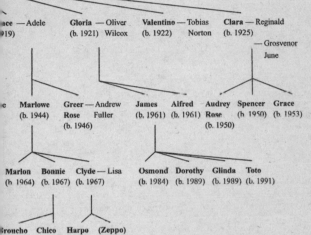

ace — Adele   **Gloria** — Oliver   **Valentino** — Tobias   **Clara** — Reginald
919)   (b. 1921) Wilcox   (b. 1922) Norton   (b. 1925)

                                                            — Grosvenor
                                                              June

e   **Marlowe** **Greer** — Andrew **James**   **Alfred**   **Audrey** **Spencer** **Grace**
    (b. 1944)   Rose   Fuller   (b. 1961) (b. 1961) **Rose**   (b. 1950) (b. 1953)
                  (b. 1946)   (b. 1950)

Marlon **Bonnie** **Clyde** — Lisa   **Osmond** **Dorothy** **Glinda** **Toto**
(b. 1964) (b. 1967) (b. 1967)   (b. 1984) (b. 1989) (b. 1989) (b. 1991)

Groucho **Chico** **Harpo** **(Zeppo)**
b. 1996) (b. 1996) (b. 1996) (expected)

Includes all Liberties named in the book,
except for David W. (b. 1916, d. 1919)

Prologue

FADE IN

1 Ext. Liberty House—Night—Present Day

Bay window, small in the distance, illuminated. The house is a large turreted Victorian, seen in dark silhouette against a darker sky. It is surrounded by a stone wall. Camera TRACKS IN toward an open gate, then TILTS up to show a large, ornamental L in the ironwork above the gate.

DISSOLVE

(A series of setups, each closer to the illuminated window.)

2 Front Drive, Liberty House

We move up a tree-lined drive, the window intermittently visible through the bare branches overhead.

DISSOLVE

3 Tennis Court, Liberty House

In shadow, the court has a forlorn air, its net torn and drooping.

DISSOLVE

4 Stables, Liberty House

The stables do not look as if they housed any living inhabitants. An unfastened door moves with the wind, moaning softly on its hinges.

DISSOLVE

5 *Swimming Pool, Liberty House*
The pool is empty. Dry leaves swirl across the cement bottom and collect in the corner.

DISSOLVE

6 *Garage, Liberty House*
Several ghostly shapes can be seen parked outside the old-fashioned wood structure. These shapes have the vague familiarity of long-buried memories—an oblong, flat, coffinlike shape, a shape curved like a whale's back, a low shape with sharp dorsal fins.

DISSOLVE

7 *The Window*
The camera TRACKS in on a fully illuminated bay window, framed by curtains that have been tied back. Suddenly, the light within goes out, and the CAMERA HOLDS a few seconds on the darkened window. A faint light comes up inside. The camera TRACKS in through the window.

8 *Int. Mae's Bedroom—Night*
REVERSE ANGLE of window, with window seat and large quilted cushions. The camera PANS past small cluttered writing desk, quilted, cushioned armchair, and low dresser to a dressing table—the skirted kind—fronted by a low cushioned French Provincial stool. On the dressing table, amid a collection of cosmetic and perfume bottles, are a highball glass, half empty, and an Oscar statuette, which doubles as a wig stand, holding askew a silver-white wig. Under the Oscar is an old metal film canister. Attached to the table is a wood-framed tilt mirror, large and round. In the mirror we can see, dimly, a woman lying in bed. RACK FOCUS brings the woman in the mirror into focus, and we can see that she is reading something by the dim light of the bedside lamp.

9 *Mae's Bedroom*
REVERSE ANGLE of the woman in the mirror. The bed is canopied and heavily curtained. It and the wall behind it are covered with quilted satin. Next to the bed is a small round

nightstand, crowded with telephone, lamp, ashtray, paperback books, and the paraphernalia of the invalid. The camera TRACKS in on an elderly woman propped up against a mountain of pillows. She is wearing a fur-trimmed bed jacket. She is pale and thin, as if from a long illness, with long, thick white hair pulled back low behind her neck, and she wears half-glasses on the end of her nose. Her rings—none of them a simple gold band—catch the light as she holds a sheet of paper in her hand. She reads intently. A file folder stuffed with additional papers lies open across her lap. The camera TRACKS into a CLOSE SHOT as the woman turns the page over.

She picks up something from her lap that reflects light with a dull gleam—a small chain of some kind, with a thin plate. She rubs the plate, brings it close to her eyes, and squints at it, as if trying to make out something that is difficult to see.

                              MAE
(In a voice choked with shock and horror) Rosebud?

She lets the papers fall, unheeded, on the bed and stares, unseeing, at some internal vision. Her fists clench.

                              MAE
(Her voice rises in outrage) Rosebud! *(Now with full histrionic fury, fist raised)* Rosebud! I'll—

Suddenly, she sits up very straight and clutches her chest. All of the papers fall to the floor. She gasps. Her mouth and eyes open wide. She blinks once, then reaches for something on the nightstand, fumbling amid the small bottles, glass, and wadded-up tissues. She knocks over the lamp, and it goes out, plunging the room into darkness. We hear labored breathing, a faint cry, and then nothing. In the darkness, some pale rays of moonlight from the window appear on the floor and on the papers and chain, which lie on the floor. We hear running footsteps.

                                        FADE TO BLACK

I felt a flash of blood along my neck and in my cheeks.

They had put my name on the marquee, just under the neon sign. WELCOME HOME TO PARADISE, GILDA! it said.

I leaned my head on the steering wheel and closed my eyes. This trip had been a big mistake, and I was in no shape to withstand the emotional upheaval. This was not a good time for my first trip home in nine years.

The last visit had also been funereal, occasioned by the death of my ninety-three-year-old grandmother, Eve Liberty, the family matriarch. My life had been relatively stable then, my relationship with Liz in its honeymoon phase, my job at the insurance company dull but steady, and the kids old enough to need less supervision. My son, John, then fourteen, had made the trip with me. So had Liz, over my objections.

Everyone had adored Liz. Liz had an auspicious name, as far as the Liberty clan was concerned. I glanced up again at my name on the marquee, large as a Sunset Strip billboard. Names meant a lot to the Liberties.

It had all started with my grandparents. The myth of their immigration has worn threadbare from all the voices that have caressed it: how they stood, hand in hand, on the lower deck, tear-filled eyes raised to the Lady with the Lamp as their ship glided into New York Harbor in 1915. Shortly afterward, before a bored immigration factotum, my grandfather began reinventing himself as an American. "Adam Liberty," he said, when asked for his name. "And this is my wife, Eve."

With a stroke of the pen Adolph and Eva Liebowitz became

Adam and Eve Liberty. Imagine my grandmother's surprise: only three months married, she scarcely remembered to answer to "Liebowitz." Now she was someone else.

Soon, like so many pioneers before them, my grandparents had followed their dreams west and arrived in Los Angeles shortly after Carl Laemmle opened Universal City. And when Laemmle, popularly known as "Uncle Carl," ran out of relatives to hire, he hired my grandfather as an assistant cameraman and my grandmother as a seamstress in the wardrobe department.

At the same time, no doubt intoxicated by his newfound power to name things, Adam Liberty, with considerable aid from his wife, began begetting new beings to name. He named them after the gods of his personal pantheon: Mae, Lillian, David, Douglas, Wallace, Gloria, Valentino, and Clara. And all of his children begat children, and they, too, were named in this fashion. So the family grew and thrived, producing, among others, a Clark and a Scarlett, a Marlon, a Marilyn, a Shane, and a Dustin, though out of deference to Eve's mother, the first girl was always given the middle name Rose. So Scarlett was really Scarlett Rose, just as our cousin Camille had been Camille Rose, our cousin Audrey was Audrey Rose, and my older sister Lana was Lana Rose.

When my grandparents had had enough of Hollywood, they looked for a place to retire where they could live on their memories and tell stories to credulous natives. If there hadn't been an Eden, Ohio, they would have had to invent it. And because they wanted to keep their fingers on the pulse of the film industry without actually having to put up with film people, they bought the Paradise, a small theater there.

If anyone asked him, "Why Ohio?" my grandfather would reply, "It's restful out here in the heartland, with all those farmers. Not restful for the farmers, you understand, but it suits Eve and me just fine."

Meanwhile, three generations of young Liberties had pursued the Hollywood dreams of their forebears; some had enjoyed long careers there, while others had burned out or given up after a season or two. Sooner or later they all seemed to be

drawn back to the bosom of the family by the magnetic person-
alities of my grandparents, populating Eden County, Ohio, with
an unusually high number of exotic names and even more
exotic talents.

Given all these developments, and the two versions of De-
Mille's *Ten Commandments*, it was downright astonishing that
we had nobody in the family named God.

So Liz, with her suggestive name and her Cleopatra-like
charisma, had been welcomed into the family with open arms
when she'd shown up at Eve's funeral with me. My son, John,
on the other hand, had puzzled them. They refused to believe
me when I said that he wasn't named for anyone: they thought I
was being coy. They spent the whole week guessing. John Barrymore? John Garfield? John Huston? John Wayne? Surely not,
they said, that awful Helen Hayes–Robert Walker anti-commie
film from the fifties!

Frankly, I thought that anyone who would name their twins
Bonnie and Clyde had no room to talk.

They were all gratified by John's musical talents. It was a
long way from playing in a garage band to scoring a major mo-
tion picture, but the Liberties liked to think of themselves as
cheerful and optimistic—a role they were as ill suited for as
Jack Nicholson was for Jesus.

In fact, funerals ranked high among the family's favorite
events, second perhaps only to deathbed scenes. Funerals
brought out the best in everyone. Whatever they had once been—
electricians, sound techs, assistant set designers, script girls, edi-
tors, assistants to the second assistant director—when it came
to a funeral, everyone was a star. They had the wardrobe and the
makeup, and they could produce on cue every nuance and in-
flection the occasion called for, from histrionic grief to subdued
weeping to unspoken pathos to stoic resignation. They were all
capable of playing any of the roles available: the dutiful and
stricken son or daughter, the long-suffering but stalwart son- or
daughter-in-law, the boor, the martyr, the rake, the prodigal, the
callous youth, the critic, and the hypocrite, not to mention the
impresario who oversaw the whole affair.

By the end of my grandmother's funeral, I had had a headache that lasted for days.

And now I was back, older, sadder, and more fragile than before.

If I could have thought of a way out of the whole ordeal, short of death, I would have taken it.

But I couldn't. In the first place Maesie had been my favorite aunt. She had been the iconoclastic exception that proved the rule about oldest children being more cautious and conservative. Perhaps that had been because she'd been a twin and had left all the cautiousness to her sister Lillian. Of all the movie-mad Liberties, Mae Liberty had achieved the greatest success onscreen, and she had the Oscar to prove it. She also had the temperament—great tempests of rage that cowed everyone around her, separated by interludes of wit, charm, humor, and self-directed irony. Even as a girl, though, I had not been intimidated by Aunt Maesie. I had enjoyed my aunt's rages, and identified with them. I imagined they spoke for me. So my fondness for Maesie constituted my first reason for coming back.

As for my second reason . . .

I opened my eyes and looked up at the marquee again. My legacy: the Paradise Theatre. In spite of its name, it had begun in 1916 as a distant cousin to the emerging motion-picture palaces of its day. For years its facade had been not merely unpretentious but plain. Weathered brown wood had risen above a functional marquee. But that had been before Maesie took over in 1970. In a gesture of sheer extravagance, she had purchased the facade from a theater in Illinois that was about to be torn down and had the whole thing reconstructed, stone by stone, column by column, mosaic tile by mosaic tile, and cherub by cherub, on the front of the old Paradise. She'd had a new sign constructed, trimmed in neon lights, which dwarfed the marquee. The building looked as incongruous in its small-town setting as King Kong would on Fifth Avenue.

Shortly afterward, the bottom had dropped out of the small theater business. The video and cable-television markets had exploded. Chain movie theaters had divided like cancer cells and expanded like tumors into mall parking lots all across America. Even unpromising markets like Eden, Ohio, got their own chain theaters, typically, as in Eden, in a shopping center on the edge of town. Independent theaters in urban neighborhoods and small towns stood vacant and crumbling, with no one to inhabit them but the ghosts of long-dead lovers. Or they became bookstores, bakeries, antique malls, and furniture stores.

I didn't know much about the theater business, but I knew that much.

"I don't want a movie theater," I'd said when my mother broke the news to me over the phone. "I mean, I appreciate the gesture and all that, but I don't want it. Why would she leave it to me?"

"You do have an MBA," Florence pointed out with some asperity. "It's the only one in the family."

That was true. My family had moved to Eden just before my high school years, so afterward I'd gone to UCLA and then New York in an attempt to put as much distance as possible between me and my immediate family. In fact, at twenty-one that had been my only clear career goal: to be where my family was not. I went to work for an insurance company, answering letters and calling policy holders to explain to them why they should be carrying more insurance than they were. One day I realized that my greatest aspiration was to become a claims adjuster, so I could get out of the office, drive around, and meet interesting people. The next day I enrolled in a night course at CUNY.

One thing led to another—or several others. I hadn't especially enjoyed my MBA work, but I had persisted because it set me apart from the rest of my family—and it annoyed them. The work was exhausting, coming as it did on the heels of my day job. I ended up marrying the guy who sat next to me in accounting class because he had invested so much time in getting me through it and because he wore me down. George was good-looking, smart, serious, and nice. He was the nicest person I'd ever met. He had almost no sense of humor. He was Ashley Wilkes, and I gradually came to the realization that I wanted

Rhett Butler. Or I wanted Scarlett O'Hara, but that's getting ahead of the story.

By the time I finished my MBA, I had been a claims adjuster long enough to know that getting out of the office was not my long-term career goal. New York traffic gave me headaches, and the people I met were not in the best of moods when I arrived. Pregnancy did nothing to improve my outlook.

When at last George and I called it quits, I was a paper pusher again, with a house in the suburbs, a one-hour commute, and a third-grader. I sold the house, moved to an exorbitantly priced sublet in the city, enrolled John in a private school, and fell in love with the girl next door: Liz. We blended our families and cut our rent in half. My job bored me to tears, but with four kids I was willing, as so many have been before me, to sell my soul for a decent salary and a dental plan.

And what did I have to show for it now, but an MBA, an IRA, and a broken heart? Even my boss had encouraged me to take an extended vacation and spend time with my family. Everyone, it seemed, could live without me.

So I had come home, and I was being welcomed with open arms. They couldn't wait, I thought sourly, to get their hands on me, to start interfering in my life. The theater was supposed to lure me back and keep me here.

"But I don't know anything about the theater business," I had whined on the phone, reverting, as I always did with my mother, to an earlier incarnation of myself.

"I'll come for the funeral," I had told my mother at last. "But I'm not staying and I'm not going into the theater business."

I started the car and took a last look at the Paradise over my shoulder.

I didn't recognize any of the movie titles on the marquee. No wonder the place is falling apart, I thought. I can change that at least.

2

The sign on the marquee proved to be the most innocuous part of the family welcome—a prelude to what was awaiting me at the familial estate, Liberty House.

My mother, Florence, eyed me critically.

"It's hard to believe that in all of New York you can't find a stylist to cut your hair properly," she said. She turned my chin from side to side, running her eyes up and down my face. She lifted a strand of frizzy, light brown hair streaked with a gray that matched my eyes. "And honestly, Gilda, all that gray! Douglas, come and look at your daughter! She looks older than we do."

My father hugged me.

"Where's Liz?" he asked. "I thought you two would have patched things up by now. I always liked that girl."

"Don't say that, dear," his wife admonished him. "That's probably why they've split."

I was reminded of why I had always stayed with my aunts Mae and Lillian at Liberty House during my infrequent sojourns home. We all pretended that it was because my parents had moved to a smaller house once their daughters were gone, and because their various projects took up all the available guest space. The real reason was that my mother and I got along better if we weren't sharing living quarters.

"I liked Liz, too," said my aunt Adele. She gave me a peck on the cheek, which risked getting her false eyelashes entangled in my hair, and then pulled back to study me. "Your mother's right about your hair, dear," she whispered. Adele's hair was on the tawny side of tangerine—not a popular color with seventy-five-year-olds. "But don't worry! I'm sure Gloria can do something with it in time for the funeral."

"Did I hear my name taken in vain?"

I shrank back. Gloria Liberty Wilcox had worked for eighteen years as a studio hairdresser. Some of the highest-paid heads in Hollywood had submitted themselves to her merciless hands. She knew how to style hair that would look exquisite on film and stand up under the hottest lights. Her bag of tricks ran to toxic chemicals long since banned for general use. Her own silver coiffure looked positively radioactive. As she approached, she was preceded by a wave of L'Air du Temps potent enough to choke a buffalo. It beat back the strong, sour smell of permanent-wave solution that had hung in the air, an odor that could have emanated from either Adele or Gloria or both, from the look of their hair.

I backed into a bear hug from my uncle Wallace, Adele's husband. Usually I smelled him before I heard him, but Gloria's cologne had triggered a sensory meltdown. His liquid eyes told me how much he'd had to drink.

"She still looks good to me," he said, spinning me, bending me backward, and pretending to bite my neck. "Tastes good, too." He favored me with a diabolical leer. His claim to fame had been a series of bit parts in horror films produced by the Val Lewton unit at RKO during the forties.

He lifted me upright, and I was toe-to-toe with my aunt Clara.

"Darling," Clara said, waving a cigarette holder as long as a stiletto and offering a cheek. "Have you put on weight?"

"Hullo, Gilda!" I saw my uncle Oliver reaching for my hand and instinctively pulled it back. He pitched forward and took a pratfall at my feet. He looked up at me with a goofy smile and asked, "Are you decent?" He roared with laughter as if he had written the line himself. He had once directed B comedies at Universal, and he loved practical jokes. My hand had been buzzed so many times that I feared nerve damage. In his presence I tended to park my hands behind my back for safekeeping.

It was sort of like returning home to Transylvania to discover that everyone has turned into a vampire except you, only the truth was, they'd been vampires when I left.

"Aw, lay off her, boys and girls." That was my favorite uncle, Val. "The kid's been gone for nine years, and you're making her wish it was nine more." He smiled at me. "Hello, sweetheart," he said. "How's tricks?"

"She's not a kid anymore, Valentino," said a new voice in the round tones of a classically trained actress. The accent was cultured and vaguely British, though its owner was not. "She's the owner of the Paradise Theatre." The voice made the Paradise sound like Albert Hall.

"Hello, Lillian," I said. "I'm really sorry about Mae."

I could see at a glance what Mae's death had cost her. It was hard enough to lose a sibling, I supposed, but to lose a twin must be devastating—even though there had been some tension in the relationship in recent years. Lillian herself walked with a cane. She stood barely five feet high and looked light and fragile as a dry leaf. The impression passed as she drew herself fully erect. She was the undisputed matriarch of the family now, and she played the role larger than life.

"Thank you, my dear," she said. She sounded like Ethel Barrymore conferring a knighthood.

By the time dinner was over, I had grown thoroughly sick of my family. The topic of the evening was my failed romance with Liz, romance being a topic on which all of them claimed some expertise. And they were all reading from the same melodramatic script—except for Uncle Val, who shrugged at me apologetically.

"Why don't you send the girl a dozen roses and an apology?" said my father. "I don't suppose that's occurred to you."

"I haven't done anything to apologize for," I pointed out irritably.

"All the more reason!" my father exclaimed. "Women love

unnecessary apologies! It makes up for all the ones you've missed."

"Don't bet on it, darling," my mother said to him.

"If I sent her a dozen roses, Dad," I said, "she'd probably switch the card and give them to her new lover."

"Aha!" Wallace said, peering at me cannily. "Now we're getting somewhere. She has a new lover!"

"Of course she has a new lover!" Gloria said. "Any woman who . . . lets herself go the way you have, Gilda—if you don't mind my saying so—is asking for trouble. A man feels—or, in your case, a woman feels—taken for granted, dear. If you want to keep the romance alive, you must—."

"I remember I quarreled with Avery once," Lillian interrupted, in the dreamy voice we associated with her memories of her first husband. Avery Gardner had been a matinee idol, and the passion of Lillian's youth. He had died tragically in a car accident at the age of thirty-four, but his memory was kept alive in what the Liberty kids called the Avery Gardner Myth Cycle. We could recite them all by heart, including this one. "When I came down to breakfast the next morning, there was a bouquet of wildflowers he had picked himself and a note saying that every flower was a kiss and an apology. He always gave me wildflowers afterward, whenever we quarreled."

"Must have been a challenge in winter," Uncle Oliver said predictably, "unless you called a truce then."

"I don't think Gilda wants to keep the romance alive at all," my mother pronounced. "I think she enjoys being tragic, and going about with that hangdog look."

Uncle Oliver tut-tutted to himself. "Got to keep 'em laughing, Gillie," he said. "Life's too short for tragedy."

"I wasn't aware I was looking hangdog, Mother," I retorted indignantly. "Quite the contrary, in fact. I thought—"

"That's the spirit!" Wallace cheered me on. "Don't give up the ship, eh? Why, if another fellow took *my* girl away—or if another girl took my girl away, I'd—"

I saw myself as Mickey Rooney to Liz's Judy Garland, but it wouldn't play. I wondered where all the other children and grandchildren were tonight. I was the only person at the table who was not a senior citizen. Perhaps the younger generations were eating at card tables in the other room, as we had always done when I was a child. More likely, the ones who lived in Los Angeles were still struggling to clear their calendars for the funeral, or getting in a last workout at the health club, or leaving detailed instructions for their agents.

"I think it's very wise of you to retreat from the field, Gilda," Lillian said. "As soon as Liz hears that you've inherited a theater, she'll come around soon enough, you mark my words."

"Sure," Clara agreed. "After all, she could hardly be in love with this other person. It's probably just sex." Clara had always been a gamine, a petite, youthful woman bursting with suppressed energy, and she had changed little over the years. She was a kind of latter-day Anita Loos, and she could drop sex into any conversation with a mischievous sparkle that disarmed the most staid of her listeners.

I had the impression that Val winked at me, but I wasn't paying attention anymore. My thoughts had turned inward, and I was cultivating the kind of out-of-body experience I had perfected as a teenager. Their voices droned on in the background, a soundtrack as familiar to me as the dialogue from a favorite cult film I hadn't seen in years.

The Addams Family, for example.

"She didn't!"

"She did!"

"You're making it up!"

"I'm not!"

I looked at my sister. I had found Betty, whose real name was Lauren "Betty" Bacall, in the last booth at Oscar's. Oscar's was an Eden institution that had been so named out of deference to my family by its former owner, who had apparently failed to notice how few Academy Awards we'd actually managed to collect. Betty had one hand wrapped around a mug of beer.

" *'Rosebud'?* She said *'rosebud'?*"

"The nurse heard her," Betty said. "The nurse was very definite, on account of Maesie was screaming, she said."

"Whatever happened to 'Give them champagne, and be gay—be very, very gay'?"

"*Dark Victory?* Oh, God, that was ages ago! Is that the last time you were home? She's been through a million others since then."

"But she didn't even approve of *Citizen Kane!*" I objected. "I mean, when she finally saw it, she admitted it was a great movie, but she never approved of what it did to Marion Davies."

"Actually, the last I heard it was going to be *Camille,*" Betty said. "She always did like that movie, even after . . . you know. Adele did over her room in all these godawful flounces and enough quilting to crash-land a space shuttle, and we'd hear Maesie in there, rehearsing."

Some people spend years planning their funerals. Maesie had spent years planning her death. She had intended to script her deathbed scene with the meticulous care of Hitchcock, but without the macabre sense of humor. She would scour classic movies to find just the right exit line, rehearse her latest favorite as diligently as an ingenue, then abruptly discard it when she happened on a new favorite. And no matter how extravagant her enthusiasm for the newest candidate, she would soon be assailed by doubts, her loyalty would wane, and her script would appear among the kindling in the fireplace.

Adele was her partner in crime. Adele had once been a set designer at Paramount, after which she had retired to Eden with

Wallace to run a hotel, The Studio Inn. The inn had provided her with a new stage on which to exhibit her talents ("Every Room a Different Set, and Every Guest a Star!"), but there was a financial limit to how many times twenty rooms could be redecorated, so Adele's services had always been available to her relatives. Now that her daughter, Greer, owned the place and her own role had declined to that of consultant, Adele had even more time on her hands. For Maesie, she had designed a whole series of bedrooms of varying styles and motifs.

"The thing is," Adele would confide to other family members, "Mae just can't decide who she wants to *be* when she dies."

Now Mae had died, and she hadn't been anyone she wanted to be at all.

"Oliver used to joke that she ought to say 'Mr. DeMille, I'm ready for my close-up.' But *Camille*! I ask you! Maesie, for all that went wrong in her life, was hardly the suffering martyr type, now, was she? But 'rosebud'? It's so . . ."

"Clichéd?" I prompted. "Obvious?"

"Well, clichés have never been a problem in our family, have they? I mean, we'd just as soon beat a dead horse as a live one any day of the week."

This from an animal lover and animal-rights activist who would never beat any horse, alive or dead. My sister had always collected animals the way dirt collects dandelions. She'd spent a brief time as an animal trainer on a ranch outside of Los Angeles, and her animals had appeared in several films on which she'd worked as a wrangler. But in the end her standards had been higher than the Humane Society's and to make a long story short, she'd ended up picketing a picture she was supposed to work on. She'd moved to Eden, married a genial veterinarian, and the two of them now ran a kind of private animal shelter on a farm outside of town.

"So why did she say it?" I asked. "What did she mean?"

Betty hunched closer. "Wouldn't you just love to find out?"

I stared at her. "No. Oh, no," I said. "I'm not *that* curious."

"Don't be ridiculous. Of course you are. We all are. Why not?"

"Because every time I come home I feel like I've walked into the middle of some cheesy B movie. At dinner it was a melo-drama, starring me and Liz. Jesus, Betty, can't they get some new writers? It was the same damn script they used for my divorce."

"They don't write dialogue like that anymore," my sister said in the sententious voice of a true Liberty.

"Thank God!"

"No, but seriously, Gilda . . ." She shifted. "She was reading something when she died."

"What?"

"Nobody knows."

"What do you mean, nobody knows?" I was interested in spite of myself.

"Just that. Nobody knows. The nurse found them on the floor—a bunch of papers, maybe some letters, and a file folder."

"Probably her investment reports."

Betty shook her head. "The nurse said it looked more like a bunch of letters than bank statements. But she didn't pay that much attention. She just picked them up off the floor and put them on the desk."

"And then what?"

"Nobody knows." Betty waggled her eyebrows suggestively. "Nobody's been able to find whatever she was reading when she died."

"And we should care because . . . ?"

"Because of 'rosebud.' Because she must have been reading something that made her say that, and maybe something that upset her so much, it killed her."

"She had a bad heart, Betts," I pointed out. "She'd already had one heart attack. It wouldn't have taken much."

"Yeah, but why that word? Aren't you curious? Remember all those Nancy Drew books we had as kids? The ones where Nancy was always snooping around in abandoned houses?"

"Am I missing something? What we have in our family are not abandoned houses but overpopulated ones."

She shrugged. "Yeah, but still. I just think it would be fun to investigate."

"It'll probably turn out to be a very simple thing," I said with a straight face.

Betty stuck her finger down her throat and made gagging noises.

I reached into my breast pocket for a pack of cigarettes, ignored Betty's glare, and lit up.

"I thought you quit," she said.

"I did. Several times."

"Gilda—"

I rolled my eyes at her and inhaled deeply.

"Okay, I'm sorry." Betty looked mildly contrite. "I know you've already gotten an earful about Liz. But seriously, Gilda. Are you okay?"

"More or less," I lied. "One good thing about being home is that our relatives drive me to distraction, immediate family included, and what I'm being distracted from is thinking about me and Liz."

She squeezed my hand. "In that case, you're in luck," she said. "Maesie's funeral gives them all the opportunity to turn in the performance of their lives."

"I can't believe she said 'rosebud,' " I repeated.

"Yeah. God, if she'd known that was going to be her last word—"

We finished the line together. "She would have died."

4

"Nope, I can't do it. I can't do it, and I won't."

Booker Gower shook his head, closing his eyes for emphasis.

"I mean no disrespect to your sister, Lillian, when I say that she must've got Gower Funeral Home mixed up with Universal Studios or Columbia Pictures. And maybe she thought I looked like Cecil B. DeMille, which I don't, and it isn't just because I'm black."

Actually, now that I thought about it, Mr. Gower did bear some resemblance to DeMille after the great director lost his hair. Mr. Gower had a wide, curly gray halo that circled his head from ear to ear. But he also had a pair of eyebrows and a mustache that looked like they'd been purchased from some bygone Fuller Brush salesman, and he used these to advantage. He was a stocky man in his early seventies, not much taller than Lillian.

"But if she thinks I'm going to let six wild horses pull her coffin through the streets of Eden, she's got another think coming. Folks like your sister get these notions in their heads, they don't stop and think about the liability. What am I supposed to do, I'd like to know, when those horses decide to stop for lunch at Hamburger Heaven? Or maybe they'll take a notion to visit the county courthouse. And it isn't just the liability I'm talking about. Your sister picked out a deluxe coffin, and it's a fine piece of work. It ain't Samsonite. If that thing was to hit a light post or fall out onto the street, your sister would get more than she bargained for in the way of a send-off."

Peachy Gower finally interrupted his tirade.

"Pop! Turn up your hearing aid! It's not *wild* horses she wants, it's *white* ones! The color white!"

"Oh, *white* horses." The old man scratched his jaw. "Well, I don't know about that. I suppose we can find 'em all right. But I still say it's looking for trouble. It doesn't take much to turn white horses into wild horses, if you ask me. If they bust that coffin wide open and leave Maesie sitting in the middle of Main Street, it won't be anybody's fault but hers."

"We'll work something out." Peachy winked at us.

Peachy had been one of my best friends when I was growing up. I had gotten to know her on summer visits to my grandparents. Then, just before I started high school, events had conspired to push my parents into an early retirement from their singing and dancing careers, and we'd moved to Eden. At that socially graceless age, Peachy and I were united by the weirdness of our families, though we found each other's families endlessly fascinating. Both families were on humiliating public display—Peachy's at the funeral home, and driving around town in a hearse; and mine at the Liberty School of Dance, where my parents stunned our Ohio neighbors with their Fred and Ginger, Nelson and Jeanette routines. Through Peachy, I'd learned more about the undertaking business than most people want to know. Not counting her, I was probably the only living person I knew who'd lain inside a coffin. It was not a bad place to hide when my parents were giving a public performance.

In high school we'd shared the goal of putting as much distance between ourselves and our embarrassing families as we could. If anybody was more surprised than I was when Peachy joined the family business, it was probably Peachy.

When I was a kid, there had been two funeral homes in Eden, Ohio. In the language of the times, one had been "white" and one had been "colored." Then, the year after I'd graduated from high school, the owner of the white funeral home, Mr. Drysdale, had suddenly quit the business and moved. Now there's a McDonald's where his funeral home used to be, on North Main Street.

It took some white people longer than others to get used to

the idea of patronizing a black-owned funeral home. But Mr.
Gower's efficiency and straightforwardness had won them
over. You didn't get crocodile tears or even strained sensitivity
from Mr. Gower. If he was sorry that somebody had died, he
said so, and if he wasn't, he didn't. On the other hand, you
didn't get a sales pitch, either. If you wanted advice, he gave it
to you, that was all. And he'd been known to advise a cheap-
skate's widow to plant the man in a pressboard box, the way the
old skinflint would've wanted to go.

Mr. Gower's wife, Alma, had always provided the warmth
in the business. They'd made an effective team, offering both
practicality and sympathy. Peachy had always seemed to me
to combine their traits, and now that she was running the
business, I presumed her clientele still appreciated the quali-
ties that Gower Funeral Home had built its reputation on.
With her braids and avant-garde wardrobe, she looked more
like a Benetton model than a small-town undertaker.

Mr. Gower was semiretired. He and Alma spent the winter
months in Florida, and much of the rest of the time spoiling
their grandbabies. But he put in appearances on ceremonial occasions, and Maesie's funeral was certainly that.

Too vain, even at eighty-two, to wear bifocals, Lillian squinted
down at her list. I knew she was having trouble reading her own
writing, but in keeping with family policy, I didn't offer to help.

"Next," she said with uncharacteristic hesitation, "let's see. I
suppose we should discuss the graveside service."

"Assuming the coffin arrives in one piece," Mr. Gower
grumbled.

"Yes," Lillian said firmly, "assuming that. Of course, Sophie
will want to scout the location when she arrives. But you might
just draw me a diagram—"

I groaned inwardly. I saw what was coming. No family occasion went unrecorded on film or, nowadays, video. The Liberties would consider their performances wasted if they were not
captured for future generations to snooze through at family
gatherings. My cousin Sophia, Scarlett's daughter, was a documentary filmmaker. She lived in Santa Cruz and liked to make

social justice films with an action agenda. I wondered what they had threatened or bribed her with to induce her to shoot the funeral. They were probably letting her show up in jeans and hiking boots. Maybe I could be her assistant, I thought.

At this point the door flew open and Adele sailed in, breathless.

"My goodness, Lillian, why didn't you call me?" she gasped. "I had no idea you were coming here first thing this morning. If I hadn't called Flo, I wouldn't have known. You should have called me! You know I take an interest in these details, and I think I have something to contribute." She said this last with an injured air, and her eyelashes descended like a second-act curtain.

What she had to contribute I could only guess at, and so, from the look that flickered over her sister-in-law's face, could Lillian.

"Adele, Gilda was available and willing," she said, "and I didn't like to bother you so early."

"Lillian, good heavens, it's no bother at all," Adele replied magnanimously. "After all, this is Maesie we're talking about. Now. Have you chosen a color palette yet?"

Mr. Gower, who had risen belatedly at Adele's entrance, sat back down in his chair with the air of a soldier who foresees a lengthy campaign. At the words "color palette," his eyebrows had leaped across and met low over his nose like a pair of crash-dancing caterpillars.

"Because," Adele went on, oblivious, "I was thinking shades of purple and complementary colors. It's spring, after all. Maesie's wearing that white dress, of course, and I see her holding a small nosegay of violets and lilies of the valley. The pallbearers could wear lavender shirts, though I can't decide whether white or black tuxes would be best. Black is distinguished, I suppose, but so common, and I feel Maesie would have wanted to make a statement, don't you?"

"I'll be outside, Aunt Lilly," I mumbled, making my getaway.

I was taking my first puff when I heard Peachy's voice behind me.

"Wait up, girlfriend!" She linked an arm through mine. "Let's take a walk and leave the negotiations to the older generation."

"I thought you'd want to mediate."

She shook her head and her braids brushed my cheek.

"I was willing to mediate between Pop and Lillian," she said. "That would have been possible. But Adele's just turned the discussion into a three-ring circus, and you couldn't pay me enough to stand in the middle of that and play ringmaster."

"Did you see your dad's face when she said 'color palette'?"

Peachy laughed. "She'll have him ripping the lining out of that coffin and replacing it with lavender satin. Funny, though, that she should pick purple, of all things. It would be the worst color for her."

"Yeah, unless she's planning to have Gloria dye her hair again before the funeral," I offered.

We looked at each other.

"You don't think . . . ?"

We burst out laughing.

"Well, punk is one look she hasn't tried," I gasped.

"Lord help us, can't you just see that woman in a Mohawk?" Peachy snorted.

"I hope she'll go for the body piercing."

"And maybe a tattoo," Peachy said. "A rose tattoo?"

"The purple rose of Cairo?" I could feel the tears tickling my cheeks. "Please," I begged, "let's not start. I won't be able to face her over the dinner table."

"You know she'll make your uncle Wallace dye his hair to match."

"Bite your tongue! Purple is one of Wally's favorite colors. He'll get my cousin Al to do his makeup and show up at Maesie's funeral looking like a ghoul."

"Well," Peachy said, "in that case, I hope your cousin Sophie shoots it in color."

I groaned.

"Have they gotten worse, Peach, or is it me? Have I just forgotten?"

"Girl, they were always strange," she reassured me.

We'd been ambling aimlessly and now we'd reached Main Street. I stopped and took a deep breath. The white crab apples that lined the street were in full bloom, clouds of white swaying gently in the May sunshine. This was Eden at its best, a small-town paradise.

"So," I said, giving her arm a squeeze. "What about you? You happy here?"

"Comfortable," she acknowledged. "I'm comfortable. I guess some days I'd go all the way to 'happy.'" She grinned at me. "I'm happy right now."

I grinned back. "Yeah, me, too. So how's the funeral business?"

"I like it. Now isn't that a kick in the pants? But it turns out that I'm putting my psych major to good use. If a family's in crisis, there's nothing like a death to bring everything to the surface. Half of what I do is family therapy."

"My family must be a real challenge to you."

"Honey, I gave up on your family a long time ago!"

"I'll bet you're good at what you do," I said.

"I am. I'm a good businesswoman, and I like working with people. I do some volunteer work, I get involved with local politics from time to time, I spend time with my kids."

"How's your love life? Is Magoo still hanging around, trying to figure out why you dumped him?"

We had nicknamed Peachy's ex-husband, Mitchell, "Magoo" because he missed everything except the most obvious. Needless to say, the divorce had come as a great shock to him, in spite of every attempt Peachy had made to talk things out.

And yet, as soon as the words were out of my mouth, I felt a sharp pain in my chest and my color rose. Thinking of my shock over Liz's betrayal, I realized that the nickname applied just as well to me. But if the thought crossed Peachy's mind, she didn't show it.

"Oh, God, no! He's got himself a new girlfriend, and from the look of her, the word 'subtle' is not in the girl's vocabulary, so they'll probably get on just fine. She's nice to the kids, though, and they think she's funny. No, I've been seeing this guy from Columbus, real sweet and sensitive."

"I'll bet his first wife trained him," I said.

She laughed. "As long as I don't have to," she said.

We'd been walking south on Main Street, under the crab apples, our shoes brushed by fallen blossoms blowing across the sidewalk. I was gradually developing the uncanny sensation of having slipped behind the curtain to where the rough, unfinished side of the scenery was exposed.

"Say, Peachy, speaking of local politics, what's going on around here? Half the storefronts we've passed are vacant, and this one is on the way out."

We stopped in front of a shoe store. The glass was completely covered by GOING OUT OF BUSINESS! and SALE! signs.

Peachy shook her head. "Sad, isn't it? Mama bought me my first pair of grown-up shoes in that store."

"Remember those shoes you bought for the senior prom? They dyed 'em to match your dress and they got that peach color perfect. Remember that? How come they're going out of business?"

"Same reason everybody else did, I imagine," Peachy said. "Megaverse."

"I saw that store as I was driving into town, in that new shopping center across from Eden Center, where the chain theater is," I recalled. "That shopping center wasn't here the last time I was home."

"No, it opened maybe three, four years ago. Business in the downtown area wasn't great, but most of the old established stores were hanging on. Then Megaverse moved in and offered everything the downtown businesses did and more, sometimes at cheaper prices, and with plenty of free parking. I'm lucky they don't do funerals or sell coffins—yet."

"Is parking downtown that big a problem?" I asked, looking around me in surprise.

Peachy shrugged. "You might not find a place right out front of where you want to go, but you won't have to walk any farther than you would in the Megaverse parking lot. Trouble is, it feels farther to people because they can't see their destination. In the Megaverse parking lot, you can't see anything else."

"I would've thought people were loyal to the family-owned businesses."

"Most people are—or try to be. But if things are cheaper at Megaverse, they can't afford not to shop there. Plus, they can buy everything from geraniums to insurance there. It's tough for a small business to compete."

"Hey!" I said, stopping in front of another empty window. "This is where the bookstore was. Don't tell me that's gone!"

Peachy didn't say anything.

"Peach, this is creepy! I'm beginning to think that the movie theater is one of the few businesses left downtown besides your funeral home."

"So maybe you'll understand why people in Eden have so much invested in keeping it open, why they have such high hopes for you as the new owner."

I turned and studied her face. "I hope you're kidding, but you're not, are you?"

"Gil, a lot of people blame your aunt Lillian for what's happened to downtown Eden," Peachy said seriously. "They'd never say that to her face, of course, but you know what long memories people have. They think things started downhill when she sold that land to the developers who built Eden Center."

"I never understood that," I admitted. "When she bought that land, she and Mae were talking about a drive-in theater, with a flea market on the weekends. I thought that's what she bought it for. And then she ups and sells it to that development company. She made some excuse about planning for the future and safe-guarding her investments, and claimed the company had made her an offer she couldn't afford to turn down. I suppose that might have been true, but I sometimes wonder whether Mae ticked her off somehow, and she sold it out of spite or because she could see that they couldn't collaborate in business. That's when their relationship became strained, but maybe the real break happened before the land was sold instead of after."

"At least they were still on speaking terms," Peachy observed.

"Not at first, though," I said. "Mae really did stop speaking to her for a while, even though it didn't last. But, Peach, I'm not responsible for my aunt's mistakes. I've got my own sins to answer for. So if you hear anybody suggest that I've got a duty to ride to the rescue of Eden's downtown business district, I hope you'll put them straight."

"I'll try," she said. "But you have to see it from their perspective, too. If the theater goes under, Eden will lose one of the architectural wonders of small-town America—the one thing, besides its annual harness race and its college, that puts it on the map. Julius Cole will buy it, tear it down, and we'll get another bank building or something."

"Oh, right. Uncle Julius. I don't think I ever knew what he did for a living."

"I don't know if he calls it his profession, but his hobby is buying and selling real estate."

I was feeling overwhelmed.

"Is the theater really in danger of going under, do you think?"

"Gil, you're the one with the account books. Don't you know?"

"I haven't seem them yet," I said. "I haven't even met with Maesie's attorney. I have to do that this afternoon."

She smiled. "Girlfriend, you've got your work cut out for you—whether or not you take the theater. But seriously, Gilda, much as I'd love to have you around, I'm not going to pressure you to stay. Small-town life suits me, but it's not for everybody. I just want you to be happy."

These days, tears seemed to be perpetually waiting off camera for their entrance cue, and they heard it now.

"Thanks, Peach. I really appreciate that. Maybe I can find someone who wants to buy a movie theater."

5

"You can't sell it. I'm sorry, Gilda, but under the terms of the will, the property cannot be sold for five years. That's not atypical for legacies of this type."

Mr. Hermes leaned back in his chair and regarded me placidly. He was a handsome second-generation Greek-American with an air of infinite patience.

"Not even within the family?" I suggested. On the way over I'd been running through the family tree in my head in an attempt to identify some relative who might want a movie theater of their very own.

"No," he said.

"What happens if I refuse it?" I asked. "I mean, you can't force me to own a movie theater I don't want, right? There must be title transfers to sign off on and everything. So what happens if I say no?"

"The property would be divided among the surviving siblings," he said, "who would become joint owners."

I felt a sledgehammer hit me right between the eyes. The surviving siblings: Lillian, my father, Wallace, Gloria, Valentino, and Clara. If the funeral was any indication, they were as ill equipped for a joint business venture as the Romans, Christians, and lions in a biblical epic. Adele would want to do the place over and color-coordinate everything down to the tickets. My mother would want to stage tap dance competitions in the lobby and would offend Adele at every turn. My father would try to smooth things over between them, while keeping an eye out so that Wallace didn't burn the place down running the pop-

28

corn machine under the influence. Oliver would hold up the ticket line doing card tricks or would run people off with whoopee cushions in the seats or plastic bugs in the drinks. Val, a retired electrician, would take one look at the wiring and insist on shutting the theater down for renovations. Clara and her greedy husband, Grosvenor, would refuse to spend a penny on this venture, Gloria would take her part against my mother, and Lillian would stop speaking to everybody. Every sibling would accuse every other sibling of trying to run the show. The chance that they would agree on which films to book, if they ever reached that stage, would be nil.

Mr. Hermes cleared his throat. "There is," he said, "a financial legacy that accompanies the property if you decide to accept it."

I narrowed my eyes at him. "What kind of financial legacy?" I asked.

"Something in the neighborhood of five hundred thousand dollars."

I sat up straighter. "Some neighborhood! That's not a legacy, that's a bribe!"

He just looked at me, open-eyed and guileless. "Your aunt did feel that it might help you make up your mind."

"So who gets that if I turn it down? Her brothers and sisters?"

"No, it goes into a charitable trust, which the family—the siblings and their offspring—will administer."

Another recipe for disaster, as Maesie very well knew. Before long, the supporters of the actors' retirement homes and the American Film Institute's film restoration project would be having it out with the animal-rights activists and the disabled-children advocates, and pretty soon nobody would be speaking to anybody.

"In any case," Mr. Hermes continued, "the siblings will all be receiving generous legacies in their own rights."

" 'Generous'?" I echoed.

I had always assumed that Maesie had sunk a substantial part of her savings in the Paradise, which, as I understood it, lost money every year. My aunt had had expensive tastes in wine and spent money on a few other indulgences, but she had not had an extravagant lifestyle.

"The movies made your aunt a wealthy woman," he said, "and the Paradise was the only bad investment she ever made, from a monetary standpoint. At the time of her death, I'd estimate her net worth in excess of three million."

"Jesus!" I was shocked. "Why couldn't she give me something I really wanted, like the name of her stockbroker? Anyway, if anybody should get the theater and the money, it should be Lillian."

"Gilda, your aunt made this will only a few months ago, after her first heart attack, when she knew she was seriously ill. She believed that perhaps you were at a crossroads in your life and that you might need an opportunity to . . . to take some time off and, well, take stock. She wanted to safeguard the future of the Paradise, too, there's no denying that. And she thought you could do that. She didn't trust Lillian's business judgment. She claimed, whether rightly or wrongly, that Lillian had made some bad business decisions. And, of course, Lillian is getting on; Mae was concerned about that. But she did believe that she was acting in your best interests as well."

As he spoke, a bubble of grief rose up in my throat and burst. I began to cry for both my losses: Maesie, who had, in her undemonstrative way, given me a steadying and uncomplicated love; and Liz, my soul mate, the one whom I'd always imagined myself growing old with until the day she'd revealed that she'd fallen in love with someone else and walked out the door.

Mr. Hermes handed over a box of tissues with the practiced air of a man who had women sobbing in his office every day of the week. I wondered what his undergraduate major had been.

"There are," he said, "two stipulations attached to the legacy."

"I was sure there would be," I said wryly, cynicism battling nostalgia for the upper hand.

"First, you have to keep the Paradise name."

Well, that was innocuous enough. If I was going into the movie business, which was looking likelier by the second, I didn't see any point in changing the name of the theater. To what? The Rialto?

"Second, you have to keep Duke on. He's one of the projectionists, and he knows a lot about the business. Your aunt thought he would be a great help to you."

I cast my mind back to the last family funeral.

"Pale, skinny kid with bottle-thick glasses? Is that Duke?"

"He's your cousin Ronald's grandchild. Lillian's greatgrandchild, Shane's boy. I believe that makes him your first cousin, twice removed." He gave me an unexpectedly puckish little smile. "But *you* may not remove him. And I doubt you'll want to. He's been running things, for all intents and purposes, ever since your aunt fell ill."

"He's just a kid, though, right?"

"He's seventeen."

I sighed. "Right. As long as she was leaving me people, why didn't she leave me a fifty-year-old business manager?"

"I'm sure your aunt's accountant would be happy to advise you. I would suggest that you talk to her, in any event, for her perspective on the theater's financial record and prospects. I'd also suggest that you talk to Duke and the staff, and to anyone else who can give you background information on the theater. You might even . . ." He trailed off.

"What?"

He shook his head. "Never mind. I was going to suggest— well, maybe I'll just say this: you might talk to your cousin Greer's husband, Andy Fuller, at the bank. His perspective would be valuable, as long as you understand where he's coming from."

I nodded. "The bottom line," I said.

"Exactly. And I don't have to tell you that there's more to a movie theater than that."

"Mr. Hermes," I cautioned him, "you're showing your age."

He laughed. "Do you know what I think? I think it would be fun to run a movie theater."

* * *

With the family gathering, I didn't have time to go looking for advice, but it came looking for me. Everyone, it turned out, had an opinion about how to improve the Paradise's chances for survival, except for those, especially among the younger generation, who didn't expect it to survive. Duke's father, my cousin Shane, thought that it should become some kind of virtual reality theater, with individual booths wired with a selection of virtual reality tapes—an idea that struck me as a throwback to the old kinetoscope parlors. My cousin James talked up IMAX, but I told him that it would never work since I couldn't sit through an IMAX film without feeling queasy. By dinnertime, my elbow was black and blue from all the people who had grabbed it to pull me aside and advise me. It sort of matched my eyes, which were an unbecoming pink from all those times when I was ambushed by memories of Liz. Everywhere I went—Liberty House, my parents' house, downtown—I experienced sudden flashbacks of Liz in that place, and my heart was wrenched. I was spending a lot of time in the bathroom, where I could cry in solitude and attempt to repair the damage afterward.

After dinner Andy Fuller, the bottom-line banker, waylaid me between the kitchen and the dining room, with my hands full of dirty dishes. My cousin Greer had met him when she was temping for MGM in the sixties and he was an accountant. As I'd understood it, he'd been a casualty of the change in ownership in 1970, when a Las Vegas financier took over the company, and they'd moved to Eden, where he'd worked his way up to president of Eden Commercial Bank. He was an energetic guy, who'd probably copied the phrase "Can-Do Attitude" off a flip chart at some motivational seminar and taken it to heart.

He relieved me of a stack of plates.

"I know you're still adjusting to your legacy, Gilda," he said, "and I don't want to intrude, but if you should need any financial advice, I want you to know that I'd be happy to help. You can't sell anytime soon, I know, but we might be able to put our heads together and figure out a way to maximize your profits."

When they weren't advising me on my business affairs, my

family members were scrutinizing my love life. Everyone who hadn't yet had the opportunity to express an opinion on the Gilda-Liz breakup did, with my mother and aunt Gloria serving as chorus. My uncle Val's solicitude was just as bad, since it made me feel like an emotional wreck who needed special handling. Thankfully, Aunt Clara was too self-centered to give my love life any thought, and Aunt Lillian had other things on her mind.

So did Aunt Adele, who, along with her daughter, Greer, called a family conference to discuss hotel arrangements. Happily, Andy had business to attend to at the bank or we would have gotten a cost-benefit analysis of each option. But Greer had the reputation for being just as canny as her husband when it came to business matters.

"Should I hold a room for Betty, in case she shows up?" Adele asked anxiously. "And if so, which one? I thought about the *Casablanca* room, but she might be offended by that, or maybe it would just make her sad, I don't know. I don't have time to do it over into a *Big Sleep* room—"

"Considering the occasion," Val murmured, "that's just as well."

"You could put Jimmy there, if he and Gloria come," Wallace proposed, highball in hand. "Health permitting, and all that."

"Why do you say that?"

"Well, he was in that remake, wasn't he? *Big Sleep Two? Return of the Big Sleep?*"

Adele's habit was to ignore her husband whenever inebriation rendered his commentary irrelevant.

"And it's so frustrating not to know who's getting along these days! Even if I knew who was coming, I wouldn't know who's on speaking terms with whom and who needs to be separated from whom!"

"Maybe we'd better send out for copies of all the tabloids, eh?" Oliver proposed.

"The real problem, if you ask me, is the *Little Mermaid* room," Greer said. "I told Mother at the time that it would be damned inconvenient if we got a convention of seniors with no kids, but she insisted."

"But I like that room!" Oliver protested. "That one's my favorite, with all the seaweed and the little colored lights!"

"If you'd listened to me and done Dracula's castle, you wouldn't be in this pickle," Wallace said, a little sulkily.

Meanwhile, more and more family members were arriving by the hour, until the town was teeming with Liberties. And these were no huddled masses, either, but flamboyant Southern California transplants hung with beepers and cell phones, sporting ponytails (the men), buzz cuts (the women), some dreadlocks and a lot of moussed, blow-dried hair (both sexes). Empty-sleeved double-breasted designer jackets draped the shoulders of the more formally attired. In the younger women's outfits, there was more cloth in those jacket sleeves than in the skirts. A group of them together looked like a Quentin Tarantino movie cast crossed with a Fellini. At Liberty House, you couldn't move an inch without stepping on a Liberty. Half of them were on the phone to L.A.

Somewhere in there my mother took me aside.

"I wish you'd speak to your aunt Lillian, Gilda," she said.

"Why? What's wrong?" I asked, dreading to be pulled into a family conflict.

"She's tearing the house apart looking for something, and she won't tell us what," said my mother. "Honestly! She's going to work herself up into a heart attack of her own if she's not careful! If she'd tell us what she's looking for, we might be able to help, but she won't."

"I'll keep my eyes open, Mom," I said. That was the most I was willing to promise. I suspected that the real problem had less to do with the state of Lillian's health than the state of my mother's frustrated curiosity.

My last airport run of the day on Thursday was at ten-thirty that night, to pick up my son, John. My father volunteered to ride along to keep me company, but I suspected that he couldn't shake the habit of worrying about his daughters out alone at night. For my part I hardly needed company, socially overstimulated as I was, but I looked forward to spending a little quiet time with him.

It turned out something was on his mind: the theater. He had a few ideas of his own for turning the theater around. He talked about them all the way to the airport.

At the gate my son gave me an awkward hug, blinking in the sudden glare of the airport light, and then looked me over with the air of nervous apprehension the young get when their parents' lives turn messy.

"You okay?" he asked.

I knew he wanted me to say yes, so I did. His height always came as a shock to me, whenever, as now, I hadn't seen him for a while. Intellectually, I knew he wasn't in the fourth grade anymore, but emotionally I was always expecting Opie instead of Ron Howard. He was wearing jeans and a T-shirt, and I noticed a pierced ear I'd never seen before. When he bent down to pick up his bag in the baggage claim area, I detected a tiny ponytail sprouting out of the back of his head. My boy had gone Hollywood.

He seemed to think running a movie theater would be "cool" but admitted he couldn't quite picture me threading a projector.

"I could take a look at your sound system, Mom," he offered benevolently, in the indulgent voice of the wired addressing a technophobe.

My father, meanwhile, had returned to the topic of innovations I could introduce. "I know it's a risky business, honey," he said. "Trying to survive as an independent theater these days is tough. You're a David going up against Goliath chains like Cinemark and AMC and Odeon. But I still say you can beat 'em if you're smart enough, and I really do believe that with some of these ideas of mine, you can kill the competition."

As it turned out, I didn't have to. Somebody did it for me.

6

The next night was the visitation, a custom I could live without.

"Why do they want to look at a dead person, Peach?" I asked. "And why would a dead person want to be looked at? It creeps me out."

"I know how you feel," she said, "but a lot of folks don't feel like they ever got a chance to say good-bye."

"And they think she can hear them if they say it now?"

"Some of them probably do. But for a lot of them, seeing her one last time gives them a sense of closure. They don't like to think that she just disappeared, you know? They don't like to think that the last time they saw her was the last time they'll ever see her."

"Yeah, but you're talking about normal families. I mean, look at them!"

Gloria and her son Alfred, a Hollywood makeup artist, were standing by the open coffin, doing a number on Maesie's makeup and hair for the edification of anyone who would listen. I could smell Gloria's perfume from across the room. Adele was fussing over some potted plants, moving them around until their arrangement suited her. Wallace, potted himself, was standing by, a tree of some kind swaying in his arms, waiting for Adele to tell him where to put it. My mother was staring at the organist in a way that worried me; any minute now she would go over and critique the woman's playing or offer to sing along. My uncle Val and my cousin James, both of them electricians, were off in a corner talking earnestly together and sketching invisible circuits on the wall with their index fingers. Val's longtime partner, Tobias, a writer, was sitting alone with that dreamy look he gets when he's studying my family for material. My cousin Clark and his daughter Josephine, a retired and active stunt performer, respectively, were attracting attention by reenacting a stunt in the middle of the carpeted floor. Oliver was furtively tugging at the edge of the rug they were standing on, hoping to topple them into a row of funeral wreaths; if he succeeded, they would go down like dominoes, and the last one would land on Maesie's upturned toes. My cousins Ronald and Marlowe were both talking on cell phones, hands pressed to their free ears. And the whole scene was being captured for posterity: Sophie was operating the video camera, with plenty of assistance and advice, and my cousin Spencer was taking still photographs.

And then the public arrived. The press was already camped out on the lawn of the Victorian house as if it were the Dorothy Chandler Pavilion on Oscar night. Some well-known faces showed up in the crowd, but I thought sadly of the ones who were missing among Lillian's and Mae's contemporaries: Davis and Shearer and Hayworth and Stanwyck, Wayne and Welles and Kelly.

Meanwhile, there were other faces to contend with—well-known and not so well-known. Visits home strained my underdeveloped memory. Sometimes I remembered faces but not names, and sometimes I didn't remember either.

"Gilda! Don't tell me you've forgotten!"

The pudgy man swayed his hips suggestively. Had he taken me to a dance? Won a local hula hoop contest? Taught me the twist? I searched my memory banks and came up dry.

"My Elvis imitation at the junior talent show! Say, I still remember that comedy routine you did. Every time I think of it, I have to laugh! You were always such a cutup!"

A comedy routine? *Me?* Surely he was mistaken.

"Gilda! It's so good to see you again, dear! Still a size seven-B?"

"Gilda! Long time no see! Wrap any houses lately?"

"Hey, Gilda! Heard you were back in town. What d'ya say we go bowling for old times' sake one of these nights?"

Bowling?

"Gilda! Well, it's about time. Now, tell me all about yourself and what you're doing these days. Have you kept up your writing?"

These people had a completely different memory of my childhood than I did. To hear them talk you would have thought I was something of a daredevil, a merry prankster, a social magnet. What I remembered was humiliation, isolation, and self-doubt. We couldn't all be right, could we?

I heard "Rosebud" intoned in my ear and turned to find Betty and my oldest sister, Lana, behind me. Lana was a film editor in Los Angeles, but she didn't have that Hollywood look about her. She was dressed in a navy pinstripe pantsuit and wore her brown hair pulled back in a snood. I was dressed in a charcoal-gray double-breasted pantsuit myself, with my best silk tie skewered to a tuxedo-tucked gray shirt. I hoped to look as good as Lana did at fifty, but at the rate I was going, my face would look like a road map of my disappointments and frustrations.

As if reading my mind, she nodded in the direction of our aunt Clara.

"So tell us, Betts, did she have another face lift since I was home last?" she asked.

"I think so," Betty said. "It's hard to keep track."

Clara's face lifts were the source of great amusement to us. She was the only one in the family who didn't look like a Liberty, since she'd replaced her Liberty nose, narrow with a bump in the bridge, with a sleeker model. She'd replaced her first husband with a newer, sleeker model as well, and our guess was that she was trying to ensure that people didn't mistake her for his older sister—or, God forbid, his mother. Her claim to fame was a popular series of light comedies in the fifties beginning with *Unlucky in Love* and ending with *Guilty as Sin*. She'd supported two husbands on her actress wages, which was no mean feat, given Grosvenor's expensive tastes. Grosvenor had once worked in special effects, but for as long as we'd known him, he'd sustained the illusion of always keeping busy without ever having an identifiable job. He was sixty now, but we couldn't remember a time when he hadn't been retired.

"If she did," Betty added, "I'm sure she went to the best surgeon."

We giggled. Two of Grosvenor's most annoying habits were his infatuation with costly things and his irritating tendency to go on and on about why whatever it was he had was better than what you had. He was obsessed with brand names and hierarchies, sort of like a walking *Consumer Reports* minus the "Best Buys." As far as he was concerned, the prices of goods reflected their worth. If someone had described him to me before I met him in the flesh, I would have dismissed him as a screen type, not a real person.

"It's not really his fault," we would all say. "After all, with a name like Grosvenor, how could he be anyone but who he is?"

Clara considered him very wise and had adopted his attitude toward material goods.

"I swear, that cigarette holder of Clara's should be registered as a deadly weapon!" I observed. "If we get through this weekend without one cigarette burn in the crowd, I'll be astonished."

"She's a walking fire hazard," Lana agreed. "That dress has way too much fabric, and it looks highly flammable."

"It's a new look," Betty said. "Cocktail hour at the funeral home."

"So what do you think about 'rosebud'?" Lana asked me.

"I try not to think about it," I said, giving Betty a look.

"But don't you think it's odd, after all that preparation?" Lana persisted.

"Sure," I admitted. "But people probably say odd things when they're dying. I wouldn't know."

"Well, *I'd* feel better if we could find the file she was reading when she died," Betty said.

"Me, too," Lana agreed.

"Gilda!"

I felt a tap on my shoulder. My cousin Shane was towing a lanky kid with thick glasses, a smattering of acne, and unruly dark blond hair. The kid's skin had the mushroom pallor of someone who spends too much time indoors.

"Remember my son, Duke?"

I flinched at the reminder of how mismatched the kid was with his name and covered it up with a cough.

"Yeah, sure." I shook his hand, which was moist. "Hi, Duke. I hear we'll be working together."

Duke shrugged and said nothing. He studied the floor.

"Aunt Maesie used to call Duke her right-hand man," Shane persisted cheerily. "Isn't that right, son?"

Duke shrugged again. "I guess," he mumbled.

"Duke knows everything there is to know about running the theater," Shane said, clapping him on the back. "Anything you need to know, just ask him."

"I will," I said.

Duke pushed his glasses up with an index finger and continued to study the floor.

"He can even take the projector apart and put it back together," his father bragged.

Duke raised his head then, like a horse that had scented something. As his father talked on, his gaze rested on someone across the room and his eyes changed color from a pale blue to a darker shade. He frowned.

Startled, I turned away from Shane to follow Duke's gaze. His father broke off and looked to see what we were staring at.

"Oh," he said. "Julius is here."

The Liberty kids had always called Julius Cole "Uncle Julius" because he was a good friend of Maesie's. He had reciprocated by stocking his pockets with candy and sending us extravagant presents for our birthdays. They were often the kinds of presents our parents wouldn't buy for us, and we loved him for it. Nine years ago, at seventy-two, he had been a handsome, trim man who didn't look a day over fifty-nine. I knew his age because Maesie had once commented that he was a year younger than she and Lillian, so she reserved the right to boss him around. But not many people claimed that right. I didn't know much about how he'd made his money, only what Peachy had told me—that he bought and sold real estate. He might well have been wealthy before that, though, since I supposed you needed money to buy real estate in the first place. He radiated success. He was one of the town's leading citizens.

He was also reputed to be something of a ladies' man, and the way in which Maesie deflected inquiries on this subject had always led Lana, Betty, and me to speculate that she had once been one of his conquests, if you could use such a word in describing iron-willed Mae Liberty. But as I'd grown older, I'd sensed some tension in their relationship. Maybe it had been there all along. Mae had been married four times after all, yet she'd never married Uncle Julius.

"Gilda," said a familiar voice in my ear.

I felt a kiss planted on my cheek and looked up at my ex-husband, George.

"I'm sorry, sweetheart," he said. "I know you and Maesie were close."

I felt swamped by my past. My eyes teared. "Thanks, George," I said. "It was good of you to come."

I reached up and touched the newly sprouted hair along his jawline.

"Is this your idea or Honey's?"

Honey was his second wife. They had been married less than a year, yet I detected her influence in his clothes, which were less conservative, more fashionable, than his usual style. And he was wearing contact lenses.

He blinked at me and smiled somewhat sheepishly.

"Like it?"

"Yeah, I do," I said. I felt only gratitude to Honey for making him as happy as he deserved to be. "I like the whole look."

"Sorry to hear about you and Liz," he said. He meant it, too; that's how nice he was.

"Thanks," I said again. What else was there to say?

But our tête-à-tête was interrupted by a commotion at the front of the room, which was having a ripple effect on the crowd. Duke was standing by the coffin with Julius, surrounded by people with shocked expressions. Duke's hand gripped Julius's arm.

"I just don't want him to get near her," he said to his astonished mother. He spoke in a low, tight voice audible in the hushed room. "I don't want him to touch her."

Shane was making his way through the crowd.

"What's going on here, son?" he asked, glancing nervously at Julius.

"I don't want him to touch her," Duke repeated. "She wouldn't have wanted him to. She knew all about him."

Shane traded surprised looks with his wife and Julius.

"I don't know what you mean, son," Julius said gently. "Maesie and I were good friends. We'd been friends a long time."

"Not anymore," Duke persisted. He still hadn't released his grip on Julius's arm. "She knew all about you, and she hated you."

My eyes shifted. I scanned the crowd to see how people were reacting. And then I was engulfed by déjà vu. Only it wasn't déjà vu, exactly, but rather a feeling of recognition. All eyes in the room were riveted on the scene around the coffin—except for one pair. Where I should have seen eyes, I saw a curly mop of black hair. I didn't recognize it, but it belonged to a woman. She was writing in a small notebook. It was like that moment at the tennis match in *Strangers on a Train*, when Farley Granger, who plays the protagonist, spots the psychotic killer, played by Robert Walker, because his is the only head in the stands that isn't turning from side to side.

She must have felt my stare, because from across the room she raised her eyes to mine. She gave me a long, slow wink.

7

"Duke, you're making a scene," Shane cautioned him sternly. "This is not the time—"

"It is if he's going to touch her," Duke responded stubbornly. "She would have hated that."

"Duke!" his father admonished him.

"It's all right, Shane." Lillian's commanding voice cut him off. "Leave the boy alone. I don't want him to touch her, either."

She gave Julius a frosty look that made the crowd hold its collective breath. I was shocked. I knew that Lillian had never gotten along especially well with Julius, but she seemed to tolerate him for her sister's sake. Now she appeared willing to break with funeral protocol to push him away.

She and Julius stared at each other over the coffin, oblivious to the attention they had attracted.

"I'm not going to touch her, son," Julius reassured Duke, a bit wearily, I thought. He disengaged his arm and turned away. "Maesie was always full of life, and that's the way I want to remember her."

"You do that," Lillian retorted, narrowing her eyes.

I felt a hand gripping my elbow.

"What was *that* all about?" my sister Betty was whispering excitedly in my ear.

"Beats me."

"Boy oh boy, if looks could kill, Uncle J. would be a dead man!"

The room was buzzing.

" 'She knew all about you,' " Betty repeated portentously. "What did *that* mean?"

Lana joined us. "What's up with Duke? I mean, I know he was close to Maesie, and he's always been a little strange, but . . ."

"Is he totally wigged out or what?" Betty agreed.

"Please, guys," I pleaded. "That was my business manager."

"Then you'd better start learning about the business pretty darn quick, Gil," Lana said.

"Lillian was pretty steamed, too, though," I pointed out.

"Yeah," Betty said. "Think she knows something we don't know?"

"About what?" Betty's husband, Teddy, joined us. He had boyish good looks, mussed dark blond hair, and the faint odor of alcohol about him. "Sorry I'm late," he said. "Obstetric emergency."

Betty kissed him and smoothed his hair. "How'd it go?"

He grinned. "Mother and six kittens are doing well, thanks. So what'd I miss?"

"Where'd you come in?" I asked.

"The part where Duke was going on about Julius not touching Maesie and Lillian was agreeing with him."

"You know everything we do then," I assured him.

"Maybe Mae and Julius were secret lovers all these years, and she just found out that he was unfaithful to her," Betty speculated.

Lana rolled her eyes. "Betts, the man's a notorious Don Juan. You'd have to be blind and deaf not to know that he fools around."

"Well, Duke is practically blind," Betty said. "Maybe he was the one who didn't know about Julius."

" 'Practically blind'! That's my projectionist you're talking about!" I wailed.

"Don't worry, Gil." Teddy patted my hand. "He's a great projectionist."

"Well, I still don't think they were referring to Julius's love life," Lana said. "Everybody knew about that by the time his wife left him, and that was years ago."

"Wait, guys! I've got it!" Betty cried. "What if it wasn't Maesie he screwed around with but Lillian?"

" 'Screwed around with'?" I echoed. "Lillian?"

"You know what I mean," she said. "Maybe he seduced and betrayed her, and Maesie only found out recently.

"Hey!" She grabbed my arm and Lana's excitedly. "I just remembered! Lillian's middle name is Rose. She's the sister who got Rose, not Mae! So maybe *she's* 'Rosebud'! I wonder how we could find out."

"Now, Betts," Teddy said, "you're not going to go digging into your aunt's love life. It's none of your business. Leave it alone, sweetie."

She seemed to relent. "Well, maybe you're right."

But I felt her crossed fingers on my arm and glanced up at her. She grinned at me.

And then Julius himself was in our midst, giving us hugs all around. In my teens I'd had a crush on him, and I still found myself tongue-tied in his presence. He had the kind of Cary Grant good looks that just got better as he matured and the easy charm to go with them. His hair was white now, but his eyes were the same intense blue they'd always been, and they had Grant's mischievous sparkle.

"Well, the boy's upset," he was saying. "He's feeling possessive about Maesie, and I can understand that. She's been his patroness and mentor all his life. He's going through a rough period. We all need to cut him some slack."

He turned to me. "I hope you'll bear that in mind, Gilda. You're the one who'll be working with him."

I didn't answer. I was thinking that maybe we could just hire a therapist and transform staff meetings into group therapy sessions. I could talk about Liz and Duke could talk about Maesie, and the therapist could say useful things like "I hear you saying that you're feeling hurt and abandoned."

Julius took my hand and my ears turned red, just like that. I couldn't see them, of course, but I could feel them, glowing like exit signs.

"I want to wish you the best in your new enterprise, honey," he said. "I mean that. And if there's anything I can do to help, just let me know."

"Thanks, Julius," I mumbled. "I will."

He gave me a dazzling smile that bared his teeth, added his other hand to the pile, and gave my hand one last meaningful shake. Then he was gone.

"Well, he seems to have taken it well," Lana observed.

"He's a charming guy," Betty said. "Vengefulness doesn't suit his style."

"Neither does magnanimity," I said. "We'll see."

My family doesn't believe in doing anything by halves. And in their book an event without a postmortem, as we were accustomed to calling these family gatherings before they had turned so funereal, was incomplete.

So we all retired to Liberty House after the visitation to gossip some more. Presiding over the kitchen was Mae and Lillian's housekeeper, Ruth Hernandez, an energetic and spirited woman who had been in her twenties when she'd moved east with Mae from Los Angeles. She had never married but always claimed that she remained single by choice, and I'd never had any reason to doubt her word. She had an endless string of boyfriends, and she managed them as efficiently as she managed Liberty House. It was hard to imagine two strong-willed women like Mae Liberty and Ruth Hernandez enjoying a peaceful coexistence in one household, but even Maesie had never wanted to cross her.

In the living room, I saw Grosvenor setting up the video camera on a tripod. I ground my teeth. "I wish they'd turn that damn thing off," I growled.

"And deprive the Liberty film archive?" Lana said. "Not a chance."

Grosvenor was bending Andy Fuller's ear about his camera— QVC was the only brand he'd consider, the others couldn't touch it for clarity, et cetera, et cetera. Andy was trying to look interested over his yawns, and Sophie was pointedly ignoring the whole business.

Shane arrived with Duke, whose fumbling apology to the group in general and Lillian in particular seemed sincere.

"Thank you, dear," Lillian said. "I sympathize completely. Julius is an odious man, and now that Maesie's dead, I can say so."

Everyone looked uncomfortable.

"I don't know, Lillian," Andy Fuller ventured. As a banker he must have felt uneasy to hear one of his principal clients abused in his company. "He's always been good to the kids."

"If you mean to suggest that he's purchased their affections cheaply, I would agree with you," she said severely. "He buys cheap and sells dear—that's the secret to his success."

"Oh, come on, Lilly," my father admonished her. "You're being too hard on him. You can't hold his success against him."

"Oh, but I do," she said.

"Well, well," Uncle Wallace said appeasingly, "to each his own, eh?"

"Smile, everybody!" My cousin Spencer had arrived on the scene, Nikon around his neck. It was a Kodak moment.

The youngest Liberties arrived, fresh from the baby-sitter, wide awake and ready to party. Groucho and Chico, the twins, and Harpo had all been born last year, and Zeppo's arrival was imminent, from the look of my cousin Clyde's wife, Lisa. They lightened the tone of the gathering.

"I thought Kate looked well, didn't you?" Aunt Adele observed to me. "In the tabloids, they make her look like she's at death's door."

"Mother, the tabloids make Demi Moore look like she's at death's door," Greer said.

"Even so, Greer, at your mother's and my age you don't like to hang out near open coffins," Aunt Gloria put in. She made a small gesture and I was engulfed with a tidal wave of L'Air du Temps. "The corpse might look better than you do."

"Speak for yourself," Adele said, somewhat huffily, patting her tangerine hair and lowering eyelashes heavy with mascara. If I were she, I thought, I'd never lower them in public, for fear I wouldn't be able to lift them up again, but she must have had well-developed eyelids.

"Maesie looked younger in her coffin than she did when she played Queen Elizabeth," my cousin Al, the makeup man, said. "Now *that* was some makeup job!"

"Dreadful movie, though," my cousin Marlowe, the agent, said.

"Smile!" said Spencer, and a flash went off.

I was keeping an eye on Harpo, who had broken from the herd and just discovered one of Scarlett's crutches. Scarlett, who worked as a film editor, had had polio as a child and walked with two crutches.

Harpo reached out and seized the rubber tip. I dived and caught the other end just before it fell on Betty's foot. I picked up the baby to distract her.

"Listen, Betts, there was a woman at the funeral home tonight that I haven't seen before," I said, giving the baby my fist to gnaw on. "Curly dark hair, short and slim, black pantsuit. Know who she was?"

"No, why?" She dug an elbow in my ribs. "Interested?"

I gave her a look. "Only because she had an odd reaction to that little contretemps between Duke, Julius, and Lillian."

"Which was?"

"Well, no reaction at all, I guess. She was writing in a little notebook."

"A notebook? How weird. Well, maybe the fight reminded her of something, like to call her ex-husband about the alimony check."

I shook my head. "I don't think so."

"Anyway, I can't think of who you mean. I don't remember anybody like that."

Together we said, "We'll go to the tape," and burst out laughing. Whenever something like this came up and somebody didn't remember it, we'd joke about the family archive. Everything, after all, was recorded on film or on video.

"Hey!" George was standing at my shoulder, finger poised in the air, taking in me with a baby in my arms. "That reminds me of something."

"Sleepless nights?" I said. "Colic? Strained carrots on your best tie? Unmentionable stains on your white shirtsleeves?"

"That's it!" He grinned and held out his arms.

I handed over the baby. He patted her padded posterior, took a deep breath, and made a face. "That reminds me of something, too," he said. "Will you excuse us a minute?"

He departed with good grace, just as our son appeared.

"Mom, some of us thought we'd go into Columbus to catch some music. Want to come?"

The state capital was twenty minutes down the road. It didn't impress a bicoastal urban sophisticate like John, but it was livelier than Eden.

"You're going now?"

"In a little while. Audrey says Lillian looks pretty tired, anyway. She doesn't think we'll be missed."

My cousin Audrey, Clara's oldest, was a recording studio executive and a good contact for an aspiring musician.

"You guys go ahead," I said. "I'm not up to it. But thanks." I was touched that I'd been invited.

"Getting old?" That was Tobias Norton, Uncle Val's partner.

"Yeah," I admitted. "I'm getting older and you're getting younger. It's not fair!"

Tobias laughed. At seventy-seven, he was two years older than Val, but he carried his age well. They had been together since I was in high school. I'd never figured out how Val had persuaded him to move to Ohio and live inside the force field that was the Liberty family, but Tobias claimed to like small-town life. As a writer he preferred to live with a minimum of

distractions, he said; my family seemed to me a veritable Grand
Hotel of distractions, but he did seem immune to it. And he and
Val maintained strong ties to the gay community in Columbus.

"So did you gather any material tonight?"

He smiled enigmatically. "Perhaps."

"I noticed you weren't the only one studying the scene for in-
spiration," I said. "There was a woman with curly dark hair
who was writing in a notebook. Know her?"

"I saw her," he said. "Don't know her. Why?" He cocked an
eyebrow at me. "Interested?"

"No," I repeated. "I just want to know why she was taking
notes at a visitation."

"Come on, Gillie. This is Uncle Toby. You can tell me."

"Not on your life! Whatever I tell you is liable to appear in
the *New York Times Book Review*. Anyway, there's nothing to
tell. It's just that too many weird things are happening."

"Weirder than usual?" Val joined us. "How quickly they
forget!"

"Well, first there was this 'rosebud' business, and then the
missing papers or whatever they were, and then Duke freaks
out about Julius, and then Lillian sides with him, and in the
middle of it all is this chick nobody can identify and she's writing in a notebook." I took a breath. "All I'm saying is, if we're
going to be the lead story in next week's *National Enquirer*, I'd
like some advance warning."

Spencer popped up over Val's shoulder like a moon rising.

"Smile!" he said.

How any of the actors in my family ever made it to an early
makeup call was a mystery to me. They all stayed up half the
night and ate breakfast about the time other people were thinking about lunch. Somebody made a beer run after midnight, and
at one the living room still hosted a lively contingent, although
Lillian had already disappeared upstairs. And what with all the
uncles and aunts and cousins and second cousins and cousins
once or twice removed and their families, we could have cast
Exodus and still had a few people left over to chisel the tablets
and operate the machinery that parted the Red Sea.

By two o'clock, Betty and I had killed most of a bottle of scotch by ourselves in the kitchen. Ruth Hernandez had stacked the dirty dishes and rinsed the glasses and retired some time ago. I was waxing more maudlin by the minute. My words had grown fuzzy around the edges.

"I don't care what anybody says," I said. "The thing about Maesie was, she lived her life." Elbows on the scarred wood table, hands spread and facing palm to palm, I pumped them up and down for emphasis. "She lived her life."

"Amen," Betty said.

"She had a lot of tradegy, I mean, tragedy, but she just kept going."

"Kind of like the Energizer bunny," Betty agreed solemnly.

"The who?"

"You know, the little pink guy with the drum. Wears shades."

"Oh, yeah, him. Well, that's just my point. She had her ups and her downs, but she never—"

"D'jyou know she won the Oscar the same week she found out she was pregnant with Camille?"

"I never heard that."

"S'true. The very same week."

The profound implications of this coincidence rendered us momentarily speechless.

"Camille was always a little wild," Betty said at last. "Remember her funeral?"

"I never did figure out what happened to her," I said.

"Me, neither," Betty said. "All I know is that it was something gynecological, like maybe some kind of fast-growing cancer they were trying to cut out. Nobody ever explained it. Camille was the first person I ever knew who died."

"Me, too."

"Oh, come on! You hung out with Peachy. You must've seen lots of dead people."

"I saw some, sure, but they weren't people I really *knew*. I mean, there was Mr. What's-His-Name from the drugstore who always gave us suckers—I saw him laid out. And that older lady from the library who had the heart attack in the middle of Readiculo the Reading Clown. But I didn't *know* them."

"And then Giulietta had that motorcycle crash. After that, I used to imagine what it would be like to be in a coma, lying there dead to the world with everybody standing around you, talking to you."

"Yeah," I said. "And what if you could hear the doctors talking, even though you looked like you were asleep? That's what I used to think about. What if you heard them saying they were going to pull the plug and you couldn't tell them not to? That's what creeped me out."

"Well, they said there was extensive brain damage," Betty reminded me.

"Yeah, I know that's what they said, but you never know, do you?"

"No, you don't. 'Cause look what happened to her mother. That was some kind of surgery."

Giulietta had been Camille's daughter, though who her father was, nobody knew for sure. She had been raised by Maesie after her mother died, when Giulietta was only seven. And then she had died in the hospital after a motorcycle crash had left her in a coma. She was only eighteen.

"I can't imagine outliving my daughter and granddaughter."

"Me, neither." Betty perked up suddenly. "Hey, they were both Roses! Camille Rose and Giulietta Rose. Maybe that's what Maesie was thinking about when she died! Maybe she even saw one of them coming to get her!"

"But you said the nurse said she sounded angry. Why would she sound angry if she was talking about them?"

"No, you're right." Betty sighed. "It doesn't make sense. Unless . . ."

"Unless what?"

"Nothing," Betty said, deflated. "It's too late, and we're too drunk, and the funeral is too damn early in the day for anybody with the kind of hangovers we're going to have. And my animals all wake up even earlier than that."

It was two-twenty by then, and everyone had finally cleared

out and gone up to bed or gone home. John and his party had gone in search of a livelier crowd. I dragged myself to the door to wave Betty off. I felt dog-tired and depressed. I toured the downstairs, turning off lights. At the foot of the stairs, I remembered something else and went back to the living room. The camera was still on, but the tape had long since run out, and its transparent eye stared glassily at the vacant room.

"The party's over," I said, and switched it off.

"Come on, Gilda! Wake up!"

Betty was bouncing on my bed. In my sleepy confusion I fell backward in time and thought we were kids again. I rolled over, nestled into the pillow, eyes closed.

"Hey! Come on! Wake up! You'll never guess what happened!"

I opened my eyes. Big mistake. The light hit some nerve at the back of my head and my whole skull started to throb in pain.

"This had better be good," I said.

"It is! You're now the owner of the only movie theater in Eden, Ohio!"

That got my attention.

"What are you talking about?" I demanded groggily.

"The Eden Center Theater burned down last night. Clyde called Marlowe, and Marlowe called Adele, and—"

I was sitting up by this time. "You can skip the gossip chain. What happened?"

"Nobody knows! The first call to the fire department was around one-twenty, but the whole place was already in flames by the time they arrived."

"I don't suppose it was arson," I ventured.

"Well, it wasn't somebody smoking in bed." She smirked. "So, how does it feel to have the field to yourself?"

"I'm not sure," I said slowly. "I've got a real bad feeling about this."

"You mean, just because Maesie's chief rival went up in smoke on the eve of her funeral? Or is that your hangover talking?"

"Both. How come you're so chipper this morning?"

"I've been up for two hours already with the animals. I'm not over my hangover; I've just gotten used to it. So, anyway, I kind of like the idea that somebody firebombed the chain theater as a farewell gesture."

"You would. Look, it makes a great movie, but it won't play in Peoria. If this fire *does* turn out to be arson, the cops' suspect list is going to have 'Liberty' written all over it."

"They'll love it! Mom will do Dietrich in *Witness for the Prosecution*, Aunt Lilly will play the Russian countess in *Murder on the Orient Express*—"

I groaned and flopped back down on the pillow. "Oh, please!"

"Well, all I can say is, I hope you sold them the insurance on the place. Otherwise, you'd be the logical suspect."

I groaned again.

"Anyway, you have to admit we have a lot of pyrotechnic talent in our family. Wait'll the police find out that Grosvenor worked on *The Towering Inferno*!"

"Grosvenor is hardly the type for sentimental gestures," I pointed out.

"Well, if he did it, he'll have a hard time keeping it secret," she said. "He'll be dying to brag about it. Then there's Daphne. She does special effects, too, and she's Lilly's granddaughter, so she might have done it."

"Betty! We don't even know if anybody did it yet. Maybe it was just faulty wiring."

"And if that's the case we know who would be capable of helping that along." She appeared to ponder this scenario. "Of the electricians, I think I like Val over James for it. James is only a nephew, after all, and Val was always closer to Maesie, I thought, than to any of the other siblings. No, wait a minute! Maybe Julius did it. You know, kind of a farewell gesture to Maesie.

"Well, one thing's for sure," she said after a pause. "If it was arson, the arsonist will be at Maesie's funeral today."

That was probably true. I couldn't think of anybody who wouldn't be at Maesie's funeral, except for the president perhaps, and that was only because he was touring Latin America.

The main event, as I had begun to think of it, started at ten at the Methodist church. Methodism was big in Eden: the local college was Methodist, and there was a Methodist seminary just outside of town. Most of the Liberties went in for more flamboyant religions than Methodism—we had some Episcopalians and a few Catholics—but most of these designations became operative only on ceremonial occasions. We learned early to worship the God of Charlton Heston and to associate Him with the smell of popcorn rather than incense. But Maesie had chosen the simplicity of Methodism when she divided her loyalties late in life. Val claimed it was because the service let out in time for her to prepare for the Sunday matinee.

The day was bright but chilly. Nearby churches and businesses had posted signs inviting funeral attendees to park in their lots, but that did little to ease the congestion. The police were preparing to block off Main Street for the funeral procession and their presence added to the confusion. Tempers were frayed by the time people squeezed through the front door of the church. There they were engulfed by the overpowering scent of flowers and perfume.

"Gilda, you haven't seen Julius, have you?"

My mother looked worried.

"No, why?"

"He's supposed to be a pallbearer, but he hasn't shown up yet," she said, scanning the sea of faces.

"You don't suppose he's boycotting because of last night?"

"I can't imagine he would. Not Mae's funeral, surely!"

"Well, if he doesn't show, remember that Betty's been lifting all those feed sacks. She could probably carry the coffin on her shoulder all by herself."

Mother gave me a look. "Tobias has already volunteered." Then she frowned again. "How strong do you have to be?"

She knew as well as I did that the strongest thing Toby lifted on a regular basis was a pen. She was deferring to my expertise as Peachy's confidante.

"Not that strong, Mom, if there are six people," I reassured her. "Don't worry. He'll do fine."

Reserved seating for the family took up half the church. Everyone else who hadn't come early enough to get a seat stood, rich and famous shoulder-to-shoulder with the humble and obscure. I found myself checking out the fire exits, in case there was a pyromaniac among them.

The siblings, who sat together in the first row, had resisted all of Adele's attempts to color-coordinate them. There were six of them now—Lillian, Douglas, Wallace, Gloria, Valentino, and Clara. A seventh, David Wark Griffith Liberty, had died during the Spanish flu epidemic of 1919, while the director he was named for was filming *Broken Blossoms*. But Lillian was the only one alive now who would have remembered him. So Mae's death must have frightened them all, marking as it did the beginning of the long parade to the cemetery in a way that their mother's death had not.

George sat on one side of me and held my hand. John sat on the other, his face rigid with the effort to fight back tears.

But what the whole production desperately needed was a tyrannical director, a skillful script doctor, and a ruthless editor.

Each of the siblings read a biblical passage, taking care to show their best side to the audience, and they all exceeded their time limit. Then my mother sang a hymn. Then half of the siblings spoke about their dead sister. Then the minister spoke about her. Then my parents sang a duet. Then the youngest three siblings spoke. Then James's twins, Dorothy and Glinda, read a soppy piece about angels. Then James's eldest, Ozzie, brought his six-year-old brother, Toto, up to read a prayer to God to take care of Maesie. Then, to my embarrassed surprise, John got up, retrieved his guitar from behind a wreath of gladioli, and sang a song he'd written in Maesie's memory. Then the lights went out and a bar-size big-screen TV was rolled out, and we watched a video about Maesie's life, made by Sophie and her aunt Grace, while John hummed and strummed in accompaniment. Then the video presentation turned into a kind of sound and light show, and I glimpsed Audrey at a console, wearing earphones.

Then, just when I was hoping for the final credits, or at least an intermission, other members of the audience began making their way to the front. Some spoke movingly, some told funny stories, but I was past caring. I needed a bathroom and a cigarette. My exit was blocked on one side by the standing crowds and on the other by the advance up the aisle of an older woman who was being helped by my father. I recognized her as one of Maesie's old cronies from the Hollywood days, a film editor with three Academy Awards to her credit. When she finished speaking, the lights went down again. I made my escape as they began to roll a compilation of scenes from Maesie's films.

Peachy followed me into the women's room.

"Don't give me that look!" she said. "I nixed the production number. Said we didn't have the insurance to cover it. And I vetoed the eighty-two white doves on the grounds of sanitation."

"Well, thank God for that! Am I the only person who *isn't* speaking at this extravaganza?"

"Just about," she admitted, following me outside. "The horses don't have lines, so anything they say will be ad-libbed."

"You didn't!"

She shrugged. "The lady wanted six white horses, she got six white horses. They've got some spots on 'em, and they're old and kind of pokey, but I think they'll manage to drag a coffin through the streets of Eden without breaking a sweat."

"As long as I don't have to ride one."

"No, your horses are all under the hood. Got you a nice white limo with a bar."

I blew out a puff of smoke and grinned at her. "Peachy, you're the best," I said.

"I know it."

"Julius ever show?"

"Not yet. We've got Tobias on standby. Now I have to get back, but I'm dying to talk." She leaned close with a wicked smile and said, "I hear you smoked the competition last night."

"That isn't even funny!" I protested, but I was speaking to her retreating back.

The horses, when their turn in the limelight came, looked bored with the whole affair. In spite of his resistance, Mr. Gower drove the impromptu hearse because he apparently didn't trust anyone else to do it. Behind the hearse came the fleet of white limos holding the Liberty clan, and everybody else was behind that. At the tail end was a Jeep full of fraternity boys on dung duty.

The whole procession moved slowly down Main and turned onto Oak Street. The horses stopped in front of the Paradise for a few minutes of silent contemplation before moving on.

"When I die," my father said, "have 'em stop in front of Hamburger Heaven so I can catch one last whiff of it before I'm planted."

To say that I hoped the graveside service was shorter than the church service would be an understatement of epic proportions. My shoes were killing me.

I lingered on the edge of the crowd to smoke a cigarette and spotted the dark-haired woman from the visitation. She was apparently alone again. She was wearing dark glasses, so I couldn't read her expression. She wore a blue-gray pants outfit, with parachute pants and a floor-length coat. She also wore, I now realized with a start, a very funky pair of lace-up black boots that reminded me of combat boots. I caught myself staring at them, then raised my eyes to find her looking at me. At least I thought she was looking at me; it was hard to tell with the glasses. She smiled at whomever she was looking at and then melted into the crowd.

The minister's voice was a distant murmur. I closed my eyes against the pain in my head, heart, and feet.

"You should never wear shoes like that to a funeral," a low voice said close to my ear. "Especially a Liberty funeral."

I opened my eyes and shifted them right. A curly dark head had materialized at my shoulder. It appeared to be intent on the minister.

I tried to think of a snappy retort and failed. I settled for the truth.

"If I'd worn combat boots, the damn funeral would last the rest of my life, because that's how long I'd have to hear about it from my mother," I said.

"Might have been worth it, though," she said.

The next time I turned my eyes in that direction, she was gone.

The "Amens" around me were loud with finality, as if the right response would cut the ceremony short. And then suddenly it was over, and Gloria and Adele were handing out roses from the display on top of the coffin. Clara was posing for the cameras, shoulders rolled delicately forward as if she were taking her cue from an old mourning picture. Oliver had his rose between his teeth.

10

Back at Liberty House the camera was rolling and the booze was flowing. The Liberties generally preferred to mix their sympathy with something stronger than tea. We laid out a buffet lunch in the dining room, so the kitchen and dining room were crowded with family and friends, unwrapping, reheating, stirring, dressing, and rearranging food. There was another crowd in the large living room, a room that mixed modern comfort and antique style. Ties were yanked loose or removed, dress jackets were discarded.

I saw Jack Lemmon sampling clam dip and Joanne and Paul dressing a salad. Duke slumped morosely in one corner, surrounded by kids his age who I assumed worked at the theater. Adele was showing off an antique breakfront to a small group and one of them was sketching it. Gloria had her fingers in the hair of a woman who had an executive look about her; my aunt appeared to be examining it critically and was shaking her head. Uncle Wallace was ensconced behind the bar, where he was pouring white wine for an elderly actress who was deep in conversation with Mr. Gower. Lillian was holding court from a high-backed chair by the fireplace. The star from one of those martial arts films was trying to have a conversation with Andy Fuller, surrounded by adoring kids who were hoping for a karate demonstration. Ozzie stood on the fringes, feigning the lack of interest appropriate for a thirteen-year-old. A flamboyant young starlet type who must have come with somebody was batting her false eyelashes at my cousin Clark, a sixty-one-year-old body builder who looked to be around fifty, and he was flexing his muscles nonchalantly in response, as if it took superior strength to carry a platter of ham from kitchen to table. Sidney Poitier was getting his ear bent by Uncle Oliver, who I sincerely hoped was not about to pull a live mouse out of Poitier's coat pocket. The only person missing was Julius Cole. I passed Toby in earnest conversation with a small group of people whom I took to be writers.

"Tarantino's crap!" a middle-aged man insisted, his face red. "Pretentious nonsense! And his imitators are worse!"

"You're only saying that because you're in Ohio, sweetie," a woman responded acerbically. "If we were back in L.A., you wouldn't have the guts to criticize him."

Sidney Lumet was on the phone in the kitchen.

I slipped upstairs and changed into jeans and tennis shoes. From down the hall an insistent voice reached me.

"I'm telling you, Richie, he's shopping the same damn minotaur script that Zukow pitched to us last year. 'A gender-bender *Splash*,' he called it, as if audiences want to see Keanu Reeves topless the same way they want to see Hannah in a bikini! 'After *Hercules*,' he said, 'audiences will want more Greek mythology.' 'Al, animated mermaids are in,' I told him. 'Computer-generated dinosaurs are in,' I said. 'Not cow people. You seen any cow people on the screen lately? Angels, Al,' I said. 'Angels are hot. Bring me angels.' "

When I returned to the living room, everyone had stopped speculating about Julius Cole's absence, and was congratulating my cousins Sophie and Grace on the biopic and my cousin Scarlett and my sister Lana on the compilation of scenes from Maesie's films.

"I didn't know they were going to show it at the *funeral*, for heaven's sake," Lana muttered to me.

"Dottie was a big help." Scarlett acknowledged the bent little woman whom my father had just settled into an armchair. It was Dottie Alexander, the film editor.

"Oh, I'm a storehouse of useless information," she said in a creaky voice. "And it helps to be older than God. People do what you ask them to, and do it quick before you drop dead on 'em."

"I hadn't seen some of those films in ages," my mother said. "I didn't remember half of them."

"Well, we didn't include everything, you know," Scarlett said.

"I'm glad you included my favorite scene from *Never Say Never Again*." Gloria sighed. "I cry every time she says good-bye to him—every time! Even this time, when it popped up in the middle of everything else, it just gets to me . . . right here." She tapped her chest theatrically.

"And that scene from *Within These Walls*, when her daughter is dying!" my cousin Greer said. "Talk about bringing things back! They showed that scene over and over when Camille died, and then even on the local news when Giulietta died. She must have grown to hate that scene."

"We talked about that, Greer," Scarlett said uncomfortably, glancing at Lillian. "But in the end we thought it should be included because it played such an important role in her life."

"Quite right, Scarlett," Lillian reassured her. "It was an artistic decision Mae would have appreciated."

"I liked the scene you were in together, Lilly," a neighbor said. "Was that the only film you ever did together?"

"*Within These Walls,*" Lillian said. "Yes, that was the only one."

What nobody said was that Lillian had never been quite as talented or quite as successful as her sister. I had rarely seen any hint of jealousy or bitterness in her attitude toward Mae, but I wondered, not for the first time, what it must have been like to be Mae's less brilliant twin.

"I never saw that scene from *Edith's Folly*, where she played a drunk," my cousin Shane said. "That was pretty amazing! I'm kind of surprised it wasn't censored." He glanced at his father.

"I seem to recall that there was some controversy about it," Ron replied. "Is that right, Mother?"

"Oh, heavens, yes!" Lillian said. "It went back and forth to the Hays Office a million times before they were satisfied that Edith died a sufficiently miserable death."

"And in the process, got Mae an Oscar nomination," my father pointed out. "The Production Code drove us crazy, but it wasn't all bad."

"Personally, I liked being reminded of how funny she could be," Andy said.

"That scene from *Fair Game* made my sides ache," Val agreed. "I've never laughed so hard at a funeral!"

"They should have let her do more comedy," Lillian agreed. "She always wanted to, but the studio had other ideas. She fought very hard to get that part in *Fair Game*."

A miserable-looking Duke came in to call my cousin Clyde to the phone. As a cop, Clyde was always getting calls that interrupted his participation in family gatherings. Clyde handed baby Harpo to his wife, Lisa, and left the room with an air of resignation.

I nudged Lana, and she gave me the arm of her chair to sit on. In our immediate vicinity, people were on to Mae's husbands.

"I was so surprised to see Frank," one woman said to another. "I thought they weren't speaking."

"Oh, things got better between them, I think, these last few years," the other said. "The poor man doesn't look healthy, though."

"Which one was Frank?" I asked Lana in a whisper.

"Between Jack and Phil," she said. "Husband number three. Cameraman."

My cousin Marlowe caught my attention from across the room, where he was listening to Clara. He waggled a finger at me from hip level.

"What's Marlowe doing?" I asked.

"He's giving you the high sign," Lana said. "He probably wants to be rescued from Clara."

I ambled over.

"Gilda! There you are! I have theater business to discuss with you." He turned to Clara. "Do you mind?" He took me by the arm and guided me away before she could answer.

"Theater business?" I asked.

He grimaced. "Sorry, I just had to get away from Clara. Know what she wants me to do?"

"Plan her comeback?"

"You knew about this?"

"No, that was just a wild guess. Is that really what she said?"

Marlowe was an agent at CCA, and he represented some of the hottest names in Hollywood.

"Well, if Mae could have a comeback in her seventies, Clara says, why can't she?"

"Mae made two movies. That's a comeback?"

"Mae only wanted to make two movies. Our Clara is a bit greedier than that." He offered me a cigarette, took one himself, and lit them both.

"Isn't she always?"

"It would be one thing if she would take the kind of roles I could get for her, you know?"

"Such as?"

"Oh, you know." He gestured vaguely. "Small supporting roles. Dotty aunts, pleasant grandmothers, cameos on *Falcon Crest*. Or commercial work. But she won't take those. 'If you think I'm going to hawk denture adhesive, you have another think coming!' she says."

"She has a point."

"Yeah, well, *my* point is that Maesie had more talent in her little finger than Clara ever had or ever will have. There's always the possibility I could pair her with another golden oldie, like Hepburn or Matthau, you know—a *Whales of August* thing or even maybe a *Dirty Old Men* thing. She could manage that. But she said she wouldn't do an 'old lady's film.' She threatened to go to William Morris."

"And you said . . . ?"

"I said it was a good idea. I said she shouldn't mix family with business, that it would spoil our relationship and drag everybody in the family into any disagreements we had."

"Does Grosvenor want her to act again?"

"Oh, Grosvenor. He probably wants her to do anything that would support his expensive tastes. You know that new entertainment center he bought last year? He's just itching to get his hands on Clara's legacy from Mae so he can replace it with something newer and, according to him, more advanced."

Betty was waving at me, so I excused myself.

"Gilda, you remember Dr. Genesee," she said. "Dr. Genesee was Mae's doctor."

"And mine, and everybody else's," I said, shaking his hand. "How are you?"

"Oh, not anymore," he said. "I'm retired. Only kept on a few of the old standbys, like your aunt. I was ready to make way for the younger generation."

"And this," Betty said, with an emphasis I didn't understand, "is Helen Beverly, the nurse who took care of Maesie."

"Yes, I remember," I said, shaking her hand. "You used to work in Dr. Genesee's office."

"So, tell Gilda about 'rosebud,' Helen," Betty urged her.

"There's not much to tell," Helen said. "It's just the last word I heard her speak before she died."

"She said it three times," Betty prompted. "And she was shouting?"

"Not shouting, exactly," Helen said, frowning. "What would I call it? Kind of like a cry at first, as if she were in pain, and then like she was getting angry. But I was down the hall, you know, not in the room with her."

"And when you went in there were papers on the bed?"

"Not on the bed," Helen corrected her. "They'd fallen on the floor. Your aunt had been reaching for something on the night-stand, I guess—perhaps the call button or phone or maybe a glass of water. She knocked the lamp over, you know. So I think the papers had fallen off the bed and were scattered on the floor."

"But you picked them up and looked at them?"

"At first, I was too busy doing CPR to pay any attention to them, but when the paramedics arrived, I picked them up."

"And looked at them?"

She shook her head. "Not really. I just glanced at them and then put them on the desk."

"You said you thought there was a letter," Betty pursued.

"That was my impression, yes, and a file folder. But there was a lot going on that night, Betty, so I wouldn't want you to hold me to anything."

Dr. Genesee spoke up. "She's right, Betty. There was a lot of confusion that night."

Betty gave in gracefully. "Okay, but whatever it was, you never saw it again?"

"Not as far as I know," Helen said, "but then I haven't been back here since I left that night—well, early the next morning actually."

"See, the puzzling thing is that nobody claims to have found papers on the desk later," Betty said. "Unless . . . you didn't put them under something, did you? Or *in* the desk?"

"Oh, well, I may have, I don't know," Helen said with a smile. "Sometimes I can't even remember what I had for breakfast."

Dr. Genesee laughed. "Sometimes I can't even remember if I *had* breakfast." He gestured toward the buffet with his empty plate. "So I'm going to make darned sure I get lunch."

Betty raised her eyebrows at me when they'd gone.

"What?" I said.

"I wish you'd seen Mae's desk before they cleaned up her room. There was lots of stuff on it, sure, but the top layer was all date books and bills and paperbacks and stuff. If somebody says they set papers on a desk, they don't move other things to do it, especially not in a moment of crisis."

"Have you asked Ruth about it?"

"Yes," Betty said. "She doesn't remember seeing anything like that when she tidied the room the next day."

"Well, then, who was in Mae's room that night?" I asked, intrigued in spite of myself.

Betty threw up her hands in an impatient gesture. "That's the whole problem. I know who was there the night she died, but by the next afternoon, which is when Ruth went in to clean, a lot of people had been in and out of the house. Anybody could have taken those papers."

"But why would they?" I persisted. "Why would anybody even be looking at papers on the desk, anyway?"

We were interrupted by my father's voice, raised to the level he used to fill a large auditorium.

"Clyde has an announcement," he said.

My cousin Clyde looked more like a teenage Roddy McDowall than a police officer. He said awkwardly, "It's about the theater fire. Somebody was in the theater when it burned down. They've found . . . well, a body."

11

Everyone stared at Clyde in stunned silence, as if they were waiting for further clarification.

"That's it," he said after a minute. "That's all we know."

"But who is it?" Lillian demanded.

"We don't know yet, Aunt Lilly," he said firmly, suddenly becoming a cop. "Once we know who it is, the next of kin will be notified first."

"But suppose it's Julius," she countered, extending the silence.

Wallace, standing next to her, actually dropped his jaw in astonishment.

"Don't be silly, Lillian," Adele said at last. "Why ever would it be Julius?"

"Can you think of any other reason why he would have missed Mae's funeral?"

"Perhaps he's ill," Gloria volunteered.

Lillian snorted. "He was fine last night. That man would have dragged himself to the church for Mae's funeral if he were on his deathbed. He wouldn't have missed his last opportunity to gloat over her."

"Now, Lilly," Andy Fuller put in appeasingly, as if negotiating a delicate financial transaction. "Julius was very close to Maesie. Perhaps he didn't feel he could handle her funeral. Some people can't."

"*I'm* handling it, goddamn it!" she said, as if he'd insulted her. Tears had sprung to her eyes and begun to trickle down her cheeks.

"Lillian's right," my mother put in. "Julius wouldn't have missed Mae's funeral for the world, whatever his motivation."

"But, Flo, we shouldn't go jumping to conclusions," my father said. "After all, there's no reason why it should have been Julius's body in the theater."

"He *owns* the place!" Lillian exclaimed.

A thrilled buzz circled the room.

"What do you mean?" my father asked.

"Just what I said. He owns the damn theater! He owns the building, he owns the shopping center, and he holds stock in the theater chain!"

My father went pale. The implied treachery to the Liberty family and to Mae shook him profoundly. I was feeling faint myself.

"That can't be true!" he said.

"No, Lilly, you've got it wrong somehow," Wallace said.

"No, Julius wouldn't—" Gloria began.

"It's a national chain," Oliver said with the air of adding helpful information.

"Oh, for God's sake, Ollie, it's based in Cleveland!" Lillian retorted. "Some national companies are, you know. It's not Paramount or Sony! And even if it were, he could still own a controlling interest, even from Eden, Ohio. Ask Andy."

Everyone swiveled in the direction of the banker in the family. Apparently, none of the Liberty siblings had ever made a movie about the stock market.

"Well, of course it's true that anyone can own stock in a company," Andy said cautiously.

"So does he own stock in that chain—what is it? Cineglobe?" my mother asked him. "You must know."

"Now, Florence, you know I can't tell you that, any more than I could disclose what I know about your own investments," Andy said.

"I'm not invested in anything that could ruin the Liberty family," she said tartly. "And if he is, and you knew about it . . ."

"Now, Flo, be reasonable," Andy pleaded. "Don't you think you're exaggerating just a bit? One Cineglobe theater in Eden,

Ohio, would hardly ruin the family, even if Julius owned it outright."

"Well, does he?" This time it was Clara, who was working herself up into a fury, I could tell by the glint in her eye.

"Of course he does," Lillian said. "Ask Duke."

Now all eyes were on Duke, who was trying to melt into the floor.

"He owns it," Duke said hoarsely. "Maesie knew about it, too. She'd known for a month or so. That's why"—his voice shrank to a whisper—"I couldn't let him touch her."

"I don't understand," Adele said, bewildered. "You're saying he owned Mae's competitor?"

"I think it's more accurate, Adele," Lillian replied, "to say that he *was* Mae's competitor. And now he's Gilda's. Unless, of course, he's dead."

"But I don't understand," Adele repeated. "He was one of her dearest friends."

"Maybe he wasn't dear enough," Lillian said.

"What do you mean, Lilly?" Wallace asked.

"She means that Julius Cole is a bastard, Wally," Clara explained with asperity. "Personally, I've never liked the man."

"But he's like one of the family," Gloria protested, sinking distractedly into the nearest chair and ending up on Tobias's lap. Toby gave way gracefully.

Val laughed unexpectedly. "If we had any more like him in this family, Gloria, we'd really be in bad shape."

Andy cleared his throat. "I'm not saying you're right about . . . well, any investments Julius might have made, but I think I should remind you that he's a businessman and—"

"Oh, that's right, Andy!" Val seemed to me to be in a peculiar mood, more peculiar even than everyone else's on this most peculiar occasion. He seemed to be enjoying himself, but his enjoyment verged on giddiness. "We'd forgotten that he was a businessman, boys and girls! We can't hold him to the same standards of loyalty, honesty, and friendship that we hold everybody else to!"

I saw Toby tug discreetly at his elbow.

"Well," Gloria said, "I don't think we should be talking about him like this behind his back. After all he's been to this family, I think he should at least have a chance to defend himself. Oliver, I want you to go get Julius on the phone right now."

Oliver started and for once the comedy was unintentional.

"But, uh, Gloria, uh, what should I say?"

"It's perfectly simple, Oliver," she said sternly. "Just ask him if he owns the Eden Center Cineglobe theater—or rather, if he owned it."

Ollie did some more comical throat-clearing and toed the carpet.

"Well, uh, but . . . I mean, just like that?" he asked.

"Just tell him the question has come up," Gloria said.

Ollie left the room reluctantly, stirring up the audience. It clotted in every corner of the room, coagulating around whispered conversations. Half a dozen people reached for their cell phones and left the room. Most of the writers had produced notebooks and were taking notes. Lillian's son Ron, the producer, had moved in on her with his arm across the shoulders of another Hollywood type.

All the movement and noise stopped abruptly, as if for a reel change by an inept projectionist, when Ollie reappeared.

"Julius isn't there," he announced weakly. "But I left a message."

The din started up again, and I suddenly realized that I was rubbing my temples to relieve the headache that had begun this morning with my hangover.

I heard Lana's voice beside me.

"Don't worry, sis," she said. "When it hits the big screen, you won't even recognize it."

12

Some family members seemed reluctant to discuss Julius Cole's business affairs until and unless his death was confirmed. That in itself seemed odd to me. The clamor for revelation died suddenly and was replaced by a thick fog of silence.

Even Betty became more secretive. She would call me on the phone, and even then she would whisper.

"You don't really think that could have been Uncle Julius they found, do you?" she'd ask.

"I don't know what to think," I'd say, over and over again. "Why should it be? But then why should it be anybody? How could one single person get trapped inside a burning theater, unless he fell asleep and was overcome by smoke inhalation? And how can anybody fall asleep in a movie theater these days? In the first place the staff comes around to clean up after every show, and in the second place the sound is usually loud enough to cause premature deafness."

"Did you know about Julius and the Eden Center theater?" my mother demanded.

"Mother, how would I know?" I retorted irritably. "I'm the one who just arrived in town, remember?"

"Well," my father said philosophically, "we'll just have to wait and see, won't we? I can't help but think that Lillian is mistaken."

Meanwhile, I had a theater to run.

Stammering and looking everywhere but at me, Duke had cornered me just before he left Liberty House with his family on the night of the funeral. He seemed to be mumbling something about contractual obligations and I gathered that the long and short of it was that we should reopen the theater the next night to avoid lawsuits by the distributors.

"Lawsuits?" I squeaked. That was just what I needed to make my return home complete.

He blushed and stammered some more, and what I got out of that was that everybody would probably give us a break because of Mae's death, but that we shouldn't push it.

I shouldn't worry, however, he reassured me, because the staff knew their jobs well and would continue to do them. The concession stand was well stocked, and I needn't worry about film ordering yet. He, of course, would project. In his blundering but kindly way, he guaranteed that everything would run smoothly.

But it didn't turn out quite like he promised. There was one small hitch in our plans: they depended on him. And at four-thirty the next afternoon my projectionist/business manager was picked up by the police for questioning about the disappearance of Julius Cole. We were three hours away from showtime.

I doubt that they restricted Duke to one phone call. I don't doubt that he called me first.

"I'm really sorry, Gilda," he said, "but I . . . uh, I'm in the police station right now, and, uh, they don't think I'll be out in time for . . . well, you know, the, uh, early show."

My heart skidded to a halt. "What?" I screeched.

"I'm really sorry about this," he said. He sounded miserable.

I could feel myself hyperventilating. "But you're the projectionist!" I wailed.

"Yeah, well, I told them that."

"Isn't there somebody there I can talk to? Who's in charge?"

He handed me to a detective sergeant, Dale Ferguson, who had been my lab partner in eleventh-grade chemistry.

"I'm sorry, Gilda," he said. "But we really need to talk to him."

"Dale," I pleaded, "cut me some slack here. I'm the only

show in town tonight, and without a projectionist I've got no show."

"Look at it from my perspective: I've spent my day running a taxi service to the airport and taking statements from your family members and various other Hollywood types in the back of a police cruiser. From the amount of electronic communication equipment they're wearing, I'd suspect they were all drug dealers if I didn't think that it was some kind of Southern California trend in fashion accessories. I sympathize, Gilda, I really do. But we're investigating a disappearance here, and it's no secret, I guess, that we might be investigating a murder. We're not arresting Duke; we just need to talk to him. And we need to talk to him now."

I knew what he meant. My own son, wearing jeans, had looked endearingly scruffy and low-tech in that crowd of uncles, aunts, and cousins when he'd given me an awkward hug that morning and headed home to hawk maps to the dream factory. But Dale's problems were not my problems.

"You're not still holding that sulfur dioxide thing against me, are you?" I asked. "Or that little acid hole in your letter jacket? Or that blue stain on your favorite shirt?"

"Gilda, believe me, I'd help you out if I could," he said. "I should probably warn you that I'll need to talk to you in the next few days if Julius doesn't turn up. I had to start with the people who were leaving town." And then, just before he put Duke back on, he added, "Good luck with the theater, Gil. I mean it. Oh, and Gil?"

"Yeah?"

"Maybe you should stay away from the concession stand," he said. "Just a little friendly advice from a former lab partner."

Then Duke was on again.

"Duke," I said morosely, "what am I going to do? I don't suppose we have one of those self-threading projectors, do we?"

This was greeted with a moment of silence on the other end of the line. I supposed that for the first time Duke was taking in the extent of my ignorance.

"Call Tod Welch," he said, his voice suddenly taking on a

businesslike tone. "He was the manager at the Eden Center. If he can't do it, he can tell you who his other projectionists were. If that doesn't work, call Harry De Soto. He's an old-timer, and he's clumsy with the platters, and he talks a lot, but he can probably do it. Their numbers are on the wall by the phone behind the concession stand.

"Everybody else knows their job," Duke continued. "Remind Rashid to check on the ice and the soda-fountain canisters. Remember to make two pitchers of lemonade before the first show." .

"The first show?" I echoed despondently.

"Well, you know—just in case they don't let me out of here in time for the second. Oh, and you should probably pick up a couple dozen lemons on your way in. And some flashlight batteries. If anybody wants advance sales, just ask them to wait until tomorrow."

I was scribbling madly.

"The cops get free popcorn whenever they come in." I could hear him ticking off items on a list in his head. "Check the toilet paper in the women's john during the early show. Nobody gets their money back because they didn't like the picture, and that goes double for Mrs. Mooney, who always tries. Don't let the kids hang on the concession stand and clean the glass between shows—the girls know that. Oh, and if you get Harry, tell him there's no smoking anywhere in the theater—especially in the projection booths. Also, don't let him handle the platters. He's a klutz, and if he drops one, we're in deep shit.

"If something goes seriously wrong, like, if the film breaks and the projectionist can't fix it, or if somehow the reels get screwed up on the platters, which shouldn't happen because I set it all up, or if there's a power outage . . ." He took a breath. "Just give everybody a rain check and a free bag of popcorn. Most people know what's going on, so they probably won't kick. And anyway, they're going to give you some time before they start complaining. You know, like a honeymoon."

"How long?" I asked.

"Well, hopefully I'll be back tomorrow night," Duke said gloomily. "I'd better be."

There was something in his voice I didn't like.

"Why?" I asked faintly. "What happens tomorrow night?"

"We get a new film in," he said. "*101 Dalmatians*. A kiddie show."

After he hung up, I sat at the kitchen table and cried. Tears of self-pity gushed from my eyes, coursed down my face, and dripped off my chin until I looked like an escapee from *Stella Dallas*.

When I had cried myself out, I reached for the phone again. One week, I told myself. I'd do it for one week. Then Duke could take over and I'd go back to writing insurance policies.

Unless, of course, Duke got arrested for murder.

Despite the pleasant May sunshine outside, the theater lobby was dim when I first let myself in, using a key Lillian had passed on to me with some ceremony. I took a deep breath, filling my lungs with the scent of popcorn mingled with the faint, musty odor of a well-aged building. I had been here many times in my life, had once even been permitted as a child to sit on a high stool behind the ticket window and push the button that dispensed the tickets with a gratifying *whoosh*. I had even worked here, off and on, mostly behind the concession stand and on cleanup duty. But either I hadn't noticed very much, didn't remember very much, or everything had changed.

During my two summers as a theater employee, there had been only one theater and one screen. The theater had included a main floor and a balcony. The balcony had spooked me considerably. I had hated to be sent to clean up there, dreading the suspicious wads of paper and even an occasional condom when Mae showed *One Million Years B.C.* and *Barbarella*. The last time I had come home, the balcony was already a separate theater, and a third theater, long and narrow, had been added on the side after Maesie purchased the building next door.

The ticket window of my childhood no longer existed. In my

preteen years, the ticket machine had been moved to an island just inside the entry. There had never been much need for crowd control, and Mae had never replaced the old velvet ropes that used to separate the arriving spectators from the departing ones. I couldn't remember when I'd last had my ticket torn, but Mr. Bamberger, who smelled of Sen-Sen and had always seemed old to me, was probably the one who had done it. My grandfather had busied himself in the projection booth and at the concession stand, while my grandmother sold tickets and chatted with the customers. Later, Mae had become a regular projectionist and taken over the business when my grandparents finally retired. Mrs. Johnson, the kindly lady who for years had filled in wherever she was needed but who probably appeared on the books as an usher, had also retired at some point and been replaced by a series of college students.

Even the concession stand had been moved from the back of the main lobby to the side lobby, at the entrance to the third theater. Duke had told me that I could find the lights in the small office behind it, and I did. I was running short of time to indulge my nostalgia. I needed a projectionist.

Of course I got Harry. That was how my luck was running. Tod Welch wasn't answering his phone, and I didn't much blame him.

As I waited for someone to show up and tell me what to do, I grabbed a flashlight off the shelf and took a brief tour of my new property. At least the organ pipes were still in place, high on the wall to the right of the main theater stage. For the first time I noticed the elongated Art Deco lights on the walls, which were also no doubt original. To the left of the main theater stage, there was a clock on the wall. It shone brighter than the exit signs, reminding me that we were now two and a half hours away from showtime and counting.

I looked in on the other theaters, but I avoided the dark stairways and passages that led to the mysterious upper regions of the buildings. As a kid, I had loved to play hide-and-seek up there, in the realm of spiders and mice, where the old marquee had gone when it was retired, along with stacks of plastic letters that could be used for writing messages to the ghosts of old vaudeville performers. I had never encountered a ghost, nor had one ever answered my messages, but I had never lost hope that the old dressing rooms above the stage were haunted.

I was less familiar with the new building, which had a long hallway connected to a long, narrow room above the third theater. My flashlight played over dark shapes huddled together. Some seemed to be old electrical equipment, some furniture, some boxes.

In the dim light I peered at the yellowed pages showing in the top of the nearest box. They were forms headed "Time Register," and they had been filled in in pencil. I felt an odd sensation to see the names of people, Asa Walker and Dorothy Good, who had worked here the year I was born, 1951. I wondered if they were still alive.

I have always been captivated by historic records. There is something about handling old papers—crisp and brittle or worn soft with age, yellowed and age-spotted and smelling of mildew and must—that always gives me goose bumps. And I don't necessarily mean the Declaration of Independence, or the manuscript of "Ode on a Grecian Urn." In fact, the more ordinary the artifact, the more it fascinated me as a casual record of everyday life. So I propped my flashlight on a nearby box and began leafing through the papers, feeling my hands turn furry with dust. If I looked through all the boxes stashed in various corners of the theater, I thought, maybe I could find records dating back to 1916. I didn't have the time to do it now, but I couldn't resist a peek at the box just under the first one. It contained more time registers, neatly filled out in pencil, with slots for the doorman, relief doorman, ushers, cashier, operator, janitor, assistant janitor, candy attendants, bill posters, and manager. I tried to imagine a time when all those people were employed by a single small-town theater.

And then my eye fell on a familiar name: Julius Cole. According to this record, during the week ending July 12, 1940, someone named Julius Cole had worked ten hours as an usher at the Paradise Theatre.

The light from my flashlight, which had been dim to start with, suddenly wavered and died, leaving a kind of ghostly imprint of the name on my retinas.

"Hey!" a voice shouted. "Are you up there?"

I dropped the flashlight on my foot.

Harry De Soto was a wizened old guy in khaki work pants and a well-worn Hawaiian shirt. He had a bad shave, a bad cough, and uncombed white hair, and he smelled of pipe tobacco. I saw a pipe stem sticking out of his pants pocket.

I gave him credit for finding his way to the projection booth. Then he stood there and contemplated the projector with a look I couldn't interpret but found dismaying. I contemplated it with him. It looked like a projector, all right, only bigger and more antique than I remembered. What looked less antique was a column of gigantic steel platters, about the size of a Godzilla pizza, which took up much of the space in the booth. There was film mounted on one of these platters, but I couldn't see how it would be mounted on the projector.

"I never did get the hang of these platters," Harry said after a minute, "but I reckon we can figure 'er out."

Sweat popped out of my pores like quills on a porcupine.

"You can call me an old coot if you want to," he said, "but sometimes the old ways are best." He pulled a film end off the top platter and squinted at it, then pressed it to his bottom lip.

He's crazy, I thought. He's going to eat the film. Then I won't have a projectionist or a film.

But he seemed satisfied with just a taste.

"Now you take them carbon lamps we used to use." He tilted his head up and down to get the best view out of his glasses, studied the film end, turned around and studied the projector, raised his glasses up and parked them on top of his head, studied it some more, coughed, caught his glasses as they fell, and settled them on his nose again. He talked throughout this procedure. "Them lamps had to be adjusted just so. You couldn't get the carbons too far apart nor too close together, or you wouldn't get the arc. But them lamps were better lamps than these ones they have now.

"Of course, you can call me an old coot if you want to," he repeated. I hadn't called him anything. I had barely gotten a word in edgewise since he'd walked in the door. "You can say what my doctor says, which is, 'Where do you think you got that cough, you old coot, if not from them carbon lamps?' And then you had to be sure you had enough carbon to get through a whole picture. You didn't want to be changing in the middle. But them lamps were a better lamp than anything they've got today, and I don't care who hears me say it."

I didn't think there was anybody to hear him except the ghosts of people who probably agreed with him.

He'd threaded the film through a series of pullics mounted to the same post the platters were mounted on. Now he dragged the leader over to the projector and was threading it in somehow. Seeing the film stretched out in midair that way made me nervous, and I broke in.

"Are you sure that's how it goes?" I asked anxiously. "I mean, it seems like it should be enclosed or something."

It didn't seem to occur to him to take offense.

"That's how she goes," he said placidly. "And then she comes down through here like this and through this here and back over to this empty platter here."

As he said it, he stretched the film back across the seemingly

vast space between the projector and the platter and fastened it
to the platter's core.

"And Bob's your uncle, as the Limeys say," he said, then stood
back to admire his handiwork. "I think that's how it goes," he
added.

It didn't look to me as if this setup could possibly be right,
and I wondered if Tod Welch had come home yet, or if I could
find an instruction manual for the projector in the hour and a
half I had left.

"Now, young lady," he said. "What did you say your name
was?"

"Gilda. Gilda Liberty."

"Oh, Gilda. There was a famous lady named Gilda in a movie
way back in the forties."

"I was named for her," I said.

He ignored me. "Of course, that was before your time. This
Gilda—she was kind of a shady lady. Rita Hayworth played
her, and I'll tell you something, that Rita Hayworth was a real
honey! You wouldn't know anything about that, but she was
what we used to call a hot tomato!"

I didn't bother to try to convince him that I knew who she
was. If by some miracle he could get the projector to run, silence was a small price to pay for it.

"She married the sheik of Araby, she did," he told me. "Rita
Hayworth, I mean, not Gilda—she was married to this Nazi
who was in the Mafia."

I wondered if all of his renditions of movies were as freely in-
terpreted as this one.

"And she got up onstage and sang, 'Put the blame on Mame,
boys,' " he said. To my surprise, he began mimicking Gilda,
peeling off an imaginary glove and then twirling it, hips bump-
ing to an inaudible drumbeat. "She did this striptease and oh,
boy! That was really hot stuff in those days!"

I flashed on my balcony-cleaning experiences and winced.

"She had a daughter with one of those funny A-rab names,"
he continued. "But then she died of that old-timer's disease."

"Alzheimer's," I couldn't help correcting.

"When I heard she'd died, why, I just couldn't get that tune out of my head. 'Put the Blame on Mame.' It was real sad how she died."

We observed a moment of silence.

Then he said, "So, now, Rita, we got to check the sound. So you run down to the theater and tell me how it sounds."

"Oh, I was supposed to tell you," I said. "Duke asked me to remind you not to smoke."

He gave me a slow conspiratorial wink, which I dreaded to interpret.

I went downstairs to the dark and empty theater. To my amazed relief, the trailer suddenly appeared on the screen, and when the numbers counted down to zero, a picture appeared. There was no sound. I looked up and saw Harry's face framed in the small window next to the projector. He stared at the screen and then I saw him cup his hand behind his ear. Then he held his hand up to me and disappeared. I was just on the verge of losing hope when the sound blasted me out of my seat. I raced back up to the booth.

"It's a little—" I wheezed.

"I know, I know," he muttered. "Used to have one speaker, then two or three. Now they got speakers all over the damn house. Dolby, they call it. Ain't good enough to have sound coming from one direction, you got to have it all around you. Well, you can call me an old coot, but what I say is, you only got two ears and they're stuck to the sides of your head, and they only hear in one direction.

"Now you take smoking," he said, suddenly changing the subject abruptly. "Used to be worth your life to smoke in a projection booth. I mean it; you were taking your life into your hands with that old nitrate film we used to have. Them were the days! And hot! You like to died in the booth, summer and winter, it was so hot. Now, if you was in the audience, why, you could smoke like a chimney and nobody would bother you! Nowadays, you got this fireproof film, and flame-retardant seats, and circuit breakers, and I don't know whatnot, and none of you young people smoke."

I opened my mouth to speak, but I didn't get the chance.

"And now they got it where you can't smoke anywhere in the theater, when you could light a match to a reel of film and nothing would happen." He shook his head. "You can call me an old coot if you want to, but I say I got to go sometime and I might as well enjoy myself while I'm here. Try 'er now, Rita."

I didn't realize at first that he'd switched subjects on me again. When I did, I zipped downstairs to check the sound level.

The sound was fine, and the picture was in focus, as far as I could tell through my middle-age eyes. We went through the whole process two more times and were finishing the last sound check when I heard voices in the lobby. It was time to face the troops.

I had met them all at Mae's funeral. They were all college students. There were three young women with long hair on the blond side: Amy, Amanda, and Jennifer. I couldn't tell them apart. Two of them were here tonight, but I wasn't sure which two. The fourth musketeer was a darker-skinned young man named Rashid.

"Where's Duke?" he asked with the air of someone who was accustomed to giving short shrift to the supporting cast and dealing directly with the star.

"He won't be here tonight," I said as lightly as I could manage. "He has to talk to the police about Mr. Cole's disappearance. The police are questioning everyone," I added, "and I guess it's his turn. So we're on our own."

"Duke won't be here?" one of the blondes asked, with such astonished apprehension in her voice that I felt my bravado sag.

"He said," I reported lamely, "that everyone knew their jobs." They exchanged glances.

"Who's projecting then?" Rashid asked. His English had the clipped accent and intonation of Indian or Pakistani English.

"Harry De Soto."

"Harry De Soto?" he echoed, alarm in his voice. "The old guy?"

"He is," I affirmed a bit stiffly, "an older gentleman."

"I heard he was ninety-five," the other blonde said to the first one.

"He tells dirty jokes sometimes," the first blonde confided. "Only they're so old, they're not even all that dirty, you know?"

I nodded. "He called Rita Hayworth a 'hot tomato.' "

"Who's Rita Hayworth?" the second blonde asked.

Then everybody set to work and made a good show of appearing to know what they were supposed to do. They put their heads together to figure out what I could do and came up with some unskilled gruntwork they thought I could handle. So I carried ice from the ice maker to the ice bin under the soft-drink machine. I refilled the straw and napkin dispensers, which turned out to be harder than it looked for somebody with my mechanical ineptness. I ended up taking the dispensers into the candy closet, because I didn't want to figure them out in public. I spilled half a box of straws on the floor.

"She could make lemonade," one of the blondes proposed to the other.

The other blonde turned and regarded me speculatively.

"Why don't you restock the candy in the display case?" she said.

Humbled and depressed, I did that. Even then it took me ten minutes in the candy closet to find the jujubes and another five to find the Twizzlers.

"That looks great, Gilda," one of the blondes complimented me.

I looked up at her from where I squatted.

"No, really!" She laughed. "Don't worry! You'll get the hang of things! Except for the projection, there's nothing really that hard. It's not like you've done it before, right?"

"Actually, I have," I admitted. "When I was a teenager."

"Oh, well," she reassured me, "that was ages ago. You'll do fine!"

"Thanks, Amy," I ventured gratefully.

"Amanda," she corrected me gently, just as I heard Harry in the background, asking where Rita was.

The first customer arrived at seven-fifteen for a seven-thirty show. It was Victoria Binkley Bopp, whom I'd never forgiven for pushing me off the diving board in the summer after seventh grade. She had a husband in tow and three sullen kids.

After a cynical appraisal of my abilities, Rashid had given me a job to do: I held a small metal counter in my hand and pushed the button for every ticket sold to the main theater attraction. I greeted my assignment with skepticism.

"Doesn't the ticket machine tell you how many tickets are sold?" I asked.

He shrugged. "Not for the individual theaters. So we do it when we think we might have a sellout in the main theater. It's not like the airlines; we can't overbook and then offer people free movies to give up their seats."

"You're expecting a sellout?" I said faintly.

I almost missed the next group of four while Victoria was bringing me up-to-date on her life. From where I was standing, I could see her kids hanging off the concession counter.

"Gilda! *Cómo estás? Qué placer verte de nuevo!*"

It was Señor Lopez, my eleventh-grade Spanish teacher.

"Oh, hi, Mr. Lopez. Good to see you, too. I'm . . . uh, good, I guess," I said.

He waggled a finger at me. *"En Español, Gilda. No me digas que lo olvides."*

"Uh, well, I, uh, I remember some," I managed, while clicking off the next party. *"Estoy bien, gracias, y usted?"*

He laughed and clapped me heartily on the shoulder. "Bravo, Gilda! *Estoy muy bien!*"

The next person in line was Willard Braxton, who'd had a crush on Betty all through high school and was always trying to enlist my aid in his campaign. He threw his arms around me and made me push the counter button in surprise.

"Gilda! We sure have missed you around here! It sure has been dull!"

"Oh, yes?" I said vaguely, trying to figure out whether my count was one or two off.

"Yeah, things'll be different now, though." That was Marci

Sturdevant, Lana's best friend in high school. "You were always such a cutup!"

"I was?" In my astonishment I missed the next three people in line.

"Gilda, I said to Chuck, I said, 'I don't care what the picture is tonight, we're going.' " That was the school librarian, though I was damned if I could remember her name. This was turning into a reception line. I should have passed out name tags at the door.

The aforementioned Chuck held up his hands. "I didn't object. Did you hear me object?"

"We wouldn't miss this for the world!" his wife said. "Your first night!"

"Kind of like a premiere, isn't it?" That was Mr. Blumenthal, whose wife gave piano lessons and had, for many years, played piano at the dance recitals at my parents' school.

The line was out the door, and my count was hopelessly confused.

"But where's Duke?" someone asked. I think it was Mrs. Hobbs, the mayor's wife, who owned a gift shop downtown.

"He's, uh, he's not here," I said. I'd been so rushed and so stressed out that I'd forgotten to script an answer to this question. "He's taking the night off."

From what I knew of Duke, this sounded improbable even to me.

"I saw him down at the police station," somebody said in the self-important voice of a busybody. "He's not in trouble, is he?"

"No, no," I assured them. "He's just being interviewed, like everybody else."

"*I* haven't been interviewed," said the busybody, sounding miffed. She turned to someone near her and asked, "Have you?"

"This is all about Julius Cole, isn't it?" somebody asked.

"I think it was terrible, the way he died in that fire," somebody else said.

"They don't know if it's Julius, though, do they?" another person asked.

"Well," said Mrs. Lacey, my tenth-grade art teacher, "whoever it was, we all came to support you tonight, Gilda, so that the police can see that we don't hold you responsible for that other theater burning down."

I dropped the counter.

That was the moment the Liberties had chosen for their arrival en masse. With my mother in the lead, they swept past the line and pushed their way into the circle around me. People fell back to let them through.

"You held seats for us, Gilda, I hope?" my mother said.

Why would I have held seats for them? I hadn't had a clue they were coming. And since, in true Liberty style, they had arrived at the last minute, and since half the town had turned out for my opening night, the best I could do was to put them in the upper section of the balcony theater to watch *Microcosmos*, a nature documentary.

Adele and Gloria walked out after half an hour, shuddering.

"There are plants eating bugs in there," Gloria told me reproachfully.

"You wouldn't have liked the others any better," I said. "There are animals eating plants in them."

Adele raised a suspicious eyebrow at me and went off to study the decor.

Uncle Ollie and my father loved the film, as it turned out. Uncle Wallace liked it, too.

"But I never did see Anthony Hopkins," he said, exhaling whiskey fumes.

We let that pass.

"It was great, honey," my father said.

"Lots of action," Uncle Oliver agreed enthusiastically. "Some of those bug battles were just as exciting as the old sword fights."

My mother didn't venture an opinion, but she looked reasonably content. Grosvenor was bending the ear of anybody who would listen on the subject of how the film had been shot and recorded. He'd stationed himself near the newspaper and magazine clippings on the wall, so that when people stopped to read about the film, he could spare them the trouble. I didn't see Clara, so she was probably in the rest room, primping.

The other half of the town was waiting for the nine-forty-five show, so I couldn't take much time out to talk to my family. Rashid had given up on the counter idea and cut me loose to meet and greet. What I really wanted to do was hide out in a projection booth. But on the other hand I really didn't want to watch Harry, either, or listen to his monologues. The first screenings had gone off without a hitch, and I had a sense of impending disaster.

Thinking she had a new pigeon, Mrs. Mooney was asking for her money back. Tempted as I was to hand her over to Rashid, I took the first real step in acknowledging that I, Gilda Liberty, MBA and former insurance executive, was in the theater business: I told her no.

Around ten-fifteen, when things had quieted down and I was breathing my first sigh of relief, Peachy showed up with a bottle of champagne. I poured a glass for each of my coworkers, Peachy, and myself.

"I wish Duke was here," said the one who wasn't Amanda.

I was thinking the same thing.

And then, suddenly, there he was.

"Hey," he said. "How's it going?"

We beamed at one another and then at him.

"Well, I'd like to propose a toast," said Harry with a flourish. "To Rita!"

"Who?" said Rashid.

We toasted Rita and Gilda, and then Duke, for keeping the

theater going after Mae got sick, and then Harry, for stepping in in an emergency, and then Rashid, for overseeing things while Duke was gone, and then Amanda and Amy, for running the concession stand so efficiently, and then finally Peachy, for bringing the champagne. By the time we'd run out of people to toast, we'd run out of champagne, but Duke wanted to toast Maesie. He remembered a can of beer in the refrigerator and so we toasted her with that, even though it was a little flat.

Rashid was gloating over a sellout night—unheard of in anyone's recent memory of the Paradise.

"How did they know it was my first night?" I asked. "You'd think I had sent engraved invitations."

"This town is like that, Gilda," Duke said. "Everybody knows everybody's business."

"Some of them think Gilda burned down the other theater," Amanda told him. She glanced at me. "You didn't, did you?"

"Of course she didn't!" Rashid said with a conviction based less on loyalty, I thought, than on acquaintance with my incompetence.

"*You* didn't, did you, Duke?" Amanda asked him.

He hesitated, drained his cup of beer, and said, "I would've if I'd thought of it. I wish I'd thought of it."

"Gee," Amy said, "I wish Jennifer was here. Then this would be like a real going-away party."

I choked on my beer. "Going away?" I echoed. "Who's going away?"

I glanced at Duke and saw with alarm the realization dawning on his face.

Amy looked at Amanda. Amanda looked at Rashid.

"Well," Amy said, "we all are. This is finals week, and our exams are over on Thursday. Well, actually, mine are over on Tuesday, so I'm leaving Wednesday. Jennifer's leaving then, too. But Amanda and Rashid will be here till Thursday."

"But it's only May!" I protested weakly.

"I'm sorry, Gilda," Amanda said. "But Eden always gets out early. We have graduation on Mother's Day every year."

"Isn't anybody going to summer school?" I asked.

"We're really sorry, Gilda," Amy said. "We thought you knew. We told Duke a while ago."

"It sort of slipped my mind," Duke said.

"But who's going to run this place?" I asked.

"Don't look at me," Harry put in. "I've got a fishing trip planned with my son-in-law."

"Don't worry, Gilda," Duke said. "Once summer school starts, we'll find some more students to hire."

"When is that?"

"It's only two weeks from now."

"Two weeks!"

My euphoria had been short-lived. This didn't seem like the moment to announce that I was due back at work in New York a week from tomorrow.

"You could probably hire some of the Eden Center people."

Duke frowned ferociously. You would have thought someone had suggested to John Wayne that he hire a couple of out-of-work cattle rustlers to help out on the drive.

Then everyone else left and Duke and I were alone.

"I can lock up, Gilda," he said. "I'm staying here tonight."

"In the theater?" I asked, taken aback.

"Upstairs," he said. "I have a room upstairs. I stay here lots of nights."

"Oh," I said. "So how did it go tonight—at the police station?"

He shrugged noncommittally. "Okay, I guess. They just asked me a bunch of questions. How about you? Any problems?"

"No," I said. "Everything was fine."

I wondered whether both of us were lying or if only one of us was.

I found the house in an uproar when I got home. My mother was there.

"Oh, Gilda, good," she said. "I'm glad you're here"

That was my first surprise: she actually sounded relieved to see me.

Then she handed me my second.

"Your aunt's been arrested," she said.

"My aunt?" I glanced around the living room to see who was

missing. Clara and Gloria were kibbitzing in the corner. Then I heard what my mother was saying.

"Adele and Wallace went down to the station with your father to see what can be done," she said. "I'm sure there's some misunderstanding behind it."

"You mean *Lillian*?" I gasped as I took it all in. "*Lillian's* been arrested? Whatever for?"

"Breaking and entering," my mother said crossly. "Can you picture that? The police claim she tried to break into Julius's house."

15

"I didn't break anything," Lillian insisted haughtily. "I only entered."

We were sitting around the living room, holding a late-night family summit of sorts. It was an intimate little group: my parents, Wallace and Adele, Gloria and Oliver, Val, and Clara. No one else from my generation was there. I was there because I happened to be living in Liberty House.

"But where did you get the key, sis?" my father asked.

"It was Mae's key," Lillian said.

"You should have heard the story she told the police," Adele complained. "She said that Mae was Julius's executor, and now that Mae had predeceased Julius—"

"Who may not be deceased at all," my mother pointed out.

"Oh, he's deceased, all right," Wallace said. "They told us that much. Identified by his dental records." He flashed his own fangs to illustrate.

"Oh!" Gloria exclaimed, and crossed herself. As far as I

knew, she wasn't Catholic, but she seemed to feel some sort of gesture was in order.

"Poor Julius!" my father said.

"Was it smoke inhalation?" my mother asked.

Adele reclaimed the floor. "So now that Mae had predeceased Julius, she said, which she couldn't have known about . . ." Here she gave Lillian another significant look. "She was worried about the will, because she couldn't find Julius's will anywhere—"

"Is that what you've been looking for, Lillian?" Gloria asked.

"It can't be that," my mother told her. "She was looking before he died."

"So," Adele continued, with a glare for her interrupters, "she says she went to Julius's house to look for his will." She dropped both hands on the arms of her chair and sat back. "Even Wallace doesn't believe that story!"

"I don't care whether he believes it or not!" Lillian snapped. "And I don't care if you do!"

"Well, but, sis," my father said in his most conciliatory tone, "we're only trying to help. Adele's a little upset, but she's only trying to help."

"I don't recall asking for her help, or anyone else's for that matter," she said.

"She *drove* to his house?" my mother said. Then, to Lillian, "You *drove* to his house at that hour of the night? You haven't had a valid license for years!"

"Sergeant What's-His-Name had to call us," Adele said. "She wouldn't even call her own family when she got arrested!"

"I didn't get arrested," Lillian said evenly, "I got picked up."

"So they haven't filed charges?" Val asked. It was his first contribution to the discussion.

"They haven't *yet*," Adele said pointedly.

"Well," my father said, "I doubt they will."

"Course not," Ollie said. "Just a big misunderstanding, eh, Lilly?"

"But I still don't understand why you went to Julius's house," Gloria said to her. "At that time of night?"

"And all by herself!" Adele added reproachfully, as if suggesting that her attitude might have been completely different if only she'd been invited along. "Flo's right, Lilly. You can't see well enough to be driving at night."

"Nobody has to understand anything," Lillian said. "Nobody has to believe anything. This is a private matter."

"But, Lilly," Wallace objected. "It won't be private if you're arrested. And now that we know Julius is dead—"

"Of course it won't be private," Adele said. "We'll all be involved. And we have our own reputations to consider—and our children's. Think what a scandal would mean to Greer and Andy, especially Andy. His position at the bank could be jeopardized."

Because I happened to be looking in her direction, I saw Clara lift her head on the word "reputation."

"But Douglas said she wouldn't be arrested," she said nervously. "She won't, will she? So there's nothing to worry about." She fumbled for her cigarettes and fitted one into her holder.

I was on the second pack of the day myself. Any more time around my family and I'd turn into a chain-smoking, caffeine-addicted alcoholic.

"The point is," Adele said, "the police are now looking for Julius's killer. Any strange behavior around Julius will draw their suspicions."

"But surely, Adele, they don't think Lillian killed him!" Gloria said, shocked.

"I thought he died in the fire," Oliver said, his brow creased with bafflement.

"Well, they're not going to suspect Lillian of setting fire to the theater, Adele," my mother said. "I think we can rest assured of that."

"Why do they think Julius died in the fire?" Val asked.

Everyone turned to look at him in surprise.

"What do you mean?" my father asked.

"Just that," Val said. "Why do they think he died in the fire? I know he was found in the burned theater, but why didn't he get out?"

They stared at him. I decided to put my two cents in, since Val had put his finger on the question I'd been asking myself.

"Val's got a good point," I said. "Most people who die in fires die of smoke inhalation—usually because they're asleep when the fire starts. That could have happened to Julius, I guess, but it seems so unlikely. What would he have been doing asleep in the theater late at night? And if he was asleep and the fire was accidental, then there wouldn't be any question of murder. But if the fire was set, then somebody would have had to go around spreading gasoline or kerosene or something to make sure the place burned down, and they could hardly do that without waking him up if he'd fallen asleep."

"You mean he was drugged?" Wallace asked.

"Either drugged or already dead," I said. "Are you sure the police said they were investigating Julius's murder, or did they say they were investigating his death?"

Adele and Wallace looked at each other.

"I'm *sure* they said 'murder,' " Adele said in the cautious tones of uncertainty.

Wallace frowned. "I thought so, too."

"Well," Lillian said, "he got no more than he deserved."

"Lilly!" Gloria gasped.

"Sis, I don't think you should—" my father began.

"What Douglas is trying to say," my mother continued, "is that if that's your opinion, you should keep it to yourself, Lillian—at least until the police arrest Julius's killer."

"In the meantime," my father announced, "we have a theater to run."

My heart sank and I reached for another cigarette. This was the moment I'd dreaded. I'd been too honest when my father had gotten around to asking me how things had gone at the theater that night. Now he broadcast my troubles to the rest of the family.

"We'll help you, Gilda," Wallace volunteered.

"Of course we'll help!" Adele said.

"We'll all help," my mother agreed.

"Absolutely," Lillian said.

They had the eager, enthusiastic faces of the little animals who'd done Cinderella's housework for her. How could I say no?

Once the meeting was declared over, I went to empty the coffee grounds into the flower beds along the back porch, a long-standing practice of Mae's. At the back door I paused when I heard a conversation in low voices between two people standing on the porch.

"*You* were quiet tonight, Clara." It was Val.

"You were pretty quiet yourself," she shot back.

It occurred to me that Lillian wasn't the only person who wasn't telling everything she knew.

Betty was bouncing on my bed again. I'd had this dream already, and I hadn't liked it the first time around.

I didn't look at her. "I don't recall leaving a wake-up call," I said.

"You'll never guess what's happened now!" she said.

"Lillian got picked up by the police," I said sleepily. "I remember."

"Gillie, that's old news! I mean what's happened since then."

I rolled over reluctantly and stared at her.

"Julius Cole's house burned down in the middle of the night!"

"It couldn't have," I objected mildly. "Lillian and the cops were there in the middle of the night. They would have noticed."

"I told you, this was *after*," she insisted. "It burned down after they left."

"That's not funny, Betts!" I cautioned her.

"But it's true!" she crowed. "And the reporters on the scene are calling it 'suspicious'—a 'fire of suspicious origins.' "

"Betty, we didn't have this many fires in the city!"

"Makes you wonder, huh?"

I closed my eyes again. Maybe if I clicked my heels together three times and said, "There's no place like home," I would end up back in my New York apartment with Liz and the kids.

But Betty interrupted the attempt.

"Gilda, did you see Grosvenor last night?"

"I saw him at the theater, yeah."

"But afterward," she said, "while Lillian was at the police station and after."

"No, he wasn't there."

I accepted that my new day had started, whether I wanted it to or not, and got up. I did some stretching exercises.

"Don't you think that's significant?"

"What I think," I said, "is that if I were Grosvenor June and had a reputation for expertise in pyrotechnical special effects, the one thing I would never do is try to burn down a real house in my immediate vicinity."

"But you're not him," she pointed out. "Are you?"

Detective Sergeant Dale Ferguson wasn't prepared to give anything away when he got around to interviewing me that afternoon. The only confidence he entrusted me with at first I could have figured out for myself.

"Just between us, Gilda," he said, "I wish your aunt had never gone near the Cole house."

"So are you going to arrest her?" I asked.

He sighed. "Not much point in that," he said. "She had a key, however she got it. If she decides to say in court that the man asked her to go water his dieffenbachia, we can't prove he didn't."

"At eleven o'clock at night?" I asked skeptically.

He shrugged. "If Lillian Liberty Van Nuys says it, you know damn well there's not a potential juror in this town who's going to doubt her publicly."

He narrowed his eyes at me. "I don't suppose you know what the hell she was doing there at eleven o'clock at night?"

"Well, I doubt she was planting firebombs," I said. "Anyway, if I'm going to rat on my family, you have to give me something in exchange."

"Like what?"

"Julius Cole's cause of death."

"You'll hear about that at the inquest."

"Tell me now."

We were sitting in a small, pleasant interview room in the new police station. The table we were sitting at was round, there was carpeting on the floor, the lighting was unobtrusive, and there was no sign of a two-way mirror. The only thing about the room that was the least bit intimidating was the lock on the door that had to be released by someone working behind the counter.

"Okay," Dale said. "He was shot."

"Where?"

"In the head."

"Front or back?"

"Back."

"So he didn't see it coming."

"Not unless he had eyes in the back of his head. And according to the skull we have—"

I winced.

"Sorry," he said penitently. "I forgot he was a friend of yours."

"I don't know," I said. "I guess I didn't really know him very well. I used to have a crush on him, which kind of put a damper on our conversations."

He nodded. "That was before . . . ?"

"Obviously."

He nodded again. "I liked Liz," he said.

"Yeah," I said. "Me, too."

"Sorry," he repeated.

"Me, too," I said.

"So," he said, "how's the insurance racket?"

"If you're going to ask me if I sold Julius a policy, I'll throw this telephone at you," I said.

"Touchy, aren't you?"

"All the Liberties are touchy. Me, I'm the restrained one."

"That's not how I remember it."

"Yeah?"

"Yeah," he said. "Way I remember it, after the successful experiment on my shirt, you dipped Donna Waymeyer's braids in the same acid."

"I got tired of hearing about how long her hair was—like growing hair was a talent and we should give her a medal or something."

"If I'd been a cop then, I would've arrested you."

"Yeah? So arrest me now. Or is there a statute of limitations on assault with a deadly depilatory?"

"I'd have to arrest myself as an accessory before the fact. I seem to recall it was me egging you on."

"So I take it you don't suspect me of plugging Uncle Julius in the back of the head?"

"Not unless you've changed your weapon," he said.

"I guess you don't think I could fire a gun," I challenged.

"Oh, I think you could fire a gun," he said. "Whether you could load it is another question. Anyway, tell me about the last time you saw Julius Cole."

I told him. He took notes.

"Didn't you guys have enough money left over for a tape recorder?" I asked. "Or do you have one hidden behind your tie?"

"Too intimidating just for a friendly chat," he said. "Not that you were ever easily intimidated. So did Julius mention any appointment he had that night?"

"Nope."

"Did you get the impression he left in a huff after his little squabble over the coffin? Or that he left because he had someplace to go?"

I shook my head. "He just left," I said. "Maybe he would've stayed longer if he hadn't fought with Lillian. I don't know."

"See anybody walk out with him?"

I closed my eyes and replayed the scene in my mind.

"No," I said. "Andy Fuller was standing with him by the door, probably trying to smooth things over. But he didn't walk out with him, I don't think."

"Did you see any other signs of hostility or anger toward him? Other than Lillian's and Duke's, I mean."

"No." I didn't like where this was leading. "Didn't anybody see him at the theater that night?"

"One kid who worked there. And the manager—what's his name? Tod Welch. He's the one who loaded the film for Cole."

"The film? What film?"

"The film he wanted to watch that night. The second show in one of the theaters was over by eleven-thirty, and he asked Welch to set up a film for him. Welch turned it on, he figures, around eleven-forty-five and left the theater just after midnight—around twelve-fifteen."

"So Julius was killed some time between twelve-fifteen and when?"

"Fire chief estimates twelve-thirty, twelve-forty-five at the latest, as the time the fire started. Whoever killed him, if he saw the fire, was probably out by one."

"But what was it?" I persisted. It really bothered me to think of someone sneaking up behind Julius Cole while he was watching a movie. "The film, I mean. What was it? Was he previewing it or what?"

"Welch doesn't remember," Dale said, "except that it was something 'old,' which to him could mean the seventies. And we don't have a lab report yet, so we don't know if we'll be able to identify it, but we did find a significant portion of it intact. Why? Do you think he was watching that volcano movie or something and it got too realistic?" He grinned.

"No, I just can't figure out why he'd be there watching a movie at that hour."

"Because the theater wasn't available till then?"

"On a Friday? He had all day—or maybe up to four o'clock."

"Well," Dale said, "maybe he had other things to do during the day. Maybe he took care of routine business affairs during the day and watched movies at night."

"What were his routine business affairs?" I asked.

"Say, who's interviewing who here?"

"Well, how many people would've known where to find him? Who knew he owned the theater? Most of the people in my family didn't know it," I pointed out. Right away, I could have kicked myself for saying "most."

He didn't rise to the bait, though. "He owned a development company, J. C. Enterprises. I don't know much about his business affairs yet, but as I understand it, he bought and sold real estate. And then sometimes, of course, he hung on to it, like he did with Eden Center."

"Is that who Lillian sold the land to?" I asked, surprised. "J. C. Enterprises?"

"She says not. She says it was another company, one with a kind of funny name: the Pison Corporation."

"But Julius owned that, too?"

"I gather it's one of those wholly owned subsidiaries."

I was silent for a moment. Thinking out loud was getting me into too much trouble.

"So are you assuming that Julius had an appointment with someone at the theater that night?"

"I'm assuming that if he didn't," he said, "someone followed him there, either from the funeral home or from anyplace he might have gone between the funeral home and the theater."

He let that sink in.

"I don't suppose you've identified anyplace else," I said gloomily.

"Not at present we haven't," he said, "but I'm still working on it. See, I don't think you sit down to watch a movie if you're expecting someone to come in and interrupt you. You might if you were at home, watching it on a VCR, but not in a movie theater."

"Hmm. So you're looking for a killer who's also an arsonist, or for a killer *and* an arsonist? A killer and two arsonists? What?"

"Did I say I was looking for an arsonist?" he asked innocently.

"You're not?" I was floored.

"I don't know yet," he said. "The arson investigation on the theater isn't completed. Now the other case—the Cole house—is different. That's not my case, but I saw the place and even I could tell it was suspicious. You could tell there were several points of origin. Whoever set that fire wanted that house gone. But between you, me, and the four walls, if the theater fire was arson, it was a damned professional job. One point of origin, and no obvious signs that an accelerant had been used."

"But where did the fire start?"

"Ask me to read the file, why don't you?" he protested, not very seriously. "I don't suppose there's any harm in your knowing that, as long as you remember it's not official. I'm not an arson specialist. But most of the fire damage was done to the projection booth. The seats in the theaters were damaged by smoke and water, but the fire loss is concentrated in the booth. The manager says they were storing some newsprint advertising supplements there, not far from the projector that was running. Fire chief doesn't think the fire would have spread very fast unless there were flammable materials nearby."

"But what you're implying is that it could be purely a coincidence that the theater burned down just after Julius Cole was murdered. Coincidences like that don't happen!"

"Not in real life they don't," he agreed placidly. "Only in the movies."

17

Grosvenor was standing out on his front lawn, chatting with curious neighbors, when I arrived. There was a police car in the driveway. Clara was nowhere in sight, despite the camera crews gathered around the rhododendrons and the reporters checking their makeup in the news vans' rearview mirrors.

"Gilda, I'm being set up!" Grosvenor announced loudly and dramatically when he spotted me.

The camera crews perked up and I saw several cameras hoisted onto shoulders and pointed in my direction, in case I turned out to be somebody important.

"Yeah?" I said noncommittally. "What's going on?"

Grosvenor seized my arm and turned me away from the cameras. He steered me toward the front door of the Junes' modern ranch-style house.

Inside the front hall he glanced around, then focused his attention on me.

"The police think I burned down Julius's house," he said confidentially.

"Why would they think that?" I asked.

"You know," he said.

"Because you're a pyrotechnician? Because that's your specialty—bombing things, burning things down?"

"My point exactly," he said, nodding and looking wise. "So why would I be dumb enough to do something like that in my own backyard?"

"You might do it," I said mildly. I'd never been able to bring myself to call him "Uncle Grosvenor." "But I hope you wouldn't

101

be dumb enough to leave your materials and equipment lying around."

"Gilda, I'm telling you, I was set up," he insisted. "Someone wants the police to think it was me."

"Depending on how expertly it was done," I observed, "the cops might have a hard time swallowing that. I wouldn't think there'd be a lot of call for arson in Eden County. I don't think we have much local talent."

"Ridiculous!" he said. "Any firefighter could do it."

That gave me pause. Was it true? And if so, could volunteer firefighters do it as well? That would tend to broaden the pool of suspects.

"For that matter," he said, "anybody could learn how to do it from the Internet. Even you could do it."

"They have arson lessons on the Internet?" I asked incredulously.

"Of course," he said. "You can learn how to do anything on the Internet: build bombs, burn down buildings, hijack planes—"

He broke off as an officer appeared in the doorway carrying a large plastic bag.

"What's that?" he asked as the officer edged past us.

"Probably clothing and shoes," I guessed. "They're probably testing for residue. I hope you did a wash this morning."

"My shoes?" he echoed. "They're taking my shoes?"

I turned and walked away. Here it was, payback time, or so I suspected, and I actually felt sorry for the guy. He was arrogant enough to assume he'd thought of everything, from fingerprints to residue on clothing. I doubted they'd match anything at the scene of the fire to Grosvenor's workshop. But it was just possible he hadn't thought about shoes.

I stood and watched the officer stash the bag in the trunk of the cruiser. I wondered what in the hell Grosvenor had hoped to accomplish by burning down Julius's house, if he'd burned down Julius's house.

I doubted that the prosecutor could build an arson case on the basis of trace residue on a pair of shoes. I thought of reassuring Grosvenor on that score. But no, I didn't feel *that* sorry for him.

* * *

I was supposed to meet Duke at four o'clock, after school let out, for a guided tour of my new property and my first lesson in running a movie theater. I arrived early, let myself in with a key, armed myself with two flashlights, and climbed to the third floor. I felt guilty about what I was doing, but I told myself that I needed to know exactly how much trouble my business manager was in.

I found a pull chain just inside the hallway and gave it a yank. The bulbs inside the blackened metal fixtures might have been original from the faint yellow light they gave off. The old marquee was right where I'd last seen it, all those years ago. The floor was dusty, an unhealthy environment for anything but dust mites to live in, and a path had been worn clean from the porcelain sink at the top of the stairs down the hall to the first door. I opened what I thought was a closet door tucked into one corner and found a toilet. Both the sink and the toilet appeared to be in working condition, and on top of the former were a razor, a toothbrush, and soap. Inside the first door off the hallway my flashlight found an old-fashioned push-button switch.

I drew my breath in in surprise. Here was Duke's lair, his private pad, hidden away from the prying eyes of the Liberty family—or at least all eyes but Mae's. When it came to her theater, I doubted that Maesie had missed anything.

And I wondered what she had made of it. For one whole wall was devoted to her. There were movie posters from her movies, pictures and articles clipped from magazines and newspapers, press books, gossip columns, studio publicity photos, and even a dust jacket from an old unauthorized biography. I sneezed, but the tears that started in my eyes weren't entirely caused by the dust. Here was Mae as a girl, barely older than Duke, playing a waitress in her first film, her beauty eclipsing that of the more prominently placed star even then. Here was a publicity photo of Mae as a Fox starlet, all soft-focus radiance. Here was Mae in her Academy Award performance, sending her lover back to his wife without telling him that she was dying of a rare blood disease. Here she was in her forties, modeling a dress for some charity function, and in her fifties, playing a business executive, and on up to the publicity still of Mae in her late seventies, flashing her signature smile and displaying her wrinkles unabashedly. It was a Mae Liberty museum and Duke was its curator and only visitor.

I was relieved to see that the rest of the room was more typical for a teenager—or at least for a certain type of teenager. The theme was science fiction, as indicated by sci-fi posters, comic book covers, and other paraphernalia. Science fiction and movies. The kid lived most of his life in a fantasy world.

In one corner was a futon and next to it stood a set of cinderblock bookshelves loaded down with science fiction novels. Against the wall opposite the bed was a desk made from two antique file cabinets and a wooden door, also venerable. But on top of the desk was a computer, and it looked brand new to me. The monitor was large, perhaps eighteen inches, the CPU was housed inside a tower that included a CD-ROM drive, and there were speakers on either side of the monitor. The printer was a color laser printer and next to it was a scanner. Next to the desk was a stand with another CD player, and I counted four large speakers, one mounted in each corner of the room. A set of earphones was tossed casually on the bed. There was a reading lamp on the floor next to the futon and another lamp on the desk. Three wooden crates seemed to serve Duke as a dresser.

The wall sockets into which these various pieces of equipment were plugged looked new, I was happy to see; I just hoped the old theater's circuits could handle the strain. There were no windows.

I had seen what I had wanted to see, and I was more than a little ashamed of myself. I wasn't about to start hunting around for a gun.

When I turned out the light, the ceiling winked at me and I looked up, dazzled by a sky filled with stars and planets and moons. They must have absorbed the light while it was on and now they glittered in the dark. I was enchanted.

When Duke arrived, he took me on a more thorough tour of the building, from the old boiler room under the main theater, with its mysterious piles of old pipes, to the backstage storage area, where the sound system was, to the old dressing rooms over the stage. The whole building was like a rabbit warren, riddled with small closets and storage spaces, and everywhere you looked there were vestiges of its past, from film posters to press kits, from sandwich boards to an old water fountain, from long-forgotten reels of film to dust-covered splicers. And in the spaces left over there were boxes and boxes of old records. Duke told me that the second building, the one Mae had bought and converted into a third theater, had once been a bank and then an insurance company. He showed me an old safe mounted on the wall of the long storage room, where I'd found the employee records the day before.

That reminded me of Julius Cole.

"Duke, do you know if Julius ever worked here?" I asked. "I mean, years ago, when he was a young man."

If he had, Duke had never heard about it.

Then we climbed to the third floor and, with a shy pride, Duke showed me his room.

"This is where I stay," he said simply.

I felt an odd mix of emotions. Was his willingness to bring me here an expression of trust? Or did it simply constitute a facing up to the inevitable—that as the new owner, I would eventually discover his hideout? It occurred to me that he was holding his breath, waiting for me to register shock or disapproval, waiting for me to lecture him about how primitive the living conditions were and throw him out.

"This is really nice," I said, and I felt rather than saw him breathe again. "It must be really good for you to come up here and get away from the family."

"Yeah," he agreed, pushing his glasses up and looking around, as if trying to see the place through my eyes.

I pretended to study the Mae Liberty gallery for the first time. "This is quite a collection," I said, and sighed. "Wasn't she beautiful?"

He didn't speak, but in a telling gesture he reached out a finger and touched one of the photographs softly on the cheek.

Then he said, "She was really good to me. Nobody else treated me the way she did."

"What do you mean?" I asked. I was curious about their relationship. I knew how Maesie had treated me, but I realized I had never noticed how she had treated other people.

Duke looked embarrassed. He seemed to be struggling to find the right words. Then, gazing at the photograph, he said, "She took me seriously."

I nodded. "You were her business partner."

"I bought all this stuff with the money she paid me," he said with a gesture that took in the computer and stereo equipment. "It's not like we made a lot, either." Then he looked self-conscious again, as if it had occurred to him that it might be inappropriate to mention money around his new boss.

"She's the one who asked Uncle Val to rewire this room so that I could have all my stuff here," he said. "My folks complained that I was spending too much time here, but she talked them out of it. She knew this was where I wanted to be.

"But it's convenient, too," he said, as if he needed to persuade me to let him stay. "See, all the prints have to be checked when we load them onto the platters. A lot of theaters don't do that, but it isn't right; they should. Sometimes the last place that had the print screwed it up. You know, like maybe they had a break and didn't splice it back together very well. If you don't fix that, you'll have a break, too. We've even gotten reels that were loaded backward. Once that happens, you can't just stop and fix it while the audience is sitting there, you have to give them their money back. So I have to put in a lot of hours, and I work late at night."

I nodded, more convinced than ever that I didn't want anything to do with handling the films if that many things could go wrong with them. At the same time, my respect for Duke was increasing by leaps and bounds. How had the kid managed all these months to go to school and run a movie theater at the same time? He did look tired, but I don't think I would have lasted a week on his schedule.

"I want you to be my business partner, too," I said. I had given this a lot of thought over the last few days. "I'm not really sure why she left me the theater, but—"

"She liked you best," he said quickly. "She thought you'd be good for the Paradise. She thought you'd take care of it."

We were both feeling our way.

"Why didn't she leave it to you?" I asked gently.

"I'm just a kid!" he blurted out. "I still have to finish high school. Not that I want to. But I have to. That was our agreement. And, anyway, I don't know much about business—profits and taxes and stuff like that."

"I'll bet you could learn," I pointed out. "You already know a lot about running a theater."

"I'm not outgoing enough," he confessed. He pushed his glasses up with his forefinger. "Grandma Eve and Grandpa Adam used to talk to everybody who walked in the door, that's what Maesie said. And she was like that, too. She knew what kinds of movies everybody liked; she even talked them out of movies she didn't think they'd like. They'd come to buy a ticket for a movie and she'd say, 'Oh, you won't like that one. That one's too violent for you. I'd rather have you see this one.' And they'd take her advice, or else be sorry they didn't."

I was startled to see tears in his eyes.

"I tried to do that after she got sick," he said softly. "I tried to run things just the way she wanted them, and talk to people and all. And everybody was really nice to me. But I just can't do it the way she could."

My own eyes teared up again at this vision of his struggle to be the person he thought she needed him to be. It must have been agony for this shy, withdrawn, awkward teenager to stand in the lobby every night and try to think of something to say to people.

"Oh, Duke," I said, and suddenly I had my arms around him. "Maesie loved you just the way you are. She didn't want you to become somebody you're not, not even for the good of the Paradise. Maybe that *is* why she left the theater to me—because she thought I could do the things you couldn't. She probably knew I'd recognize how talented you were, and we'd share the responsibilities. That's what I'd like to do—work out a partnership. If you're willing, that is."

I felt his chest heave. After a minute he backed out of the hug. His glasses were steamed up.

"You don't have to do that, Gilda," he said.

"I know I don't have to," I replied. "I want to. I'm willing to learn from you, but there's probably a lot you do that I won't really want to do, like projecting."

"You really ought to learn that, Gilda," he said.

"Okay, okay, I'll learn, but I don't want to take over that job," I said. "And now I really need a cigarette. And we need to talk some more."

He shrugged. "It's your place," he said. "You can smoke up here or in the office, just not in the public areas."

"Let's go to the office then," I proposed. I found the dimness of the third floor depressing, and I didn't especially want to contaminate his living quarters with my smoke.

As he turned out the light, he asked, "So what did you really think, the first time you saw my room?"

I glanced at him in surprise. He grinned sheepishly and pointed up at his starlit ceiling.

"The stars were still glowing in the dark," he said.

I laughed. "Way cool," I said. "I thought it was way cool."

Duke led as we descended the stairs. I was wondering whether I could ever get used to spending so many of my waking hours in the dark, like a bat, when Duke spoke.

"I didn't kill him, Gilda," he said abruptly. "And I didn't burn down his theater, either. I don't have an alibi or anything; I was here by myself after the visitation. And I'm not sorry somebody did it. Maybe I even wish it was me. But it wasn't."

"Thanks for letting me know," I said.

I was still looking at his back when he said, "Do you think they're going to arrest me?"

"Not for having an argument with him," I reassured him, "if that's what you'd call it. Not even if you'd punched him in the nose. There's a difference between that and killing somebody."

"So I guess I missed my big opportunity, huh?" he said wryly.

In the tiny office behind the concession stand, he insisted I sit in the only chair, an old wooden swivel chair. He hunted up an empty bottle for me to use as an ashtray and propped himself against a low file cabinet.

"Grandma and Grandpa Liberty used that upstairs room as an office," he explained, "but Maesie did a lot of the office work at home. You could use that upstairs room again if you wanted. We're just using it for storage now."

"You mean as an office?" I said. "You're not suggesting I move in here with you? I don't know you that well yet."

He blushed just as deeply as I thought he would, but he smiled, too.

"So," I said. "Let's talk about you. You have one more year of high school and then what?"

He shrugged. "My parents want me to go to college. Maesie wanted me to, too."

"What about you? What do you want?"

He looked at the floor.

"I'm happy here," he said.

"How are your grades?"

"Pretty good, actually," he said. "I like to read and stuff, and I'm pretty good at math and science. I don't do so hot in Spanish."

"*Yo tambien,*" I assured him. "So what about Eden College? Want to go there?"

He pushed his glasses up and toed the floor. "Could I go to Eden College and work here, too?"

"I don't see why not," I said. "You might not be able to carry a full load, but if you're a good student, you could probably work it out. I do agree with Maesie and your folks that you ought to go to college, though you don't have to go right away, as far as I'm concerned. But eventually you'll need it to keep yourself employable. After all, we don't know what's going to happen in the theater business in the next ten or twenty years."

I didn't point out that if the last twenty years were any indication, it was unlikely to support Duke's paperback habit for long.

"That would be okay, I guess," he admitted.

"Can you get a scholarship?"

I knew that Eden College cost a bundle, and generous as I was feeling toward Duke, I didn't yet know what I was in for as the owner of an independent theater in the middle of a dying downtown.

"They have scholarships for local kids," he said. "But Maesie left me money, too."

"Good," I said. "So it's a deal? Fifty-fifty on the theater profits, assuming there are any, we make all the big decisions together, and you get a college education in your spare time."

I held out my hand.

"Deal," he said, and shook it.

We grinned at each other.

"So where do we start?"

I had the nagging feeling that I'd forgotten something. Just before we unlocked the doors that night, I realized what it was. I'd forgotten to tell Duke that I was due back at my old job a week from today. Then I realized that I was thinking of the insurance company as my "old job."

Careful, Gilda, I cautioned myself. You've been carried along this afternoon on a flood of emotion. That's no way to make career decisions. You don't want to make any promises you don't want to keep.

18

Peachy was tearing her hair out over Julius Cole's funeral arrangements.

"There's no family to speak of," she said. "His first wife is dead, and the second wife, whom I finally tracked down, could care less and can't think of anybody who could. No children."

"Doesn't that make it easier?"

I had dragged her off to play miniature golf, one of those completely frivolous activities we used to indulge in as kids. I thought it would relax her. The problem was that we were having a cold May, and though we were both wearing jackets, the wind was picking up and rain was threatening.

I gave my ball a little tap. It bounced off the edge of the cup, hit Peachy's ball, and knocked it into the corner.

"Sorry!" I said.

"Anyway," she continued, rubbing her hands to warm them up, "it should have made things easier, not having to deal with Coles. And it should have made things easier just having to deal with Andy Fuller, who is the executor."

"Except that Greer comes with Andy," I said, making another lackluster attempt to get my ball in the hole.

"And who comes with Greer?" she asked.

"Oh, God! Adele! I'm really sorry, Peachy," I said contritely. "If I could do anything about my relatives, I would."

"You could bump off Adele as far as I'm concerned," she said darkly. "Why can't she content herself with horning in on the motel business and leave Julius Cole's funeral alone? Is she a frustrated director or what?"

111

She gave her ball a nudge, which sent it back down the straightaway, almost to the tee. She stalked after it.

"If it were up to Andy, he'd leave everything to me," she said. "Julius would get a first-class funeral—"

"No visitation, I hope," I put in. "If the fire department had just let the fire burn a little longer, he'd already be cremated. Then we could have just scattered what's left of him over the Eden Center parking lot. Or, better yet, scattered him over what's left of his house. Nobody would have even noticed a few more ashes."

I realized that my whole attitude toward Julius had shifted once I'd learned about the Eden Center theater. I had adjusted pretty quickly to the idea of his being dead.

She ignored my suggestion. "Then Greer puts her two cents in, saying that maybe since Julius was so important to the town and all, we ought to come up with a list of people who should make speeches."

"I would've thought after Mae's funeral, everybody would be all talked out."

"You'd think so, wouldn't you? And then along comes Adele, with 'Julius would've wanted this' and 'Julius would've wanted that,' until she aggravated me so, I swear, Gil, I almost broke down and said the one thing you can never say in the funeral business!"

"Which is?"

"Don't matter what he wanted, the man's dead!"

With that she gave her ball a whack that sent it sailing over the side. It landed with a thud on another straightaway several yards away.

"Oh, good!" she said. "I'm already up to the windmill hole. That means I'm almost done."

In the end Julius's funeral was a model of restraint next to Mae's, even though the whole town turned out for it. The local dry cleaners must have been up all night to meet the sudden demand for the dresses and suits that had been dropped off casually after Mae's funeral. Andy Fuller, wearing the somber look of a banker who has just lost one of his biggest depositors, gave a short speech about Julius's love for the community. This was the big theme of the minister's eulogy, too—Julius's habit of putting the needs of the community before personal gain.

I had noticed a certain amount of restlessness and muttering during Andy's speech. It increased in volume as the minister praised Julius's generosity.

A man behind me said in a voice that carried several rows, "He left us Megaverse, that's what he left us, and an empty downtown."

A woman's voice said, "Well, thank God he died before he came up with any more community needs to be generous about."

Another voice said, "Somebody should have burned him out ten years ago."

I was a little shocked. In the first place, I didn't know what Julius Cole had to do with Megaverse, though I now knew what he'd had to do with Eden Center. Was that what they meant—that by building Eden Center, he had opened the door for Megaverse? Or was he more involved than that? I would have to ask my parents.

In the second place, I had thought of Julius as a well-respected citizen. Even if people had disagreed with some of his business decisions, he had certainly been responsible for a great many of Eden's development projects, which must have provided jobs for Eden residents. And even if they felt strongly about some of his decisions, as they had about Lillian's, I would have expected them to keep those feelings to themselves out of deference to his stature in the town.

In the third place, this was his funeral. You don't expect a hostile crowd at a funeral. But these folks seemed to have come here to bury Caesar, not to praise him.

The service was mercifully short, which explained Adele's sour expression. Most of the Liberties trooped out to the gravesite. I suspected they didn't want to miss anything. As we circled the grave, I studied the faces around me. Dr. Genesee was there and Helen Beverly, his former nurse, was with him. She was wearing sunglasses, but she applied her handkerchief to her face so much that it was clear she was weeping. Lillian's face was stony, with a slight downward curve at the edges of her mouth, which suggested bitterness. My parents were somber. Adele also looked bitter, but perhaps for different reasons. Wallace was gazing into space, Oliver was asleep on his feet, and Gloria was frowning at the back of the minister's wife's head—or rather, at her hairdo, I guessed. Greer was blowing her nose, though more from allergies than from grief, I thought, and Andy's face was unreadable. Val and Tobias were standing shoulder to shoulder, closer than they typically stood in public. Their heads were down, so I couldn't see their expressions. Grosvenor was looking around the cemetery. Clara was wearing a slight smile; her expression could only be described as satisfied. Betty winked at me as my gaze swept her face; her husband, Teddy, had already gone back to work. My cousin James's kids were climbing all over the tombstones, and Clyde the cop, who was probably supposed to be helping Dale Ferguson observe everything, was observing his cousins with a look that said he wanted to arrest them. Dale was doing what I was doing, scanning the crowd. When our gazes crossed, he raised his eyebrows at me.

"Call me later or come by," my mother said as we left the cemetery. "I have something I need to talk to you about."

I groaned inwardly. At seven-thirty the theater would be teeming with little people clamoring to see *101 Dalmatians*. I'd been hoping to put off my headache until then.

At Liberty House I changed into jeans and a T-shirt and went downstairs to the study to sit at Mae's desk. It was time to try to figure out the Paradise's finances.

I was skimming a six-month summary of ticket sales when Lillian wandered in.

"Let me know if you need help with anything," she said.

"I will." I didn't lift my eyes from the page.

"I mean, if there's anything you don't understand, I might be able to help," she said. "Just ask."

"Okay," I said.

"Sometimes things get misfiled," she persisted, "and then it's hard to determine where they belong. Just let me know if you find anything like that."

A small warning bell went off in my head. She's been looking for something, my mother had said; find out what she's been looking for.

"Why?" I asked casually, eyes still on the page. "Anything missing?"

"Not that I know of," Lillian said, and left the room.

I put down what I was reading. Misfiled? So she was looking for something that might have been misfiled? Like what? Whatever Maesie was reading the night she died?

But for the life of me I couldn't figure out what it could be. A new will? Something that cut me out and left everything to Lillian? It didn't sound plausible. According to Mr. Hermes, the attorney, Lillian had received a generous legacy from her sister's estate, in addition to sole ownership of Liberty House. Her lifestyle was not very extravagant. Did she want the theater? But that didn't make sense, either. Lillian seemed to accept that she was too old to run a movie theater, and she seemed happy to have me do it. Unless she thought that Duke, her great-grandson, should own it—or that she should own it on Duke's behalf. That hardly explained the level of anxiety, though, that my mother had described—unless my mother had been exaggerating. I mentally reviewed the past few days, when I'd been too preoccupied with my own problems to notice other people's.

No, I thought, if my mother had been exaggerating, Lillian wouldn't have been caught inside Julius Cole's house. But what did he have to do with anything?

"Oh, my God!" I said out loud. "What if they were married?"

I remembered the conversation I'd had with my sisters after the visitation. What if Maesie had once been married to Julius Cole? They didn't have to have been married when she died; they could have been married once upon a time. Mae was the marrying kind. What if she'd had five husbands instead of four?

That would explain Lillian's remark about finding something that had been misfiled. Perhaps she was looking for a marriage certificate. My thoughts tripped over themselves as they rushed out.

What would be the purpose of a marriage certificate now? Unless there was a child we didn't know about, which seemed far-fetched, Mae's only child was dead. And Mae had predeceased Julius, so her heirs would be hard-pressed to claim any part of his estate.

If there had been a marriage, I couldn't imagine that it had lasted very long. In the first place, I would have heard about it. In the second, Julius was, as Lana had pointed out, a notorious philanderer, and Mae would never have put up with that. They had also seemed to be on good terms for ex-spouses. I was well aware that my own relationship with George was the exception that proved the rule about the lifelong enmity that divorce generates.

But perhaps it wasn't a marriage certificate Lillian was looking for. Perhaps she'd told the truth when she said she'd been looking for Julius's will. Maybe she had reason to believe that someone else in the family stood to inherit part of Julius's estate. But why? Had his sexual adventures given him a hitherto unknown branch on the Liberty family tree?

And did any of this have anything to do with the theater?

My next thought made my heart jump. Were we all wrong about who owned the Paradise? Suppose Mae had gotten in over her head when she'd renovated the theater and put up the new facade. Suppose she'd been forced to sell. Who would be a more logical choice than her old friend Julius, who would have agreed to keep the whole thing secret and permitted her to continue running the business? Suppose Lillian had been looking for a deed to the theater property. Maybe I didn't own a movie theater after all.

To my utter amazement, I greeted this prospect with disappointment rather than relief. But I *should* be relieved, damn it! I told myself. I can go back to New York and get on with my life. As the tears sprang to my eyes, I thought, What's the matter with me, anyway?

I blinked back the tears as soon as I recognized the weakness in my latest theory. Mae's will was quite recent, Mr. Hermes had said. She wouldn't have left me a theater she didn't own. Besides, according to Mr. Hermes she'd been worth three million.

"I give up!" I said in exasperation.

That was my father's entrance cue.

"What are you giving up?"

"Oh, hi, Dad," I said. "I don't know. I'm giving up trying to figure out what's going on around here."

"Oh, what's going on around here," he echoed. "I know how you feel."

"Dad, was Maesie ever married to Uncle Julius?" I asked. "Or did they ever . . . I mean, might they have . . . ?"

"Been lovers?" he finished for me. "As to that, I can't say. She was never married to him, though. I'd have known."

Not, I thought to myself, if you weren't invited to the wedding.

"There was always something between them," he mused. "I thought maybe they'd get together in the end. I could be wrong, but I got the impression that Julius wanted it."

"But Maesie didn't?"

"I don't know, Gilda," he said. "I honestly can't say. But their relationship was deep." He settled into a nearby armchair.

"Then why did Lillian hate him?"

He interlaced his fingers under his chin. "You'll have to ask her that, honey," he said. "I honestly don't know. She implied that it was because he owned the Eden Center theater, but that doesn't sound like the whole story to me. She's never liked him."

"So what are you doing here?" I asked him.

He nodded at the desk. "Same as you, I imagine. Going through Mae's papers. Trying to straighten things out, pay bills, close accounts. Val and I are her executors, you know."

"Mom says she wants to talk to me," I said. "Know what it's about?"

"Yes, as a matter of fact, I do." He got up and came over to the desk, pulled open the top drawer, and extracted a business card. He laid it on the desk in front of me.

I squinted at it. " 'S. Styles, Private Investigator,' " I read. I picked it up and frowned at it, then at him. "Who's this?"

"That's what we were kind of hoping you'd find out for us," he said. "We have some bills and some receipts from him. Apparently, Mae hired this guy for some reason. We need to know . . . well, if he finished the work and if we owe him any money. And if he did finish the work and still has something to give us, I guess we'd better get it."

I gazed at the card thoughtfully and tapped it on the desk. "Does Lillian know anything about this?"

"She says not."

"I suppose you want me to be, uh . . ."

" 'Discreet' was the word your mother used."

"Well," I said, "I suppose I could say I want to have my lover followed to see if she's cheating on me." I quirked my mouth at him. "Seems a little late for that, though."

Duke was already leaning over the concession counter studying something when I arrived at the theater.

"Howdy partner!" I greeted him.

"Hey, Gilda," he said. "How was the funeral?"

"Short," I said. "Whatcha lookin' at?"

"Release schedules," he said.

I leaned over the counter, shoulder to shoulder with him, and studied the list.

"Can we get some with people in them I've heard of?" I asked. "Like this Julia Roberts film or this one with Tommy Lee

Jones—I've heard of them. Can't we get those? Or are they too expensive?"

"It's not usually the expense that cuts us out," he said, "though now that the Eden Center theater is gone, maybe they'll give us what we ask for."

"But don't we have to bid for things?" I said.

"Not very often anymore," he said. "Universal's the only company that requires a bid, and even then it's not clear why we bother. Mostly we get what the distributors want to give us."

"What do you mean?" I asked. "Are you saying that we don't even get a shot at any of the blockbuster movies?"

"Yeah, that's what I'm saying. We can tell them what we want, but it won't do much good. Most of the time they just call our booker and tell him what they're sending. And as an independent theater, we don't have much clout." Duke pushed his glasses up. "See, the distributors, they don't care about keeping us happy, they only care about keeping the chains happy, because the chains are bigger customers. Not necessarily in this market, but nationally. So now the big movies go to them automatically, without any bidding. We used to bid against the Eden Center for whatever was left over. And then we basically got whatever they didn't want. Now the distributors don't even pretend that the process is fair. So once in a while they throw us a bone, but that's about it.

"Mae never believed that the old way was fair. She never thought the bids were really being looked at. She wanted to sue them in the worst way. You know, it was like a monopoly or something."

"Why didn't she sue?"

"I guess she just ran out of time and energy." When he straightened up, he was almost a head taller than I was. "But you could do it if you wanted to," he said hopefully.

"Not this week, kid," I said. "Let's see how it goes."

By the time the first show's audience had left, there didn't seem to be a clean surface in the entire movie theater. The concession counter was sticky, the ticket counter was sticky, the bathroom door was sticky, and the faucet handles were sticky. I had a bruised shin from holding one tyke up to the water fountain. Rashid was in the men's john mopping up a flood that had occurred when somebody threw a whole box of Gobstoppers into the toilet and flushed. Amanda looked less like the pretty college student she was and more like an extra from *M*A*S*H*.

The adults had taken one look at the horde of kids waiting to get in and had stayed away in droves. I didn't blame them a bit.

I heard screaming and turned around. Duke was lugging a kid out of the projection booth. He carried the kid all the way out to the sidewalk, where, red-faced, he told the kid to stay put until his mother came or he'd never get in to see another movie at the Paradise.

"There've been times in the past two days," I confessed to my sister Betty on the phone later, "when I began to think maybe I had a calling, you know? I thought, well, bringing joy and pleasure into people's lives—that's not a bad life's work." I raised my foot and peeled a squashed jujube off my shoe. "This is not one of those times."

The next morning I lay in bed, exhausted. I've been in town almost a week, I thought, and it's aged me ten years. It wasn't just the physical exhaustion, which was real enough. It was the emotional exhaustion as well. And if the grown-ups of Eden, Ohio, were resolved to give me a honeymoon period, their kids weren't in on the deal. Last night the theater had been overrun with Macaulay Culkins, apparently cloned by the same photo-copying process that Disney had used to create the original hundred and one dalmatians. My dreams of bringing joy and laughter to the masses had crashed against a wall of sticky-fingered, hyperactive munchkins. What I wanted to bring them was not joy and laughter, they had too much of that already.

I spent what was left of the morning in Mae's office with my father.

"It's kind of nice having you around, Gil," he'd said the night before.

And the truth was that I was enjoying these little father-daughter work sessions. Mostly we just read in companionable silence, but sometimes we ruminated out loud when we discovered something interesting and I was reminded of why Mae had chosen my father as one of her executors: he had good business sense. At the same time he was unpretentious, which made him more willing than most of the family to admit he didn't know something.

Lillian found lots of excuses to visit the office and ask us how we were doing. I had the sense that she was never very far off camera; I felt spied upon.

"Say, Dad," I asked him at last, "do you have any theories about what it is Lillian's been looking for?"

He put down what he was reading and took off his reading glasses. "No," he said, "I don't. But it's occurred to me that it might have something to do with that private investigator."

I nodded. "That's occurred to me, too. But what?"

"That's what you'll have to find out, Gilda," he said.

Val showed up in time for lunch, which was typical of him. He wasn't really very interested in Mae's business affairs, and my father seemed to accept that Val's role was to be a kind of archivist for her more personal papers: correspondence, diaries, and any other autobiographical material we might find. Mae had known everybody from Hollywood's golden years and she had received letters from many of them. Val was going to organize everything, expurgate anything that he judged too painful or damaging for the public eye, catalogue the remainder, and ship it all off to USC, whom Mae had designated in her will as the recipient.

The five of us sat down to lunch—Val, Lillian, my father and I, and Ruth Hernandez. Ruth had begun her career eating in the kitchen, but shortly after she had come to work for Maesie, they had instituted their lifelong habit of eating together, whether in the kitchen alone or in the dining room with guests. Everyone knew Ruth and respected her as a member of the family. For her part, Ruth had never been intimidated by Mae's and Lillian's famous friends.

She was the first to speak when Lillian asked, for the umpteenth time, whether we'd found anything interesting that morning. Even after all these years she still had a Spanish accent, and her language was a colorful and eclectic mix. I'd always thought that maybe that was why she'd gotten along so well with Louis B. Mayer.

"Lilly, they're going to tell you if they find anything," she scolded Lillian. "Why do you have bugs up your ass? If you lost something, tell us all, everybody, and everybody will help you look for it. But you're going to drive everybody crazy always looking, looking, looking and then asking everybody what they know. And you're going to get arrested if you go looking in somebody else's house again. In the jail they got no places you can look. So you'd better tell us what you want."

I saw Val hide his smile behind his napkin. Then he said, "She's right, you know, sis. You really ought to confide in us."

But Ruth turned her guns on him. "You're the one to talk, Mr. Cat-That-Ate-the-Parakeet! Don't think I don't know about the times you were in there with Mae, whispering behind closed doors! There is plenty of trouble, tippy-toeing around in this house, and it all starts with secrets! There are too damn many people keeping too many secrets, and you're all going to get tangled up someday and fall down in a big pile, and then you'll be calling for me or Gilda to come untie the knot!"

I started to hear my name mentioned as one of the family troubleshooters. I couldn't even untie my own knots; I was in no shape to straighten everybody else out.

"I don't know why you talk as if I were some kind of maniac," Lillian said coldly, "wandering about the house at all hours looking for something. I'm not looking for anything in particular."

I gazed at her in admiration. That was the response of a great actress: flat denial. I couldn't have pulled it off.

"But if I *were* looking for something," she continued, "and hadn't told any of you what it was, that would indicate that it was something private." She looked pointedly at Ruth. "There is entirely too little privacy in this family and in this house."

She had the situational ethics of all great role players, be they actors or politicians or lawyers. Under normal circumstances—

which is to say, when her own curiosity was targeted at another family member—she was no defender of privacy.

"I for one am not interested in whatever it was that Val and Maesie discussed behind closed doors," she said haughtily.

I was, but it seemed an inopportune moment to say so.

"As you say, Lilly, it was private," Val agreed evenly.

"Well, but could you just tell us if you knew Uncle Julius owned the Eden Center theater?" I asked hesitantly. When he looked at me in surprise, I added, "I'm just trying to figure out how many people knew about it."

"Why?" he asked. It was a reasonable question.

"Because whoever killed him either knew he'd be there or followed him there," I offered lamely.

"And you think I killed him?" Val said rather defensively.

"No, of course she doesn't think that," my father said uneasily.

"Gilda doesn't think that, Valentino," Ruth put in, "but you've got to listen to what she's saying because the police might think it. They're going to be looking at all the Liberties, now that they know about the theater."

"But we were all here," Val protested. "I don't know the exact time frame of the murder, but if the theater was seriously damaged by the time the firetrucks arrived on the scene at one-thirty, we should all be in the clear, because we were here, a lot of us, until one-thirty at least."

My father shifted uncomfortably in his chair.

"And if no accelerant was used," Val continued, "that fire must have been burning for a while."

"Who told you," I asked, "that no accelerant was used?"

"Clyde," he responded, seemingly unperturbed. "Who told you?"

"Is that how he put it?" I pressed.

"What do you mean?" he asked.

"Well, if you say 'no accelerant was used,' that means somebody was there to use or not use it," I explained. "You're implying arson."

"I see what you mean," he said slowly. "I don't know whether he used those words or not, come to think of it. I just assumed it was arson, because it would be too great a coincidence if the place just happened to burn down right after somebody was killed there. But it's true the killer might have done something— even something inadvertent—that could have triggered an electrical fire."

"Like what?" my father asked.

"I don't know," he admitted. "I'd have to think about it. A stray bullet could have done it, I suppose."

"A bullet?" Lillian appeared startled. "I thought he died in the fire."

Val shook his head. "Somebody shot him in the back of the head. The fire came later—or I assume it did. Could've come during, I suppose."

I didn't bother to ask Val how he knew Julius had been shot. He'd obviously been milking Clyde for all the inside details on the case, just as I had with Dale, and Clyde had probably given him what Dale had given me.

"Valentino, you know too much about electricity for your own good," Ruth told him. "You'd better keep your mouth shut."

"Oh, now you think they're going to round up electricians?" he scoffed. "A minute ago they were going to arrest all the Liberties."

"You just watch out they don't arrest somebody who's a Liberty and an electrician both," Ruth retorted.

"But Val was right a minute ago when he said he should be in the clear because he was here," my father observed.

"Of course, Lilly went to bed early, as I recall," Val said wickedly, grinning at her.

Lillian looked daggers at him but didn't deign to reply.

"You leave Lilly alone!" Ruth chided him. "You'd think losing one sister would make you grateful for the ones you got left."

That put a damper on the conversation for the remainder of the meal except for a few innocuous remarks about the weather.

When it was over, my father went off to play golf and Val excused himself to go grocery shopping. Lillian went back to doing what she'd denied she was doing. And I went to see a detective.

20

I hadn't called to make an appointment. It occurred to me that detectives were frequently out of the office, but I assumed there'd be a secretary, and this way I could gather some first impressions before I actually had to confront the man. His business card, at least, had been reassuringly restrained—no cutesy logos (big eyes, spyglasses, fingerprints), catchy mottoes ("The Truth Shall Make You Free, but Your Spouse Will Pay" or "No Stone Left Unturned" or "Dirty Laundry Our Specialty"), or even straightforward advertising ("Free Estimates: Shop and Compare").

I almost missed the street entrance, which was wedged between the defunct shoe store and a venerable news shop downtown. Stairs inside led up to a door. I opened the door onto a hallway and walked into *The Maltese Falcon*, down to the smoked-glass-paneled wooden doors, one of which had painted on it S. STYLES just where SPADE AND ARCHER had been in the movie. The walls looked like they hadn't been painted since the forties, when a slightly garish shade of aqua must have been in fashion.

I opened the office door and went in, expecting to find an anteroom with Effie behind the desk.

But it was just an office with no anteroom. Two side walls were lined with dusty file cabinets. A huge battered desk that looked like army surplus stood between the windows, which faced me, and I could make out the shape of a computer to one side of the desk. The backlighting made it hard for me to see the person behind the desk, but what I noticed first was the feet: I was looking at the bottoms of two feet propped up on the desk.

Feeling embarrassed that I hadn't knocked, I hesitated, considered retreating, then decided it was too late, so I advanced a few steps into the room. My eyes adjusted a little to the light, and I was looking at a familiar head of curly dark hair. The reason it looked so familiar was that it was down. The person behind the desk was asleep.

I hesitated again, then turned around to leave.

"Going so soon?" a voice said.

I turned back.

The head came up. She yawned broadly, stretched, and then, crossing her hands over her chest again, regarded me through half-closed eyes.

Even at that I felt probed.

"Siesta time," she said.

"Sorry," I said.

She shrugged.

"I can come back," I volunteered.

"It took you long enough to get here." She yawned again. "You might as well stay."

"You were expecting me?"

"Let's say I was expecting someone from your wacko family," she said. "Not you, necessarily."

She reached behind her desk. I half expected her hand to come up holding a gun. Instead it was holding a fire extinguisher.

"See?"

I walked forward and laid the business card on the desk in front of her. She pulled her feet off the desk, dropped them to the floor, and leaned forward to give it a brief glance.

"Don't tell me," I said. "You're S. Styles."

"Okay," she said. "Don't tell me you're G. Liberty. See if I care."

There was a wooden chair in front of the desk, just like the one Spade and Archer had. I sat down.

"Mind?" I asked.

"I don't charge rent," she said.

She was as small as I remembered, but she looked smaller, dwarfed as she was by the massive desk, file cabinets, and computer. Today she was wearing khaki pants, as far as I could tell, and a white button-down shirt about three sizes too big, open at the collar with the sleeves rolled up. She had delicate features and unnerving dark eyes.

I suddenly wanted a cigarette very badly. "Mind if I smoke?" I asked.

"Advice is free, too: quit."

"That's not very original," I said.

She opened a desk drawer, took out a tacky ashtray from the New York World's Fair, and set it on the desk.

"Give me one," she said.

She'd taken me by surprise again. "You smoke?" I asked.

"Hardly ever."

So I angled the pack at her. She took a cigarette and the lighter I offered her, lit up, passed the lighter back across the desk, sat back, and looked at me.

"You seem to know why I'm here," I said. "I wish I did."

"Why do you think you're here?"

"Everybody's a shrink," I said.

"So sue me."

"I'm here because my parents wanted me to come and find out whether we owed you any money," I said. "Or, rather, whether Mae owed you any money."

"That's what your parents said they wanted," she said. "What do they really want?"

"They said they wanted to know if you had anything for us," I said, flicking my ash at the tarnished globe. "Any reports that you'd completed for Mae but hadn't delivered yet—anything like that. But just hazarding a guess I'd say they want to know why Maesie hired you in the first place."

"My good looks and charm," she said. "Also my low overhead."

"I was coming to that. Why would a private investigator want to locate in a small town like Eden?"

"You obviously haven't gone shopping for office space in Columbus recently."

"No, but it strikes me that the rents are higher because that's where the customers live."

She laughed. "Babe, you've got enough going on in your family to keep me on a retainer for the rest of my working days, if they'd be willing to hire me. Anyway, the point is, most customers don't go shopping for a private dick in their own backyard."

"I can't believe you actually said 'private dick'! You must have the same scriptwriter my family has."

"Babe, I wouldn't touch your family's scriptwriter with a ten-foot pole," she said. "But I'll say 'private vagina' if it will make you feel any better."

I didn't know how to take her. If I'd been any other Liberty, I would have taken offense. But what she said about my family pretty much coincided with my own view of them.

"So, what? You're saying that people will drive to the country for a private investigator, the way they would to buy a car?"

"Let me put it this way: if you'd hired me to prove that your spouse was getting it on with your business partner, would you want to run into me in the produce aisle at Kroger?"

This hit a little too close to home.

"I see your point," I said.

"And if it turned out she wasn't getting it on with your business partner, you wouldn't want to have to introduce me to her in that same produce aisle, now would you?"

She sat back and blew a series of perfect little smoke rings.

"I don't have a spouse," I said, for lack of anything better to say.

"I know," she said.

"Goddamn it!" I said. "What did Mae hire you to do? Investigate me?"

"No, that was on the house."

I could have thrown the ashtray at her.

"Well, who the hell *were* you investigating?"

"Lots of people. Your family, and miscellaneous others, including Julius Cole. Uncle Julius to you."

"Uncle Julius?" I echoed.

"I think I ought to tell you that your aunt Lilly has already come to call," she added.

"Lillian?"

"It was either your aunt Lilly or the dowager empress," she said. "I tend to think it was your aunt Lilly playing the dowager empress, but it could have been the other way 'round. Say, did anybody ever tell you that *you* could use a new scriptwriter?"

I nodded. "My ex did, more or less."

"Which one?"

I glared at her.

"Look, why don't you just tell me if my family's in some kind of trouble or not?"

She shook her head. "Sister, don't you know that by now?"

"I'm not asking about their mental condition," I snapped. "I'm asking about their legal condition. They may be nuts, but as far as I know, they're not psychopaths. I'd just like to know if somebody's about to be arrested."

She raised her eyes to the ceiling.

"Do I look like a fortune-teller or a palm reader? If you came here expecting me to channel Maesie for you, you're out of luck."

I was tired and cranky, and she was treading heavily on my last nerve.

"Look, why don't you just tell me about Uncle Julius," I said in exasperation.

"What do you want to know?"

"Why was Maesie investigating him?"

She turned partway around and gazed out the window for a minute, giving me the benefit of her profile.

"I don't know for sure that she was investigating him," she said at last. "I'm just guessing that part. You could say that it all started with her autobiography."

"Her autobiography?" I parroted again. "I didn't know she was writing one."

"I'm not sure she was," she said. "That's what she told Lillian, and that's what she told me at first. Maybe that's how it started. But I didn't really believe that that's what she was up to, and after a while she stopped mentioning the book."

"That's how what started?"

"The investigation. She called me in, she said, because she was sick and couldn't do the legwork anymore that she needed to do in order to confirm background details. So she'd ask me to find answers to specific questions."

"About Julius Cole?"

"Not necessarily. At first they appeared to be all over the map, her questions. But one way or another a lot of them came back to him. The ones that didn't, well, I figured I just didn't know the connection."

"Give me a for instance."

She looked at me. "You know I'm violating client confidentiality just talking to you about this," she said.

"Your client's dead, for crissake!" I expostulated.

"I told your aunt Lilly I wouldn't do that."

"I'm not the dowager empress," I said.

"True," she said, and grinned at me.

"We could play twenty questions," I suggested dryly. "For example, I'll bet you're the one who told Mae that Julius owned the Eden Center Cinemas."

"That's a yes," she confirmed. "She asked me to find out something about his business affairs—what companies he owned, or owned stock in, things like that."

"And you found out that the company with the funny name—the development company that Lillian sold her land to—belonged to Julius Cole."

"Lock, stock, and barrel," she said. "The funny name, by the by, is Pison. Mean anything to you?"

"Sounds like 'poison,' " I observed.

"You sound like the kind of English major who spent too much time studying dialects and reading *Huck Finn* and too little time reading your Bible."

"Oh, and I guess you were the star of your Sunday school class."

"Touché." She tipped her chair forward and it gave an ominous creak. She got up and walked over to one of the banks of file cabinets. She found the drawer she wanted, opened it, rummaged through it, and came up with a battered black Bible. She leafed through it till she found her place, then began to read:

" 'And a river went out of Eden to water the garden; and from thence it was parted, and became into four heads. The name of the first is Pison: that is it which compasseth the whole land of Havilah, where there is gold.' "

She shut the book.

"So jolly old Uncle Julius was a four-headed monster who saw Eden as a piece of real estate that he could turn into gold?" I asked.

"Something like that," she agreed. "I think it's fair to say that he was at least two-faced."

"And did Mae suspect that he owned the theater? Is that what she hired you to find out?"

"No, I think that came as quite a shock to her," she said, putting her own cigarette out, half smoked. "At least she turned pretty pale when she read the report and asked me if I was sure it was right."

"But you were right?"

"You don't have to be Nero Wolfe to figure out the significance of a piece of information like that, even when you don't know the principal players all that well. I double-checked my facts before I gave them to her."

"Then why was Mae having him investigated, if she didn't realize that he owned the theater?"

"Remember, I'm just guessing that he was the focus of the investigation," she said. "Now we come to a 'for instance.' " She leaned back in her chair, elbows on the armrests, fingers interlaced. "She asked me to bring her any new stories I could find about Avery Gardner's death."

"Avery Gardner!" I exclaimed. "Lilly's first husband? How does *he* come into it?"

This was getting weirder by the minute.

"So I went down to the Columbus Public Library, because it has better parking than Ohio State. And I start checking the *New*

York Times Index and rolling out the old microfilm to read about the Gardner story, and along comes this nosy librarian." She glanced at me. "You know how bored librarians get when they don't have somebody to help, so she kind of creeps up behind me and starts reading over my shoulder, I guess, though I didn't hear her. And all of a sudden I hear a voice in my ear saying, 'Oh! You're interested in Avery Gardner! Oh, he was one of my favorites! Have you checked the *Los Angeles Times* yet? It's not indexed like the *New York Times*, but if you have the dates, we can find the stories.'

"So once I crawled back inside my skin—I swear, some of those librarians wear those thick rubber soles just to see you jump!—I said that I would love to see the *Los Angeles Times* and that made her happy, so she went off to get it. And when she came back with the microfilm, she said she happened to remember that there had been several big spreads in the L.A. papers because she once had another patron who was interested in the same topic—Avery Gardner's death.

"At first, you know, I figured it had to be a schoolkid, writing a report, but then I thought it was a funny topic for a school report, even these days when you can write term papers on Jell-O. So I thought maybe Maesie had come in before, but if she had, why send me out to do it all over again? So I asked about this other patron. It had been years ago, she said, but she happened to remember because he was such a charming gentleman, and it seemed so odd that a businessman would be interested in Avery Gardner's death."

"Julius!"

"I described Julius Cole and she said that sounded right, though she repeated that it had been ages ago. So I asked her if she could remember when. Know what she said?"

"She couldn't remember?"

"Nope. She could remember perfectly well, because she was pregnant at the time and kind of self-conscious."

"I'll bet," I said wryly. I could remember distinctly how it felt to have Uncle Julius's charm turned on you like a searchlight, making you acutely aware of all your imperfections.

"It happened eight years ago, in 1989."

She sat back and looked at me, obviously waiting for me to react.

I flipped through my mental files, but it was hopeless. All my dates were in deep storage.

"I give up," I said. "What happened in 1989?"

She looked at me. "This is *your* family we're talking about!"

"Well, I don't retain numbers, okay?"

"I thought you were in insurance."

"You don't have to be a mathematical genius to be in insurance," I said defensively.

"No, but it helps," she said. "Jesus, remind me not to buy any insurance from you."

I was about to descend to the level of I-wouldn't-sell-you-a-policy-if-you-were-the-last-person-on-earth. "Look," I said, "if this little reminder costs extra, you can put it on the tab."

"Your aunt Lillian sold the Eden Center property to Julius Cole in 1989," she replied, and then added, "No charge."

I stared at her. "I don't get it," I said slowly. "Are you saying that the deal had something to do with Avery Gardner's death?"

She nodded. "That's what I think."

"Like blackmail?" I asked. "Is that what you're saying? Are you suggesting that Lilly had something to do with Gardner's death and that Julius found out and blackmailed her into selling him the property? I think you *do* know my family's scriptwriter!" I was on my feet, waving my arms in frustration.

"You don't like it?" She looked slightly offended. "I think it's brilliant."

"You would," I retorted. "You're sitting in a seedy office, playing Sam Spade. You've probably got a bottle of bourbon in your bottom drawer."

"Never mind what I've got in my bottom drawer," she said. "No need to get sarcastic. Tell me what's wrong with my theory."

I put my fists on my hips. "Well, in the first place, Lillian adored Avery Gardner. If you'd ever heard her talk about him, you'd understand."

"There's a thin line between love and hate," she said sententiously.

I groaned.

"Okay, that's not original, either," she said. "But it's true. Anyway, I never said she killed him; you're the one who invented that little scenario. I'm just guessing that there was something funny about his death."

"Like what?" I threw up my hands. "What could be funny enough to induce her to sell land she didn't want to sell, especially when she knew her sister would be angry? No," I corrected myself, "not angry. Furious."

"Maybe he was with another woman when he died," she said. "Or maybe she was with another man."

"Oh," I said, and sat down. She watched me turn this over in my head. She knew my family well enough, all right, to consider this a plausible explanation. I wouldn't say Lillian would have died if her beloved Avery had been exposed to the world as an adulterer, but she would have been deeply humiliated. And if she herself had strayed, she would certainly not want that to appear in her sister's autobiography. Her degree of anxiety was beginning to make sense to me.

"It was a very long time ago," I protested weakly.

She didn't say anything.

I took out another cigarette. She nudged the ashtray in my direction and swallowed any antismoking lectures that rose to her tongue.

"Was there anything in the newspaper reports that made you think all this up?"

"He wasn't at home when he died," she said. "He was on his way home from a party, and he was about half an hour away from his house, but on this wooded road. Apparently, he felt it coming on and pulled off the road. He died in his car. But it was two-thirty in the morning."

"He was young for a heart attack," I observed.

"Thirty," she said. "It happens. Nicotine addiction, for example, raises your blood pressure."

"*You* raise my blood pressure," I pointed out. "Smoking calms me down."

"I suppose his death could have been drug-related," she said. "Lillian wouldn't have wanted that to get out, either."

"There were always drugs in Hollywood," I agreed. "But where does this lead us? Lillian said that she didn't know Pison was connected with Julius; okay, maybe she lied about that. Maybe she's known all along that he owned the Eden Center theater. That would certainly explain her obvious dislike for the man, though it seems to me she's always disliked him. But are you suggesting she killed him in order to suppress this secret about Gardner's death, whatever it is?"

"Of course not," she said. "Are you?"

"Of course not," I said. "Anyway, why now? If she were going to get him, she would've done it years ago. No, this is just stupid."

She let the silence stretch.

"So, look," I said, "do you have any unfinished reports on any of this? You said Mae asked you to find out other things, too. I don't think I even want to know what they were. But I guess if you have anything, I'll pick it up and pay whatever she owed you."

"I already told Lillian that I delivered all my reports to Mae before she died, and her account is all paid up," she said.

"You told Lillian that?" I asked.

"Yep. Has she found 'em yet?"

"Not as far as I know," I said, sighing.

"Of course, she may think she's looking for notes for an autobiography," she said. "I couldn't tell."

"I don't suppose you know anything about 'rosebud,' " I said wearily.

"Rosebud?" She frowned. "Oh, Mae's dying word. I read about it in the paper. Well, I've never believed anything I read in the paper. I figured it for something your family would invent."

I nodded. "Well, thanks, anyway. I need to do some thinking about all of this."

We stood up and shook hands. When I turned around and

headed for the door, I saw two posters on the back wall, on either side of the door. One was Dick Powell in *Murder My Sweet*; the other was Bogey, Astor, Lorre, and Greenstreet in *The Maltese Falcon*.

I tapped Bogey on the chest.

"I guess you always wanted to be him when you grew up," I said.

"No," she said, "I wanted to be the gunsel, but I was too tall."

Someone was pounding on the door. I pulled the pillow over my head and pretended not to hear.

I have to get my own place, I thought, with only one set of keys.

"Gilda!"

It was my mother. She pulled the pillow off and glared at me.

"Didn't I train you to answer your mother when she called you?"

"Mom!" I whined. "I have a splitting headache, and I have to be at the theater in two hours! I just want a little peace and quiet."

"I'll give you peace and quiet," she said. "First just tell me what he said."

"What who said?" In my enlightened state I was confused by the pronoun.

"The detective. Isn't that where you've been?"

"Oh, the detective," I said. "It's not a he, it's a she—Ms. Styles."

I was stalling for time. Part of what I wanted the peace and quiet for was to figure out whom I was going to tell what and when.

"All right, then, what did she say?"

I sat up in bed and crossed my legs. I reached for my pack of cigarettes.

"Gilda, you smoke too much," my mother scolded me.

"That's what she said," I replied.

"What else?"

"She said that she delivered all her reports to Mae before Mae died and that we don't owe her any money," I said.

"Reports on what?" my mother pursued.

I sighed. "It had to do with Mae's autobiography," I said. "That's what Mae told Styles. She just needed help filling in some details."

This seemed the safest route to take, since it was what Lillian believed. After all, I told myself, I didn't know for certain that it wasn't true.

"Her autobiography?" My mother frowned. "I didn't know she was writing an autobiography."

"She told Lillian," I said.

My mother crossed her arms over her chest. Her style tended toward hippie chic: long skirts and oversize blouses, belts worn loose and low on her hips, or pants suits made from natural fibers. She had frosted hair, which she usually wore pulled back in a bun of one sort or another, and lipstick. In my view, her natural look made her the most attractive of the sisters-in-law, though I wasn't deceived by it. She probably spent less time at it than Adele and Gloria, but what time she spent was deliberate and well invested.

"Gilda, when somebody's writing an autobiography, they hire a research assistant, not a private investigator," she said skeptically.

"I wouldn't know," I said.

"So what kinds of details did Mae want filled in?" she asked.

"I don't know, Mom," I said. "We didn't go into that much. The only thing I know for sure was that this Styles checked up on Uncle Julius's business affairs for Mae, and that's probably how Maesie found out about the theater."

"Gilda, none of this makes any sense."

She marched over to the chair where I'd flung my bathrobe that morning as if she couldn't stand seeing it there any longer, swept it off the chair, and headed for the closet to hang it up. This was one of my mother's most irritating habits—her tendency to straighten up after me. On her way to the closet she picked up a pair of sneakers I'd left in the middle of the floor.

"Mom, I'm going to wear those shoes!" I complained.

"When? Two hours from now?" Her muffled voice came from inside the closet. She was taking a suspiciously long time, as if she'd found other things in there to tidy up.

"Liz probably left you because she was tired of picking up after you," I heard her say.

"Liz was an even bigger slob than I am," I retorted. "Mom, I'm forty-five years old. When do I get to leave my shoes in the middle of the floor if I feel like it?"

She reappeared. "When I'm dead. But if I come back to visit and trip over those damn shoes, Gilda, I swear I'll haunt you for the rest of your days."

"Now there's an incentive," I grumbled.

"Now why in God's name would Maesie want information on Julius's business affairs for her autobiography? His other affairs I might possibly see, but his business affairs?"

I shrugged. "Mom, did Maesie ever have an affair with Uncle Julius? Dad says no, but he doesn't always pick up on those things."

"I don't know, Gilda," she said. "I always thought he wanted one, but whether he ever had one or not, I couldn't say. There was something strained in their relationship, though, in spite of how close they appeared to be."

"Do you know why Lillian never liked Julius?"

"Not really, but I can guess," she said. "His kind of charm, combined with his reputation for philandering, made him oil to Lillian's water."

" 'Philandering,' Mom?" I teased her.

"Well, I'm not going to say 'screwing around,' like you young people do," she said.

It had been years since I'd thought of myself as a "young person," and since Liz had left, I'd been feeling ancient. Come to think of it, the last time I'd felt like a young person probably coincided with my last visit home, nine years ago. Nothing like a visit to the old homestead to put you in your place.

I waggled my eyebrows suggestively. "Do you think Julius the Philanderer ever tried to seduce Lillian, Mom?" I asked.

"I don't know that, either, but it wouldn't surprise me," she said, folding a T-shirt that was hanging from a doorknob. "He's the kind of man who would chase anything in a skirt, and Lilly was quite a beauty in her youth."

"Did he chase you?"

"Wouldn't you like to know," she said archly.

"Only if he caught you," I said. "Mom, do you know if anybody in the family went by Rosebud?"

"Betty asked me that," she said. "I don't know of anybody. It sounds kind of like a pet name, doesn't it?"

She had opened several dresser drawers in succession and found them empty.

"As long as we're reviewing family history," I said, "do you have any ideas about why Grosvenor June would want to burn down Uncle Julius's house?"

"I haven't the foggiest," she said. "Do you really think he did?"

"Well, I don't think it was the Wicked Witch of the West," I said.

She was scanning the room and finally spotted a corner of my suitcase sticking out from under the bed. She dragged it out and then stared in dismay at its contents.

"Gilda, for heaven's sake! You've been here a week already and you haven't unpacked! Look at this mess!" She stooped down and lifted a tangle of panty hose and underwear. If she was trying to embarrass me, she was out of luck. "I can't even tell what's dirty and what's clean. Can you?"

"The dirty stuff's turned inside out," I said. I knew she didn't expect me to have a system.

She shot me a look of alarm.

"You're not thinking of going back!"

I flopped back down on the bed. All conversations with my mother seemed like reruns.

"I said I'd come for the funeral, Mom," I reminded her wearily. "That's all I promised. I haven't made up my mind."

"But, Gilda, you have a theater to run!" she protested.

"I also have an employer in New York who's expecting me back on Monday," I said.

I didn't mention that when I'd called my secretary to check in a few days ago, she'd responded with "Gilda? Oh, Gilda!" as if my charming smile, bad math, and cranky editing were just a distant memory to her.

"Anyway," I said, "Duke can run the theater. He can probably run it better without me."

"But we've all agreed to help you out!" she said. "We can't help you out if you're not here!"

She'd shifted, as I knew she would, into emotional blackmail.

"Sure you can, Mom," I said. "You can help me out by helping Duke out."

She sat down on the bed, her eyes on the T-shirts she was folding.

"You know, Gilda, I've kind of enjoyed having you around again," she said.

"You have?"

I couldn't think why.

"I was kind of looking forward to having you around longer," she said.

"You didn't have anything to do with Maesie's decision to leave me the Paradise, did you?" I asked, my suspicions aroused.

"Certainly not!" she said, offended. "I was surprised when she did it, though it made a certain kind of sense, and I knew she always liked you best."

"She did?"

Everybody seemed to know that but me.

"Of course she did. She liked you for the same reason that

you and I never seem to get along very well, because you're such a . . . I don't know . . . an individualist, an iconoclast."

This coming from a family that had its own resident vampire was saying something. Or maybe what she was saying was that I was the only person in the family who had any interest in being normal. Iconoclasm is relative.

"I just don't know, Mom," I said.

"You don't like your job at the insurance company, do you?" she asked.

"Not much," I admitted.

"Do you get to see Liz's children anymore?"

"Not much."

I felt tears welling up in the corners of my eyes and turned my head so that she wouldn't see. Losing the kids on top of Liz's defection had been hard. They still called me sometimes—mostly when they were mad at their mother—but even the phone calls had tapered off after the first few weeks. But I couldn't talk about it with my mother. I couldn't talk about it with anyone; the words clogged my throat.

"You don't have to live here, you know," she went on. "You could move into your own apartment or even buy a house of your own. That's something you could never afford to do in New York."

It had never occurred to me to live in Liberty House if I stayed in Eden. The suitcase under the bed should have tipped my mother off on that score. But I was dangerously close to breaking down and couldn't speak. It took all my powers of concentration just to hold back the tears.

"You might enjoy the slower pace here for a while," she said. "This is the fastest-growing county in the state, and the Columbus metro area is one of the largest in the country."

I thought of a bumper sticker I'd seen once: MY MOTHER—TRAVEL AGENT FOR GUILT TRIPS!

"And who knows? There are places in Columbus you could go to meet people," she said. It dawned on me that this was her code for gay bars when she added, "You might meet some nice girl you like even better than Liz. Where there's life, there's hope, as your grandmother used to say."

It wasn't like my mother to wax sententious, as she must have recognized herself. I felt her hand patting me on the hip.

"Why don't you have a good cry and a nap and think about what I've said? I do love you, Gilda, even when we don't get along."

"Me, too," I managed before she slipped out of the room.

I didn't bother to point out that I couldn't think and cry and nap all at the same time and that thinking was likely to ruin the nap.

And tonight I had to start training a new crew. Which was hard, since I wasn't yet trained myself.

Actually, Thursday night wasn't so bad, if you discount my parents' duets behind the concession counter. It started, as usual, with my mother, who habitually sings to herself. Then my father joined in. Pretty soon they were cranking out a medley of love songs, perhaps inspired by the romance we were showing up in the balcony. Then the popcorn started popping, and my dad did a Fred Astaire imitation, helping himself to two pretzels and using them as drumsticks. Soon the two of them were dancing in the narrow space they shared with Rashid, who was waiting on customers, and I can't imagine how he did addition in his head with all that ruckus. From where I was sitting at the ticket counter, I was so distracted by them that I pretty much waited for the customers to tell me how much they owed me, and I hoped they were right, because I knew I'd have to answer to Duke if I screwed up. But I was watching my parents out of the corner of my eye because I was worried that at any minute they'd vault the concession stand or start dancing on top of the counter.

Oddly enough, though, my parents' performance didn't embarrass me the way it would have twenty or even ten years ago. At fifteen, I would have looked for a hole to crawl into. At thirty-five, I would have pretended that they were going senile. Now, at forty-five, I considered their antics the least of my worries—unless they broke the counter. And their dance routine did have the added appeal of keeping the peanut gallery enthralled.

No, Thursday was relatively trouble-free in Paradise. Friday night was another matter.

On Friday night Betty showed up with two dalmatians from the Dalmatian Rescue League and a fistful of brochures to hand out. The dalmatians were the best-behaved players on our team.

Adele showed up with cut flowers and spent the first half hour arranging them in the middle of everything on the ticket counter. Grosvenor and Clara arrived with a high-tech portable CD player so that we could have sound in the lobby. To my ungenerous regret, Grosvenor's good humor and self-confidence seemed completely restored. Clara was wearing a spectacular dropped-waist beaded dress right out of the twenties that made her look like the ultimate flapper, even though half the Jazz Age had already gone by before she was born. My parents complained that music in the lobby would disturb people watching the movies in the theaters, but it was clear that they regarded the CD player as competition for their own act behind the concession stand. Gloria, not to be outdone by Adele, whizzed past with some plastic flower arrangements for the bathrooms that exuded a sickly chemical odor that was probably supposed to be floral air freshener. It didn't seem to occur to anybody but me that the only thing people wanted to smell in a movie theater was popcorn.

Grosvenor plugged the CD player in and blew a circuit, causing Duke to pop out of the projection booth with a look of sheer horror on his face. In the dimness of the half-lit lobby, somebody screamed, and I heard a child start to cry. Wallace had just come out of the rest room in a cape and full makeup. Taking advantage of the temporary darkness, one of the dalmatians—or perhaps both of them—ate Adele's flower arrangement. My sinuses were enormously grateful to them, but it touched off a spat between Adele and Betty as soon as the lights came back on.

My parents started singing "Tomorrow." As my vision cleared, I saw Oliver leaning on the ticket counter and my eyes focused on his tie. I leaned across the counter, took hold of it, and pulled him toward me.

"What is it, Gilda?" he said, feigning innocence.

In the background, some of the youngest of the new arrivals were screaming because the lights had come on and they'd gotten their first look at the dogs, who still looked hungry.

I unclipped Uncle Ollie's tie clasp and emptied it out in the flower vase.

"It was just a little water, Gilda," he protested sulkily.

"Not one squirt, Ollie!" I told him sternly. "Not one!"

Lillian arrived with Greer, lugging a lifesize portrait of Maesie that she wanted put up in the lobby. Now. She caught her cane in the door.

My parents were singing "By the Light of the Silvery Moon" and waltzing around the ticket counter, to the delight of the dogs. The dalmatians were barking and snapping at their heels, causing more terror and turmoil among the younger set.

Val and Tobias showed up with a large box, which they set on the ticket counter so that I couldn't see around it to sell tickets until I'd opened it. I stared at the shiny metal machine.

"It's a cappuccino machine!" Val announced enthusiastically.

I groaned inwardly: one more piece of equipment I'd have to learn how to operate.

"Gee, guys," I said, "you shouldn't have!"

There were skirmishes breaking out all around me as Liberties took sides in the Adele-Betty dispute.

Behind me, Gloria was doing her Loretta Young imitation, as if she were a gracious hostess welcoming people to our home. Ollie pretended to trip over a jujube and took a pratfall that shook the whole building. It was the only spilled jujube that the dalmatians had missed, and now one of them was throwing up in the vicinity of Adele's shoes.

I closed my eyes. When I opened them, S. Styles was standing in front of the ticket booth, her eyes swimming with suppressed laughter.

"Five-fifty," I told her.

"What a deal," she said, looking around.

Then Tobias plugged in the cappuccino machine and blew all the circuits.

In the darkness and pandemonium that ensued, I could distinguish two voices. The first was Duke's; he was calling my name and he was hysterical.

The second was low and close and familiar.

"Sister, I'll bet the insurance business was never like this!"

First thing the next morning I heard the same voice on the phone. After the previous night's festivities, I'd slept in, dragging myself out of bed around noon. I was indulging in my usual healthy breakfast, coffee and cigarettes, when the phone rang.

"Know who this is?" the voice asked.

"S. Styles," I said. "But you sound a little funny."

"It's probably the concussion," she said.

"The what? Are you the person who got hit when I knocked over the vase in the dark?" I was instantly contrite. "I thought it just got one of the dogs."

"I didn't get hit by the vase," she said. "So don't worry; I'm not suing anybody—yet."

That sounded ominous.

"Okay, I give up," I said, now more irritated than contrite. "Am I supposed to be implicated in this injury in some way?"

"Not you," she said, "but maybe somebody you know. You know anybody wears strong, very sweet perfume?"

"Aunt *Gloria* clobbered you? What did you do, criticize her hair?"

"Aunt Gloria, huh?" She seemed to be thinking this over. "She packs a mean ashtray, I'll say that for her."

"Are we playing twenty questions again, or are you going to tell me what this is all about? Is this by any chance the New York World's Fair commemorative ashtray we're talking about?"

"It is."

"Ouch!"

"I was walking home after the movie," she began. "Well, first I stopped in at Oscar's and then I walked home, and I happened to walk past my office. And I thought I saw a light moving around in there. At first I thought I must be imagining it—maybe it was some weird reflection from the streetlights or something. But as I kept looking at the window, I decided it wasn't my imagination, so I went up. I was very quiet."

"Were you wearing those boots?" I asked.

"I was very quiet," she repeated. She sounded miffed.

"How many drinks at Oscar's?"

She ignored me. "The door was closed and locked, so I slipped the key in quietly and got the door open. There was light from the windows, but I didn't see anybody and there was no light in the room."

"The old behind-the-door trick," I said. "Isn't that one on your licensing exam?"

"I could smell the perfume, so somebody was there or had been there. But maybe they'd seen me coming. It occurred to me that they might be behind me in the dark hallway and I turned around to see, and wham!"

"You never even looked behind the door?" I asked incredulously.

"Look, in the first place, there's not much space there, and in the second, once I thought of the hall, it was more important to check that out first, so they wouldn't get away by slipping past while I was looking behind the door. I didn't expect some idiot to come tearing out and clobber me! Whoever it was should have been relieved that I wasn't checking behind the door."

"Lulled into a false sense of security."

"Exactly."

"And this perfidious perfume-wearing prowler had the audacity not to be lulled."

She greeted this observation with a short but meaningful silence. Then she said, "I bet I could get a lot of money if I sued."

"What are you going to do? Call for a police lineup and smell them all?"

"Don't be too sure I can't get fingerprints off the ashtray," she said tartly.

I snorted. "Not if it's my family, you won't! They've made too many detective movies to leave fingerprints."

"Then I'll bet I can get traces of perfume," she said.

I seemed to have moved past alarm into giddiness. I was having a hard time taking this seriously anymore.

"Why don't you just hire a bloodhound and hope there's only one person in the entire town of Eden who wears L'Air du Temps?" I suggested. "Anyway, what makes you think it's one of my relatives?"

"Intuition," she said. "Also the fact that the *L* drawer was standing open in one of the file cabinets."

"But this person didn't take anything?"

"She was in the wrong file cabinet," she said. "She was in the historical cabinet, not the one for active cases."

"Are you saying there *is* something she could have taken?"

"Are you going to tell her to try again? God, I don't even have my office completely aired out yet."

"I thought you said you'd given everything to Mae before she died."

"I gave her reports, sure," she said. "You think I didn't keep copies? What kind of businessperson do you think I am? I got hard copies in the file and another set on disk. She didn't even touch the computer."

"Give her a break," I said. "She's seventy-something. They didn't have computers in those old detective movies."

She gave a short laugh. "*I* should give *her* a break? Babe, your relatives don't need a break, they need a psychiatrist. And maybe a lawyer," she added darkly.

"So you are going to sue?"

"What do you think I'd get?"

"Free hairstyling for life. Her life, of course."

"Forget it!"

I sighed. "So what do you want me to do? I assume there's a reason you're telling me all this."

"I just thought you might be interested to know that the criminal activity in your family is escalating, that's all."

"Do the cops know about the perfume?"

"No, I kept that little tidbit for your ears only."

"Thanks."

"Seriously, babe," she said, "something screwy is going on in your family, and I hope it's not connected to Julius Cole's death, but if it is, you'd better find out and put an end to it before somebody else gets killed. I mean, even if Julius's house was empty when it burned down, what if the house next door had caught fire in the middle of the night? Or what if I happened to have one of those soft skulls you're always reading about in detective fiction?"

"I don't read detective fiction."

"Okay, one of those soft skulls I'm always reading about in detective fiction. I could be dead, and Ms. L'Air du Temps could be facing a very long prison term."

"All right, point taken," I said. "But you're not off the hook, either, S. Styles. You could have told me you had copies of those reports. Maybe if you'd just handed them over, this wouldn't have happened."

"I can't just hand over my reports to any Tom, Dick, and dowager empress who strolls into my office and asks for them!" she expostulated. "They were Maesie's, and they were confidential."

"Well, don't you think I'd better see them now, before anybody else gets hurt?"

So she agreed that I could look at them, but it would have to be tomorrow; she had a softball game today.

"You're not going to play softball with a concussion!" I

protested. "I don't think you're supposed to do anything except lie around."

"No, I don't think I could get the catcher's mask on without causing brain damage. But if I don't play, I have to sit on the bench and yell insults at the other team's pitcher."

"That," I told her, "should come easy for you."

I went looking for Gloria. I finally tracked her down playing cards with some of her cronies at the Paradise—not the theater but a retirement community. They were playing in a recreation room, with two men hard at a game of Ping-Pong at the other end of the room.

"Oh, Gilda!" said one of the friends. "I hear we missed all the excitement at the theater last night."

"Gloria, I need to speak to you," I said. "Now."

"My, that sounds ominous!" another friend said. "Has somebody else died?"

At the mention of somebody else dying, Gloria dropped her cards, revealing half her hand.

"They haven't, have they, Gilda?" she asked anxiously.

"Come with me and I'll tell you," I said.

We sat on a sofa in the lobby. I had to sit closer to Gloria than I usually liked to sit, in order to keep our conversation private. She played with her rings.

"Now, Gloria," I began, "please tell me what you thought you were doing at Styles's office last night."

"Whose office?" I had to hand it to her: She looked genuinely puzzled. But then acting talent runs in our family.

"You know who I mean," I said sternly. "S. Styles. The detective."

"What detective?" she asked blankly.

"The one Maesie hired," I said. "The one you hit over the head last night."

She looked at me. "Gilda, honey, I know you had a rough night last night," she said. "Have you been drinking?"

No, I thought, but your perfume is giving me a buzz.

She reached out and patted my hand. "Honey, maybe you ought to lie down," she said. "You don't look so good."

"Last night—" I began again.

She nodded brightly. "I was at the theater last night, remember? And Ollie was there, and you, and your folks, and Lilly, and—"

"After," I said. "We're talking about after you left."

She nodded. "The late show started, and you said you didn't need us anymore, even though we would have been happy to stay and help clean up. I still think we should go early tonight and work on that spot where the dog threw up. We ought to scrub it good and then put a fan on it."

"So after you left . . ." I let it hang there.

Her head bobbed as if she were following my narrative as it unwound. "After we left, we went out to the Big Boy and had hot fudge cake. I said we shouldn't, after all that popcorn, but Ollie said we'd made it this far—he meant our ages—and we might as well go out in a blaze of glory. And so we went, and ran into Patsy and Tick, and . . ."

"After that?" I prompted her. "After the hot fudge cake and the confabulation with Patsy and Tick?"

"Well, after that we went home," she said. "And Ollie went back to work on his screenplay—"

I was momentarily distracted. "Oliver's writing a screenplay?"

"You didn't know?" she asked, surprised. "Oh, yes, and he's having such a good time! Tobias loaned him a book about screenwriting and he seems to think there's nothing to it!"

"Is it a detective story?" I asked suspiciously.

"No, it's a comedy about this man who marries two women, only he's got amnesia when he marries the second, so he— Gilda, what is it with you and detectives? Honey, you've got detectives on the brain!"

"To be more accurate," I observed wryly, "I've got a brained detective on the brain. What were you doing while Oliver worked on his screenplay?"

"Well, I turned on the television and watched part of *The Tonight Show*, but Jay didn't have anybody on I wanted to see, so I started changing channels. And then, Gilda, you know what?"

She gripped my wrist.

"What?"

"I saw that part from *Citizen Kane*! You know the part, right before the ball breaks, with the snow and those wide-angle lips saying 'Rosebud'? Honey, it just gave me the shivers, after Maesie and all, so I turned off the TV and went back to my book."

"What are you reading?" I asked.

"*Men Are from Mars, Women Are from Venus,*" she said. "Gilda, it's so interesting. Have you read it? But I can only read so much of a book like that at one time, so after a while I went back to this biography of Clare Boothe Luce."

"And you never went to the office of a detective named Styles?"

"I don't *know* a detective named Styles," she insisted. "I don't know any detectives—well, except for Dale Ferguson, and I don't guess Clyde counts, because he's a police officer but not a detective."

I studied her.

Then she said in a shocked voice, "Did Maesie really hire a detective, Gilda? Whatever for?"

That was the point at which I was inclined to buy her story. Instead of focusing on my accusation, as a guilty person might be expected to do, she'd apparently brushed it aside as ludicrous and seized on the one thing I'd said that interested her.

"It was for her autobiography," I said.

I'd always found it easy to lie to my family, because truth wasn't, to them, a cardinal virtue. After all, they spent their lives writing and revising their own scripts and they never scrupled to revise the past along with the present. Maybe I should have been more suspicious of Gloria for that reason, but frankly the notion that she'd been creeping around a detective's office late last night, and bashing a person over the head, suddenly seemed as ridiculous to me as it did to her.

"Her autobiography?" she echoed. "She never told me she was writing an autobiography."

"Maybe she just wanted to surprise you," I said. "Go back to your game."

"But aren't you going to tell me what this was all about?" she complained.

"When I figure it out," I said, "I'll let you know."

The truth was that I was now embarrassed by the conclusions I'd leaped to. Anybody, after all, could wear the same perfume as Gloria. It might even have been a coincidence that the prowler left the *L* drawer open. For all I knew, whoever it was might have been working her—or even his—way through all of S. Styles's files and happened to have been interrupted almost halfway through the alphabet. After all, with that many file cabinets, Styles obviously had other clients and other cases that didn't involve my family at all. She had her nerve, I thought, casting unjustified suspicions on the Liberties.

I called her from a phone in the lobby. I wanted to catch her before she left and give her something to think about between innings.

As I raised my hand to the phone, I caught a whiff of something familiar, and it gave me an idea.

"Styles," a voice said curtly.

"I have a question for you, Styles," I said. "You said you smelled perfume. Did you smell anything else?"

"How could I?"

I waited.

"No," she said at last, slowly, as if she'd given it some thought, "I didn't. Why? What should I have smelled?"

"Permanent wave solution," I said. "It's fainter than the perfume, I'll grant you, but you wouldn't miss it. She got a perm right before the funeral."

"Hmmm," Styles said. "And I take it she doesn't know what you're talking about?"

"Got it in one."

"That must have been an interesting conversation."

I was a little flattered that she didn't question my judgment or even my sense of smell. Of course she didn't question her own sense of smell, either; she didn't suggest that she could have missed the smell of the perm.

"The person who mugged you wouldn't even have to have been wearing the perfume, either," I pointed out, waving my own pungent paw in the air. "If Gloria had touched them—or if anyone had touched them, for that matter, who wore as much perfume as Gloria—or if she'd given them anything or they were wearing anything she'd handled—"

"Okay, okay, I get the picture," she said. "Do you think anybody was trying to set her up?"

I hadn't considered the possibility.

"That seems a little far-fetched to me," I said.

"So where does that leave us?" she asked. "Do you really believe that there could be two—count them—two sequences of strange events going on in the town of Eden, Ohio, at this moment, and that they're completely separate, and that one of them, at least, has nothing to do with your loony family?"

"Since you put it that way . . ." I admitted reluctantly.

"See you tomorrow!" she said cheerfully, and hung up.

On Saturday night, in an admirable show of spunk, Duke sat his new crew down in the upstairs theater and marched up and down like Patton before the American flag, lecturing them on what they could and couldn't do in our theater.

To my parents, he pointed out that in a theater, concession-stand staffers were more crucial than a song-and-dance team. To Adele, he pointed out that ticket sales were more critical than flower arrangements. To Oliver, he pointed out that not everyone had the same sense of humor he did, and that if they had come to the theater to see a romance or a drama, they might not be in the mood for comedy. He also added some poignant remarks regarding liability and insurance premiums that showed he didn't need me to explain that part of the business to him. To Grosvenor, he suggested that we were running a theater, not a dentist's office, and that the only thing he wanted to hear coming out of speakers at the Paradise was the soundtrack. To Gloria, he hinted that some people were allergic to chemical air fresheners, which I took to be a bold step in the direction of breaking to her the news that some people were allergic to perfume, too. He added what I would have if he hadn't been doing such a good job of it—the part about people wanting to smell popcorn in a movie theater. To Betty, he explained that just because kids liked to watch dalmatian puppies on the screen, it didn't mean they wanted to have a close encounter with a grown-up dalmatian in the lobby. The dogs looked so chastened that he added that he wasn't necessarily opposed to the idea of dogs in the lobby as a clever tie-in, but they had to be kept under control and out of the way, so kids didn't have to confront dogs if they didn't want to.

To Val and Tobias, he said thank you for the cappuccino machine and that he would plug it in again as soon as Val upgraded the wiring.

To everybody, he said that the movies came first. If we can't project the movie, he said, we're out of business, no matter what our decor looks like or what we're serving or how we smell.

"Duke, we were just trying to help," Gloria said in a small voice.

"I know, Aunt Gloria," Duke said, "and, believe me, Gilda and I appreciate it."

I started when I heard my name mentioned on the side of the good guys. I was still waiting for Duke to get around to lecturing me, but maybe he was going to do that in private. Come to think of it, I'd already gotten the flashlight lecture.

"We've got to get them to sign out the flashlights, Gilda," he'd said, pointing one at me when I'd arrived that afternoon. "All they have to do is sign their name next to the number of the one they're taking and then cross it out when they bring it back."

My face must have betrayed my reaction, because he'd continued patiently, "I know it doesn't seem like a big deal to you, but these things add up, and we can't afford it. It's not just the flashlights, it's the batteries, too. Because they're little, the workers forget and walk away with the flashlights. See?"

He'd gestured at the small row of bright yellow flashlights. The two empty spaces accused me of negligence.

"We lost two last night," he said, "and we don't know who has 'em. If they'd been signed out, we'd know who to bug."

His shift in tone brought me back to the present.

"We couldn't survive the next two weeks without you," he was saying to the family sincerely. "But—"

"We *would* like to survive them," I put in, so he wouldn't have to say it.

Oliver was the first to start laughing. Wallace joined in and then my parents, Val, and Tobias. The theater was dim, but from what I could tell, Gloria still looked a bit hurt, and Adele and Grosvenor were nursing resentments. Clara looked bored and impatient.

Duke asked about the missing flashlights and my mother confessed guiltily that she'd taken one home in her pocket. Nobody confessed to the second theft, but he got them to promise they'd look for it at home.

"As long as we're all here," Clara said, "I think we should talk about planning some special events."

" 'Special events'?" Duke repeated.

"Yes, you know, like a retrospective of Maesie's career," she said. "Those videos we showed at the funeral generated a lot of interest in seeing some of Maesie's old films."

"Oh, yes?" My mother's skepticism was audible.

"No, hold on, Florence," my father said. "She's right, you know. It's not a bad idea."

"Sure," Clara said. "And we should include some of Lillian's movies, and yours, and mine, too."

"And mine," Wallace reminded her.

"Of course," she said. "A retrospective of the entire Liberty oeuvre."

"You could include my movies, too," Oliver said, as if the thought had just struck him.

"What about Adele's?" my mother said dryly. "And Gloria's? I thought that wig she designed for Mae to wear as Marie Antoinette was a masterpiece."

"Why, thank you, Flo!" Gloria simpered. "That wig *was* special. But, you know, I always favored the hairstyle I created for the queen of the vampires in *Kiss of Death* because I had to work with real hair, and that girl could not sit still to save her soul!"

"I'm especially fond of the way I wired the house on *Dead End Street*," Val said, winking at me. "The way the lights went on and off in rapid sequence to suggest a supernatural presence—I always thought that was especially effective. And, of course, there's Grosvenor's work on *The Towering Inferno* . . ."

Duke was looking panic-stricken. He looked to me for help.

Grosvenor was saying, "I don't consider that my best work, though, Val. No, I'd say that the atom bomb sequence in *Atom Bombshell* represented the pinnacle of my career."

"Would you be including the younger generations?" I asked.

Clara looked doubtful, even annoyed, but Wallace said, "Yes, why not? Bring in the whole fan-damily!"

"And how many movies are we talking about then?" I asked. "Mae made, what, more than seventy in all? And, Lillian, you have another forty or fifty?"

"We wouldn't show all of the films everyone's made, Gilda," Grosvenor corrected me. "We'd only select a few representative ones."

"So we're not really talking about a retrospective of Mae's career here, are we?" my mother said.

"It could start with Maesie, of course," Grosvenor assured her. "But I think Clara's right—the renewed interest in Mae's career will spark a new interest in the Liberty family."

"And we ought to capitalize on it," my mother said, "so that Clara can start her comeback."

Clara looked daggers at my mother.

"There's nothing wrong with Clara's desire to work in film again if she wants to, Florence," Lillian reproached my mother mildly.

"But does she honestly think she can jump-start it with a film series at the Paradise?" my mother asked.

"If the publicity were handled correctly," Clara said defensively, "I don't see why not. The national press covered the funeral. Naturally," she added, "Grosvenor and I would be willing to handle the publicity."

"Naturally," my mother said.

"Hold on," I said. "Mom, Clara, give it a rest! Duke and I just want to get through the next two weeks. After that, if we're still here, we can discuss plans for the future."

"Does that mean you'll be here for the next two weeks?" my mother asked cagily.

"But I hope you realize, Gilda, that this is a golden opportunity for Clara," Grosvenor admonished me. "Timing is everything in promotion. Mae's death has created an interest now. We have to strike while the iron is hot!"

"And before Maesie's cold?" Val asked innocently.

"Gilda's right," Lillian said in a voice that suggested the discussion was over. She stood up. "First things first. We have a theater to run."

And, for a change, they behaved themselves. But I had the sense that it was only a lull in the storm.

24

"No peeking," I said.

Styles gave the sigh of a martyr. She had both hands over her eyes.

"What is it you think I'd see?" she asked. "I haven't made any special study of perfume bottle designs."

I held the tissue under her nose.

"Do I get some bread and cheese in between to clear my palate?" she asked.

"Number two," I said, and held a second tissue under her nose. She made a face. "I hope none of these is yours."

"Number three," I said, and repeated the procedure.

"Strongly floral, with an underscent of musk," she said. "I choose number three."

"L'Air du Temps," I confirmed.

"Do I get to smell perm solutions next?" she asked. "I just ask because my head aches, that's all."

I studied the bandage around her head.

"Did they have to shave your head back there?" I asked.

"I assume so," she said, "but I wasn't watching in the mirror, and it's not like at the beauty shop, where they hand you a mirror when they're done. Something was buzzing around, though."

"Does it hurt?" I asked, wincing. "Where the injury is, I mean."

"What do you think?"

We were sitting on a bench in the town park. It was pretty nippy, and the sky was overcast, but she'd wanted to get out.

I checked to see if my jacket was zipped up all the way. There was nobody else in the park except for a dog with its nose to the ground. Styles slouched on the bench next to me, but she reminded me of a compressed spring—a coil of energy waiting to be released.

"The first time," Styles began, "Mae asked for some really easy stuff—the date of the Twentieth Century merger with Fox, the date Bette Davis first challenged her studio contract, the name of some vice-president at MGM she couldn't remember. All straightforward library work; she could have called a reference librarian, like I did."

"Mae was at Fox," I observed. "I think she might have got her start there. And Greer met Andy at MGM."

"Then there were a few trickier questions," Styles continued, "such as the date of the last passenger train to come through Eden. But again strictly academic research, historical society stuff. Maybe she was testing me to see if I'd get it right.

"Then she said she wanted a kind of biographical profile of Julius Cole, with an emphasis on his financial affairs. She said she'd known him since the early fifties, when she'd come to visit her parents here. She claimed he was a good friend who belonged in the book, but she'd known him too long to ask questions about things she should know by now. It would have sounded reasonable enough if she hadn't put the emphasis on his financial affairs. I couldn't quite see what that had to do with the story of Mae's life. But again maybe she was testing me to see if I'd call her on it. I figure, hey, it's her nickel, what do I care why she wants to know?

"But because she wanted a historical perspective, I started at the other end of his life, so to speak. I knew the current stuff would be easier to come by. Basically, what I came up with was a rags-to-riches story—you know, young man starts out as an usher in a movie theater and ends up owning the whole show: the land, the theater, even a whole chain of movie theaters. Not that I found out about the chain at first."

"So he was an usher at the Paradise?"

"Yeah. I gathered that his father was a kind of bum who was out of the picture more often than not, so his mother raised him pretty much on her own. He didn't finish high school; he had to work. I can't tell you all the jobs he had, but they didn't amount to much. He worked a lot of places—hardware store, county office, car dealership, you name it. Then he got his Realtor's license in the early sixties and acquired a partner. The partner had capital, but Julius apparently had only his good looks and charm."

"Assets not to be underestimated in real estate," I observed.

"Right. But still, he kind of rocks along for a while, a house here, a farm there, a small commercial property over there. He makes a few questionable decisions, like buying the funeral home in early '71 and trying to turn it into an upscale apartment house—like Eden really needed one of those. And even if it had, people are funny about living in a former mortuary. But he probably recouped his loss when he sold it to McDonald's. Then suddenly, later that same year, he himself buys a choice corner of downtown real estate, sells it to Eden Commercial for their new headquarters, and walks away with a bundle of money. Before you know it, a lot of Eden real estate is changing hands, and the most lucrative pieces of it are all passing through Julius Cole's hands. By 1985 he's the executive V.P. of Cineglobe, Inc., a national theater chain whose president is probably a figurehead. In 1989 he buys a prime piece of real estate from your aunt Lillian and puts up a shopping center and multiplex theater. In 1991 he develops another shopping center across the road from it and anchors the new center with a Megaverse."

"So he was in on Megaverse! And in 1997 somebody sneaks up behind him in a movie theater and shoots him in the back of the head," I said.

"The end," she agreed.

"So how did Mae react to all of this?"

"Well, she only got half of it at a time," Styles said. "After I gave her the first half, she asked, 'Where'd he get his money in 1971?' "

"Where *did* he get his money?" I asked. "From the McDonald's deal?"

"I never found out," she said. "McDonald's didn't happen until '72. Somehow I didn't think your cousin-in-law at the bank was likely to be a useful source."

"He's big on confidentiality," I affirmed.

"So Mae goes away and thinks things over, and then here's what she asked next."

She handed me a piece of paper and I skimmed it.

One of these assignments I'd already heard about: Mae had asked for the news reports on Avery Gardner's death. The others took me by surprise.

She wanted to know about Andy Fuller's job at MGM—what he did and why he left. She wanted to know anything Styles could find out about a picture my father shot on location in Rome in 1950, a movie called *When in Rome*. She wanted Styles to read up on the House Un-American Activities Committee hearings in 1947 and on the Committee for the First Amendment to see if any Liberties were mentioned in the news stories. She wanted to see anything Styles could find on Clara's career. And she wanted news stories on an accident that had taken place on one of Grosvenor's sets, when a grenade had exploded prematurely and cost an actor his left hand. She asked Styles to trace several people whose names I didn't recognize.

Styles was studying my face.

"What do you make of it?" she asked.

"I don't get it," I said. "It still looks mostly like a job for a reference librarian. Some of it looks like stuff she ought to just come right out and ask the people involved. Unless . . ."

"Unless?" Styles prompted.

"Unless she thinks there's something to be uncovered in each case that somebody might want to keep hidden," I said. I raised my eyes to hers. "Is that it?"

"I don't know," she said. "You tell me. It's your family."

"You did the research," I pointed out. "What did you find?"

"You really want to know?"

"If you mean about my father, no, not really. I'm guessing my mother didn't go to Rome because she had two little kids at home and was probably pregnant with me. As I recall, his co-star in that one was some Italian bombshell who died an untimely death a few years later."

"Tosca Sabatini."

"That's her," I said. "So are you going to tell me he had an affair with her?"

"There were rumors," she said. "To confirm them, I'd have to interview people. Mae didn't want me to do that—yet."

"God! What was she writing? An exposé of the family?"

"I'm still not convinced she was writing anything," Styles said.

"And why would she ask that question about HUAC?" I asked. "She belonged to the Committee for the First Amendment herself. Wouldn't she have known who was involved on both sides?"

Styles shrugged. "Maybe she thought there was something she missed."

"You can probably look up Clara's career in any film encyclopedia," I said.

"I did."

"Spot anything?"

"Not really," she said. She consulted some notes, which appeared to be scrawled in black ink on a restaurant place mat. "Looked pretty typical to me. She also started out at Twentieth Century-Fox in her late teens, a starlet with a lot of small parts. Got her big break in *Stars in Her Eyes*, 1937, and made a string of modest successes for the next ten years. She was married to a cameraman named Reginald Baker in her twenties and had twins—Audrey and Spencer—and then Grace. She divorced Baker. Married Grosvenor June, a special-effects technician, in her thirties. Retired from film work in her early forties, and they moved here."

"What about the accident on Grosvenor's set?" I asked. "Was he responsible for that?"

"Could have been," she speculated. "I couldn't find out much. Those were the good old days, remember. Even in the fifties,

the studios were still powerful enough to contain the scandal, if
there was one."

"So how about the rest of us? Didn't she ask you to send for
my FBI file?"

"Babe, I'm sorry to disappoint you, but you don't have one."

"No way!" Now I was really miffed. "I worked on the Moratorium! I even got arrested once! I was on a planning committee
with a couple of Black Panthers!"

"Sorry," she said. She looked genuinely sympathetic. "Maybe
they lost it. Or, hey, how about this? By the time they finished
censoring things with the Magic Marker, there wasn't anything
left to read! Huh?"

"Jeez!" I said.

"The point is," Styles prodded me gently, "what did she want
all this information for?"

"If we didn't know her better," I observed, "it would look as
if she were setting up a blackmail operation."

"Right."

"But what if she *were* setting up a blackmail operation?" I
said thoughtfully. "What did she want to get out of it? I mean,
you may have noticed that my family is out of control. I could
see her wanting some leverage on them. But what for?"

"Do you think she was worried at all about whether somebody might try to put her in a nursing home?" Styles asked.

"In my family?" I said incredulously. "Listen, nobody in my
family would dare to do something to Maesie that she didn't
want done."

"Not ever?" she persisted.

I frowned. "What do you mean?"

"Suppose her illness made her feel vulnerable," Styles suggested. "Suppose she began thinking about the long term. Maybe
she'd been getting forgetful. Suppose she was worried that if
she became senile, the family would decide to move her into a
nursing home."

"Yeah?" I said doubtfully.

"Suppose she had a confidant, someone who had agreed to
hold on to a certain document and publish it under particular

circumstances. Then if anyone threatened her with a nursing home, she could threaten them right back: the day you move me out of this house, the *Times* will receive a major exposé of the Liberty family."

"You ever write a screenplay, Styles?"

"Okay," she conceded. "Maybe it could use a little fine-tuning. But where's *your* explanation? I'm doing all the work here. You got a better idea?"

"No, but I don't think she'd ever attack the family like that."

"Maybe she figured she wouldn't have to," Styles reasoned. "Maybe she figured nobody would want to call her bluff and find out what she'd do."

"Anyway, I can't imagine anyone shipping Maesie off to a nursing home if she didn't want to go there," I said. "And what would Uncle Julius have to do with anything?"

"Hey, I didn't say it was perfect!" she said grumpily. "Maybe she wanted to know whether to leave him in the will. Or maybe she was thinking of assigning a power of attorney to somebody outside the family and she wanted to make absolutely sure that he was a safe bet."

"But then why did somebody kill him?" I asked. "Unless it was totally unconnected to all of this."

"I got another theory," Styles said with the air of someone who has only been running cartoons before the main feature. She stretched and cracked her knuckles. "Want to hear it?"

"Is it better than the last one?"

"Suppose Maesie suspected that family members were being blackmailed," she said.

I gazed into the distance as I thought about the possibility. The cold finger at the base of my spine told me that she'd come nearer the mark this time.

"Suppose she wanted to know who was vulnerable?" Styles proposed.

"And she wouldn't want to ask, because nobody would admit the truth," I said. "But why would she have suspected blackmail in the first place?"

Styles remained silent, but I could feel her eyes on me.

And eventually I answered my own question. "Lillian's land," I said. "She didn't buy Lillian's explanation of why she sold the land, especially to a development corporation." I hugged myself and shivered. "She suspected that Lillian had a particular reason for wanting to raise a large amount of cash on short notice."

"Unless . . . ?" she said. Just that.

The wheels turned again. "Unless Julius Cole was the blackmailer."

We sat in silence. I fumbled for my cigarettes and lit up again. I could barely feel my fingers.

"She asked where he got his money," I recalled aloud, "didn't she?"

"That's what she asked," Styles confirmed.

"Maybe she found out," I said softly.

"Maybe," Styles said. "But we're still speculating."

"Listen," I said. "I don't like where this is going. Somebody killed Julius. If he was a blackmailer, he had to have had more than one victim. But judging from Mae's suspicions, if we're interpreting them right, several of them could have been in my family. If Grosvenor burned down Julius's house, he's at the top of my list—him or Clara or both of them. I've already had one aunt picked up on a B&E. I've had another aunt's perfume implicated in another B&E."

"You can't smell perfume on me, can you?" Styles interrupted anxiously. She dipped her head in the direction of my nose.

"Smells like alcohol to me," I said. "Maybe a little shaving cream mixed in."

She cut her eyes at me.

"You're right," she said in retaliation. "Your family is in some deep shit, babe."

"But you don't really think somebody in my family sneaked up behind Julius Cole and shot him in the back of the head, do you?" I asked, trying to sound more skeptical than I felt.

"It ain't hard," she said. "Of the ways to kill a man, that's one of the easiest. You don't even have to look him in the eye. Takes almost no physical strength. It's not even that messy."

"Thanks for sharing," I said.

"You asked," she reminded me. "I'm just telling it like it is."

"And I guess you think somebody in my family—Lillian, say, then burned down the theater and a few nights later went over to your office around midnight and clobbered you. Woman's had a busy week for a gimpy eighty-two-year-old."

"I'd prefer to think," she said, "that it wasn't your oldest relative who clobbered me."

"I'll bet you would," I said. "So who does that leave?"

"There's always your resident pyromaniac."

"Right. So am I supposed to go around checking everybody's alibi for the night of the murder by sneaking seemingly innocent questions into the conversation? No, wait a minute! If we're focusing on the killer—not the garden-variety arsonist or mugger but the killer—there aren't that many alibis to check, at least not in my family, because most of us were at Liberty House together. I'd forgotten about that."

Styles flexed her shoulders and shifted on the bench. "You don't have to do anything," she pointed out.

I didn't comment.

After a minute she said, "You can just wait for the next person to get clobbered or arrested or caught in a fire."

"Maybe there won't be a next person."

"You got a theory to explain that?"

"No," I admitted.

We sat in silence, staring out over the park. The grass had turned green and some of the trees were showing bright green buds against the gray sky. The cold had crept into my bones.

"Hey!" she exclaimed, jumping up from the bench. "Where's Waldo?"

"Who?"

"Oh, there he is. Yo! Waldo! Don't be crossing no streets now!"

The dog she'd apparently been addressing was sniffing along the sidewalk that bordered the park. He'd barely acknowledged her caution by raising his floppy ears. In fact, his whole head seemed controlled by the pull of gravity; he'd had his nose to the ground ever since I'd first spotted him.

"Where were we?" Styles said, sitting down again.

"What do you think I should do?" I asked. "I mean, what would you do if you were me? I'd be willing to hire you, if I knew what to hire you for."

She appeared to be considering this.

"You've got three options, as I see it," she said at last. "One: do nothing. I think we've already discarded that one, am I right?"

I nodded.

"Two: call a meeting of your crazy clan, show them copies of my reports, and ask them what the hell is going on."

"Gives me a headache just to think about it." I groaned.

"Yeah, but it has the appeal of straightforwardness," she said. "Anybody who has anything to explain can explain it— or not. There's a strong possibility that everything that's happened has happened because somebody's trying to keep a secret. With everything out in the open, maybe everybody will be protected."

I thought about this. "But we still have a murder to deal with," I said, "and a murderer. The police are going to keep investigating. Eventually, they'll want to arrest somebody. Besides, we don't even know yet what the secret is. I mean, making your reports available hardly constitutes an exposé and it might be dangerous for you. The killer might assume you know or guess more than you've put in your reports. Or the killer might worry about somebody else who knows something— maybe even something they didn't realize they knew until we published your reports. So what's my third option?"

"That's the one where you hire me," she said, "to figure out what the hell is going on."

"And how would you do that?" I asked.

"It wouldn't be easy," she observed, "because we can't just review everybody's bank statements to see if they're writing large checks we can't account for, or depositing them, for that matter. I think we need to investigate Julius Cole, but we won't have access to the bank records the police will have. I think we need to start with what we know: the two questionable real estate deals Julius Cole has been involved in. In 1971, without any apparent resources, he pulled off a major coup by acquiring a piece of downtown real estate and then selling it to Eden Commercial. The party implicated in that deal is Andy Fuller, either as a blackmail victim or as a covert partner, somebody who got a substantial kickback for financing the sale. Then in 1989 Cole buys land from Lillian, which nobody thought she wanted to sell and which she may or may not have known she sold to him. Other deals may implicate other family members, but I guess I'd start with those two."

"It sounds like you'd be investigating two of my relatives to find out if they had a motive for murder," I said, annoyed. "Anyway, Andy's out. He was one of the last to leave the night Julius was killed. And Lillian was upstairs in bed."

"You know that for a fact?" Styles asked. "That Lillian was in bed? For that matter, do you think your cousin-in-law would be incapable of hiring someone to do his dirty work for him?"

I shot her an exasperated look.

"I'm just saying—"

"I know, I know!" I interrupted. "Think like a cop."

"Or a prosecutor," she said. "Meanwhile, why don't you tell me who's in the frame? Julius was last seen alive at eleven-forty-five or thereabouts, when the projectionist started his movie. The firetrucks were called in a little before one-thirty and the whole place was engulfed in flames by then. So let's say the murder probably took place between eleven-forty-five or -fifty and, say, one o'clock at the latest."

"The cops are looking at a tighter frame than that," I said. "The projectionist left at twelve-fifteen, and they don't think anybody would have hung around after one, when the fire would have been obvious. I guess the murder could have taken place while the projectionist was still there . . ."

"Doubtful, though, even with a suppressor, which isn't as

silent as people usually think it is. So who was still at Liberty House at one?"

"Practically everybody," I said. "A group of people went off to Columbus earlier, looking for music, but they can alibi one another. Lillian went upstairs to bed."

"Your parents?"

"They were there."

"Duke?"

"Jesus!" I said. "You're as bad as the cops!"

"I just need to know what we're dealing with."

"No, Duke left around eleven-thirty," I said. "Betty was there, in the kitchen with me." I squinted, as if that would make the picture more vivid. "Adele and Wallace, Clara and Grosvenor, and Val and Andy Fuller were in the living room."

"Not what's-his-name? The writer?"

"No, he probably rushed home to get the evening's festivities down on paper.

"My sister Lana was out on the sun porch with Bonnie and Clyde and the babies. Spencer left with Audrey and the kids. I think Shane was in the library with Clark and Scarlett and Sophie and Greer."

She heaved a big sigh.

"Who'm I missing?"

"The name that pops to mind is Gloria, the scented lady."

I paused. "No, I think she and Ollie left earlier. Come to think of it, she said she had a cake to bake for the postfuneral luncheon. But you're not seriously considering Gloria as a prospective murderer, are you?"

"If she did this," Styles said, touching the back of her head gingerly, "I'd consider her very seriously. Or your uncle Oliver."

I shook my head. "He couldn't do it without playing it for a laugh. I really think you're offtrack there, Styles."

"So of the people Mae asked me to investigate, the only one you can't alibi is Lillian, right?"

"Well," I said unenthusiastically, "I guess."

"And Duke—we should probably throw him in for good measure because the cops are so keen on him as a suspect. And

I'm not prepared to rule out Gloria and Oliver, even if you think they're long shots."

"Well, hell, if you're going to be that way about it, I can't alibi cousins Dorothy, Glinda, and Toto!" I remarked, exasperated.

"Too short," she said dismissively.

"Okay, setting my nutty relatives aside for a moment, isn't it just possible that another blackmail victim, somebody not related to me—"

"Some Tom, Dick, or Harry," she put in, "as opposed to some Toto, Duke, or Harpo."

"Yes, somebody with a perfectly ordinary name," I agreed. "Isn't it possible that somebody like that killed Julius? Or somebody who was embittered by the way Megaverse has put the rest of the town out of business and took it out on Julius because he brought it here?"

"Sure," she conceded. "It's possible. But it doesn't explain my head injury. Of course, it's also possible that there are some unrelated events that only appear to be connected because of the time frame. We have to keep an open mind."

"Yeah," I said wryly, "you could have been attacked by a wayward spouse, driven to desperation."

"It happens," she said. "You know, you shouldn't take this so personally. It'll just prevent us from finding out what we need to know."

"But what is it we need to know here?" I asked. "That's my point. I don't want to go pawing through my relatives' dirty laundry if I don't have to. That kind of thing doesn't turn me on."

"Agreed. But how convinced are you that things are hunky-dory now and nobody else is going to die, get hurt, or get arrested?"

"Not very," I admitted.

"Now, maybe you want to take the chance," she said. "So far, your family hasn't taken any direct hits—"

I groaned.

"Well, in a manner of speaking. And maybe they're not in any danger."

"All right, all right," I said ungraciously. "You've made your point. I'll hire you to investigate Uncle Julius's death."

"You might need to finance a trip to L.A.," she said smoothly.

"L.A.? You really think that would be productive?"

She shrugged. "Mae told me I should expect to make a trip there soon. But she died before I got to go."

"Okay," I said. "But no Disneyland tickets. No Universal Studios tour. You pay for those on your own. I don't want to get the expense report and read you tailed somebody into Tomorrowland."

She grinned but didn't say anything. Then she jumped off the bench again.

"Hey! Where's that dog? Waldo!" she called. "Get out of there!"

Waldo's rump appeared from beneath the bandstand. He backed out and trotted over. At closer range I could distinguish the wrinkled, lugubrious face with the filthy nose.

"I didn't think you'd take me seriously when I told you to get a bloodhound!" I said, surprised.

"Only part," she said. "And he's been around for a while."

"His name is Waldo?" I asked.

"Yeah. You know, like—"

"Where's Waldo?"

"Well, what did you think I'd name him? Asta? Or Bogey?" She removed a handkerchief from her back pocket and wiped the dog's snout. He sat quietly and gave me a longsuffering look.

"Besides," she said, regarding him critically, "Bogey's the cat."

25

"Can you keep a secret?" I asked.

My sister Betty was helping me tidy up the small office behind the concession stand.

"I called my boss this morning and told him I needed another week, that I had a new career opportunity here and I had to decide whether to take it."

She grinned at me. "What did he say?" she asked.

"He didn't seem too happy. I guess the work is piling up on my desk."

"Gil, why didn't you just quit? Let somebody else do all that work. You know you want to."

"I don't know any such thing," I protested. "Or rather, I may know that I want to quit, but I don't know that I want to live in Eden and run an independent movie theater. 'Career opportunity' is just a euphemism for 'pain in the butt.' And now I'm up to my ears in family stuff and looking at the possibility that I'll have to cash in my life insurance to post bail for my elderly aunt."

So I told her all about S. Styles and the investigation. My job was to worm what information I could out of my family members and I thought I'd start with Betty and work up to Lillian.

Betty sat in the one folding chair crammed into the tiny space. I leaned against the shelf where the flashlights were kept, turning my back on the neat little row with its one commemorative space for the still-missing flashlight number seven. I had to talk over the noise of the icemaker at Betty's back and then stop to answer the phone, which hung on the wall a few inches away from my ear.

"Boy!" she said when I'd finished. "I never imagined it could be so complicated!" She thought for a minute. "You don't think Dad really had an affair with that Sabatini woman, do you?"

"I don't know," I said, "and I don't care, as long as he didn't murder Uncle Julius. So tell me what you know about the other people. Have you ever heard anything weird about Avery Gardner's death? Or how Andy Fuller lost his job at MGM? Or anything about Clara or Grosvenor?"

She shook her head. "I've never heard any of that stuff."

"You're a big help."

"Sorry."

"Look, what about Lillian's land deal," I said. "Do you remember anything about that?"

She shrugged. "Just what she said at the time—that she got an offer she couldn't afford to turn down.

"If I were casting this drama," she continued speculatively, after a minute's thought, "I'd cast either Adele or Clara in the role of Styles's assailant. They can both be ruthless. Of course, Mom can be ruthless, too, but this doesn't sound like her style. Besides, she'd probably be humming under her breath."

"Well, that's something."

"Uncle Ollie would muff it," she continued, "and if it were Uncle Wallace, Styles would have smelled something besides perfume. Grosvenor would never think of a weapon as low-tech as an ashtray; he'd probably carry the latest in lightweight automatic firepower. Val could do it, if he needed to, but I think he'd look guilty afterward, and he doesn't look that guilty to me. Maybe a little guilty, but not like he's just bashed somebody's head in. Lillian's definitely up to something, and she could do it, too, but it's hard to imagine her going up there by herself. Duke couldn't do it in a million years," she added reassuringly.

"What about Greer and Andy Fuller?"

She considered. "Andy could do it, maybe, but . . . I don't know. You don't think of a bank president sneaking around in seedy offices, hiding behind doors, and jumping out and attacking people."

"To tell you the truth, I don't think of any of our relatives doing that," I said.

"I don't either, but I could be persuaded," Betty said. "It would just be another movie for them. They'd pretend they were shooting a scene and that as soon as the director yelled 'Cut!' the person they'd just smashed would get up and go get her makeup fixed."

The phone rang again and I read our schedule to the caller.

"The question I have," Betty said when I hung up, "is what Mae's death had to do with all this."

"What do you mean?"

"Well, it can't be a coincidence that strange things started happening as soon as Maesie popped off, can it?" she asked sensibly. "I mean, right away, Lillian starts acting weird, and then Uncle Julius kicks the bucket. And not only does he wind up with a bullet in the back of his head but his theater gets burned down with him in it and then his house goes up in flames. That's overkill."

I was reminded of why I always enjoyed talking to my sister. For all her zaniness, she had a talent for going to the heart of the matter.

"You want to know what I think?" she asked, cocking her head at me. "I think it all has to do with 'rosebud' and those papers Maesie was reading the night she died. I think 'rosebud' means something to somebody who heard about it, and I think the papers do, too."

I had to admit that Betty's fascination with "rosebud" was sounding more reasonable all the time.

"On the other hand," she said, "if it's only Uncle Julius's murder we're concerned about, all we need to do is look for his enemies. As rich and powerful as he was, he must have had a few. And all those affairs he had—I'll bet there's enough disgruntled former lovers to cast a backstage musical."

"Disgruntlement doesn't usually lead to murder," I pointed out.

"Okay, try bitterness and hatred," she said. "I'll bet you'll find some of it. You know who you ought to talk to? Uncle Julius's ex, the one that's still living. I'll bet she knows some dirt on him."

That sounded like a pretty good idea to me, so after Betty left, I called Peachy and asked for Mrs. Cole's name and number. I had a dim memory of a pretty, plump, brown-haired woman, younger than Julius, but I couldn't for the life of me remember what her name was other than "Mrs. Cole."

After I hung up, it occurred to me that I didn't have any idea what this investigation was going to cost me. I found myself hoping that it would cost me only an arm and a leg, not a movie theater.

About that time the lights went out.

I was in the small storage closet where we keep the candy, and it was pitch dark and spooky—just a wall of blackness and the cloying smell of sugar.

I stumbled out the door and into the concession-stand area, where I could see by the light coming through the front doors of the theater. I passed through to the small office and was fumbling for a flashlight when I heard a familiar string of profanity very far off: Val.

I switched on a flashlight just as a voice behind me called my name.

"In here," I said, stopping to sign my flashlight out, cowed by my business partner's sternness.

Tobias stuck his head in the door.

"The h'electrician sends his compliments, mum," he said, two fingers tugging at the brim of his cap, "and wishes me to inform you that the h'electricity will be restored shortly. No cause for alarm. Sorry for the inconvenience, mum."

"The electrician doesn't sound very happy," I observed.

"No, mum, if the truth be told, he isn't very happy at all," Toby said sadly. "That's why he sends me on what you might call your diplomatic missions."

"I hope he pays you well."

"Not terribly well, mum, I'm sorry to say, but the work is easy for them as can withstand profanity the way I can."

We heard a new volley of curses.

"That'll be him now, mum," Toby said, raising his eyes to the ceiling. "I'd best get back before he strains his vocabulary."

And with another touch of the cap, he disappeared.

Everybody's an actor, I thought, at least in my family.

I said a small prayer to the patron saint of cinema that the electricity would be restored before the projectionist got out of school.

But the evening went smoothly after that rocky start. The dalmatians were actually proving a big draw, and some kids who'd screamed in terror the first night were dragging their parents back to visit their old pals. Gloria and Ollie were on duty. Gloria seemed to have toned down her perfume a few degrees—either that or my nose was losing its sensitivity. Ollie limited himself to verbal humor. And the electrician went to see *101 Dalmatians* and left with his own humor restored.

Gloria made a big show of handing me her flashlight at the end of the evening.

"See?" she said proudly. "I remembered!"

"That's good, Gloria," I complimented her.

I turned to put it on the shelf and then, on an impulse, held it to my nose and sniffed it. The familiar scent of Gloria's perfume filled my head.

I called her back.

"Gloria," I said, "do you remember returning your flashlight on Friday night?"

"Friday night?" she echoed. "Why, I'm sure I did. Let me think. Yes, I did. I handed it to Clara over the concession counter and asked her to put it back. I'm sure she did."

"I'm sure she did, too," I lied. "Do you remember what number it was?"

"Oh, I don't know, Gilda," she said dismissively, then stopped. "Yes, yes, I do, too! It was lucky number seven! That's what I remember thinking, because it was your first night and here I had lucky number seven!"

"Thanks," I said.

So Clara had been the last person known to have had the

missing flashlight in her possession—old lucky number seven, which must have reeked of perfume. And Clara, unlike Adele and Gloria, did not carry the smell of a recent trip to the beauty parlor. I remembered that Clara was one of Betty's favorite suspects for the Styles B&E. But had she done it alone? Or was Grosvenor involved? And what was she looking for in Styles's office? Did she know that Mae was having Grosvenor and her investigated? Did she have something to hide? If so, was it related to Julius's death?

It certainly seemed related, in my mind, to the burning down of his house. I'd decided I didn't buy Grosvenor's argument about how easily anyone could pick up the skills of arson. For once I suspected that he was selling himself short.

It was twelve-forty-five by the time I left the theater, too late to pay Clara a visit even though I knew she was probably up watching old movies.

But late the next morning she was at Liberty House, helping Lillian and Ruth sort through Maesie's clothes.

I waited until Lillian went downstairs to consult with Ruth about something in the kitchen. I'd already decided that Clara was too cagey to be tricked and that the direct approach would work best.

"Clara," I said, "I need to ask you a question. What were you doing in Styles's office on Friday night?"

I saw the telltale flicker I was watching for, but if I'd blinked, I would have missed it.

"Friday night?" she asked, frowning. "Whose office? Gilda, I was at the theater on Friday night. Helping you," she added disingenuously.

"This was after," I said. "You took Gloria's flashlight and you went to Styles's office. What were you looking for?"

Her eyes opened wide. They were the eyes of an actress who had always overplayed her parts.

"I don't know what you're talking about, Gilda."

"What *did* you do after you left the theater then?"

"What I always do," she said. "I came home and watched a movie."

There was no point in asking her which movie or what it was about, the way they always do on detective shows; she knew too many of them by heart.

"Do you know who Styles is?" I asked.

"No, who?"

"She's the detective Mae hired to help with her autobiography."

"I didn't know Mae was writing an autobiography," she said. "How far did she get?"

"Not far enough, apparently," I said, "or too far, depending on how you look at it."

"That's a shame," she said, "because even if we had some of it, we could probably hire a ghostwriter to write the rest. Are you sure we don't have something we could use?"

"Not that I know of," I said. "If you're interested, why don't you ask Lillian?"

She was busy turning out the pockets of a skirt.

"Clara, whoever broke into this detective's office panicked when the detective showed up and hit her over the head with an ashtray." I studied her. "Styles has a concussion."

"Well, don't look at me!" she said resentfully. "It wasn't me. I didn't even know this Styles person existed."

"What was Grosvenor doing on Friday night after the theater?" I asked.

"Grosvenor? Oh, he pooped out early and went to bed," she said. Then she gave me a sly smile. "Say, is he supposed to be my alibi? Is that what you're asking?"

"Not necessarily," I said. "You might be his."

She laughed.

I fingered the familiar fabric of the skirt, remembering Mae in it. It was an old one. I pictured her wearing it, saw her leaning against the fender of one of those wide tail-finned cars from the early sixties.

"She never threw anything out," Clara observed disapprovingly, reading my thoughts.

"I don't suppose you have any theories about 'rosebud,' " I commented.

"I think it was something out of one of her movies," she said.

"That's what I think. I don't think it had anything to do with the family at all, the way Betty claims. In fact, I can almost remember the scene it was in but not quite—like having a word on the tip of your tongue, you know? If we looked at her movies, we'd find it.

"Anyway," she added, shaking out a dress with a snap, "*I'm* sure as hell not 'rosebud.' "

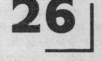

26

"Did you know that Clara and Grosvenor owned a condo at Lake Tahoe?"

"No," I said. "They do?"

"Did," Styles corrected me. "It's now part of the Cole estate. Did you know that your parents owned some investment property off Storm Road, where the new chemical plant is going in?"

"No," I said. "Is that . . . ?"

"Sold to Cole in '87, resold in '96 to the chemical company. Did you know that Wallace and Adele owned a co-op in New York?"

"Sure," I said. "I've been there. But they sold it a few years ago—oh, no! Don't tell me."

She nodded. "To Julius Cole."

We were eating lunch at a small diner in a town near Eden. The town seemed to consist mainly of the diner, an antique gas station, and an antiques and collectibles shop. We were hiding out from my family. Even the phones weren't private, unless I was alone in the theater, and lately Val had been around a lot, working on the wiring.

Some of the aforementioned collectibles graced our table.

There was one of those old glass-and-stainless-steel sugar silos, its hole encrusted with several decades' worth of accumulated sugar and grime. There was a black wire napkin holder shaped like a peacock. There was an ancient tin ashtray with little scooped-out cigarette rests. And the salt and pepper shakers were kissing cooks, a he and a she, their chef's hats awry and their spoons clasped behind their backs.

"We can't go on meeting like this," I'd said after we ordered.

"No?"

"No. Next time we go vegetarian in the Short North."

"Don't tell me," she'd said as I lit up. "You're vegetarian for health reasons."

She was eating a fried bologna sandwich. I was eating a salad that looked a little the worse for wear. Her look when I'd ordered it told me that it wasn't the right thing to order in a diner like this one, where the bologna grew up next door but the iceberg was trucked in from Florida. I'd ignored her.

"You want to hear the good news?" she asked. "All the people—well, there were only five—Mae gave me to trace show up on the sellers list. That is, at some point each of them sold property to a company owned by Julius Cole, most of them to Pison and some to J. C. Enterprises."

"I'm gratified to hear that we've developed a few suspects outside the Liberty family," I said. "But what about these sales? Did he pay a ridiculously low price?"

"I have to find somebody who knows more about real estate," she said. "You?"

"Not me," I said. "I slept through that class."

"Well, then, somebody who was awake. Preferably somebody with a good computer program. My impression, based on my own totally inexpert analysis, was that Cole paid low prices for the property he bought. Not outrageous, though, but the low side of fair. It's not like he bought thirty acres zoned industrial for a dollar."

"Lillian once said that he bought low and sold high," I recalled, "and that that was the secret to his success. But I would expect him to have bought things dirt cheap. If he didn't, doesn't that kind of undermine our theory that he was using blackmail to acquire land?"

"Not necessarily," she said. "Just because he paid a fair price doesn't mean they wanted to sell. And a ridiculous price probably would have earned him more scrutiny than he wanted. Might also have devalued property in the same neighborhood, which might be good in some cases but not in others. At the same time, I'm guessing that many of his deals were legitimate: he wanted to buy, they wanted to sell. What especially interests me are the deals he made the most money on: the bank deal, the Eden Center deal, and the Megaverse deal."

She watched disapprovingly as I picked at my salad.

"Did you know that your aunt Gloria and uncle Oliver inherited some land from your grandparents?"

"I think everybody inherited some," I said.

"Know where it was?"

"Theirs? No, where?"

"I'd say the Megaverse Lawn and Garden Shop is sitting on it."

I was stunned.

"They sold Uncle Julius the land for Megaverse?"

"Only part of it really, just a strip was theirs." She polished off her sandwich with relish and began licking her greasy fingers. "Anyway, they sold it back in '91. I'd say it took him a good six years to put together the land he wanted for Megaverse."

"So it could have been a legitimate deal?"

"Probably was," she acknowledged.

She flexed her shoulders and stretched. For someone as small as she was, the girl could take up a lot of space.

"But as Betty so aptly pointed out, it was Mae's death, not Lillian's or anybody else's, that seems to have triggered all the subsequent events," I said. "So maybe we're on the wrong track altogether, unless Mae ever sold him anything."

"Not as far as I know."

"Well, then?"

"You ever untie knots?"

"Yeah."

"I mean the really hard kind, the tight ones you really have to work at?"

I nodded.

"How do you do it? You pick at what you can see, anything you can get ahold of with your fingers, and hope it does some good. Why? 'Cause it's all you've got to work with."

"But maybe the knot we're untying isn't even the same knot as the one that's about Julius's death."

"Maybe not," she conceded. "We'll know when we get it untied."

In an expression of nervous energy, she drummed her fingers on the Formica tabletop as we waited for the waitress to bring me the change.

"Waldo sends his love," she said.

"Yeah? I didn't really think me and Waldo hit it off."

"You never can tell with him. He told me you had the most interesting feet he'd ever smelled."

I let that pass without comment.

We drove back to Eden.

"You can just drop me off at the corner," she said.

"No, I'll park," I said. "I have a meeting at the bank."

"Taking out a loan for renovations already?"

"No," I said. "It's about Julius Cole's will."

Andy Fuller had called the meeting, but nobody knew exactly why. He bustled in in a whirl of pink phone message slips, clutching an expanding file folder and trailing secretaries. At his elbow was the redoubtable Mr. Hermes, who looked calm and reassuringly genial beside Andy. Mr. Hermes carried an elegant leather briefcase.

We sat at a conference table large enough to accommodate a board of directors and their respective attorneys. Still, the table was crowded, with Liberties sitting knee to knee. My cousin Clyde, the cop, stood in one corner, gun on one hip, baby Harpo on the other. His pregnant wife, Lisa, had her chair pushed back from the conference table to make room for Zeppo. I imagined the baby sitting up in there, taking it all in, getting acquainted in utero with his or her prospective family and wondering if he or she could put in for a transfer.

"I offered to arrange this meeting," Andy began, "since it's about family matters and since you'd probably have questions for me anyway once it was over. Also because Constantine doesn't have a big enough meeting room for all of us."

Everyone laughed a little nervously.

"But I think it falls to Constantine to tell you what this is all about," he said, tapping a sheaf of papers on the table. "Con?"

"Okay," Mr. Hermes said, "let's cut to the chase, as you say in the movie business." He smiled happily at his little witticism. "I'm speaking to you now as the executor of Julius Cole's estate. In his will, Julius left several monetary gifts to employees and relatives on his mother's side. But he left the bulk of his estate to Mae Liberty."

We rewarded him with the stunned gasps he was waiting for.

"And if she should predecease him, which she obviously did," he continued, "the estate would be divided equally among her direct descendants—that is to say, those living at the time of Julius's death."

Dead silence.

I decided we were having one of those group hallucinations brought on by mass hysteria.

Grosvenor was the first to speak. His voice sounded strained. "How . . . how much would that be?" he asked.

"His assets will need to be liquidated, of course," Andy said, "and we obviously don't know yet what his property will sell for, but I'd say he was worth somewhere in the neighborhood of ten million." He pulled nervously at his tie.

Oliver whistled. "That's *some* neighborhood!" he said.

"Well," Gloria said, "I guess that should settle any questions about his loyalty to the family!"

She looked around for agreement, but her gaze snagged on Lillian, whose cheeks were flushed.

"Oh, I should think it settled things very nicely," Lillian said, her voice shaking. "How dare he!"

"Why, Lilly!" Gloria reproached her in a shocked voice.

"Oh, Gloria," my mother said peevishly, "don't you see what he's done? He's having the last laugh on Maesie, leaving us all this money he made off that damn theater chain, and Lillian's land, and God knows what other underhanded dealings."

"Well, I for one intend to have the last laugh on Julius by living to spend my share," Clara said, "and enjoying every minute of it."

"It's possible, Flo, that Julius felt guilty about the theater chain," Wallace said, and his alcoholic breath swept me like a searchlight as he turned toward his sister-in-law. "Maybe that's why he left it to us, don't you think?"

"You may all do as you like," Lillian said, pushing herself to her feet with her cane. "I don't intend to touch a penny of Julius Cole's money."

And she walked out, amid protests on all sides.

Mr. Hermes, who had stood to open the door for her, was looking a bit shaken. This was not the response he'd expected.

"We can, I, er, suppose, establish a trust fund for Mrs. Van Nuys with her share," he said, raising his eyebrows at Andy.

"Yes, yes, we'll figure something out," Andy said.

"According to my calculations," Grosvenor announced, "we'd be splitting the ten million about forty ways, is that right?"

He looked around the table for confirmation.

"If by 'we' you mean the direct descendants," Val said, "that would be about right."

"Well," Adele said, "it will be very nice for the younger generation."

Now Duke stood up. He was even redder in the face than Lillian.

"We don't want his money," he said. "Well, *I* don't. And I wish he was here. I'd tell him what to do with it."

Duke's uncle Clark tugged on his sleeve and Duke turned on him.

"Well, I *don't*!" he cried. "He just did it to make us think how smart he was! Owning the competition without us knowing, making money off it, taking money out of Mae's pockets and then turning around and giving it back to her like he was God or something. And we're supposed to feel stupid and shocked and grateful all at once—and angry, too, probably! But all I feel is angry!"

"Duke!" Gloria remonstrated.

"I think angry is a perfectly appropriate way to feel, Gloria," Val observed.

"Anyway, he thinks he's bought us," Duke said. "He doesn't give a shit how we feel."

"Perhaps then, son, you should stop worrying about how Julius feels, or felt, or what he was thinking," my father put in.

"You expect me to ignore what he was up to?" Duke asked incredulously.

"What Douglas means, Duke," said my mother, the interpreter, "is that your anger plays right into Julius's intent. Odd how we can't seem to talk about the man as if he were really dead! But getting angry at Julius won't accomplish anything for you, it just rewards his bad behavior—if that's how you see it, and I, for one, am inclined to agree with you. The thing to do is to stop being angry and start spending the man's money."

"Why, sure!" Oliver said enthusiastically. "I'll bet there are lots of things you could do with the theater if you only had the money!"

"Like keep it open," Val put in.

"And in the end," Florence said, "the fact remains that you're alive and the Paradise is still around, while Julius and his theater are both dead and gone."

"Well," Duke conceded, "if you put it like that . . ." And he sat back down.

And then Adele had to go and spoil things by saying, "Just think! You could redecorate!"

27

"So you're a millionaire?"

I rubbed my temples and leaned my forehead against the steering wheel. I had called Styles from one of those drive-by phones.

"Styles, think hard. Divide forty into ten million. What do you get?"

"A shitload of zeroes. I don't know how many."

"Yeah, me neither. But I know it ain't a million. My accountant will tell me."

"Maybe he'll want to marry you all over again," she said.

It burned me how much she knew about me, so I said, "Don't go raising your fees and padding your expense account just because I'm rich now. I still won't pay for Disneyland."

"Not even one little fling in Frontierland?"

"Not even a coonskin cap!"

"Man, people sure do get stingy when they're rich!"

"Yeah, well," I said. "Some of us start out that way. Listen, in case you haven't heard, the official verdict on the theater fire is in: they don't think it was arson, but the truth is, they're not sure."

"Now there's a verdict you can take to the bank! Where'd you hear that?"

"My cousin Clyde," I said. "I cornered him at the bank while he was still in shock and the baby had just taken a dump in her diaper. He said the fire started in the projector and must have burned steadily without anyone seeing it. They've got some nitrate residue they can't figure out, but there was no trace of an

186

accelerant anywhere. I guess it's unusual for someone to bother setting a fire and then not bother to ensure that it burns something up, although it strikes me as the kind of thing an amateur might do. If there was an arsonist, he really lucked out—the smoke detectors worked fine, even though nobody was around to hear them, and the sprinkler system didn't. But, according to the cops, chances are it wasn't arson. Unless, of course, it started out as arson, but the arsonist was interrupted, or got cold feet, or something."

"So to speak. Did they give you a figure, like the weather service does? You know, a twenty percent possibility that it was arson?"

"Nope," I said. "But if it wasn't arson, that would simplify things, wouldn't it? I mean, we'd only be looking for one arsonist."

"I guess," she said, not very convincingly. I could hear her cracking her knuckles in the background. "And we wouldn't have to look very far for that one."

Then she switched topics on me. "So . . . Cole's ex is in Cleveland. Want to go talk to her?"

"Where will you be?"

"Cruising the Hollywood freeway, babe," she said, "in my rented Mercedes convertible, with the top down and the volume up."

I drove to Cleveland on Thursday, but not before a new crisis erupted. At ten-thirty in the morning Duke called to say that he'd just checked on the film we were supposed to show that night and the film hadn't arrived yet. He didn't say that he'd skipped Civics to do it; I figured that out for myself.

"Gilda!" he pleaded. "You gotta go to Cleveland and pick up this film!"

"I'm going, I'm going!"

"You are?" He seemed surprised that it was that easy.

"I have to go anyway," I said. "So tell me where this place is."

I'd accomplished that mission. Now I was looking for Juanita Jurden Cole, sixty-two-year-old ex-wife of Julius Cole.

I had a business address at Juanita's Petals and Posies downtown. I hadn't called first. I prefer face-to-face encounters, especially if I'm looking for information. That was probably another reason why I'd grown tired of my role in the insurance business. I spent my days talking to faceless people.

Juanita's was a storefront located in a shopping center in the process of getting a face-lift. In fact, the whole neighborhood looked as if it was just turning the corner from marginal to trendy. The girl who approached me inside wore a rose-colored smock that made her look even younger than she was. Her elaborate eye makeup suggested a teenager who was trying to imitate a sophisticated swinging single.

"I'm looking for Juanita," I told her.

An attractive, buxom woman appeared from the back of the shop. She wore a pink smock with a row of pouchlike pockets across the front and "Juanita" stitched in red letters over her heart. It had been more than twenty years since I'd seen her and I hadn't been sure I'd recognize her, but I did. She had short brown hair, attractively permed and expertly colored, and more deftly applied makeup than her young assistant. She wore enough heavy jewelry to add a good five pounds to her weight, including heavy gold bangles noisy enough to call a cattle drive to dinner. Perched on the shelf of her breasts was a pair of half-glasses on a gold chain.

"I don't know if you remember me, Mrs. Cole," I said. "I'm Gilda Liberty."

"Oh, yes," she said, patting her hair lightly as if recalling just how long it had been since she'd seen me and checking to see that she was looking her best. "But I go by Jurden now, Juanita Jurden."

"I wonder if I could speak to you for a moment about Julius Cole," I said.

"I guess so," she said hesitantly, "if we can talk while I work. I have a funeral order to fill."

So I sat in a chair at a long table in the back and watched her assemble a funeral wreath. She stood, plucking flowers and greenery from several piles on the table and deftly skewering them into position, bracelets clanging together. She had a cigarette going in a glass ashtray on the table, and the smoke cut some of the sweet smell of refrigerated flowers.

"I heard he was dead," Juanita said. "I hope I heard right."

"Mmm," I assented. "You heard right."

"I'm warning you, if you came to tell me he left me a legacy, I'll faint right into these flowers and then I'll have to start over again."

"I don't know whether he did or not," I said. "His attorney is taking care of that. I'm assuming you heard how he died."

She nodded. "I'm expecting the police to come knocking on my door any day now," she said. "But I guess I have to stand in line, huh?"

"That's about it," I acknowledged, "and most of the people ahead of you so far are Liberties. That's why I'm here. To figure out who else ought to be questioned. You see, it happened right after my aunt Mae died—on the eve of her funeral, as a matter of fact."

"I heard about that, too," she said. "I'm sorry about your aunt. I always liked her."

She stood back and studied her work with a critical eye.

"You did?"

She looked over her glasses at me.

"I guess you thought I regarded her as a rival for Julius's affections," she observed. "Well, there might have been some truth to that, in the beginning, when I was still young enough and dumb enough to want his affections. Even then, it didn't take me long to notice that Mae didn't seem to want them."

I waited. Her gaze returned to the wreath and she began to fuss with the finished section.

"No, I liked Maesie, that was the funny part," she said. "In the end, of course, I liked her a hell of a lot better than I liked Julius. Somewhere in there I wondered if he'd married me just to make her jealous. Then, after a while, I cultivated the friendship, just to aggravate Julius. That was before I realized how dangerous it was to aggravate him."

"When you say 'dangerous,' do you mean he abused you?"

She arched an eyebrow at me. "Not if you mean, Did he hit me? No, nothing like that. Oh, I suppose he slapped me a few times, but that didn't really frighten me. No, he had ways of getting what he wanted without violence.

"I liked his first wife, too. Pauline. Did you ever meet her?"

I shook my head. "I don't think so."

"She was a nice woman," Juanita said thoughtfully. "A bit on the tame side for Julius, though, I would have thought. But she did me the favor of trying to warn me what I was getting into and was generous enough not to say 'I told you so' when I found out she was right."

"What exactly did she warn you about?"

Juanita glanced at me, then took a puff of her cigarette.

"Your aunt, for one thing," she said, blowing smoke. "She said to me, she said, 'There's only one person Julius loves besides himself and his mother, and that's Mae Liberty. But he can't have her, so he'll keep playing the field.' And she was exactly right. I never figured out whether he went to bed with women because he wanted to find someone else to fall in love with or whether it was just some defect in his character or his personality, you know?"

"Why couldn't Julius have Mae?" I asked. "Do you know?"

"Why, I suppose because she didn't want him! Not that way, anyway," she said. "She wanted him for a friend, though God knows why. I don't. It's kind of like keeping a barracuda for a pet."

She went back to stabbing her wreath form with flowers—mostly bloodred roses now.

"Do you think they were ever lovers?"

She smiled reminiscently. "Now there's an interesting question," she said. "Julius said they had been, but his story kept changing. 'The first time I made love to Maesie, we were in a field on a spring day, with blossoms falling all around us.' He told me that once. But then he also told me, 'The first time I made love to Maesie, we were walking on a beach on a moonlit night.' " She glanced at me sideways. "Remind you of anything?"

"Her movies," I said.

"I'm telling you, I was watching the late show one night and that movie *Moonlight Madness* was on." She pointed a gladiolus at me for emphasis. "When that beach scene came on—you know the one I mean?—with the moon on the water and the two of them there, it was like déjà vu! And I didn't think I'd seen the movie before. Well, I hadn't! I'd just heard the story from Julius, only *his* version starred him and Mae."

She traded the gladiolus for her cigarette.

"Still, your aunt was a free spirit," she said. "She was way ahead of her time in some ways. How many husbands did she have?"

"Four."

"Four," Mrs. Jurden repeated. "But I bet she never let it cramp her style. There were people in town who liked to gossip about her, called her a 'loose woman,' especially when she was between husbands. But they'd say that about any woman who was good-looking and unattached and enjoyed the company of men. Those were the same people who didn't approve of me when I married Julius, said I married him for his money."

"How did you meet him, Ms. Jurden?"

"Oh, the usual way," she said vaguely, staring off into space. "I was working as a temp and they sent me over to his office when his secretary had a baby. He kept me on and—oh, one thing led to another, as they say."

She touched her hair again in that unconscious way some women have. Her bracelets caught the light. I could imagine her in her youth, a pretty young woman head over heels in love with Julius Cole. He would have flashed his teeth at her every time he smiled, and the warmth from that smile would have melted her heart like wax.

"How much did you know about his business?" I asked.

She gave me a conspiratorial little smile. "In the early days I knew plenty—when I was working for him, I mean. I knew more than he gave me credit for. And I knew about other things, too. I used to collect message slips from all the women who were crazy about him and tease him about all his girlfriends. It was funny at the time. Afterward, when I was married to him, it wasn't so funny anymore. Not that they called the house—at least not usually.

"Come to think of it, though, I remember this one time this little girl called the house—Julius liked 'em any way, but he really liked 'em young—and I told her, 'Honey, I'm going to give you the same advice his first wife gave me: stay away from him if you know what's good for you. He's got so many girls he'll break your heart and not even notice, not even remember your name if he meets you on the street a year from now.' Well, she took it about the same way I did. You can't blame us; we were just young and dumb and inexperienced."

"Do you know of any women who might have gone by the nickname 'Rosebud'?" I asked.

"Rosebud," she repeated thoughtfully. She was wrapping a stem with thin green wire, and she frowned at it. "There was a Rosie who used to call him at the real estate office. I don't remember her last name, if I ever knew it. I don't know whether he had a nickname for her or not."

She looked at me. "It would have been a good nickname for the kind of girls he favored, pretty and young and delicate."

"Apart from ex-girlfriends, did Julius have any other enemies you can think of? Maybe somebody he crossed in a business context, for example?"

The wreath looked pretty much finished to me, though she was still picking at it. Now she glanced up at me, stubbed out her cigarette, reached for the pack, and sat down.

"Lord, I'd better sit down for this one," she said.

She nodded at the small legal pad and pen I'd carried in with me. I hadn't used them yet, not wanting to put her off.

"You going to take notes?" she asked.

"Should I?"

But she had moved on to telling her story, so I opened the notepad.

"I divorced Julius in 1973," she said. "He'd already pulled off that bank deal by then and made his first million."

I opened my mouth to ask her about the bank deal, but she cut me off.

"Don't ask me how he did it," she said, "because I don't know. I have some ideas, though. The first I knew about what he was up to was when he bought that land for an office park, just east of town. That used to be farmland, remember? I overheard him talking on the phone one night—I don't know who to. I heard him say "Oh, *he'll* sell, all right" in the really nasty tone he could get when he was about to run right over somebody. Later on I was cleaning his desk and I saw a note he'd written. It said something about somebody named Grayson and a dishonorable discharge from the Marine Corps for striking an officer and going AWOL. There was a date and a number—like a service number, I guess. I didn't think anything of it at first. Julius was in a really good mood at that time, the way he always was when he was about to make some really big deal. A few weeks later I read in the local paper where this farmer named Grayson had sold the family farm to J. C. Enterprises and there was going to be an office park there. There was an interview with the farmer, and in the article they were saying it was too bad that all the old family farms were disappearing. You could tell from the interview that the man was all broken up about it, but he said it was too hard to make a living as a farmer these days. The story even mentioned that Grayson had served in the Marine Corps in World War Two.

"I took the paper to Julius, and asked him about it," she continued. "I said, 'This wouldn't have anything to do with a little piece of paper I saw on your desk about a man named Grayson who was dishonorably discharged from the Marines, would it?' He laughed, then said I ought to just spend his money and leave the moneymaking to him."

She shivered. "That was the day I realized I was going to divorce him. I said to myself, 'Julius Cole is a coldhearted son of a bitch and he is making his money off other people's secrets. If you don't want to spend that kind of money, you'd best get out.' "

"How did he get his information about people?"

"Honey, any way he could, I imagine," she replied. "I think gossip stuck to him like flies to flypaper, and he never forgot anything anybody ever told him, so that was part of it. Some of it was pillow talk, I'm sure. There was this black-haired nurse, used to work for Wen Genesee. You know the one I mean?"

I nodded. "Mrs. Beverly," I said.

"That's her. She was crazy about him." She scooted her chair a little closer to me. "I'm telling you, it made me nervous to go in there after that. Can you imagine what he found out about people from that nurse? Why, what if you had a social disease or something? You wouldn't want everybody to know about that."

She took a drag off her cigarette. "He hired a detective sometimes, too, I think, later on," she said. "I overheard him on the phone with somebody, maybe three years back, when I went to see him with some papers that needed his signature. It was somebody he'd hired to find out something; I could tell that."

My throat went dry. "Somebody local?"

"Not from Eden," she said. "He wouldn't want somebody that close. I think he might have had informants, too. You know, somebody he had something on who would call with dirt on somebody else to keep him off their back."

"It's hard to believe," I said slowly, "that he could get away with it, that people in general wouldn't have heard or figured out what he was doing."

"Listen," she said, grabbing my wrist, "the day I left Julius Cole, I said I was through with charming men. Because that's the answer, don't you see? All the women fell in love with him and all the men respected him. And then one day he was the richest man in town. So who was left to talk about him? Not the people he'd blackmailed. They weren't about to call attention to what he was doing.

"And it was really clever, if you think about it. Most of us have done something we're really ashamed of. Some people have done worse things than others, things that might ruin their marriage or their business. But if Julius didn't want anything from you, why, he'd charm your socks off! Unless you were female and then he'd charm something else off. You might never know that he was storing up secrets to use against you if he ever needed to. And then the thing of it was, he was careful to pay a reasonable price for whatever he bought. Maybe not the best price, but something good enough that nobody would suspect the owner didn't want to sell."

"So you think he collected information randomly?" I asked, surprised. "I thought you were suggesting he'd focus on somebody he wanted something from, somebody who owned property he wanted to buy."

"He did that, too," she said. "But I'm convinced he kept a file full of secrets hidden away somewhere. Before I left him, I looked all over the house. I never found it. But that might just mean he kept it in his office."

She stood up. "It's a shame I never found that file," she said. "I would've burned it."

"Maybe somebody else did it for you," I said, and I told her about the fire.

"Well, I hope all those notes burned up in the fire," she said doubtfully. "I really do. But like I said, I never found them at the house and I looked all over it.

"You said you were worried about your family," she said, as if she'd just remembered. "If you could find that folder, I bet you'd have enough suspects in Julius's murder to keep the police busy for years. He ever buy any property from any of your folks?"

I nodded.

"Well, like I say," she commiserated, "that was a big boat to be in."

"Do you think he ever tried to blackmail Mae Liberty?" I asked.

"God, no!" she exclaimed. "If he'd done that, she would never have spoken to him again, and that would have killed him, I think."

"Did you know that he built a shopping center on the edge of town and put in a chain theater?"

"No!" She raised her hands to her cheeks in genuine shock,

bracelets clanking in protest. "He built a theater to compete with the Paradise?"

She searched my face and realized that I wasn't kidding.

"Now, I knew he was a treacherous bastard, but there's something I wouldn't have thought even he would be capable of. Well! It's too bad Maesie didn't pull the trigger. She'd never have been convicted."

She turned back to her wreath, draped a large streamer across the middle, and anchored it at both ends. "My Beloved Husband," it read.

She stood back to admire the effect, then turned toward me with a wry smile.

But I had drifted away. I was hearing Jed Leland's voice, saying to the reporter, Thompson: "I was his oldest friend. And as far as I was concerned, he behaved like a swine."

Hand on the door, I turned back. I had to be sure.

"About that detective," I said. "Does the name Styles ring any bells?"

She put a finger to pursed lips. "You know, that sounds familiar, but I just can't say for sure."

I walked out into blazing sunshine, chilled. Just who had been blackmailing whom?

"Where was this one taken?"

I was sitting on a stool across the counter from my mother, who was humming to herself and cooking. Betty, who had agreed to come along for moral support, was sitting next to me, and my father was sitting at the kitchen table, surrounded by paperwork.

I'd told my mother I wanted to look at their old photograph albums. That seemed to me to be a good way of getting them to talk about the past.

"What is it?" my mother asked, cocking her head and leaning over to look. She found her glasses on the top of her head and pulled them down.

"It looks like it was taken around Eden somewhere," I said, rotating the album and sliding it across the counter to her.

It was a completely unmemorable photograph of Gloria, Oliver, and my father standing in front of a field of weeds. It was also clearly labeled "Glendale, 1947," the way people used to do when photo albums were a family project. Like all the other photographs in the book, it had been slipped into four meticulously glued black paper corners.

"Hmm," my mother said. "That must have been the lot where Gloria and Ollie had their house built. Didn't we go out to see it, Douglas?"

"Hmm?" my father said. "The Glendale house? Is that what you're talking about? Yes, we went out there, Flo, don't you remember? It looked like they were out in the middle of no place."

"It really reminds me of Eden, though," I said doggedly. "Like out by the industrial park. Didn't you guys own some property out there?"

My sister made a small noise in her throat and rolled her eyes at me.

"Where?" my dad said. "Off Storm Road?"

"We did," my mother said, "but that was ages ago."

"Whatever happened to that?"

"Oh, we sold it," my dad said distractedly, his eyes on the paper in front of him. "Got a good price, as I recall."

"To Uncle Julius?" I asked casually.

I turned the page and pretended to study the album.

"Yes, that's right." My mother had returned to her sauté pan.

"Here's a good one of Dad," Betty said.

"Dad, you looked like a real ladykiller!" I said. "I always thought you looked good on the screen, but I figured that was just good makeup!"

"Shame on you, Gilda!" my mother reproved me, smiling. "Your father was once voted the most handsome man in Hollywood in a survey taken outside the Chinese Theater."

"That must have been after *When in Rome*," I observed waggishly.

There was an audible groan from Betty.

But he smiled good-humoredly, not a bit guiltily.

"Actually," he said, "it was after *Carefree*, and your mother has omitted to mention that she was voted the most beautiful woman in the same poll."

"Oh, look!" I exclaimed, turning another page. "Here's Clara. Is that her first husband with her?"

My mother looked up from the stove at the album I was holding up for her to see.

"I don't know who that is," she said. "That's probably why we didn't put his name down. She always had a boyfriend, never the same one twice. Except when she married, of course."

"How did she meet Grosvenor?"

My mother turned in my father's direction, frowning. "How *did* she meet Grosvenor?"

My father snorted. "How did she meet any of them?"

"Did he work on the special effects for *Tropical Port of Call*?"

My father looked at her. "That sounds right. He probably provided the wind for the hurricane."

My mother laughed delightedly. Cooking put her in a good mood, and my father rarely made a joke at someone else's expense.

"Special effects work must be hard," I commented. "I'll bet it's easy for things to go wrong."

Nobody picked up on that cue. Betty was crossing her eyes at me.

"Has Grosvenor ever told any stories about disasters on the set?"

"He might have," my father said, chuckling, "but was anybody listening?"

"There was something, Douglas," my mother reminded him. "Something about a grenade in one of those war pictures he made. The poor actor lost his hand," she told me. "Not just his fingers, like Harold Lloyd, but his whole hand! Can you imagine?"

"Well, Grosvenor was keeping bad company in those days," my father said cryptically.

"What kind of bad company?" I asked.

"Oh, well, you know," my father said, seeming to lose interest. "The usual kind."

"Did the actor sue Grosvenor?"

"Heavens, Gilda, in those days nobody thought of lawsuits the way they do now," my mother said. "The studio paid for everything, I imagine—his medical bills and rehabilitative therapy. The studios took care of their own."

"Say!" I said, as if I'd just thought of something. "You have pictures of Avery Gardner, don't you? I'd forgotten about that."

"They're in there somewhere," my mother said, moving oven racks around noisily. "I don't know which book; you'll just have to look."

But while I was looking, I became distracted by pictures of Maesie.

The camera loved her, as they say in Hollywood. Hers wasn't a conventional beauty, and it certainly wasn't an insipid, fragile beauty. She had an air about her, and her whole body projected an attitude toward life—confident, enthusiastic, fun-loving. I realized with a start why I had never remembered what any of her husbands looked like: they all seemed nondescript standing next to her.

"Look!" Betty said, and pointed. "There she is with Camille!"

We turned the page.

"Oh!" We sighed in unison. For there was Maesie with her short-lived family, Camille and Camille's daughter, Giulietta. It was hard to look at those fresh, young faces and know them to be doomed.

"Look," Betty said softly. "Giulietta's seven here. That must have been taken just before Camille died."

"That was a terrible thing," my mother said, pausing in her work to rest her hands on the counter. "I thought it would kill Mae."

"What did she die of? Betty and I were talking about her the other day and we couldn't remember."

My mother lifted a lid from a large kettle, and steam rose to cover her glasses. A fresh wave of garlic and tomato smells rolled over us. She frowned into the pot and stirred.

"I don't remember exactly," she said. "Maybe it was a ruptured cyst or something. Some surgical complication. Hand me the salt, Gilda, please."

"A ruptured cyst?" I said skeptically.

My sister raised an eyebrow.

"Well, I don't know," my mother said irritably. "I don't remember exactly. A tumor, maybe. She had some kind of gynecological surgery, and it went wrong."

"She was only thirty," my sister said. "And here's one of Giulietta." She touched a photograph showing a young woman who looked like a Botticelli model. This one was unmounted, stuck in the back of the album with the more recent pictures.

I turned it over. Stamped on the back was the processing date, 1980. The year Giulietta died.

"She was beautiful," Betty said.

"Yes, she was," my mother said, sadness in her voice. "She and her mother both."

My sister reached for another book.

"Here's an old one, with pictures of Lillian," she said. "I'll bet Avery Gardner is in here. Yes, here he is!"

We leaned over and studied him. It had been a long time since I'd laid eyes on his picture, and I really hadn't remembered how handsome he was: a slender young man with blond hair wearing double-breasted suits with padded shoulders. Occasionally, he appeared in a fedora, smoking a thin cigar. Like Mae, he had a glow about him. He always looked directly into the camera lens.

"I always forget how much Ron and Clark look like him," Betty said. "Scarlett looks more like Aunt Lilly."

"What did he die of?" I asked. "I forget."

"Heart attack," my mother said. "Poor Lillian! It was so unexpected in someone that young, but it happens."

"So it wasn't because he was keeping 'bad company'?"

"Certainly not," my mother said, "Gilda, see if you can make out this word. I can never read your aunt's writing."

She handed me a recipe card with Adele's illegible scrawl.

"Looks like 'onions' to me," I said.

She took it back and scrutinized it. "Yes, that must be right."

"So did Avery die at home?" I asked. "I mean, was Lillian there when he died?"

"No, he died in his car, coming home from a party," she said.

"Gee!" I said. "Was he by himself?"

"Lillian was at home in bed," my mother said, chopping an onion, her eyes watering.

"But was he by himself?" I persisted.

"Gilda, what are you suggesting?" my mother asked irritably, knife raised in midcut. "And why are you taking this prurient interest in Avery Gardner? I never even met the man. I hadn't met your father at the time."

My father, who should presumably know more about Avery Gardner's death, was busying himself with his papers. He was writing on a legal pad.

I shrugged. "I'm just curious, that's all. Do you think our family has more than its share of tragedies?"

"I certainly hope not!" my mother said. "What a thing to say! We have a large family, and the Liberties are extremely long-lived. It stands to reason that there will be tragedies from time to time."

I had two more topics to cover and I was desperate to finish with them. I would actually be enjoying this trip down memory lane if I didn't have to use the occasion to weasel information out of my parents.

And speaking of weasels, I still had Styles to deal with, and I hadn't yet decided how I would handle the situation.

"Here's Greer," I said.

"She must have been going to a prom," my sister observed. "Look at that hair!"

"You leave her hair alone!" I retorted. "I had hair just like that. Slept on brush rollers to get it that way, too. It was just like sleeping on a bed of nails. Then you'd rat it up till your whole scalp prickled."

"That's how you got all those holes in your head," Betty commented.

"Andy hasn't changed much," I remarked, fingering a later picture of the two of them together. "Did he work for a studio? Is that how they met?"

"I don't remember," my mother said. "I barely remember how your father and I met."

"Dad?"

"Hmm?"

"Did Andy Fuller work for a studio? Is that how Greer met him?"

"I think so, Gilda," he said. "I don't remember which one, though. I don't even remember anymore which one she was with."

I felt frustrated, but how could I blame him? I could barely remember what my New York apartment looked like, much less the life histories of every apple on our family tree. Now, I found myself thinking as I leafed through this pictorial record of intimate relationships, if I could just forget Liz. But the problem was that I didn't want to forget her, I just wanted to get beyond the stage where my heart stopped every time I encountered her image—not to mention the stage where I fantasized about reconciliations, replaying them in my head like the final scene of *An Affair to Remember*.

I gave up on finesse, persuaded by Betty's every look that it wasn't my strong suit, anyway.

"Remember that apartment Wallace and Adele used to have in New York?"

"What about it?" my mother asked, wiping her eyes with a dishtowel.

"How come they sold it?"

"How would I know?" she asked. "I assume it was because they didn't get there often enough to make it worth holding on to when they could sell it for a good price."

"Did they sell it to Uncle Julius?"

"In New York?" my mother asked, surprised. "What would Julius want with an apartment in New York?"

"Somebody's got Uncle Julius on the brain," my sister observed snidely.

"You're a big help!" I said to Betty later when I got her alone. "I thought you were supposed to be there for support! Any more support from you and I could have just marched around the house, ringing a bell and crying, 'Bring out your dirty laundry!' "

"You might as well, Gil!" she said. "Jesus, subtlety is not one of your talents."

"Well, at least I got some information," I said sulkily.

"Yeah, like that thing about Camille's death, which Mom didn't want to talk about. Do you really think they operated to remove a cyst?"

"I don't know, Betts," I admitted. "Sixty-nine was light-years away in medical history. Jesus, that was the year I graduated from high school!"

We both fell silent for a minute.

"Are you thinking what I'm thinking?" she said at last.

I looked at her. "Probably," I said, "if you're thinking that 1969 was four years before *Roe v. Wade*."

29

"This is a person-to-person call," a familiar voice said. "Is this line secure?"

There was a clatter on the line and then Ruth Hernandez's voice.

"Gilda, your dinner is hot now! You want cold potatoes, it's okay by me, but if not, you better get down here! It's a long time between now and the time the late show lets out."

And then another clatter. I opened my mouth to speak, but the noise came again.

" 'Scuse the interruption," Ruth said, and hung up.

"That answer your question? Where are you?"

"I'm at Schwab's Drugstore, waiting to be discovered," Styles said.

"I don't think that story was true," I told her.

"Babe, don't talk to me about truth!" she retorted. "I'm in the land of make-believe, deep in the heart of the dream factory! From where I'm standing, I can look out the window and see a palm tree. Looks real scenic next to my Mercedes convertible."

I had a lecture in my hip pocket to give her about truth, but not yet.

"Speaking of my Mercedes convertible, where the hell do Angelenos park? This is the first place I've been to that has a parking lot."

"I thought you were supposed to be a detective."

"So?"

"So do a little detective work," I advised her. "Also reading the signs helps."

"Meaning what?"

"Most places have a lot," I said. "You just have to look for it."

"Where? In Burbank?"

"Styles, in case you really do have a Mercedes convertible, and in case I'm paying the insurance on it, let me give you some advice. Three rules of driving in L.A. One, don't turn left. Two, don't be the first car into the intersection after the light changes. Three, don't run down any pedestrians."

"That last one explains some of the dirty looks I've been getting."

"In California they consider it very bad form to kill a pedestrian," I said. "Listen, I have to go. My dinner's getting cold, and it's one of my most basic rules of life that you never, under any circumstances, piss off the chef. I'll call you later."

As she was hanging up, I said, "Styles?"

"Yeah?"

"I'm not paying for no body piercing, either."

"Not even if I have to go undercover?"

"You want to go undercover, do it like everybody else," I said. "Hang your camera around your neck and pretend you're a tourist."

Styles had given me a key to her office so that I could call her from there in privacy, so I walked the block and a half from the Paradise after the late show. I climbed the dark stairs, using a flashlight I'd checked out of the theater. I made enough noise to wake the dead and warn any prowlers that I was on my way up. I even hummed to myself. It's okay by me, I was trying to tell them, if you want to hide in the hall and slip past me once I'm in the office. Even so, as I reached the second-floor landing, I put on the hard hat I'd borrowed from Val. If there's anybody in there, I prayed, let it be the ashtray assailant and not the guy with the gun who offed Uncle Julius.

I switched on the light inside the office and checked behind the door. Then I crept up to the desk, holding my breath, and zipped around the side to check underneath it. Nobody. Heart pounding, I sat down in the creaky desk chair. The overhead light gave the room a garish yellow glow.

I surveyed the room. If Styles had worked for Julius Cole, would she have kept the file and then given me a key to the office so that I could find it? And would she have given me any information on her filing system? I had to admit there was a possibility she thought I was too stupid to catch on. She was, after all, the professional snoop who had apparently failed to snoop-proof her own office.

Of course, she could have been setting me up.

I started with the computer. I turned it on and was shortly rewarded with the little theme chimes for Windows 95. I moused over to the little icon for My Computer, blessing the folks at Microsoft and their forerunners at Apple for making this so easy. I am not, and never have been, one of those snobs who prefers arcane programming commands to little pictures.

"It's not exactly *my* computer," I confessed to the screen in a whisper, but Windows 95 didn't care. I asked it what it was holding on its C drive and it promptly answered with a long list of files.

None of them had "Cole" in the title.

The building made all of those creaks and groans buildings make when they are old and arthritic. Every sound stopped my breathing and sped up my pulse.

I moved on to the case of diskettes. None of the labels included a file with "Cole" in the title. Two had "Liberty," but when I pulled them up, I saw that they were the same reports I had on hard copy.

I had another thought and searched the C drive for "J. C. Enterprises" and "Pison" but came up dry.

I heaved a deep sigh of self-pity and then started because it sounded so loud in the stillness. I tiptoed over to the bank of file cabinets Styles had identified as "historical" and checked for files under "Cole," "J. C. Enterprises," and "Pison." Nothing.

For good measure I checked "Cineglobe." Then I did a quick run-through of the file cabinets on the other side of the room, but I didn't find anything.

I had been there half an hour and my nerves were shot.

If Styles had once worked for Cole, that didn't mean she'd been working for him at the same time she was working for Maesie. In any case, even if Cole had been her former employer, he was dead. So what was her game? Was she really working for me now, or was she just in it for the round-trip airfare to Hollywood?

Sitting behind the desk once again, I extracted a piece of paper from my pocket, one eye on the door, and dialed the number Styles had given me. I'd decided not to confront her yet with the information Juanita Jurden had given me. If it turned out to be true, and she turned out to be a double-crossing con artist, or worse, I wanted her within slugging range.

"I don't think this is going to work," I told her, when her voice came on the line.

"Why not?"

"Because it's too goddamn creepy sitting here in a dark, empty building by myself!"

"Didn't you find the light switch?"

I didn't dignify that with an answer.

"Where are you?" I asked. She had one of those phone numbers that forwarded her calls all over the country, something I didn't understand.

"Poolside," she said, "at the Beverly Wilshire."

"Well, that's one consolation," I said dryly. "I won't catch skin cancer where I'm sitting."

"I wouldn't bet on it."

"Listen," I said, "Val's an electrician, and Grosvenor has all this advanced high-tech communications equipment. Do you think I have to worry about wiretaps?"

"Cookie, if I were you, I'd be worrying more about inherited psychological disorders than wiretaps."

"You have a point."

"I've been thinking, though," she said. "Maybe your parents aren't your real parents, you know? Like maybe you're just a publicity scheme the studio thought up when your parents' popularity slumped, and they forgot to tell you about it."

"Don't think I haven't thought of it!" I said. "When I was a kid, I used to imagine that my real parents were Jimmy Stewart and my third-grade teacher, Miss Alvarez.

"So, anyway, have you got anything to report besides the water temperature?"

"Okay, I started with Avery Gardner. The cops won't let me see the case file, assuming they could find one that old, assuming they could find one at all. This is the LAPD we're talking about, after all. The stories in the local papers—the legitimate press, I mean—all sound pretty mysterious, but nothing definite. He was on a relatively deserted road in the Hollywood hills at about two-thirty in the morning. He pulled off the road, had a heart attack, and died. He was on his way home from a party."

"Alone?"

"Well, here's where it gets interesting. Both Hedda Hopper and Louella Parsons mentioned the event in their gossip columns, but it's pretty straightforward—tragic death of a shining light of the screen, that kind of stuff. I gather they were rivals, by the way, but they were both members of the William Randolph Hearst–Marion Davies social set, and so was your aunt Mae. That means we probably shouldn't expect any shocking revelations from them. But another gossip columnist in a short-lived little Santa Monica paper I found asked, 'Who was the last person to see Avery Gardner alive?' It could have just been a publicity ploy, and I looked through the next several issues hoping she'd answered her own question, but no.

"So I got a line on a local writer who writes scandalous biographies of the stars. He's a real scumbag, if you ask me, but for a generous contribution to the deterioration of his liver, he told me that there *was* something about Gardner's death that had been suppressed. He claimed there was someone with Gardner in the car, a Paramount director named Miles Ochenberg. Says he talked to Ochenberg ten years ago—the man's dead now. Ochenberg claimed there was nothing to tell, that it happened just the way the papers had reported it. Ochenberg said the studio didn't want his name in the news reports, and he hadn't wanted to face an army of reporters, especially since his mother was ill at the time. The scumbag writer thinks there was more to it than that, but I gathered some new scandal broke out and he went after that one. He wouldn't give me anything else, and I got the feeling when I left that I should have charged him for reminding him of a possible scandal he hadn't gotten around to writing about yet."

"God! If there is one, I hope his liver gets him before he breaks the story," I said. "It occurs to me that I might save some of my relatives' lives, but they might never speak to me again to thank me."

"I thought that's what you wanted."

"No, I want them to speak to me, I just don't want them to give me advice," I said.

"Dream on," Styles said, and picked up her narrative. "So I got a line on a retired reporter for *Variety*, who covered the story. I see him tomorrow. I spent the morning on the phone tracking down a retired MGM exec, who stonewalled me when I asked why Andy Fuller left the studio, until I mentioned that Fuller was now a bank president. After that sunk in, he suggested I talk to one of my colleagues, who did some work for MGM in the late sixties. Me and the dick are doing lunch tomorrow."

"At my expense," I put in, conscious of just how much lunch could cost in L.A.

"I ran down the guy with the missing hand through SAG," she continued, "or rather I ran down his widow. She lives in Nebraska, but I spoke to her on the phone. She claims that her husband blamed Grosvenor June for his accident, says it was June who prepared the grenades. Says he always claimed that Grosvenor June was drunk or on drugs or both that day, and that he and some of the other extras had complained about it, but nobody would do anything. Nowadays, she figures they would have sued at the very least, but at the time they were offered what she called a 'very generous' settlement, and all his medical expenses were paid. He got a prosthetic hand but ended up quitting the business and moving to Omaha and opening a garden store."

"Was Grosvenor fired?" I asked.

"I gathered he wasn't," she said, "but I'm going to do some more checking to see if I can confirm a drug habit."

"What about Clara?" I asked. "Find anything on her?"

"I'm still working on it," she said.

"Poolside at the Beverly Wilshire?" I asked. I couldn't resist.

"Hey! It's ten o'clock at night!" she responded in an injured tone. "All work and no play makes Styles a bitch! You don't even want to see what I could do to the Liberty family reputation if I talked to people when I was in a bad mood."

"I can imagine," I said. "I've seen you in a good mood."

"Yeah, well, I could be out cruising Sunset Strip," she said. "Instead I'm sitting here, talking to you."

"You be careful cruising Sunset Strip," I cautioned her. "I mean it, Styles. Wear your combat boots."

I doubted that Styles had any clothes in her wardrobe that even remotely resembled a hooker's, but still.

"Say! Isn't that where Richard Gere picked up Julia Roberts?"

"I don't think so," I said. "But it's where River Phoenix OD'ed. You be careful."

"Me?" she said. "The woman is living with killers, arsonists, and muggers and she tells me to be careful."

"Okay, but just remember: not all the bodies in the L.A. County Morgue are famous."

"No, but seriously, babe," she said, "I hope you're a light sleeper. If somebody thinks Mae had the goods on them and can't find what she had, Liberty House is going to be next on the list of torch targets."

"Don't worry," I assured her. "I checked all the smoke detectors today."

30

"Guess what?"

Peachy was behind the wheel of her sporty little Mazda, the furthest thing imaginable from a hearse.

"You quit your job."

"How'd you guess?" I was a little disappointed; she'd stolen my thunder.

But, after all, her reaction was gratifying if scary. I'd forgotten that since she drove like a New York City cab driver, you didn't want to distract her with emotion. Now she swerved, cutting across the right-hand lane close enough to a Ford Taurus to cause its driver to brake, and brought the car to a halt in a cloud of dust and gravel on the shoulder.

She looked at me, radiant.

"You didn't!"

"I did."

She threw her arms around me and dragged me across the stick shift for a hug.

"Gillie, that's wonderful!" she exclaimed.

"Well, I'm glad somebody's happy," I mumbled into her shoulder.

She pulled away and searched my face. "Aren't you happy?" she asked.

"I've traded New York City for Eden, Ohio," I said. "The Met for Eden College opera; Lincoln Center, Carnegie Hall, and Radio City for the Palace Theater and the lawn at Chemical Abstracts; the Metropolitan and MoMA for the Columbus Art Museum; Central Park for a couple of state parks; and a secure job with medical and dental insurance and regular hours for a high-stress, insecure job with none of the above. Plus, as somebody just reminded me, I am probably living with a killer, an arsonist, and a burglar or two. Oh, yeah—and I've got no social life because I work nights."

"Well, look on the bright side," she said. "Your best friend lives only a few blocks away. Besides, you're rich now, girl! You don't have to worry about medical and dental insurance."

"Everybody has to worry about dental insurance, Peach," I said, as she pulled out onto the road again, causing five drivers behind us to hit their brakes. "Have you seen what it costs just to have one tooth crowned?"

"You don't have to work every night for the rest of your life, do you?" she asked.

"No, probably not, once Duke gets his new team trained," I said. "But right now I feel like I should be around for moral support, if nothing else. He says as soon as things settle down, he's going to train me to be a projectionist." I said this last as if I'd spoken my doom.

"Don't you want to be a projectionist?" she asked. "Sounds like fun to me. And it can't be all that hard."

"Don't bet on it," I said. "You should see all the little pulleys you have to thread the film through—it's worse than a sewing machine! And it's not just the projecting you have to learn. You have to learn how to check a print and make sure it's okay, with no bad splices or upside-down reels or anything like that. And anything that's screwed up, you have to be able to fix. You have to clean the projector all the time."

"It does sound complicated," she admitted. "Did Mae do all that?"

"Yeah, she was good at it," I said. "She trained Duke."

We were going into Columbus to meet Peachy's boyfriend, Tom, for brunch, the only meal I was available for.

"Let's get to the part where you're living with a gang of criminals," she said. "I want to hear more about that."

So I told her everything I knew.

"Say, Peach," I said, "you ever run into a woman by the name of Styles?"

"Oh, sure," she said. "I know her. Little scrawny thing with a big attitude. Comes across as real hard-boiled."

I snorted. "You mean she isn't?"

Peachy laughed. "Girl, my puppy and her puppy were in obedience classes together last summer at the park." She shook her head. "She couldn't get that dog to mind if her life depended on it!"

"Waldo?"

"Yeah, that was him, Waldo. Always looked like his lady friend just ran off with a boxer. I'll bet that dog is still walking all over that girl!"

I smiled. After all the personal goods she had on me, it was gratifying to have something on Styles for a change. I couldn't wait for the right moment to drop it into the conversation.

Peachy's new boyfriend seemed like a great guy. I enjoyed spending time with him, but afterward I felt depressed for the rest of the day. I didn't want him, but I wanted what they had together, and I wanted it with Liz.

I think Peachy realized how I was feeling, because when we hugged good-bye, she said gently, "Don't worry, Gillie. We'll find somebody for you, and she'll make you forget all your troubles."

31

"I need you to go to Indiana," Styles said.

"Indiana? Say, who's paying who here?"

Assuming her last report had been genuine, Styles had been

doing her job. But I had adopted a more skeptical attitude where Styles was concerned. Or, rather, I'd simply extended to her the attitude I took toward my family, in which everyone was playing a part, or several parts, like actors in a repertory theater.

"I'm busy here in L.A.," she said. "I can't afford the time to hop a plane to Indianapolis right now."

"But I've got a theater to run!"

"Quit whining!" she said. "It's the next state over. Drive west out of Columbus, you'll be there before you know it. If you hit Illinois, you'll know you've gone too far."

"So what'd you get out of lunch?"

"About a hundred grams of fat and some good skinny on Fuller. Turns out our Andy was dipping into the till at Metro and they found out when they audited the books at the time of the sale."

I whistled. "Our local bank president was an embezzler in a past life?" I said incredulously. "Why didn't they prosecute?"

"Why do you think? Because he was a Liberty, or was married to one, which was close enough. That, at least, was the opinion of my informant. He said the new owners probably would have prosecuted, but the old owners didn't, so Fuller was lucky they were the ones who found it. He was permitted to re-sign and pay restitution."

"Jesus!" I said. "Do you think he's still doing that kind of thing?"

"I don't know," she said. "He's your cousin-in-law; what do you think? Personally, I think if he is, he's stupider than I give him credit for being. But I wouldn't put it past him to have found another way to clear a little extra profit."

"In some kind of partnership with Julius Cole, you mean."

"Cole's first big break involved the bank."

"So what about the reporter you were going to see about Avery Gardner's death?"

"He canceled at the last minute, said something came up," she said. "But I can see him tomorrow if I drive out to Riverside."

"Anything else on Grosvenor?" I asked. "He's the one we're pretty sure is in hot water."

"Several of the men he used to work with told me he had a drug habit for a while," she said. "Some of the men who told me that probably still do. They claim he went into drug rehab after the accident. One guy told me the studio made him do it. When I asked why he wasn't fired, guess what they said."

"Because he was a Liberty."

"Bingo. Of course, I also gather that he was generally pretty good at what he did, when he wasn't high."

"And Clara? Did you find anything on her?"

"That's your assignment," she said. "A Mrs. Cora Appleyard. Lives in a nursing home outside Indianapolis."

I made no comment on the name. Liberties are not in the habit of throwing stones of that particular kind.

"Known on stage and screen as Nola Banks," Styles continued. "I'm told she accuses Clara of ruining her career."

Several papers on the desk stirred almost imperceptibly, as if a ghost had sighed in their direction.

"How could Clara have done that?"

"You'll have to ask Mrs. A.," she said. "All I know is that Nola Banks was slated to play the lead in *Stars in Her Eyes* before Clara took it over."

I thought I heard a stair creak.

"Wait!" I whispered to Styles. "I think I hear something."

I listened hard, the silence now as suspicious to me as noise.

"Gilda," Styles said quietly in my ear, "there's a semiautomatic in the bottom right-hand drawer."

I slid the drawer open.

"Wow! What is that, a Glock?" I mentioned the first name that popped into my head. Loudly.

Somewhere I heard another creak. Hard to tell if it was a human sound, though, or just one of the building's mutterings to itself.

"Fully loaded, too!" I enthused. "Boy, I could really get in some target practice with this baby! I'll bet it makes a nice-size hole in the target."

I didn't know what the hell I was talking about.

Now I heard, faintly, footsteps on the stairs. To my relief, they were receding. The outside door opened and closed, causing the office door to rattle softly in its frame.

I went to the window and looked down, but there was an awning in my way. I couldn't see anything.

"What's happening?" I could hear Styles's voice on the line.

"He went out. But the damn awning's in my way," I said. "I can't see anything."

"Wait," she said.

But I still didn't see anything.

"He could have gone out the back way, into the alley," she said after a minute. "Want to go look?"

"Not especially."

"If so, he's probably gone now, anyway," she said. "If not, he could be waiting just outside the street door, assuming he really went out and didn't fake it."

"You're just a ray of sunshine, aren't you, Styles?"

I was still watching the street.

"You could have waited to see if he'd open the door," she chided me. "Then we'd know who we were dealing with."

"No way! If it was the killer, he has a gun, too, only the evidence suggests that he knows how to use his."

"Go out on the stairs and use your nose," she directed me. "See if you can smell anything."

"I don't want to go out on the stairs," I said.

She heaved an exasperated sigh. "Look, go carefully, be alert, and take the gun with you."

"Styles," I whispered vehemently, "let's get one thing clear: I'm not touching the gun. It scares the shit out of me."

"So what are you going to do? Spend the night in my office?"

"Maybe I could order a pizza."

"At this hour? You're in Eden, Ohio, cookie. You can't even find a drive-through window open at this hour."

"Okay, I'll call Betty," I said. "She must have a big dog or two she could bring over."

"Good plan," she said. "You got a pen?"

"What am I supposed to do with that?" I thought she meant I

should poke the intruder's eyes out before he could draw a bead on me.

"Write down Cora Appleyard's address."

"Oh. Yeah, I got one. Shoot. I mean, give it to me."

I wrote it down. I was signing off to call Betty when she said, "Gilda?"

"What?"

"If you get killed in the line of duty, can I sing 'My Way' at your funeral?"

32

So Betty came and rescued me, along with Teddy and two large dogs of indeterminate breed who looked big enough to eat a gun but were too friendly and polite to try it. We saw no trace of an intruder, except that the back door into the alley was standing ajar.

The next morning, sleep deprived, I drove to Indianapolis.

Cora Appleyard was a plump woman with enough long grayish-yellow hair to play Rapunzel's grandmother. She was sitting in a wheelchair at a large folding table covered with craft paper. She was painting flowers on china teacups and making a very bad job of it. She had a smear of purple paint across the bridge of her nose, just under her glasses. She had sharp dark brown eyes.

"I'll bet you didn't think anybody did this anymore," she said, looking up at me as I approached. "It's a dying art."

From what I could see, she was doing what she could to hasten its demise.

"Of course, glass is really my medium," she confided to me.

"See, what I like to do, I like to buy these cheap picture frames at the five-and dime, the ones that come with glass in them, you know? And then I paint designs on them—hearts and flowers, like for a picture of your sweetie, or little ABC blocks for baby pictures, or 'Mother' inside a heart. They're real cute! And they just sell like hotcakes at flea markets! You wouldn't believe how many I sell!"

She squinted at the china cup in her hand. "I can't quite get the hang of this, though, because I'm used to painting on a flat surface. And between you and me, people don't really use this kind of cup much anymore, do they? Mugs is what they use."

She leaned forward confidentially. "These art therapists are well meaning, but they're not very practical. Half the things I make, even I don't want 'em when I'm done.

"Are you a new volunteer, honey?" she asked suddenly, catching me unprepared.

"No, Mrs. Appleyard, I've come to talk to you about someone you used to know," I said.

"A man?" she asked slyly, flicking her eyelashes at me.

"No, a woman," I said. "Clara Liberty."

"Oh," she said, and her tone shifted. "Her. What do you want to know about her for? She hasn't died?" She asked this last question hopefully.

"No, she hasn't died," I said, and prepared to stumble my way through an explanation of why I was there.

"Well, then, did you come to find out how she stole my best role away from me and ruined my career?"

I smiled at her. "That's exactly what I've come to find out," I said, hooking a chair with my foot and sitting down.

"I used to be Nola Banks," she said proudly, as if trying to impress me.

"That's what I heard," I said.

"Had my own dressing room at Fox," she said. "When they set the production schedule every year, there were always several Nola Banks pictures on the schedule—so many Temples, so many Alice Fayes, so many Loretta Youngs, and so many

Nola Bankses. I was what they called 'bankable.' There was a fan club for me in Duluth, did you know that?"

"No, I didn't," I admitted.

"It's true," she said reminiscently. "Duluth was a Nola Banks town. They were wild for Nola Banks in Duluth. One time this man wrote me a letter. He said, 'I hope you're satisfied! My wife made me stand in line for tickets to your latest picture in the freezing cold and then I got pneumonia and almost died. So would you please send me your autographed photo to help warm me up?' "

She giggled as if she'd just told a dirty joke, and her brush wobbled on the violet she was painting.

"What about Clara Liberty?"

"Clara Liberty!" she said indignantly. "Why, she wasn't nobody—except the sister of some halfway decent actresses who'd worked hard to get where they were! And I worked hard to get where I was, too, and don't you go thinking otherwise! At four o'clock in the afternoon every day I was lying down on my own bed in my own dressing room, and I was by myself! I got where I was by talent and hard work!"

I made a mental note to ask my mother if she knew what had happened at four o'clock in the afternoon at Fox every day. It sounded like they were holding orgies on the soundstages.

She narrowed her eyes at me and pointed her brush in a way that made me nervous.

"*Stars in Her Eyes* was a Nola Banks film," she said. "You look and see if it wasn't. We'd already started rehearsals. And one day I was coming down the stairs from my dressing room, and when I reached the landing, there was this pail of mop water and a mop right there and it tipped over just as I came up on it, and I tripped over the mop and fell halfway down the next flight of stairs! I could have been killed!"

She had stopped painting and her eyes were fixed on the distant scene.

"Don't ask me what happened next because I don't know! I was out cold. I came to in the hospital. I had a concussion, and a broken ankle, and a real bad hip injury. And I laid there and thought, What are they going to do about my picture? Honest to God, that's the only thing I could think about. Then my girlfriend Babs Olston came to see me in the hospital. You probably don't remember her, but she was a real good little dancer. And I said, 'Babs, I'm just worried sick about my picture!' And then she said, 'Why, Cora, don't you know that that little tart Clara Liberty is going to do your part? Mr. Zanuck said so this morning.'

"Well!" she said, getting as much mileage out of this one syllable as it was possible to get. "I knew right away what was what, and I was furious, I can tell you! Clara Liberty in a Nola Banks film? It was ridiculous! And there wasn't a person on that lot who didn't know why Mr. Zanuck had given her that part!"

"Do you think she slept with him?" I'd opted for the direct route.

"Honey, there was not much *sleeping* going on between those two, as my grandmother used to say," she said, giving me a coy wink.

"But don't you think there was a lot of that going on?" I suggested. "Old Hollywood was notorious for the casting couch."

It didn't sound like anything worth killing somebody over. So what if people found out Clara had been sleeping around? Even Ingrid Bergman had lived to receive a standing ovation on Oscar night.

"Sure there was," she agreed easily. "Where Mr. Zanuck was concerned, you could have said the same thing about half the girls on the studio payroll. But that's not what bothered me about Clara. See, I realized she had caused my accident."

"She did? How?"

"I don't know how exactly," she confessed. "I wasn't in any condition to study all the details at the time. But while I was lying there in bed, it came to me: just before I took my tumble, I'd looked down and seen Clara looking up at me. She was under the landing, kind of, leaning up against a post. And when I remembered the expression on her face as I lost my balance and went down, why, it gave me chills! And then the more I thought about it, the madder I got! Babs said, 'Let it alone, Cora! You don't know she did it. You can't prove anything.' And I said, 'I know I can't prove it, but I know what I know! She must have rigged up a string somehow and pulled that mop just as I was coming down the stairs. Because that pail shouldn't even have been there, you see. It had no business being there.' And that girl had the crust to come and see me in the hospital! 'Cora,' she says, 'I feel so bad about this—getting my big break on account of your unfortunate accident.' Butter wouldn't melt in her mouth!

"Well, when I was up and hobbling around again—it must've been two months later—I went to the studio and started asking around about that pail and mop. At first, nobody would talk, because nobody wanted to get into trouble, see? But at last I came to Manny Schine. He was a prop man and I'd known him for years. And Manny said to me, he said, 'Miss Banks, I can't tell you how that pail came to be there on the landing, because I didn't see anybody put it there. But I saw Clara Liberty carrying a mop and pail just like it not thirty minutes before your accident.' He remembered it, you see, because he couldn't figure out what she'd be doing with a pail and mop, unless she was playing a maid or something. And that's what he'd decided she was doing, before he heard the story of the accident and it jogged his memory. Now, what do you think about that?"

"That's pretty shocking," I said, "if someone would injure her rival just to get a part."

"You're darn tootin' it's shocking!" she said with satisfaction. "How do you think *I* felt? And that leg and that hip never did heal right, so before I knew it, I was out of the movies and Clara Liberty was in. Why, I wouldn't be in this nursing home now if it wasn't for that bad hip Clara gave me! If I ever get out of this wheelchair and walk again, I'll probably break it all over again, and then I'll get some kind of infection in the hospital and die."

This speech had a kind of prophetic smugness about it, yet I suspected she might be right.

"Where'd you say you were from, honey?" she asked. "A magazine?"

"No, nothing like that," I said apologetically. "Clara is my aunt and she seems to be in some kind of trouble, and I'm trying to figure out what kind of trouble she's in."

I expected her to turn her wrath on me, but she didn't.

"Clara's in trouble, huh?" she said. "Well, it's about time, you ask me. I'll bet she stepped on a lot of toes and even heads on her way up. You don't hear about her anymore, though, not even in the tabloids, and, honey, when the tabloids are through with you, you might as well lie down and die. Of course, if you did, then they'd take you up again."

She cackled merrily at her own joke.

"So you're Clara's niece, huh?" she asked, looking me up and down speculatively. "Well, honey, all I can say is, I hope you don't have anything she wants."

"What do you think?" I asked, and stood back to survey my handiwork.

"Smashing!" Betty said, grinning. "Out of sight!"

Duke was more restrained.

"Are you sure there isn't an *e* in *groovy*?" he asked.

Tomorrow night, God, UPS, and the electrical circuits willing, we would open *Austin Powers: International Man of Mystery,* the Mike Myers comedy about a swinging British agent from the sixties who has put himself into suspended animation and awakens in the late nineties to continue the pursuit of his archenemy, Dr. Evil. My poster announced our impromptu promotional gimmick: anybody who came dressed in the style of the sixties would get in for half price on opening night. Since most of the dresses being sold in the department stores these days seemed to be exact duplicates of their mod counterparts of thirty years ago, that shouldn't be too difficult.

Betty was tempting fate by plugging in a lava lamp at the concession stand. I'd vetoed the incense, on the grounds that some people, myself included, disliked the smell of it and also on the grounds that too many buildings had burned down recently.

The lava lamp cast a warm red glow on Betty's cheeks and began its ponderous bubbling.

"Far out!" Betty enthused.

"I still can't believe you saved that vinyl miniskirt you wore in junior high," I said. I was outlining my letters in psychedelic greens and purples. "And I can't believe it fits you," I added rather more morosely. I'd found a colorblock Mondrian dress, but I couldn't get it on past my hips.

"Well, you're the one with the red go-go boots," she pointed out wistfully. "Not to mention the fall."

"You might as well take them," I said. "I'll probably just go out tomorrow and buy a new pair of bell bottoms."

"Gee, thanks, Gil!" she said, pleased. "I've got extra love beads; I'll give you some."

She turned to Duke, who was making lemonade.

"Want some, Duke?" she asked. "I'll bring you some, too."

"No, thanks," he said. "I don't want to wear anything that might get caught in the projector."

"Do you have some tie-dye clothes at least?" Betty pressed him. "Because if you don't, I think I have a T-shirt that would fit."

"I'm just the projectionist," he objected. "Nobody will see me."

Betty smiled at him and hummed a little of "In with the In Crowd."

"I'm thirsty!" she complained. "Got any beer in the fridge?"

"I don't think so," I said. "We need to make a beer run."

And then I stopped, lime-green marker poised.

"How can you be out?" she asked. "I thought . . ." She glanced up at me. "What? What is it, Gil?"

"The night before the funeral," I said in a hoarse voice. "Somebody went out to get beer."

"Yeah?"

"Betts, do you remember who it was?"

"No, why would I remember?" she asked. "I was in the kitchen with you."

"Do you remember what time the person went?"

"Gil, we weren't even drinking beer!"

"I know, but do you remember, anyway?" I said. "It's important."

"Why is it important?"

"Because we're assuming that everybody who was at Liberty House that night has an alibi for Julius Cole's murder." I nodded at Duke. "That's why Duke makes such a good suspect—because he wasn't there. But somebody left to go get beer."

Betty's eyes widened. "Are you saying that whoever went out for beer is the killer?"

"No," I said with a sigh. "What I'm saying is that somebody in the family has a less-than-perfect alibi, that's all. And I wish I hadn't realized that, but there it is."

"You're saying that somebody who was at Liberty House that night *could* have been the killer?" Betty said.

"Okay, Betts, let's concentrate," I said, sliding to the floor to sit cross-legged, my back against the concession stand. I closed my eyes. "You and I were in the kitchen—"

"It was Val," Betty said. "Val brought the beer into the kitchen."

"Val? Are you being serious?"

"I'm telling you, it was Val," she insisted. "Don't you remember? He said something like 'I'd offer you ladies a drink, but I can see you're out of my league.' Something like that."

It sounded familiar, and suddenly I knew she was right. I saw him standing in the kitchen, backlit by the light from the refrigerator, smiling down at us. I remembered the conversation I'd overheard between Val and Clara on the back porch and my sense that he knew more about what was going on than he was telling. I also remembered Ruth's reports of conspiratorial meetings with Mae behind closed doors.

And then he was there again, standing in the lobby with the light from the open theater doors at his back.

"I have that toggle switch for booth three," he said. "Okay if I go ahead and put it in?"

I saw Duke glance up at the clock. "How long will it take?" he asked anxiously.

"Ten minutes max," Val said. "Longer if I blow all the circuits."

But before Duke could wind up to protest, Val held up his hands and added, "Just kidding!"

"We were just talking about you, Val," I said. "We were talking about making a beer run."

"Not for me, thanks," he said casually, moving toward the stairs. He patted his stomach. "Got to watch my girlish figure."

I trailed after him. Behind me, Betty cleared her throat obtrusively.

"But you were drinking beer before, weren't you?" I asked, as he set his toolbox down and found the wires he wanted. "At Maesie's funeral, I mean."

"That's just it," he said, unscrewing something on the back of the switch. "I drank too much beer at Maesie's funeral, as my roomie pointed out when he suggested I get on the scale."

"Oh," I said. I was fresh out of clever circumventions, so I decided to try the direct approach.

"Val," I began, "do you remember the night of the visitation when everybody went back to Liberty House?"

"And got smashed?" he said. "Oddly enough, I do."

"Do you remember going out for more beer sometime around midnight?"

"Want to make yourself useful?" he asked. He held out a small screwdriver. "Just hold that yellow wire up and out of my way while I attach this other one. If they touch, this place is history."

I pulled my hand back.

"Just kidding," he said, offering me the screwdriver again.

I took it from him and wedged it into place.

"But seriously, they shouldn't touch or we might cause an even worse disaster," he said, deftly fitting a small bunch of filaments around a screw I could barely see. "We might get Duke mad at us."

I swallowed and tried to hold my hand steady.

"So do you remember going out for beer that night?" I asked.

"Hmm?" He seemed to be concentrating on his work. "What night was this?"

"Friday night," I said. "The night before the funeral."

"The night Julius was killed, you mean."

"Right," I agreed. I was watching his hands now, not his face. "That night."

"I don't remember going out for beer," he said. "Why?"

"Betty and I were in the kitchen," I reminded him, "and you came in with two six-packs, one in each hand, and put them in the refrigerator. You made some kind of crack about us drinking the hard stuff."

"Oh, yeah," he said, withdrawing his own screwdriver. "I remember. You can let go of that now." He picked up a small plastic cap, and I wondered, not for the first time, how he managed to fit his large hands into such small spaces to do such delicate work. I sat back on a stool and watched him.

"I didn't go out for the beer, though," he said. "I was coming back from the bathroom through the entry hall and I saw Grosvenor on the phone. The two six-packs were just sitting on the table there, so I picked them up and asked if he wanted them in the fridge."

"So Grosvenor went after the beer?"

I liked that scenario better, and I didn't see how Val could lie about something like that since I could easily check with Grosvenor.

"I guess so," he said, fitting two wires into the cap and twisting it. He looked at me over the glasses he wore for close work. "Why? What are you saying? That Grosvenor bought beer on the way back from killing Julius?"

I colored at his tone of skepticism.

"I'm just trying to figure things out," I said defensively, "before somebody else gets hurt."

"Disappointed it wasn't me?" he asked good-naturedly, cocking an eyebrow at me.

"I don't know," I said. "I kind of like you in the role of avenger."

"Sort of a John Steed type," he said, "with Tobias in the role of Mrs. Peel?"

"Can he do that thing Diana Rigg could do? Can he throw himself from his back to his feet?"

"He can do the reverse," Val said, tucking the wires and caps into the small box, "as long as he has a soft surface to land on."

"Seriously, Val, do you think Grosvenor could kill anyone?"

"You're asking the wrong person, Gil," he said. "I happen to think anybody can kill someone if they're desperate."

"Do you think he's desperate? I mean, do you get the impression anything's going on with him?"

"I think he could be made desperate, if somebody threatened to take his toys away, yes," he said. "Is anything going on with him? Who knows? I try to avoid the puffed-up little son of a bitch, if you want to know the truth."

"Do you know how long he was gone that night?"

"Didn't even know he'd left," Val said. "Sorry, Gil." He removed his glasses and tucked them into a case in the breast pocket of his long-sleeved work shirt.

"What kind of beer was it?"

"What?" Val asked, startled. "The regular kind, in bottles."

"No, I mean, what brand?"

"Christ, Gil, I don't pay attention to that! I don't have Grosvenor's finely tuned taste buds."

"But he does," I said. "The point is, you can't just run down to the Sunset Drive-Thru and buy the kind of beer he drinks. How far did he have to go to get it? We live in Eden, Ohio, after all. Gourmet food shops and microbreweries are few and far between."

"Oh, I see what you mean." Val leaned back on his stool,

crossed his arms, and stroked his bottom lip. "In that case, you're right: it wasn't Bud or Miller or Stroh's."

"Coors or Mich?"

"Something more exotic, I think," Val said. "Damned if I can remember what."

"So he had an excuse to be gone for a while."

"I guess he did. But, Gilda, pessimist that I am regarding human nature, I can't quite picture him walking up to Julius and shooting him point-blank."

"Maybe he didn't shoot him," I offered. "Maybe he found Julius dead. Maybe he just burned down the theater to hide any evidence that might point to him."

"But I thought that the police had ruled out arson," Val protested.

"They're pretty sure it wasn't," I said. "But that's not one hundred percent. And you and I know that Grosvenor knows lots of ways to burn down a building."

"Except that even Grosvenor wouldn't have been so careless, Gil," Val said. "I heard there wasn't any accelerant. So what would be the point of setting a fire if you didn't make sure the place would burn down?"

"That's a good question," I said, lighting on a new thought. "Maybe we've been looking at it the wrong way around—or, at least, I have. Maybe the point of the fire was to make sure the body was found, not to make sure the building would burn down. Maybe it didn't occur to whoever set the fire that nobody would notice it until the whole place had gone up in smoke. After all, there are apartments behind the shopping center and a sports bar in the same center. Even in the dark people should have smelled smoke."

"I've been in that bar," Val said. "You can't smell anything *but* smoke when you come out. Anyway, if he wanted the body discovered, the arsonist—if there was an arsonist—could have just phoned in the fire as an anonymous tip to the fire department."

"Maybe that's what Grosvenor was doing when you saw him on the phone at Liberty House that night."

"Maybe," Val said, obviously unconvinced. "Somehow, I don't think the timing was right."

"Maybe you spooked him and he hung up before he could complete the call."

"And maybe I should pass all this on to Tobias to see if he wants to make a screenplay out of it." Val grinned at me. He stood up, snapped off the light, and we headed downstairs.

I heard his voice behind me.

"You know the other big problem with Grosvenor as murderer or arsonist, don't you, Gil?"

"Yeah, I know," I admitted. "He couldn't resist the temptation to tell somebody what he'd done and how cleverly he'd done it."

My bell bottoms flapped around my legs, giving my calves plenty of breathing room, but they got in the way of my Birkies. Every time I tripped, I was afraid my fall would slide off, though it was anchored to my head by enough bobby pins to be recycled into a cruise missile. The long hair kept falling into my eyes and getting in my way, and my love beads kept getting hung up on my MAKE LOVE NOT WAR button. I started the evening with flowers in my hair, but within half an hour I had a daisy hanging rakishly over one eye and I was shedding petals as if I'd been caught in a defoliant bombing.

I hadn't resolved the Grosvenor problem. I was hoping to discuss it with Styles when she returned, assuming that after I'd gotten her story straight I was still speaking to her. When I'd thought the killer might be Val, I hadn't really been afraid of him. I could imagine Val killing Julius out of loyalty to or love for someone else. Grosvenor, on the other hand, would only have killed out of self-interest. That made him more dangerous in my book.

I was on ticket sales, since I couldn't work behind the concession stand with all this hair. One of our new employees was sporting an Afro wig that made her look like a youthful Angela Davis, but the hair seemed pretty well attached. She was wearing a dress that I swore I had owned in the sixties—blue-green daisies on a field of white. It provided an odd contrast with her BLACK POWER button. She had removed her nose ring in honor of the occasion.

The other kid behind the concession counter had combed his punk do forward over his forehead in an attempt at a Beatles cut. It was about as effective as you'd imagine. He was wearing small wire-rims with yellow lenses. He was having a hard time distinguishing the Sprite from the lemonade.

We had violated our own rule and were playing early Beatles music in the lobby and then the soundtrack from *Hair*. Several young women in granny dresses were dancing.

Out of the corner of my eye I spotted Uncle Oliver handing out hand-rolled cigarettes that looked like reefers. I caught him by his paisley tie and said, "I hope you realize that tobacco is a controlled substance, regulated by ATF, and that you can't even give it away without a shitload of warning labels to go with it."

He gave me an exaggerated look of shocked innocence, and I let him go.

Adele, who was sulking because we hadn't let her help decorate, had nevertheless shown up in a Jackie Kennedy suit, complete with a matching boxlike handbag and pillbox hat. Wallace was in a sport jacket, Western tie, cowboy hat, and boots.

"Who's he?" a granny dress asked skeptically.

"Your president," I told her.

My mother was wearing a long flowered skirt and a peasant blouse, while my father was sporting a Nehru jacket. God knows where he found one that fit.

Betty arrived and was a big hit in her vinyl skirt and go-go boots. Somebody changed the record so that she could frug.

Val and Tobias sneaked in. Both wore dark suits and incongruous chains of plastic flowers. They each had a wire dangling conspicuously from a button stuck in one ear.

"FBI or CIA?" Betty asked them.

They exchanged a blank look.

"Don't be ridiculous," Tobias said without expression. "Everybody knows that the CIA does not engage in domestic spying." He turned his tie clip in her direction and pressed it with his index finger.

Clara arrived, very Carnaby Street down to the mod plastic jewelry. Grosvenor wore a military dress jacket and a peace symbol hanging on a cord around his neck.

By now, there was enough tie-dye in the room to clothe a Crosby, Stills, and Nash reunion concert. Some of the people wearing it had apparently indulged in their drug of choice before making the scene.

"So tell me," I said to Betty beneath the din. "Have we crossed the line into bad taste here? Have we sold out?"

"You mean because to us the sixties was a political statement and to kids today it's just a fashion statement?"

I nodded. "Something like that," I said.

"I don't know, Gil," she admitted. "I guess there are worse periods to idolize. Maybe some of the political stuff gets through."

Someone behind me cleared a throat, and I turned back to the paying customers.

My eyes struck a faded maroon T-shirt, obviously old, showing the Statue of Liberty with a gag tied around her mouth. FREE SPEECH NOW! it said. The T-shirt was under a camouflage jacket. On the jacket was a button: TAKE A PIG TO LUNCH — AND LEAVE HIM THERE.

My eyes traveled up to the face, but its eyes were scanning the room. It snagged on the impromptu limbo line my dad was leading under a broom running from a trash can to a lobby display table. In the background, the Mamas and the Papas were "California Dreamin'."

"This is too much, baby," she said. "Are you the bird in charge?"

It was Styles.

She was still talking about it when I caught up with her at Oscar's hours later.

"No kidding," she said. "I can't wait to see what you do for that volcano movie. Or *The Lost World*—that should be interesting."

"Yo, Styles," I said. "Can I focus your mind on business for just a few minutes here?"

"You haven't said anything about my tan," she pointed out.

"How much did it cost me?" I asked suspiciously. "And speaking of free speech," I said with a nod at her T-shirt, "how come you didn't tell me that you'd worked for Julius Cole?"

"What? Who told you I worked for Julius Cole?"

She looked surprised, but that didn't mean anything.

"Never mind who told me, the point is that you didn't."

"That's because I never worked for him. Why do you think I did?"

"You used to work out of Columbus, didn't you?"

"Sometimes," she said guardedly.

"Juanita Jurden, Cole's ex, said he hired a detective named Styles from Columbus."

"Ah," she said, her head coming up and her eyes shifting toward the wall. Her hands were wrapped around a mug of beer. "And you thought that was me."

This statement took the wind out of my sails a bit. Why wouldn't it be her? And then I thought of all the Liberties in Eden and wavered.

"Well?" I said, rather less sternly than before. "Wasn't it?"

"No."

"But you know who it was?"

"Not actually, no," she said.

I lit a cigarette and inhaled deeply.

"Does your family run to private investigators? Is that it?"

"I told you, it wasn't me," she said stubbornly. "That's what you wanted to know, wasn't it? Now, do you want to know about Avery Gardner or don't you?"

"Well, you don't have to be so touchy about it," I shot back. "A person who knew, before she ever met me, that my ex-husband was still my accountant has no grounds for righteous indignation. And yes, I want to hear about Avery Gardner."

I hadn't decided yet whether to trust her with my new discovery about Grosvenor's absence on the night Julius Cole was killed. She was holding something back, that much was clear. I wanted to go home and think about whether that mattered or not.

She reached inside her jacket and pulled out a photograph. She laid it on the table facing me.

It was a posed photograph of six young men, three sitting in chairs, three standing behind them, arms around one another's shoulders. They were all good-looking and dressed in the style of the thirties or forties, judging by the double-breasted, padded-shoulder suits of those wearing jackets. They were all laughing. The photograph appeared to have been taken in a restaurant or club; there were drinks on a table with a white tablecloth in front of them and the lighting was soft.

The man in the middle of the front row was Avery Gardner. My finger hovered over his radiant face.

"That," said Styles, leaning over the table to point to the man next to him, "is Miles Ochenberg."

"Where was this taken?"

"In a private club in Santa Monica, not too far from the beach."

"Not where he was that night?"

"No, not where he was the night he died."

"Who are the others?"

"I don't know all of them," she said. "This one, Jack Kronin, became a producer at Universal." She indicated a man with cornsilk hair. "And this one," she said, moving her finger to a tall, dark young man, "was a Disney animator. But now he owns a gym and a nightclub of his own. His name is Geoffrey Pullman."

"Where's his club?" I asked.

"West Hollywood."

I nodded. That and the photograph told me everything I needed to know about Avery Gardner and the secret Lillian had guarded for more than half a century.

"Where'd you get the photograph?"

"The photographer sold it to the *Variety* reporter about four years after Gardner died. I guess he was hard up. Of course, the *Variety* reporter couldn't do anything with it. I think he just felt sorry for the guy. Says he figured it was better off in his hands than in somebody else's. I think he was relieved to give it back to someone in the family."

"Do you think there are any more of these out there?" I asked, picking up the photograph.

"Could be," she said. "I think you'd better have a talk with Lillian."

"It's not worth killing somebody over," I observed.

"Not to me, and not to you, maybe," she said, "but we live in a different world from the one Lillian's lived in all her life."

"Yeah," I said. "The real world."

I laid the photograph on the table next to Lillian's place.

"I think you've been looking for this," I said gently, "or something like it."

She fumbled with her reading glasses, settled them on her nose, and looked down at the photograph. She caught her breath and then the ticking of the clock filled the silence between us.

Ruth Hernandez had gone out to some mall opening with a cousin, so we were alone.

Tears trickled down her cheeks and splashed into her neglected plate. "He *was* beautiful, wasn't he?" she said softly.

"Yes, he was."

"When he asked me to marry him, I thought I was the luckiest girl alive," she said. "I loved him so, you see. You can't imagine."

Maybe I could, I thought, but I didn't interrupt her reverie.

"He was the kindest, sweetest, most thoughtful husband," she said. "How he made me laugh! He was a good father, too."

"How did you find out about him?"

"The usual way," she said, but not bitterly. "There was a technical problem on the set and I was sent home early. He was in bed with a writer, Max somebody—I don't even remember his name. They were sound asleep."

I waited, wanting her to tell the story in her own way.

"I'd always thought we were the perfect couple," Lillian continued. "Everyone in Hollywood thought that. It's not as if . . ." She trailed off, then made another attempt. "We had a very passionate relationship.

"People assume you can tell—I know I always did—but you can't. He was very loving. We had three children, after all. They were his children. Afterward . . . after I found out, I mean, he said that he did love me and that I'd always be his best friend, but that . . . there were . . . things . . . I couldn't do for him."

"I'm sure he loved you very much," I said. I felt an empathy for her that was more than pity. I knew all about betrayal and the misery and humiliation it brought. Somehow I felt certain that Avery Gardner had loved her more than Liz had loved me, and the tears standing in my own eyes were probably at least partly an acknowledgment of that.

"I said I was willing to do anything to get him back," she said, then flicked a glance at me. "That's how naïve I was. He told me I'd never lost him, not the way I meant, and that there wasn't anything I could do. He offered me a divorce. But I didn't want a divorce. I thought as long as we stayed together I could, you know, 'cure' him. At least I'd have a chance to try. That's how I thought of it at the time.

"He cried and promised to be a good husband to me—but then he'd always been a good husband. He said he couldn't promise to be faithful, though he had tried, and at least he would be very discreet. He promised never to bring anyone home again."

Her voice was choked with pain and I could barely understand her.

"Do you know how hard it is to live under those terms—to go on living with someone, and loving him, and knowing all the time that he is living a secret life that you can't be any part of? To read articles about you and your perfect romance and to know that it's all a lie? To go on playing that role in public when your heart is in shreds? Not to know where your husband is sometimes, and who he's with, and what he's telling them about you?"

"I'm sorry, Aunt Lilly," I said, feeling closer to her than I ever had before. "It must have been agonizing."

"Maybe you think I was relieved when he died," she continued in a whisper. "But I was devastated. And after he was gone, I missed him so. I thought, Even to have half his heart or half his attention was better than this. I found myself thinking, if God would just bring him back, I'd never complain again. But it was too late."

We sat in silence for a few minutes.

"All the stories I tell about him are true," Lillian said at last. "I just don't tell everything."

"Does Val know?"

"Valentino has been a great comfort to me," she said. "Not at first, of course. He was too young at the time and he had his own problems to worry about. But somewhere along the way he guessed about Avery. I don't know how. But one day—oh, years later—we started talking about Avery, just like that. And he tried to help me understand. He said that I should never repudiate my happy memories of Avery because those were genuine. He said that Avery had loved me as much as he'd been capable of loving any woman. And he helped me understand, too, how very difficult Avery's life must have been."

My eyes strayed to the happy face in the photograph; I couldn't help it.

"Oh, I know," she said, catching my glance, "he always looked happy. And I do think he had a great capacity for joy, in spite of his troubles. But Val was right: his life was not an easy one, and occasionally he would sink into a depression that would paralyze him for days."

She smiled down fondly at the photograph.

"He was happy the night he died, though," she said. "Miles came to tell me that. It was an act of considerable compassion and charity and even courage on Miles's part, and I've always been grateful."

"Were you afraid Mae had found out about Avery?"

"I think she did find out, yes," she said. "I suppose you know that our relationship had been strained since I sold that land to Julius. But in the last month or two of her life, she treated me with great kindness and delicacy, and although she never spoke of it to me, I was certain she knew about Avery and pitied me. It must have had something to do with her autobiography—that's what I thought. So after she died I looked for any notes she might have kept. Now that I know about the detective . . . Is that where you got the photograph?"

"Yes, but she just found it," I said. "It's not out of Maesie's file."

"So anything Maesie had—notes or files or whatever—is still missing?"

"I'm afraid so. What about Julius?" I asked. "Did he find out, too?"

Her face darkened. "Oh, yes, he found out. He wanted that land, you see. I don't know whether it had to be that particular piece of land or whether he wanted it because it belonged to me and I'd never liked him. But he made it clear that he'd ruin Avery's reputation if I didn't sell it to him."

"I don't really think, Lilly, that it would have ruined Avery's reputation," I said gently.

"Oh, I know you must think I'm silly," she said, shaking her head. "After all, you and Val are . . ." She tripped over the word, even after all these years.

"Homosexual," I prompted.

"Yes. And you're perfectly good people, I know. But I was raised to believe it was wrong."

I felt a sudden empathetic pain for Val, who had been raised in the same household, in the same world, in the same moment in history.

"Anyway, it's not just that, you know," she said softly. "I'm being disingenuous. What I couldn't bear would be to have our story—Avery's and mine—spoiled by some shocking exposé, like the ones you read in the supermarket tabloids. I couldn't bear to become an object of pity," she finished with dignity.

"I rather think, Lilly, that would depend on how you handled it. You're not the first woman to have found herself married to a gay man, and you won't be the last. I agree with Val: you have to be true to Avery, to the love you felt for him and the love he felt for you. I'm willing to bet there are many married couples who would envy you that love."

She looked up at me, surprised.

"I suppose that's true," she said pensively. "I hadn't thought of it like that."

Gilda Liberty, twice-divorced marriage counselor to the stars, I thought wryly.

"So you went to Uncle Julius's house that night to look for any records he might have on Avery?"

She nodded.

"But I didn't burn the place down, Gilda. I suppose I would have, if I'd thought about it and known how to go about it. I was quite exuberant when I heard what somebody had done."

"And just for the record, you didn't kill him?"

"I wouldn't have dirtied my hands with him," she said, her eyes hard.

It was such a Lillian thing to say—a line out of some old script that she'd delivered as if it were one of the Ten Commandments—that, oddly enough, I believed her.

"And who do you think was the somebody who burned down Julius's house? Do you have an opinion on that?"

"If you mean do I think Grosvenor did it, I haven't the faintest idea," she said. "If he did, I can't imagine why."

"You don't think Julius might have been holding something over Grosvenor the way he was holding something over you?"

She looked surprised again.

"Why would he be doing that? He'd already gotten his shopping center. Two shopping centers, in fact."

"I don't know," I admitted. "But I think it's a mistake to think he was satisfied with two shopping centers. After all, he wasn't satisfied with one. Grosvenor might have had some property he wanted or something else. Can you think of anything?"

"Do you know, much as I despised Julius Cole, it never occurred to me until this instant that he might have blackmailed someone else?" She stared into the distance. "I'd always assumed it was me he was after, perhaps because he thought I spoke ill of him to Maesie. And you say he did it to other people? Threatened to expose them if they didn't do what he wanted them to?"

"His ex-wife says he did."

"Isn't that remarkable." She gave me a little smile. "This is turning into quite an illuminating conversation. May I ask why you've become involved in all this, Gilda? I'm not criticizing," she added hastily. "I'm just asking."

"One person is dead, one person has been injured, and two buildings have burned down. Our family seems to be at the center of everything, and it all seems to revolve around Mae's death. I think I should warn you, Lilly, that if somebody thinks there's blackmail material hidden somewhere in this house, Liberty House could well be the next building to go up in flames. And if the arsonist is the same person who murdered Julius, he or she may not care whether or not we're at home when that happens."

I hadn't wanted to alarm her before, but I was beginning to appreciate her toughness and I thought she and Ruth needed to be warned.

"Goodness!" she said, and her eyes wandered in the direction of the hallway. "I suppose we should check the smoke detectors."

"I already did that," I assured her. "But we need to tell Ruth—"

The telephone interrupted me and Lillian answered it. Val had given her a cordless phone after she'd broken her hip and begun walking with a cane. It had taken her some time to get used to the thing, but now she was seldom without it.

"I haven't seen him," she said into the phone. Then to me: "Gilda, Clara's misplaced her husband. Have you seen Grosvenor?"

"Not me."

"We haven't seen him." She listened briefly, then said, "Yes, I'll tell him if I see him." She hung up.

"Clara's throwing a fit because her disposal is backed up and Grosvenor is nowhere to be found," she said, and then smiled. "You know, I think I shall constantly be reminded now of what you said about married people and about Avery and me. May I keep this photograph?"

"The person who gave it to us wanted you to have it."

She picked it up gingerly and smiled down affectionately at her late husband.

"Wherever you are, dear," she said to it, "I hope you're having a good time."

I went out for a walk, wondering if the day would ever arrive when I could take such a charitable view of Liz. Lillian wouldn't have to look far to find someone who envied her her relationship with Avery. He, at least, had remained true to her in his way.

I walked away from the house, past the empty swimming pool and across the tennis courts into the woods, where I could be alone with my self-pity. I cried a little, cursed Liz a little, stomped my feet, and vented my emotions by beating a perfectly innocent tree with a stick I found. I felt better for it and gratified that no one had observed the display.

I circled around through the woods and approached the house from the back, across a field that had once served as a pasture. As I neared the old garage, which housed Mae's collection of antique cars, I noticed an odd cloud hovering over a maroon Packard. As I closed the distance, I realized that it was actually a cloud of very active flies and I could hear an unnaturally loud buzzing against the soft background noises of a spring day.

Puzzled, I quickened my pace, thinking to find a dead mole or squirrel or groundhog that the cats had killed. But the flies were after bigger game than that.

I saw the outline of a form slumped over the wheel of the Packard. I rushed forward, took one look, turned, and threw up.

The flies, their attention now divided, buzzed excitedly around me as I fought them off with flailing arms.

I retreated a few yards, gasping for breath.

Now I approached slowly, trying to accustom myself gradually to what I was looking at. But there was no way to conquer my revulsion entirely.

The figure in the car was wearing a military dress jacket, that much I could see. I could also see that there was no point in calling for emergency medical assistance or in attempting CPR. The head had fallen forward to rest against the steering wheel, face turned outward as if for one last look at the world through the open window of the car. The face—or what I could see of it through the dense cloud of flies—was reddish-black and swollen beyond recognition. The eyes were open and exophthalmic. In their corners I could see traces of something that looked like rice. Brushing away the flies and moving closer than I wanted to be, handkerchief over my mouth and nose, I could see what had killed him. Most of the cord was buried deep in his swollen neck. But the small silver peace symbol rested between his shoulders as if it had been arranged there by a killer with a macabre sense of humor.

Clara would have to find someone else to do her home repairs. As for me, my best murder suspect had just been murdered.

"Styles, so help me, you'd better not be yanking my chain! If you know something I should know, you'd better come clean!"

"Same goes for you, sweetheart, unless you just enjoy living life on the edge."

"I don't enjoy it. I want to go back to peaceful New York and be a junior executive in an insurance office again, where I only have to deal with the living."

The first person I had called after I'd found the body was Detective Sergeant Dale Ferguson. The second person I'd called was Clara. And the third person was Styles.

Ferguson and Styles had rushed right over. Clara, I was willing to bet, was still putting on her makeup.

Styles and I were sitting on the back porch, watching Dale and his forensic team go over the site. The doctor had just arrived to declare Grosvenor dead—big duh, as the kids would say—and they were about to bag the body.

"My office was ransacked last night," Styles said abruptly.

"What? Styles, I told you you needed better security—stronger locks, at least!"

"I was getting around to it," she said gloomily. "I've been busy. Meanwhile, I used the old hair-in-the-door trick to tell me whether or not anyone had broken in while I was gone."

"And that's how you knew?"

"That, the file folders strewn all over the floor, and the missing computer disks. Hair worked like a charm, though."

"What are you missing?"

"A couple of decoy disks with Liberty family names on them—you know, Liberty, Van Nuys, Wilcox, June, Fuller. I figured there was just a chance he'd only take the one with his name on it, but no such luck. I don't know why he had to rifle the files," she said resentfully. "I made it easy for him to find what he wanted and leave."

"So he didn't get the real disks?"

"No, those are locked up."

"What's on the disks he got then? Assuming it was a him."

"A virus program. Every time he calls a file to the screen, he'll get the message, 'Thou shalt not steal.' "

"Well, that's something, anyway."

"Yeah, now all we have to do is get a search warrant for every computer in Eden," she said morosely.

They were wheeling the heavy black body bag over to the ambulance.

"I'm betting on a closed casket," Styles observed. "What do you think?"

"I'm betting Peachy has second thoughts about her choice of professions."

"I don't know. She's one tough broad. She ever tell you that our dogs were in obedience class together?"

"She might have mentioned it," I said dispiritedly.

They closed the doors on the ambulance and it drove off, no lights flashing.

"There goes my favorite suspect," I lamented.

"For what?"

"For everything."

So I told her what I'd figured out about Grosvenor's little trip to the store the night of Julius's murder.

"I was going to talk to some of the people who were there that night," I said. "It even occurred to me that I could check the videotape we made, though anybody could have left the living room, where the camera was set up. Val went to the bathroom and Grosvenor was on the phone when he came back."

"If Grosvenor committed the murder," Styles said, "how might that make him a target for somebody else?"

I was chain-smoking out of nervousness. Her question startled me, and I swallowed smoke and coughed. She whacked me on the back urgently. Tears stung my eyes.

"Styles, please," I pleaded hoarsely. "It was bad enough when we had one murderer and two arsonists. You want to add another murderer to the cast?"

She shrugged. "Always a possibility. Grosvenor was strangled, not shot."

"Well, he was wearing that stupid peace medal around his neck. I considered strangling him myself. I doubt he could spell 'Moratorium,' much less identify it. But I'll bet he could have told you just how much it would be worth to a collector in twenty years."

"There you are then. You considered strangling him, and your motives had nothing to do with Julius Cole."

Clara's arrival created a small stir in the yard. She was wearing a dress and pumps and sunglasses. She chatted with Dale for a few minutes, then came over to where we were sitting and bummed a cigarette from me. She was paler than I would have expected.

"Honestly, Gilda, I just thought he was puttering around down in the basement," she said, as if I'd accused her of deliberate negligence. "How was I to know he wasn't home last night? It's not as if we slept together; he stayed up to all hours playing with his toys and then snored when he did come to bed. 'That's it!' I told him a few years back. 'I need my beauty sleep.'"

"He has a computer down there. He talks to people all over the world on that thing. That's what I thought he was doing."

I didn't bother to correct her tense. I figured she'd have to get used to using the past tense soon enough.

"That detective said I'd have to identify the body." Her voice wavered. "I don't think I can. Gilda, do you think you could do it? Please?"

"I already did it," I said, swallowing the bile that rose in my throat.

"Well, then, could you just remind them?"

"Yeah, I guess."

"So where does that leave us?" Styles asked when Clara had gone inside for a cup of tea with Lillian.

"Long on dead bodies and short on motives," I said. "Long on alibis and short on opportunity."

"You know, from the standpoint of motive," she said, "the person who stands to lose the most is Andy Fuller. If his little secret gets out, his days as bank president are over."

"The most as far as we know. There might be other secrets we don't even know about, secrets that somebody thinks we do know about. And anyway, Andy didn't have the opportunity to kill Julius. He was at Liberty House with a horde of witnesses."

"Sometimes hordes are the worst kinds of witnesses. They tend not to agree on anything."

"You mean, somebody could have sneaked out and nobody would have noticed?"

"Sure. It's not that hard in a crowd. You say to the first person you meet, 'Is the bathroom free?' And then you disappear for a half hour, and coming back, you say to somebody else, 'Can't get good help these days. I told them not to call unless it was an emergency.' "

I stirred uneasily.

"So you're saying it could be somebody like Val, who admits he went to the bathroom?"

"Jesus, Gilda, the way your family was drinking, everybody must've gone to the bathroom sometime that night."

"We should go to the tape," I said, almost automatically, then realized: we *should* go to the tape.

"Tell me again about this tape."

"Grosvenor set up the video camera in the living room that night, after the visitation."

"He did? What for? To capture everybody in their moment of sorrow?"

I cut my eyes at her. "It's just this thing my family does. Don't ask me why. Anyway, it would tell us who was in the room and who left, and we might get some idea of how long they left for. I don't know how much good it would do, since some people, like Betty and me, didn't spend much time in the living room at all."

"Still, it would be worth a look," she agreed. "We might be able to figure out how long Grosvenor was gone when he went to the store."

She followed me into the living room, where I scoured the video cabinet on my hands and knees, looking for the right tape.

"It's not here," I said, sitting back on my heels. "It ought to be here, unless Grosvenor took it."

"Why would he take it?" she asked, coming to stand over me. "Unless . . ."

We looked at each other.

"You don't think . . ." I began.

"He was your stepuncle-in-law. What do you think?"

"Off the top of my head I'd say he makes a better candidate for blackmailer than for murderer."

"So it's possible he spotted something on the video and tried to blackmail the wrong person."

"Let me ask Clara."

In the kitchen Clara was sitting with Lillian. Clara was weeping and Lillian's arm encircled Clara's shoulders consolingly. I felt awkward about disturbing them, but Lillian looked up at me as if expecting some kind of report.

"I've been looking for the video that Grosvenor made the night before the funeral, when we all came back here," I said in some embarrassment. "I can't find it."

"I don't pay any attention to that, Gilda," Lillian said. "I wouldn't know where it was."

"Clara, do you think Grosvenor might have taken it?"

Clara's eyes were red and wet. Her voice was thick. "What video do you mean?"

"The one Grosvenor shot the night of the visitation, when we got back here from the funeral home," I said. "At least Grosvenor set up the camera. I turned it off when I went to bed."

"Oh, I don't know if he had it or not, Gilda." Her voice told me she didn't care, which meant that if there had been anything revealing on the tape, she didn't know about it.

Dale Ferguson chose that minute to stick his head in the door. "Got a minute, Gilda?"

I took him through the living room, where I gave Styles the high sign. She appeared engrossed in the Liberty family film and video collection.

On the front porch I sat down on the swing and Dale chose a weathered bentwood rocker. He went over my statement about how I'd found the body, including the part where I'd vomited on the crime scene.

"We might need you to vomit again so we can match the samples," he said with a straight face.

"Just because I made a C in chemistry, you think I'll believe anything," I said. "Well, think again."

He grinned at me briefly. Then the smile faded.

"Any ideas what's going on around here, Gil?" he asked.

"Oh, sure, I've got ideas. Lots of them. Which one do you want? The one starring Grosvenor as blackmailer or the more dramatic one, where he's the killer?"

"What makes you think he was either?"

"He left here the night Julius Cole was killed. He went out to buy more beer. I don't know how long he was gone, but—"

"Not long enough, unfortunately," Dale said. "So tell me your other theory."

"Wait a minute. How do you know he wasn't gone long enough? Who said so?"

"I have a video," he said.

"*You* have the video! Oh, good, I was afraid . . . Wait, do you have the only copy or did you make a copy?"

"As far as I know, I have the only copy. Why would anybody

have made a copy? You guys have a thing about funerals in your family?"

I ignored the gibes.

"So on the video you can tell when he left and when he got back?"

"From the video I can tell when he was in the room and when he wasn't," he corrected me. "As a matter of fact, I can tell down to the second. The time counter was on."

"Really? That's unusual for us. Somebody must've switched it on by accident."

Liberties disdained counters; counters marred the image. What was the point of going to all that trouble for perfect hair and makeup if you were going to have numbers plastered all over your face? In the opinion of the most conservative faction, the presence of counters indicated a medium that was not to be taken seriously, a medium more suitable for television news than for high art.

"I can't tell you where he went," Dale continued, "only that he wasn't out of the room long enough to have driven to Eden Center and shot Julius Cole."

I thought about what he was saying.

"Based on the tape, then, did *anyone* leave the room long enough to have killed Julius?"

"You," he said. "Betty. Of course, you could have been in it together, since you've alibied each other. Lillian. Duke."

"You keep your mitts off my projectionist," I warned him. "You know that tape isn't worth shit as evidence against Duke."

"I didn't say it was," he said mildly. "I'm only telling you who it doesn't alibi. Other people came and went—not very many people sat in front of the camera for three hours. It's not clear that anybody stayed out of the living room long enough to have committed the murder, though, except for the four people I mentioned."

"I hope you've been looking for other suspects, especially business-related ones. Rivals, former business partners, people he screwed over, suspects like that."

"We have," he said, "but they wouldn't explain the number of contacts I've had with your family members, both living and dead, ever since Julius Cole died. Wouldn't explain her, either."

I turned to see Styles just stepping outside.

"Ferguson," she said, nodding at him.

"Styles." He returned the nod. "Head all better?"

"Good as it ever was."

"Pays to develop a thick skull."

"You'd know, of course."

She half smiled at him then and he returned that, too.

What was going on here? I felt like the dull-witted rival in a screwball romance.

"And now, if you women will excuse me," he said, "I'm late for an autopsy."

"Don't keep the corpse waiting on our account," Styles said.

"He has the tape," I told her after he'd left.

"What does he say about it?"

"That it clears Grosvenor of Julius's murder, and just about everybody else except Lillian, Duke, Betty, and one other person."

She laughed.

"That's what I like about you, babe! You're open to new experiences."

Grosvenor's funeral was by far a quieter affair than Maesie's. Andy Fuller and my father made most of the arrangements with Peachy, since Clara seemed to be sedated or simply withdrawn most of the time. Still exhausted and behind at work from the previous family extravaganza, most of the Liberties chose to stay put in L.A. and observe a moment of silence from their desks or dressing rooms or golf carts. Spencer and Grace and Audrey all made the trek back, more to be with their mother, I guessed, than out of love for their stepfather.

Grosvenor's sister and brother came and brought their eighty-five-year-old mother. They complained about everything, from the coffin to the cemetery to the weather.

Peachy, who looked one complaint away from a major temper tantrum, took me aside. "I appreciate that your family is trying to keep me in business, girlfriend, I really do," she said. "But please don't send me any more customers."

She'd get no argument from me. I stood at the graveside, studied the faces around me, and wondered who'd be the next to go—and whether somebody I was looking at already knew the answer. Like the rest of my family, my imagination was one big silver screen and I visualized people sitting in the light-split darkness of a movie theater, watching us and screaming, "No! Don't do it! Don't go there! He's standing behind you, and he's got a knife!" If their knuckles were as white as mine were, they were getting their money's worth.

I tried to talk to Clara at the funeral, but she was too out of it. I'd have to try again when things settled down and she emerged from whatever tranks she was taking.

Everyone ended up back at Liberty House again, and for once nobody set up the video camera. I put in my time, then changed clothes to go to the theater. My father caught me as I headed out the door.

"I keep meaning to tell you, Gilda, there's a small manila envelope full of keys in Mae's top desk drawer. Some of them are labeled and some aren't, but I'm guessing they're all theater keys. You'd better take them."

In the study I slid open the desk drawer, found the envelope, and dumped its contents on the desktop. It was a jumble of keys, all right—big and little, brassy and silver, labeled and unlabeled. I stirred them with my fingers and heaved a deep sigh.

And then my vision snagged on one. I could just make out the word "Mosler" engraved on it. I stared at it, realized what it was, and pocketed it. I swept the other keys into my hand, slid them back into the envelope, and was out the door before anyone could call me back again.

Ten minutes later I stood in the long storage room over the side theater, with its detritus of theater equipment, office equipment, and old records. I turned my flashlight on the wall and found the safe. It was a Mosler—not a big one, an office safe, not a bank safe. But it was big enough to hold what I was looking for.

The key turned easily in the old lock. Inside were several file folders crammed with papers. I carried them to the nearest room with a light—the number-two projection booth—and sat down on a stool to read.

On top of the papers in the first folder I opened was a note in Maesie's no-nonsense handwriting.

"Gilda, if you're reading this, I'm dead," it opened unsentimentally. "You must do as you think best."

"'That's it?" I answered her. "Do as I think best? What's that supposed to mean? How about some guidance here, Maesie! How about a little advice!"

I gave the papers a quick once-over. Some were notes in Maesie's writing, some were letters, some were photocopies. Some of the names they alluded to I recognized, some I didn't. But what was immediately clear was that this was a file of shameful secrets—some criminal, some merely scandalous, some shabby, but all of them destructive. Among the papers was a typed copy of real estate transactions involving J. C. Enterprises, the Pison Corporation, and several other companies whose names I didn't recognize. On the list, which was a kind of table, was a column for bank loans. Mae had highlighted in yellow the name "Eden Commercial" every time it appeared. It appeared almost every time.

One of Styles's reports, the first one, was here. The other wasn't. I checked several times to be sure.

I sat back on the stool and gazed absentmindedly into space. Every one of these names had a motive to murder Julius Cole. But which of them had done it?

I cast my mind back to the beginning—to Maesie, with her weak heart, sitting up in bed late at night, reading. To the moment when she might have read something so shocking, or so infuriating, that her feeble heart could not contain the emotion.

What had happened next?

Within a few days Julius Cole was dead. It was not an accident; someone had taken a gun with them when they had entered the theater that night. That suggested some degree of premeditation.

But it couldn't have been anyone who'd been at Liberty House that night, because the video exonerated all of them.

And then my eye fell on the splicer, which was sitting on the editing table.

I knew how it might have been done.

I called Styles.

"I'm not here, so leave a message." It was so like Styles, I thought, not to tell me my call was important to her.

"Hi, it's me," I said to the answering machine. "I'm at the theater, and I have the goods."

That ought to rouse her.

Then I called Liberty House and asked for my father. Ruth Hernandez told me he'd taken Clara home, so I tracked him down at the Junes' and asked the question I would have asked him and everyone else if it hadn't been for that damned video.

"Dad, do you remember the night of the visitation, when everybody was back at Liberty House and Grosvenor went out to get some more beer?"

"I remember the night, sure," he said. "But I don't remember Grosvenor going out. Andy went for beer, though."

I thanked him and hung up. "Stupid, stupid, stupid," I muttered to myself. I already knew that just because I'd seen Val carrying the beer, that hadn't meant he'd been the one to buy it. I should have realized that the same could apply when Val saw it sitting on the table next to Grosvenor. Someone could already have passed it off to Grosvenor before Val came along.

I called the police department and asked for Dale Ferguson. I had to hold for a few minutes, then Dale's voice answered.

"Dale, it's Gilda," I said. "I'd like to take a look at that video, if I could."

"The video?" he echoed.

"Yeah, you know, the one Grosvenor June gave you."

"Oh, yeah, I know the one you mean. June didn't give it to us, though. We got it from Andy Fuller."

"When can I come by and take a look at it? This afternoon?"

"Sure, any time. Ask for me at the reception window."

I set the phone down.

A voice behind me said wearily, "I really wish you hadn't done that, Gilda."

I turned slowly. Andy Fuller stood in the doorway. He was pointing a gun at me.

"You don't really want to do that, Andy," I said.

"You're right, I don't," he said. "But you haven't given me much choice, now have you?"

"Duke's going to be here anytime," I said, glancing at my watch. "He has a film to break down."

"Gilda, please, give me some credit. Duke's back in school, and this is Wednesday. The films don't change until Friday." He gestured with the gun. "Are those Maesie's files on Julius?"

"How's your computer working?" I asked.

He flushed. "Don't worry. I'll get what I want. But it was helpful of your father to tell you about the keys while I was around."

Then, to my alarm, we heard Styles's voice below.

"Gilda!" she shouted. "Where are you?"

Andy smiled, just a little. It was not a smile that the bank president shares with his shareholders, but something else entirely. "I might get it sooner than I think."

"Styles!" I shouted. "Get out!"

Andy closed the distance between us before my voice died and yanked me off the stool. We scuffled, but he got an arm around me and his hand over my mouth. I felt the gun against my left temple.

"What?" Styles was shouting. I heard her boot heels on the stairs, loud as a stampede. "Oh," she said, stopping in the doorway. "Jesus, babe, how many people did you leave that message for, anyway?"

I narrowed my eyes and glared at her. This would be a good time to leave, I tried to tell her. But she just stared back.

Andy took his hand off my mouth, but the gun didn't move. He gripped my forearm.

"Didn't you hear me say 'get out'?" I exploded. "Don't you ever do anything anybody tells you to do?"

"I thought you said 'get up here.' "

"I'd like your house key, please, Ms. Styles," Andy said. "You can put it right here on the table, along with any other keys you think I might need. And then if you'll put your hands up where I can see them and turn around, we're going to take a short trip down the hall. I probably don't need to point out that any move you make will force me to shoot my cousin."

"In-law," Styles added loyally, removing a ring of keys from her pocket and laying them on the table. She turned around. "I think we need to clarify here that you didn't come out of the original gene pool."

"You know what I want, Ms. Styles," he said. "It would be easier on all of us if you'll tell me where to find it."

"If I tell you, will you leave my house neater than you left my office?"

"You have my word," he said stiffly, as if that was worth a ticket stub.

"It's all locked up in my desk at home. Do you need my address?"

"No," he said. "I know where you live. Now, there's a storeroom in front of you. You're going in there."

I noticed the heavy padlock hanging open on the door, and my heart sank. Our only hope is that it will take him a week to find the right key, I thought. Please let it be a candy storeroom.

Styles walked in. He gave me a shove and I stumbled against her as the door closed. We were left in the dark. I heard the padlock snap and then the sound of retreating footsteps.

"Styles," I said, "I think I made a poor career decision a few weeks back."

"You're just depressed because things don't look so good right now," she replied conversationally.

"Right now," I said, straining my eyes in the blackness, "I can't see how things look at all. But you're probably right. Any ideas on when I can expect to see things looking up?"

She didn't answer. Instead she said resentfully, "I'll bet he's not even going right to my house. Did you see him checking his watch? Bastard probably has an important appointment he doesn't want to miss. Like we're not important. Like he can see us anytime."

I didn't know how to respond to this line of thinking. I resented Andy Fuller for several reasons right now, but it hadn't occurred to me to resent him for not shooting us more promptly.

"Styles," I said, puzzled, "aren't you scared?"

"I laugh in the face of danger, babe."

"Well, I'm glad one of us is having a good time."

Another thought struck me. "You don't think he's going to set a fire, do you?"

"If he is, he's not going to do it in the middle of the day," she said. "Give me your lighter."

"You're not going to set a fire, are you?"

I saw the flame flicker and hold.

"Want some candy?" She held the flame closer to the box. "Mary Janes! Jesus, how old is this candy, anyway? He could have locked us in with the Raisinets, but no! Oh, look! A light switch."

She hit the switch, but the bulb must have been as old as the candy. We were still in the dim light cast by the flickering flame of the lighter.

There was a small desk squeezed into one corner. She began to rifle it.

"What are you looking for? A weapon?"

"A pen. I'm writing my last will and testament. When they make the movie, I want Sigourney Weaver to play me." She wrote a few lines on a dusty invoice of yesteryear and then paused, chewing on the end of the pen. "Who do you want to play you?"

"Susan Sarandon."

"No way, babe! She doesn't look anything like you!"

"She doesn't look anything like that nun she played, either. Say, if you're going to censor my last wishes, I'll write them myself!"

"Okay. Susan Sarandon. We'll let Clara play herself. That way, she gets to have her comeback."

"Even if she turns out to be the one who clobbered you?"

"Sure. I'm in a charitable frame of mind."

"Good. Can we look for weapons now?"

"What is it with you and weapons? The man's packing a semiautomatic. Unless you got an Uzi stashed behind the Handi Wipes over there, you ain't got shit. You going to go up against him with a plumber's friend?"

"Wait a minute!" I said, slapping my pockets. "I've got a Swiss Army knife. Maybe we can take the door off, the way Peter Lorre did in *M*."

"You sleep through the end of the movie? Peter Lorre didn't make it. Besides, I don't think you've got that much time. He has to make his move before Duke gets out of school."

"I'm open to suggestions," I retorted with acerbity. "Only I'm not hearing anything but unconstructive criticism. You got a plan you want to propose?"

"Same plan I always have. Stay centered. Breathe. Extend ky."

"Extend what?"

"Ky. That's energy to you."

"Oh, no! Don't go all weird on me now, Styles!"

She didn't say anything. I think she was breathing. She was sitting cross-legged on the floor, holding the lighter like a lotus.

"Styles! Don't you dare do one of those Buddhist meditation

things where your body stays here and your mind takes a vacation in another dimension! I need your brain right here!"

She didn't answer.

"You're not one of those people who believe that virtue always triumphs, are you?"

She still didn't say anything.

"Well, maybe not virtue, exactly. That would be pushing it," I began to mumble. "Let's just say relative virtue. I mean, we are the good guys here, am I right? We haven't killed anybody to hold on to our jobs. Not that we have jobs worth holding on to, but still. Why am I talking to myself?"

"Yo, Styles!" I shook her, and she looked at me, annoyed. "Help me climb up on top of that shelf. I'm going to try to position myself over the door."

"And then what?" she asked, but she boosted me up. "Are we going to pee into plastic bags and drop water balloons on his head?"

"What's the heaviest thing in the room?"

"The desk, but I don't think we can get it up that high."

"Over there. What's that?"

"A jar of popcorn," she reported. "But it's so old it doesn't even have an expiration date on it. Must be pretty stale."

"I'm not picky," I said. "Hoist it up here."

It was a five-gallon glass jar, good and heavy. I rested it on the top shelf.

"Do you think he can see me from the hallway?"

"No, but I don't think he'll believe you vanished into thin air. Man's smart enough to be a bank president, and you ain't wearin' no ruby slippers."

"Quit grumbling! This ploy always works in the movies. You've got to startle him—lure him in."

"I'm not taking my clothes off."

We settled in to wait. Styles closed the lighter to conserve fuel. My legs and back were killing me.

"So why do you figure Fuller killed Julius Cole after Mae died?" Styles asked, perhaps to distract me. "Why not earlier or later, if he wanted to end the partnership?"

"Here's what I think happened," I said. "Mae was reading something the night she died. I think it was your second report and maybe some other material she'd gathered. Somebody found it, read it, and saw an opportunity to start their own blackmail scheme. My guess is that Grosvenor was the blackmailer, but he wouldn't have had as much opportunity to be in Mae's bedroom as Clara, so maybe Clara found it and passed it on to him.

"You didn't know Grosvenor, but he had expensive tastes. I wouldn't put it past him to have bypassed the smaller fish and gone after Andy."

"That's why they rob banks," Styles observed. "It's where the money is."

"Right. So why not start at the top? Pass me my lighter, would you? I'm dying for a cigarette."

"Jesus, Gilda, we're locked in a closet! You can't smoke in here!"

"You're way down there! Smoke rises. You'll never even notice."

"No," she said firmly. "I'm not going to get cancer from your secondhand smoke."

"You should live so long," I said wryly.

"Concentrate on something else. Grosvenor put the bite on Andy. Wait, how did he know to do that? I didn't have any information about Fuller in my report. I didn't know yet about the embezzlement."

"I don't know," I said irritably. "But I saw letters in Mae's files that seemed to have been written in response to letters she wrote requesting information. Also notes from telephone conversations, clearly labeled and dated. She still had a lot of Hollywood contacts. The missing file probably has something in it about why Andy left MGM.

"Anyway, to Andy, the touch meant that things had gotten out of hand. Julius wasn't in control anymore. And if that was the case, then Andy didn't need him. I don't doubt that the whole thing was Julius's idea in the first place and that initially he blackmailed Andy into financing his real estate empire. But Andy turned into a valuable partner, and he probably made a tidy bundle himself. He wasn't about to jeopardize it by allowing a loose cannon like Grosvenor to guard the secret of his past criminal activity. And as long as he was burning bridges, he figured it was time to get rid of Julius."

"Do you think Grosvenor hit on Julius as well?"

"I don't know if he did or not," I admitted. "He might not have understood the connection between Julius and Andy."

"Well, then, speaking of burning bridges . . ."

"Do I think Andy is an arsonist? No, I don't really think it's his style, although he may have persuaded Grosvenor to fire-bomb Julius's house for some reason or other—maybe to safeguard Grosvenor's corner on the blackmail market. I'll bet he persuaded Grosvenor to set up the video camera the night he killed Julius."

"Okay, so tell me how he worked the video thing."

"Give me the lighter and I'll tell you."

"No."

"Okay, I won't tell you."

"Fine. Suit yourself."

At this rate, by the time Andy showed up again to blow us away, Styles and I wouldn't even be speaking to each other.

"Here's your damn lighter," she said. "Only one!"

I fumbled in my pocket for my cigarettes, lit up, and inhaled deeply. "Where was I?"

"The video."

"Oh, yeah, the video. Well, I realized that if Julius's murder was premeditated, and it seemed to be, maybe we were making a mistake to concentrate on people without alibis. I mean, if you were planning a murder, wouldn't you set yourself up with a good alibi?"

"I guess. Hey, you're bouncing that smoke off the ceiling!"

"Sorry. Anyway, the video turned out to be the most important piece of evidence in establishing who was where, when, and for how long."

"Or, at least, who was in your living room and for how long."

"Right. And the counter made it too good to be true. We never turn the counter on. Mostly, in our family, we're making entertainment, not documentary."

"So what are you saying? The counter was faked? The numbers were added later like subtitles?"

"Hey, not bad, Styles! I hadn't thought of that, but it could have been done that way. No, I was thinking of something called a blue screen process."

"What's that?"

"It's the process they used in *Forrest Gump*. You ever see that?"

"Yeah. I wondered how they did it."

"I don't have a lot of technical training, but it has something to do with shooting a subject—Forrest Gump or Andy Fuller or whoever—against a blue background, then you put that tape into the editing machine with another tape and make a composite by dropping out the blue background."

"Sounds hard. Subtitles sound easier to me."

"Yeah, you could be right. But blue screen isn't that hard to do, really, and he might have avoided the really tricky matches— sitting in a chair of a certain height, for example."

"Does Fuller have the training to do something like that?"

"I don't know," I confessed. "But it wouldn't be hard to find somebody who did. All you really need is a video camera, an editor, and a blue sheet or backdrop or something, as I understand it. *I* don't have the training, after all, but I've been around film and video enough to know something about the blue screen process."

"So, the night of the murder, he gets Grosvenor to set up the camera."

"Sure, that was easy. All he had to do was stroke Grosvenor's ego and give him the opportunity to show off his superior equipment. Then, at some point, he wanders over and turns the counter on. He hangs out in the living room, in full view of the camera. Sometime around midnight he announces he's going out for more beer. He goes to the theater—probably Julius has mentioned he'll be there, watching a movie—and shoots Julius. He's got cold beer stashed in the back of his car, something imported, supposedly out of deference to Grosvenor's refined tastes but really to explain the length of his absence. He returns, meets Grosvenor in the front hall, and hands him the beer. Nobody really knows how long he's been gone, because in a crowd like that people don't. He goes back to the living room and positions himself in front of the camera again. The next morning, the day of the funeral, while everyone's sorting themselves into cars, he ducks into the living room and retrieves the tape. He takes it to somebody who can edit it to his specifications and—voilà! The perfect alibi!"

"But a professional editor will be able to tell that the tape's been manipulated, right? I mean, you can see that it's a composite if you're looking for that."

"No, that's the beauty of it! The resulting tape is a new master. As long as the two tapes match exactly and he's not sitting in a chair that isn't there or sticking his arm through somebody's chest, there's no way to tell."

"Well, if you're proposing that we let ourselves get killed in order to give Andy Fuller a chance to mess up and get convicted, you've got another think coming."

"Styles, which one of us is risking permanent spinal injury by standing on a high shelf in a small, hot closet, waiting to drop a jar of popcorn on his head?"

"Pas moi."

"You got that right. Anyway, I think Grosvenor's murder was pretty messy. Surely they'll come up with some forensic evidence from that, don't you think?"

"I don't know," she said. "Fiber evidence is overrated."

"Shhh! I hear something!"

"That's him, all right," Styles said. "I recognize the Florsheims."

"Get him in here," I whispered.

We heard him fumbling with the lock. Then the door swung

open and light flooded the room. I hadn't quite reckoned with the blinding effect of even the pale light from the hallway on eyes accustomed to pitch darkness.

"Where's Gilda?" he said.

I had to hand it to Styles. She was a damned good actress. She looked so blank even I began to think I wasn't there.

"Gilda?" she asked.

"My nosy cousin," he prompted.

"How would *I* know where she is?" Styles said, as if annoyed to be asked such a stupid question.

He had to think about that.

"How about if I just shoot you?" he said at last. "Then I can go look for her."

She shrugged, looking bored with the whole conversation.

I heard him move and his gun arm appeared below me. It occurred to me that that was my primary target, especially given his most recent proposal. I dropped my bomb on it and then jumped.

I heard him cry out, but he pulled his arm back. I landed on the floor in a bed of broken glass and popcorn kernels. I lunged for his legs, but he stepped back.

"Goddamn it!" he shouted. "You broke my goddamn arm, Gilda!"

Unfortunately, the injured arm was still holding the gun, which he transferred to the other hand.

"She didn't mean to," Styles said. "She meant to break your skull, but her aim's a little off."

I shot Styles a look. Once the action got under way, her contribution had been to duck. With allies like her, who needed enemies?

"Get up!" he said.

I got up slowly, picking glass out of my butt.

"Let's go," he said. "Put your hands up, both of you, and keep them up!"

He waved us past him with the gun and then followed us down the hall.

"Downstairs," he said. "Turn left."

Styles, who was leading the way, stopped.

"I know it's none of my business," she said mildly, "but if this were my show, I wouldn't want to walk out of here without checking to make sure the safe had been cleared out and I had all the evidence Mae Liberty was holding against me."

He stopped, too, and looked at her.

"It's just a suggestion," she said.

What the hell is she up to now? I thought. We'd have a better chance to make a run for it or summon help if we could get outside.

"Okay," he said, "show me the safe."

"You need a flashlight," I said.

"All right," he said, "we'll all go into the projection booth and get one."

But he didn't go in, as I'd hoped he would. He stood in the doorway with his gun in Styles's back and watched me. I couldn't pretend the flashlight wasn't there; it was out on the table, where I'd left it. The files, however, were gone.

I led the way to the safe. It was locked, just as I'd left it. The key was in my pocket. He tried to open it, wincing as he moved his injured arm, and failed.

He turned to me and gestured with the gun again. "Open it."

"No."

He stepped behind Styles. He must have poked her in the back with the gun again, because she flinched. Now I was facing the two of them, but he couldn't see her face.

She shifted her eyes right and nodded almost imperceptibly in that direction. I felt a surge of panic. What does she want me to do? I thought frantically. Then I saw her flex her right hand. I flashed on an image of Styles behind home plate, down on her knees, signaling the pitcher. She arched her hand a little as if she were wearing a mitt.

I fished out the key. "Here's the key," I said. "You open it."

And I pitched it in the direction of his right hand—the one at the end of his injured arm, the one without the gun.

What happened next happened in a blur. Styles whirled around. Her hands were up in his face. Then somehow she got hold of his gun hand and he was flat on his back. He squeezed off three shots, but they all hit the ceiling. I was dancing around, trying to keep the flashlight trained on him so that she could see what she was doing.

"Move back till I get the gun!" she shouted.

Somehow she flipped him over and pinned him, bending his arm at the elbow and then jamming his wrist.

He released the gun with a moan.

She picked it up and pressed it to the back of his neck.

I stood, stunned. It was probably just as well that somebody else had heard the gunshots and called the cops. I heard sirens in the background.

"Wow!" I said at last. "What was that?"

"Staying centered, breathing, extending ky. Aikido. Japanese martial art."

Impressed as I was, I still wanted my share of the credit.

"I thought I was the one who extended the key," I said.

She laughed. "That helped. Also that dopey stunt in the closet. It encouraged him to underestimate us—put him off his guard a little."

Within the hour, as we were cooling our heels in the police station, Styles was already critiquing her technique.

"I should have cold-cocked him when I had the chance," she said regretfully. "I should never have let him get those three shots off. But in aikido we're trained to open our hearts to our attackers and extend positive energy. I did that, all right, but I can see I have room for improvement in the self-protection department."

"Hey, the guy's got a broken arm and a broken wrist," I consoled her. "You did okay."

I got out of there in time for the early show at the theater, and by midnight I was beyond exhaustion. That was when I first realized that I had given only the most fleeting of thoughts to Liz when I had faced death that day. Styles's nonchalance had somehow kept me focused on staying alive, and I realized that I liked being alive, with or without Liz.

The next morning I paid Clara a visit. She lived in the kind of pretentious, two-story faux colonial you would expect the Junes to live in, with all kinds of high-tech security equipment to keep out the riffraff.

There was a plumber in the kitchen, working on her disposal, so we sat in the living room.

She appeared alert, and I came straight to the point.

"I want that file, Clara."

"What file?" She overplayed her innocence the way she always had onscreen. If anyone had a future in Hollywood, it was Styles, not Clara Liberty June.

"The one you found in Mae's room after she died."

"I don't know what you're talking about, Gilda."

"The one that makes reference to your big break in *Stars in Her Eyes*."

Her own eyes darkened. "That's nothing but malicious slander what Cora says about me!" she snapped. "She's just jealous, that's all! She always resented my success!"

"I might believe that, but concussions just seem to follow in your wake."

She paled. "That detective knows something, doesn't she? She's talked to Cora, hasn't she? Does she have a file on me?"

"If you don't give me that file," I said evenly, "my next call will be to the *National Enquirer*."

"You wouldn't!"

"Try me."

Actually, I doubted that the tabloids would be interested in a scandal that old, but it was typical of Clara's self-centeredness that she assumed they would be. She got up and left the room, then returned with a large envelope.

"What are you going to do with it?" she asked.

"Destroy it."

She handed it over.

"You showed it to Grosvenor, I assume?"

"Certainly not," she said. "He would have held it over me for the rest of my life."

"So was Grosvenor with you when you broke into Styles's office?"

"I told you, I didn't tell him anything about the file."

"But he must have found it?" I prompted her.

"Yes, he found it. But I had no idea he was going to use it for anything. I suppose—well, he had his heart set on a Jaguar."

"A Jaguar?" I echoed, incredulous.

"He probably went to Andy for a bank loan. Maybe he mentioned something about Andy and MGM, I don't know. Andy didn't have to kill him! After all, we would have paid him back when we got our share of Maesie's estate."

I didn't think she was that naïve, but I didn't challenge her. What she'd said was, after all, probably a milder version of the truth.

"So whose idea was it to burn down Julius's house?" I asked. "Yours or his?"

"Not mine!" she said, so quickly and adamantly that I was sure the idea had been hers.

"Anyway," she said self-righteously, "it was a community service, wasn't it?"

I tended to agree with her, but I wasn't going to let her off the hook.

"And the theater?"

"We didn't have anything to do with that." This time her voice was perfunctory, almost bored. I tended to believe her.

I went home and called Dale Ferguson.

"You never told me if they identified the movie Julius was watching when he died."

"Oh, yeah, funny thing about that," he said. "It was one of your aunt Mae's films, an old one called *Betrayal*. Pretty ironic, wouldn't you say?"

"Pretty ironic," I agreed. "So they had enough film left to tell?"

"Yeah. I guess because it was wound tight on a reel. Well, not a reel, exactly. One of those platter things."

"Which platter?"

"What?"

"Can you tell where it was, the part that didn't get burned? Top or bottom?"

"Hang on."

In a minute he came back on the line.

"I'm looking at a picture of it now. I'm not an arson specialist, you know, and burn scenes can be deceptive because things shift around in a fire. Everything that was in the booth fell when the floor collapsed. But I can see some platters here, one on top of another, it looks like. There's no film on the top one, and I seem to remember assuming that the film on the bottom one was protected by the top one. Why? Do you have a theory?"

"No." I tried to sound disappointed. "Well, I had a theory about the solvent we use to clean the gates, but I guess it won't work. You know me and chemistry."

He was still laughing when he hung up, which was fine with me. It kept him from trying to make a connection between solvents and the position of the unburned film. There wasn't one.

Then I paid my second visit of the day, this one to Val.

Val and Tobias lived in a beautiful Victorian on a tree-lined street where half the trees seemed to be in bloom. When they didn't answer my ring, I went around to the back and through the gate into the garden, where I found them on hands and knees, planting.

"Hey, Gilda! Pull up a stump and stay awhile!" Val greeted me.

"Pull up a weed or two while you're at it," Tobias suggested.

I settled on a broad stump just off one of the paths near where they were working. At my feet the lilies of the valley and violets were in bloom, and I could smell a heady perfume.

"What's on your mind?" Val asked.

"Do I look like I'm on a mission?"

"You look like you came to talk."

"I know who burned down the theater," I said.

"No kidding!" He sat back on his haunches, rubbing one hip with his hand, and glanced at Tobias, but Tobias wasn't managing to look very surprised. Toby was a writer, not an actor. "Who?"

"You had a part in it," I said, "but it was a very small part. I'm guessing, though, that the news of Julius's death was pretty unsettling for you."

He looked at me with interest.

"How did I do it?" he asked, as if genuinely curious.

"You mean, how was it done? I don't know all the details, but I'll admit I'd like to hear them. I'm guessing Mae wrote Julius a note, telling him she knew about the Eden Center theater and asking him to watch one of her films there, for old times' sake, after she died. I don't know whether she specified a time, but I think she would have, to minimize the risk to other people. And it would have appealed to her flair for drama. You know, 'At midnight, before my funeral, please watch this film and think of me.' Something like that."

"What film?" Val asked, watching me carefully.

"*Betrayal,* a film with a highly suggestive title. You delivered the print, I think, along with the note, after she died. But this wasn't just any print. Now, here's where it gets tricky, because I don't know enough about film stock. But some of the film survived the fire. So I'm guessing that she didn't just hand over an original nitrate print. Can you tell nitrate from safety film?"

"A careful projectionist probably could," Val said. "An experienced projectionist would know immediately."

"Okay, so Maesie wouldn't risk anything too obvious. The film ran a hundred and three minutes—I looked it up—and the film that survived the fire was on the take-up platter. I think somewhere in the final reel of the film—knowing Mae, it was probably at the climax—she spliced in some nitrate to replace the safety film. Then she did something—I don't know what, but you probably advised her—to create friction as the film passed through the projector gate. From what I've read about nitrate, it probably wouldn't take much, just a strip of some rough material glued to the surface of the film, for example. When the nitrate passed through the film gate, the friction caused a spark, and the whole thing went up in flames. That would explain the nitrate residue they found.

"I doubt she expected to burn down the whole theater, that was just luck. She thought Julius would call the fire department and that would be the end of it. At best, she would have inconvenienced him, but she would have scored a small victory.

"So," I concluded. "That's my theory. What do you think?"

They exchanged looks again.

"*I* think it's going to be fun to have her around all the time," Tobias said to Val.

Val grinned at me. "You're right about the chances of burning the place down," he said. "When I heard the whole theater had gone up in smoke, I'll admit to a sense of elation that we'd succeeded beyond our wildest dreams. Well, Mae had. She knew she was coming to the end of her road, so to speak, and she was furious at Julius when she found out about the theater. She did ask my advice, but the scheme was basically hers. I was just the delivery boy."

He smiled reminiscently. "You can't imagine how pleased Julius was when I handed him the sealed envelope and the film canister. He said he was touched she'd remembered him that way. I'll bet even when he saw the title, he thought she was having her little joke."

"He probably couldn't resist bragging about it to Andy," I said.

"I thought that, too, when I heard Andy had been charged," Val agreed. "Andy knew he owned the theater, after all. He probably told Andy he had a very important date with Mae there at midnight."

"Andy was the only one he could tell," I said, "and he was the wrong person."

Val stood up and stretched his back, hands on his hips. "I can't feel sorry for the guy, though," he said. "As far as I'm concerned, he got his comeuppance."

When I left, Tobias handed me a small bouquet of lilies of the valley and violets.

"Violets, the flowers of remembrance," I said, touched. "Thanks, Tobias."

I had agreed to destroy the material Clara gave me, but I hadn't agreed to destroy it unread. In the privacy of the small office in the theater, I extracted a file folder from the envelope. I didn't want the responsibility of all those secrets, though, so I leafed through it, looking for a clue to the things that still puzzled me. What had Maesie been reading the night she died?

I found it on the bottom of the pile.

It was a letter to Mae from Mr. Drysdale, the man who had once owned Eden's other funeral home.

It read:

Dear Mrs. Carlton,

For many years I have been expecting to receive your letter, so I was not as surprised as you may think. I am sorry to hear that you are in poor health. I hope the rest of your family is well.

You have asked me several questions regarding the death

of your daughter, Camille, and I will answer them honestly to the best of my ability.

You have asked about the medical procedure that led to her death. You must understand that I have no medical training and am not fully qualified to assess the quality of her medical care. But I will say that I have seen, in the course of my work, many women, young and old, who have died as a result of this procedure. Based on my experience, and what I saw when I prepared your daughter for burial, I have no reason to question the competence of the physician who attended her. Indeed, I would have to say that he was unusually careful, given the illegal nature of the procedure and the carelessness with which it is often performed. I am sure you can understand that any medical procedure involves risks. That is why I have always supported the legalization of this particular procedure, because legalization ensures that it will be carried out in sterile surroundings, supervised by trained professionals, and that patients will be given the kind of information and follow-up care that they need.

You have asked whether I know the identity of the person who performed the procedure. I do not.

Finally, you have asked whether I know the identity of the father of your daughter's baby. I cannot say that I know it for certain; I have never confirmed what I suspected at the time. But I am returning to you now an anklet that I removed from your daughter when I laid her out. It should have been removed at the hospital, but it must have been overlooked by the emergency room staff who rushed to save your daughter's life. I have kept it all these years because I could not, in good conscience, bring myself to throw it away.

You will say that I am a thief, that I should have returned it to you at the time. Yet I had both unselfish and selfish reasons for not doing so. I genuinely believed that what the anklet reveals would add to your pain. But I will also confess to you now that I had selfish reasons for not wishing to make enemies in certain quarters. The man to whom I refer subsequently became my enemy and forced my relocation. However, we are all too old now, you and he and I, not to speak the truth.

I hope this has been some comfort to you. God bless and keep you.

Sincerely yours,
Thomas A. Drysdale

I picked up the envelope, turned it over, and shook it. A small piece of jewelry dropped into my hand.

The chain was badly tarnished, but someone had cleaned off the narrow plate in order to read the inscription engraved on it.

To my darling Rosebud, with all my love. J.C.

It was a cool, clear spring day. The sun shone brightly on a green world.

I was out behind Liberty House, lighting a match to a small pile of kindling, newspaper, and firewood. A slight breeze sprang up, playfully stirring the flames, and then faded away.

I was thinking about Julius Cole and Maesie, and their long and troubled relationship. I wondered whether Mae had ever realized, until the moment of her death, just how troubled it had been—how bitterly Julius had resented her rejection of him as a lover.

But had he really loved her? Was that really his story, how he had loved and lost? Or had he acted out of ego and hurt pride? Could you really love someone you were that angry with?

Abruptly, I thought of Liz. I was looking forward to the day when I could be angry with her, without the complications of love and grief. But perhaps anger was just as painful as love, and just as destructive.

I put the first of the folders, with all of its contents, into the fire and watched the paper curl and turn to ash.

I wondered if Julius had ever planned to reveal his treachery to Maesie. Had he looked forward to the day when he could tell her that he'd attacked the two things she'd cared most about, her daughter and her theater? Or was it enough for him to know how badly he'd hurt her? Did he revel in his secret power without feeling tempted to speak about it?

I didn't really understand Julius Cole's obsession with power over people. I didn't want that kind of power over anyone, not even Liz.

I dropped two more folders into the fire.

"You must do as you think best," Maesie had written. I supposed that if Julius were still living, I would have had to decide what to do about him, and I was relieved that that particular decision had been taken out of my hands. I didn't even see the point now of confronting Dr. Genesee and Helen Beverly about the abortion. If they had performed the abortion on Camille and on other women, they had done so conscientiously, and I was convinced that they had acted with compassion.

I fingered the anklet in my pocket. I couldn't even be sure that Julius hadn't loved Camille, even if he'd loved her only as an extension of her mother. Love for him had been so bound up with ego and power that he might not have been able to extricate one from the other.

But Maesie would not have forgiven him. When I thought about the small fire that had consumed the theater, it seemed perfectly plausible to me to imagine Mae's ghost standing by, feeding the flames with her fury until the building, and Julius himself, were engulfed and annihilated.

Styles had promised to destroy all her files on the case.

That left only one.

I opened the last file and scattered its contents over the flames. They curled and blackened and crumbled.

I followed the smoke upward with my eyes until it became a thin black line against the blue sky and then dissipated.

Please turn the page
for a brief commentary on
Orson Welles's *Citizen Kane*.

be removed while making *Citizen Kane*, the next major film for RKO, *The Magnificent*

A Note About
Citizen Kane

At twenty-three, Orson Welles enjoyed considerable notoriety after his Mercury Theatre radio production of H. G. Wells's *War of the Worlds* caused a national panic. Hoping to capitalize on the publicity surrounding this incident, RKO brought Welles, John Houseman, and their Mercury Theatre players to Hollywood.

After several attempted projects, Welles began work on *Citizen Kane*. According to one famous account, the script was largely written by veteran screenwriter Herman J. Mankiewicz, an acquaintance of newspaper magnate William Randolph Hearst and his mistress, actress Marion Davies, while bedridden with a broken collarbone and a fractured leg. Critical to the success of the film were Houseman, credited as Welles's assistant; cinematographer Gregg Toland; composer Bernard Herrmann; and the young editor Robert Wise, later a great director in his own right.

The film survived attempts to suppress it by rival studios under pressure from Hearst, but it did not do well at the box office. Welles never again worked in Hollywood with the freedom he enjoyed while making *Citizen Kane*. His next major film for RKO, *The Magnificent Ambersons*, was edited while he was out of the country. Despite a long and troubled relationship with Hollywood, however, Welles would live to see *Citizen Kane* become one of the most highly praised films in the history of cinema.

—DELLA BORTON
January 1999

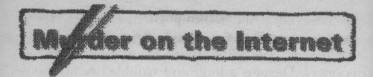